Blood Posse

Blood Posse

PHILLIP BAKER

St. Martin's Griffin
New York

ISBN 0-312-13030-9

First published in Great Britain by Picador, a division of Pan Macmillan Publishers Limited

First St. Martin's Griffin Edition: July 1995
10 9 8 7 6 5 4 3 2 1

To Raquel, Aaron, Alicia, Camille,
and to Gail

Blood Posse

Chapter 1

Sirens holler and scream, howling as if World War Three had started. This constant whining we are used to. But today there is an urgency in the cry from the government wolves. The directions in which the wailing sirens echoed is also different. At first our ears had instinctively cocked towards the chambers of hell—East New York and Brownsville, where black folks were forever cutting each other's throats. Helicopters with black numbers painted on their bellies hover overhead. They resemble agitated flies trying to avoid the swat. They circle the Flatbush area, chopping up the air and adding to the confusion.

It's a dog's day afternoon in mid-July 1970. Tempers are rising into the upper nineties, like the gauge on the thermometer. Everyone is doing their own thing, caught up in the city's intricate web, snared in a rat race where strength is vital, but more so one's endurance.

The local cops had just been around, turning off the hydrant, our only means of escaping the tortuous heat. The beat cop O'Hara had barely finished barking. "You kids better find something to do before something happens to you." The smell of alcohol was ripe on his breath as he bent down to wave a threatening finger in our faces. He almost fell over as he stared into our eyes, looking like an old lion who had seen many battles, but was now relegated to a lesser place in the pride.

"Suppose there's a fire, for Christ's sake," he slurred, balancing his hands on his hips and looking up into the pale blue sky. His face was red as a beet and made him look comical. "There's gonna be some sore heads on this block the next time I'm called out." He rocked unsteadily on his heels and barked: "Go to the park and play like other kids. The street's no place for young boys." His red-glazed eyes dropped on me lazily. "I expect better from you, Danny Palmer. I don't think your father would be too pleased to know what you've been up to. Would he now?" he growled.

"No, sir," I answered innocently keeping my head down. The water from my sneakers, T-shirt, and jeans formed a puddle at my feet.

His partner dragged himself from his squat around the driving seat in the police cruiser. The guts from a Hero sandwich spilled down the front of his uniform. Mayonnaise trickled down the side of his chin. "Holdup in Sheeps Head Bay," he shouted with a mouthful. "Some lunatic's got the bank under siege."

"Christ," O'Hara growled regretfully. He shuffled his hip holster, tucked in his chin, and tried to look cocky and vigilant. "Now be off with you." He gave me a feeble push, then staggered back to the cruiser.

I turned to my main man, Nathan, and cursed as the car went speeding down the street, sirens blasting as it reached the end of the block.

"Jive-ass motherfucker. Acts as if he was never a kid. What he expect us to do anyway?"

Nathan smiled and patted me on the shoulder. "Chill out, Danny. Ain't no cop can stop us playing Skelly, right?" There was mystery in Nathan's dark green eyes, his face an intricately woven mask of mischief. He was slightly taller than me. The water dripped from the ends of his braids like an icicle thawing. His sister, for whom I had a secret yearning, had sat earlier, patiently doing both our braids, using the back of the comb to swat away our hands when we impatiently tried to feel how much she'd done.

The chalk lines from previous Skelly games were still visible in the middle of the street. We found a few bottle stoppers and got down to some serious action.

The gods smiled in favour of my opponent like the golden sun that ruled the day. "Shit, Nathan, you a lucky dude!"

"What you mean lucky, nigger? Who taught you to play this game anyway? The art of Skelly is in the fingers, man." He wiggled his index finger in front of my face.

Determined to beat him, I got down further on my hands and knees, mindless of the heat rising in misty haze from the ground.

Traffic was light along the block. The young and restless played in the streets, sidewalks, and driveways. Cars were parked along both sides of the tree-shaded avenue. Occasionally a speeding car would race down the block trying to avoid the main flow of traffic on the busy Linden Boulevard.

The residents were out in their numbers. Fat women squatted on steps with their skirts clasped between their legs. The men were on ladders slapping paint around windowframes. They groomed the outside of their houses, trying to maintain the standard set by the previous Jewish owners. Limbs were hacked recklessly from trees and flowers perished at the hands of young mischievous children. Black folks had no patience when it came to trimming hedges or keeping gardens.

The only evidence that the area was once a middle-class Jewish community was a handful of aged sitting tenants lazing around in deck chairs plotted on the sidewalk and watching the world go by. They were left behind as a legacy living out their ninety-nine-year leases. Their previous landlords had sold them out to the blacks and Hispanics who were slowly creeping up on the area like cancer. Some were fortunate, having been given prior warning that they were about to be sold down the river. The unfortunate ones had woken one day to find angry black faces confronting them. It was like a farmer finding a chicken hawk in his fowl coop.

The new home owners, anxious to pay their steep and demanding mortgages, threatened the vulnerable tenants with violence if they didn't clear out. Confused, the old creakers had slipped back into their apartments finding it hard to believe that the Schullers or the Hochburgs had delivered them into the hands of such evil gentiles. They called the police in the hope that the law would rescue them from their nightmares. The police sadly confirmed their worst fears. They were about to drown in a sea of black people who had no sympathy with their suffering. They were left alone without family and friends, struggling to complete the arduous course, on life's endless marathon.

On hot days they'd bring their deck chairs on the sidewalk, lapping up the sun, breathing the humid, choking air and cursing the army of black kids who had invaded their lives. The kids fell on them like the atomic bomb on Hiroshima, and had the same disastrous effect as far as they were concerned. From their deck chairs they scoffed at the devastation that rapidly replaced their old traditional modes. There were street dances that lasted all day and into the night. Ghetto blasters with loud crazy music blaring. Fights that made the Vietnam War look like a squabble in a school playground. And there were open hydrants that exploded and drenched little black bodies wiggling under cold needles of water. Not to mention half-naked boys playing funny games in the middle of the street and bringing cars to a stop, causing the drivers to hoot loudly.

Nathan's luck was still holding out. "Yo! This shit ain't fair! Got a contract with these cars or what, man? Just when I'm busting your ass."

"Ain't my fault," he shouted over the heavy sound of the car's engine kicking over like a stampede of buffaloes.

Reluctantly, we got up from the ground taking our very sweet time to jig out of the way. The driver huffed, cursed, and pulled off with a screech of tires shaking the parked cars and narrowly tearing the skin from our hides.

Waves of disgust rippled over the age-old scars on the old-timers' faces.

With the mood for Skelly broken, we fiddled aimlessly with the steel clamp placed on the hydrant. Nathan frowned despondently, knee deep in the dirty puddle caused by the excess of water from the hydrant. "No use, man. Let's hop down the next block see what that little Haitian punk's up to." He dried the beads of water from his copper-toned forehead using the end of his faded summer shirt.

The old-timers watched us suspiciously as we approached them on the sidewalk.

There was Max, a pleasant old man who always dressed like he was still working for the city morgue. Max occupied the apartment on the second floor in my parents' tenement housing. Sitting with Max were two men and one woman, his friends from neighboring houses. Walking-sticks supported them in their deck chairs. They weren't afraid, just mistrustful.

I remember Max telling my mother one day: "Life is all over for us old-timers." His voice was hoarse and the cold rattled on his chest. "No one remembers the good we've done," he said, sadly. "The Jewish community don't care what happens to us. Many old-timers like myself have no wish to live. We welcome death but are afraid to take our own lives." There was anger in his eyes as he spoke. "Mrs Palmer, I'm fortunate. You're an understanding woman. You put no pressure on me even though I pay only seven dollars and fifty cents for an apartment you could easily get two hundred dollars a month for. Please don't be upset with me if one day I go out on the subway or sit in the park and let one of these human vultures take me out of this miserable world."

There was sympathy in my heart for Max and the other old-timers. Nathan thought they were pretty funny and enjoyed making their lives a misery with his childish antics. Bouncing with a bebop lean, Nathan grabbed Max's straw hat from his head as we passed.

"Bring that back, you moron!" shouted Max, trying to lift his tired frame from the chair. The old lady poked lamely at Nathan with her walking-stick.

Not wanting Nathan to call me a punk I joined him in mocking laughter as we ran screaming down the block, throwing the hat around to each other. We shuffled past spacious driveways and plane trees. Their long arms swept the faces of the three-storey brick houses.

Crossing the busy Linden Boulevard we played daredevils, dodging the speeding cars and laughing as a Cadillac ripped Max's hat to shreds and missed us by a fraction of an inch.

Linden Boulevard is more than just six lanes of traffic running for miles in either direction. It is steeped in a romantic culture with sturdy houses on either side of the street, ranging from Victorian through art deco to postmodernist. The architectural wonder reflected the history of the Irish exodus from the potato famine, the Italians' flight from Fascism, the Jewish, Polish, and Czech escape from Nazism, and the black Americans' migration from the South.

There was a football game taking place in the center of the block. Strong black men in their teens showed off their sporting prowess. They were dressed in shorts and T-shirts and drenched in sweat.

Tall trees shadowed the area, keeping it in permanent darkness. In the fall the narrow street and sidewalk would be carpeted with brown water-soaked leaves that seemed to cry out when trampled under foot or run over by cars.

We stood gaping as Cool Dave Green leaped into the air like a giant frog and picked off an interception then sprinted to make a touchdown. He threw the ball down and rocked triumphantly to the sound of the Crown Heights Affair band that was practising in a basement nearby.

The heavy sound of music seemed to mushroom from out of the earth, rolling off the cars and two-storey semi-detached houses. The crisp, vibrant sound of the drums echoed down the long driveways, where children played away from the scrutinizing eyes of their elders.

The action on the block was electric. There were no sitting tenants or white family-owned houses. Black people were in their element, making noise and hanging from fire escapes. Speakers were on windows, hammering out a variety of ethnic music. There was the smell of soul food and fat dripping on hot coals coming from a barbecue.

Nathan jacked up in front of a driveway where some young girls were skipping a double rope. He screwed up his face and rested his hands on his hips. "Hey! Paula, this where you been all day, huh? Mama gonna tear your butt."

The young light-skin girl, her long ponytails jumping up in front of her, pretended not to hear her brother and continued skipping, mumbling a few quiet words every time her feet cleared the ropes.

"Girl, you deaf or what?" Nathan picked up a large stone and hit her hard on her frail little legs. She fell to the ground screaming.

"Now get your raggedy ass home." He kicked her up her can.

Paula got up from the ground and limped out of the driveway, rubbing her weeping eyes. She reached halfway down the block then turned and jeered. "Stinky, you wet your bed."

Nathan made a gestured move as if to give chase. Paula went into overdrive, her little feet doing the Charleston down the block.

Paul Semere was sitting on the steps of his house looking

bored and listless. He tightened his nostrils as we took a seat beside him. "Shit! You guys smell and look like y'all been dipped in a cess pit," he sneered.

"The only cess pit around here is your goddamn mouth," replied Nathan.

"See you still got your arms." Paul gave him a bitter stare out the corner of his eye.

"That's right!" Nathan waved his arms around defiantly. "All that voodoo shit don't work on guys like me."

"Give it time, man. My mother said whoever stole that money from her room their hands gonna drop off, and that ain't no jive."

'Hey, punk, you accusing me or something?' Nathan stood up, swelled up his chest, ready to throw down.

"Me and you were the only ones in the house when the money went missing." Sweat started to bust out on Paul's face. Water dripped from the bridge of his broad nose. He was ten shades darker than the average nigger. And he was ugly, too. He was dressed like the footballers, with a pick stuck in the back of his Afro.

I got up and threw the egg-shaped ball as it landed at my feet. The ball ended up in a garden across the street where some folks were having a barbecue on a lush lawn surrounded by a low fence.

I felt like a piece of shit, especially when the footballers started to chant abuse. A short bald-headed man rested his paper plate to one side and picked up the ball. He sized it up in his hands, intent on impressing a few women with paper plates on their laps. The ball sailed through the air swiping leaves from the trees then ended firmly in Dave Green's hand.

I returned to the steps where the argument between my two friends had reached high tide. Paul was slowly drowning.

Nathan was on his feet and pointing at Paul. "Any time you feel brave enough to take me on then you welcome, sucker.'

Paul needed help.

"Man, this here's the worst summer there ever was," I interrupted before punches started flying.

"Not even a bicycle between us," Paul hastily replied, only too glad to get a rueful Nathan off his back.

"Ain't no use beefing about not having one," Nathan said. "All we gots to do is go and steal us some."

Paul instinctively gave him a suspicious glance. "And where we gonna keep them there bikes when we get them?" Not waiting for an answer, he continued: "My father would bust my ass if he knew I went stealing."

"Parents sure strange," I said. "Ask them to buy you one, they say, 'No! Got better things to do with sixty bucks,' and when ya goes out and gets yourself one they thrash the dear life out of you."

"That's because y'all West Indians got your heads stuck up your ass," Nathan sneered. "I once heard Paul's dad telling him to go and find the strap so he could whip his butt. My father could never tell me that shit."

"OK, Mr Smart Ass, you the one made the suggestion. Where we start looking? There ain't no nigger around here got none and that's for sure," Paul said.

"Carnarsie," Nathan answered dryly. He gave Paul a look that could stop time. There was always a reservoir of hate inside him ready to overflow on Paul. He turned to me and mumbled as if Paul wasn't there. "Them there Italians got all kinds of bicycles laying around up there ready for the taking."

Paul gave him a long, cold, sinister stare as if saying, "Like how you took my mother's money."

"Suppose we gonna fly there," I bantered.

"That's right, Danny. Right on the back of a bus." Nathan looked at each of us in turn, searching our eyes to see if he could find any signs of fear. He found none. "You West Indian boys sure thick in the head. Everything someone got to spell out to y'all."

The muscles in Paul's face tightened at the mention of West Indians and their inferiority. I had seen that hardened look on many occasions, especially when Nathan wanted to remind us that we were foreigners and scorned by the majority of Afro-Americans.

"Man, why you don't lay off that West Indian bullshit for a change?" Paul said.

"Jive niggers. You guys are nothing but a set of punks." Nathan sprayed me through his gapped tooth.

"Not so." I dried my face.

"Are too."

"Man, been hopping trucks in Jamaica from when I was knee high," I lied.

"Man, you still knee high, motherfucker. You might have hopped a boat over here, but I'm certain you ain't never hopped no truck, unless it was one of those donkey carts."

The argument ended up pretty much the same way it always did, us proving to Nathan that we were just as bad and wild as himself.

We rolled onto Church Avenue and hopped the first bus that came along. Black faces, hot and sweaty, gaped at us with mixed feelings from inside the crowded bus. The windows were open, a poor substitute for the air conditioning system that never seemed to work on those old buses, especially the ones heading for New Lots and Brownsville, the heart of rowdy nigger and Puerto-Rican territory.

Cars hooted and drivers shouted abuse as we clung to the sides of the bus, bouncing up and down like trained monkeys. Paul and myself took the side windows, resting our feet on the large silver bumper conveniently hanging off. Nathan was on the back, riding that old bronco for what she was worth.

"Ready to run! You guys spot any cops," Nathan warned. Black fumes from the exhaust burnt our noses. The driver revved the old, tired engine in another one of his attempts to dislodge us. He missed none of the numerous potholes along the route. We must have looked a strange sight—three fourteen-year-old boys hanging on the sides of the B35.

After riding on the bus for four blocks we jumped off, veering south. Hostile white faces gaped at us from inside as we hopped the Ralph Avenue bus. The back windows were closed and condensation dripped down the sides of the glass. The sound of the air conditioning was louder than the bus engine.

Bottles and stones bombarded us as we rode further into Cracker neighborhood, passing sturdy residential houses with flower gardens and trimmed evergreen trees.

The run that was slowly taking on the appearance of a helter-skelter trip came to an end when we jumped off in front of Carnarsie High School. There wasn't a black face in sight.

White folks held onto their bags tightly as we passed. Some crossed the road.

Nathan made his way around the school grounds like an old tracker familiar with difficult terrain. He led us nonchalantly towards a bicycle rack encased in the school's compound. The owners of a neat row of bicycles were sweating on the handball courts. We could hear the balls crashing on paddles and rebounding against the wall.

Nathan fiddled with a padlock chaining four racers together. Paul and myself looked on anxiously, glancing sideways occasionally to see if anyone was coming.

The lock finally gave way, relieving some of our mounting tension. Paul was practically on his toes, would have probably run away had it not been for his fear of Nathan.

The operation was a success. Our feet turned like windmills as we raced along Ralph Avenue screaming and cutting through cars.

Being young, restless and energetic we rode right past our area straight out to Sheeps Head Bay. The area was like Coney Island on a Friday night. People were all over the place buzzing with excitement. Cops were directing traffic. Loudspeakers were shouting coded messages to law officers with their guns drawn. There was a bank holdup and the robbers were holding hostages.

We raided a fruit stall on Church Avenue and made our get away, leaving the stall attendant shaking his fist and cursing us in Yiddish. The sea was a few minutes' ride away. After gorging ourselves on fruit we dived into the polluted water with our clothes on.

Nathan was happier than I'd ever seen him. He smiled at Paul and sang, "Bye, bye Miss American Pie, rode my Chevy to the levee but the levee was dry."

We picked up a chase by an Irish gang on the way home. The gang was hanging out on the corner of Church and Seventh Avenues under the overhead train lines. They seemed to be looking for some action and were glad when they saw us riding, exhausted, down the street.

They gave chase but their choppers were no match for our racers. They finally gave up chase when we reached civilization, the teeming streets of Flatbush.

The humid evening crept over the city. The weekend rush had started. Thieves and muggers laid in wait for healthy pay packets. Commuters were moving around at breakneck speed trying to get off the streets. The game of musical chairs had started, where the penalty for missing the last bus or train home would be costly.

The mouths of the subway stations were choked with people. Riding home was like playing Russian roulette. Cars were at a standstill and people jaywalked across the roads. There were minor car accidents and people threatening to end each other's lives.

The football players were relaxing on the steps, enjoying a cold beer, when we rode imperiously on the block. There was a sudden pang in my heart when I saw Nathan's older sister, Nadine, seductively passing her long slender fingers through Dave Green's long nappy hair. Who does he think he is, I thought, clenching my fists and feeling bitter. Just because he was the star for Tilden High football team didn't give him the right to my girl.

Her beauty was captivating, like an ancient goddess. Her young breasts rested lightly on Dave's shoulder and her light bronze complexion tingled with natural oils. She combed a handful of his hair and whispered softly with a smile into his large, floppy ears. Her long, curly Afro brushed the side of his face.

Nathan knew I was hurt. He shrugged his shoulders and smiled. Guess she wanted older guys! But shit! What was wrong we me? My mother always complimented me on my large brown eyes. "They're like a raging fire out of control," she said. My complexion was velvety dark, even if I was a little on the short side and slightly underweight.

The bicycles were shocking out like Liberace's diamond rings. A few guys from the football team offered us ten bucks apiece for them.

"Ten bucks," Nathan's eyes sparkled with greed. "Man, all we got to do is go and get some more tomorrow. With thirty bucks we can go partying tonight."

"Hey, man, thought you wasn't going."

"That's before I got this here cash, Danny boy. Besides, my

honcho Super Dice came around and gave me a special invitation. He says to make sure I bring you and him along." He threw back his head and gestured towards Paul.

"That dude's hot," I said. "Everywhere he goes there's trouble. Heard he done pass through every gang in the city."

"He's a sick cat," Paul screwed up his face. "The last day of school him and a few guys were calling me names. They looked like they were stroking for a fight. Lucky for me my father was waiting outside the school to take me over to Pitkin Avenue to buy some skins."

"You guys got it all wrong," Nathan made a face as if to confirm our stupidity. "Super Dice's the original homeboy from right here in the Fifties. He likes you guys, honest to God."

"What d'you think my name is? Willie Neck Bone?" Paul said. "Super Dice might be from right here in the Fifties but me and Danny ain't. Him and his boys always beating on West Indians."

"We ain't got to like the dude to go along to the party. Think of all the girls that'll be there."

Nathan smiled a thin smile. "There'll be so many broads there even you two jerks might score." He paused and looked into Paul's eyes and said invitingly: "Just for you I'll get that little girl in the eighth grade down in the locker room and you can have your way with her."

Paul smiled mischievously. "Danny can get some too?"

"As much as he wants," said Nathan, breaking out in the silly song he'd been singing all day about Miss American Pie and this will be the day that I die.

Chapter 2

The party was held in the gymnasium of our local junior high school. Someone had tripped the locks on the side doors to gain entrance. A live band from Wingate High hammered away some heavy sounds. The gymnasium was packed. Everyone was tripping out on acid tabs and reefers that were handed out freely by a foxy chick at the door as we entered. Hard drinks were on sale a buck a cup. There was Mad Dog wine, Night Train, Thunderbird, and rum. The chicks looked fine on the dance floor. Their hair finger-waved and slicked down on the scalp. Some sported marcels and pageboys. The guys all had big Afros that bobbed up and down in the smoke-filled atmosphere, stinking of reefer. Feet were sliding and knees shaking to the wild and crazy dances that were rocking the discos—Funky Chicken, Mashed Potato, the Bump, and the Hustle. Nathan was freaking out on the dance floor dressed in his Sunday best. A black suit that was two sizes too small and a pair of off-white sneakers.

Paul and I had given him our share of free drugs. Nathan had convinced us that's what Paul's secret flame from the eighth grade and her friend needed to get them going.

The two chicks were under his spell and bumping him on either side, swinging their hips like pendulums. Paul waited rapturously for Nathan to give him the all-clear signal.

We'd withdrawn to the sideline after a few embarrassing dance refusals. We weren't rejected because of our threads—definitely not. My sharkskin pants glistened under the overhead lights. I was jazzing my expensive multi-colored playboy shoes that I'd spent an hour buffing. I was well within the scope of fashion. Deep down I knew the reason we weren't accepted but sincerely hoped things would get better.

I nudged Paul. "Get in the groove, Homie, your time's coming up real soon. Nathan got those girls so hot they'll be melting before they reach the locker room."

"The sucker looks like he's about to welsh on me." Paul was doubtful. "Every time I give him the eye he ignores me." He paused and shook his head. "Man, this isn't our scene. Even when they stoned out of their brains they still don't like us."

The atmosphere in the party had reached fever pitch and I was running a temperature. Miniskirts were rising. The music had toned down to a lovers' serenade. Bodies were locked together in warm embrace. Occasionally a smiling couple would slip away downstairs to the locker room.

"Hey! Danny, do you think they'll ever accept us?" Paul took a sip of his 7-Up.

"Sure, they'll accept us. In a few weeks when we start high school you'll spot the difference. Them older kids are more mature. Many of them won't even know we're West Indians. We're already sounding like Yanks. All we got to do is eat shit and think Yanks and we're in."

"That's it, Danny. Why should I have to give up my Haitian roots just to be accepted?"

"Forget all that Haitian bullshit, man. We're Yanks now."

"Don't know about that." Paul shrugged his shoulders.

The band staggered to an abrupt halt. The drummer held the shimmering cymbals. Super Dice shuffled from out of the crowd and wheeled around the dais taking the mike from the pretty female singer.

Bodies froze in the midst of the Bugaloo and turned their attention to the dais where the willowy stature of Super Dice wheeled around and did an impressive James Brown shuffle. He sported a baseball hat turned around backwards.

"Yo, home team, chill out!" he shouted. "Everybody happy." He turned the mike towards the crowd with all the assurance of a stage actor.

The crowd near lifted the roof with their tumultuous shout of "Yes!" Surprisingly, even Paul joined in the shouting.

"Take it down, y'all," Super Dice shouted. "Yeah, real easy like." He waved his hands over the crowd like the conductor of a symphony orchestra.

The noise gradually subsided and attention was once again focused in his direction. He flicked a red bandanna from his back pocket and dabbed his forehead. "Things changing, brothers," he said gravely. "The gangs are closing in on our turf. They're getting greedy and want to expand. The Tomahawks gang and their punk leader, Sugar Bear, want control of the Nineties, Flatbush, Crown Heights, and the Clarkson area. What we gonna do, brothers? We just can't let them roll in and take over, right?"

"No way!" shouted Nathan, rocking unsteadily on his feet. The crowd was fired up by the threat. They mumbled among themselves until Super Dice's voice filled the room once more.

"Brothers, we all know what happens when an outside gang take over an area. They control all the action and got no respect for the residents. We the only area in this city that don't have a gang. Brothers, if we don't form one soon then we gonna pay with our lives like the people of Fort Apache Bronx and Brownsville under the hands of the Tomahawks and X-Vandals. The Savage Skulls executed one of our brothers last week on the corner of Church and Utica."

Super Dice had planted the seeds of discontent and he waited to reap the inevitable outcome. His deep, soulful voice sprayed through the speakers and his milk-white sneakers scuffed on the Formica floor. "Check out our walls and handball courts," he shouted in disgust. "Graffiti! Yes, motherfucking graffiti! The gangs done put their slogans up. Even those banana-boat nappy-heads got their names up. Total dis!"

He screwed up his face painfully and threw his hands angrily. His eyes wandered over his intoxicated flock. The acid tab was already creating illusions in their brains while the alcohol and speed heated their blood. The marijuana laced with angel dust summoned their thoughts to immediate dangers and insecurities. "All isn't lost! Oh, no, brothers! Right here in this very arena we got some of the toughest guys in the city." He raised an apologetic hand and threw a kiss to the she devil of Brooklyn. "Sisters, you ain't forgotten neither, we need Debs."

"Right on, brother!" shouted Charmane, a smooth-complexioned girl sporting a Mohican haircut. She was dressed like a rebel—bleached jeans and belly-showing tank blouse.

Super Dice paid her a compliment. "Hold tight, sister Charmane. Ain't no girl quicker than you when it comes to handling a blade. In fact, there are only a few guys in this city that can match your speed."

The crowd whistled and catcalled their respect for Charmane's notoriety. She revelled in the applause, wiggling her round ass and shaking her fist in the air.

Super Dice waved for silence, then continued. "Yeah!" He sighed like a gospel preacher. "Me and a few of the brothers have started putting a gang together, one that can protect us against outside intruders. We looking for a few more recruits. The name of this gang, or should I say our gang, is the Jolly Stompers." He cast his dark, sunken eyes to where me and Paul were standing. "Only Homeboys need join up because we taking no prisoners once we start rolling. All in favor say aye."

West Indians weren't considered Homeboys even though we lived in the area.

Super Dice laughed, delighted with the response from the crowd. They hailed him as a messiah. A deliverer, one who would rescue them from the foreigners and head-hunting gangs.

Looking around at the excited faces it dawned on me that me and Paul were the only ones that didn't have prior warning about the reason for Super Dice keeping the party. He'd moved from gang to gang with only one intention—becoming a leader. He got his wish.

Chills shook my body when I considered the local psychos and school bullies that joined the new gang.

Super Dice used his experience to further incite the crowd. "We're gonna be strong, brothers, stronger than the Suni Gods who claim to be the givers and takers of life. Together we gonna kick ass. Let me hear y'all shout, Jolly Stompers. Let's tear the roof off this motherfucker."

For five minutes there was loud chanting and stomping of feet. I didn't know which way to turn, neither did Paul. The crowd's reaction towards us earlier was enough to suggest we weren't part of their group. "Why were we invited?" I asked myself. My thoughts were interrupted by Super Dice's chilling voice amplifying through the speakers.

"Easy, crew!" he shouted. "Easy. Take it down real low.

Brothers, we gonna initiate the birth with a little sacrifice. Our name will be feared above the Devil Rebels, Tomahawks, and Vandals." He raised his hands in command. The lights went out, plunging the gymnasium into total darkness. An ominous hush fell over the crowd. Bodies moved around in the darkness. Feet shuffled hastily beside me. My immediate thought was that Paul had taken advantage of the dark to grab some of the flaunting miniskirt ass that teased our sexual appetites.

"Paul, chill out," I whispered discreetly. Something was wrong, drastically wrong. My heart started to race. There was no answer from Paul. A feeling of claustrophobia and dread enveloped my brain.

A fight had broken out beside me and bodies were scuffling on the floor. The darkness provided no clue as to who was fighting. There was a shuffle of feet making a fast exit, then a choking, gargling sound replaced the scuffle on the floor.

My concern started to mount when the gargling became one of desperation. I dropped to my knees and felt for whatever lay perishing. A warm, sticky body writhed under my touch. "Paul! Paul!" I shouted excitedly.

The lights flickered on as suddenly and mysteriously as they had gone out. My hands were dripping with blood, Paul's blood. I was frozen in terror, locked in disbelief. My mind put on hold.

The crowd screamed as they gathered around, waxed in terror. Stiff hands covered mouths. Vomit erupted from a few unsteady bellies.

My knees were soaked with the life juice rushing from Paul's neck like an open dam. His feet kicked violently and his hands found the large knife plunged into his throat. He tugged with his last burst of strength, trying to remove the fatal weapon.

Nauseated and unable to move, completely horror-struck, my eyes beamed down on Paul's body as it twitched and remained silent. He'd painfully passed over to the other side.

Super Dice wheeled on to the dais from somewhere in the crowd and took the microphone. "Chill out, Stompers! Quiet down! Don't be amazed. Heads got to roll when taking power."

Robot-like bodies turned towards the dais, giving their sadistic bloodthirsty leader their undivided attention. He said in a cold, chilling voice: "That's just the beginning, brothers. We gonna rule this here turf with an iron hand. Only with blood will we command the respect that's due to us." His eyes locked with mine and burnt through my nervous body.

I was on my feet, alienated from the crowd, blood still dripping from my extended hands. My eyes darted around the room, unable to focus on anyone or anything.

Super Dice poisoned their minds. "I want to hear y'all shout 'blood', Stompers. Shout it loud."

The echo chamber on the amplifier was switched on, expanding the word "Blood! Blood!" The drug-intoxicated youths started shouting "Blood" and stomping their feet.

Fear gripped every inch of my five foot six structure. Was I to be their next victim? Their chants and stomping exploded in my brain, driving me mad. My senses demanded I make haste away from the infectious madness.

Super Dice made his way slowly off the dais, his followers making an avenue for him as he charted a menacing course toward me. Nathan was beside him holding a clenched fist over his head and shouting, "Blood!" My blood.

Distorted faces moved towards me fueled by their thirst for more West Indian blood. I turned quickly and headed for the main doors, jumping over Paul's body and moving like the eye of a hurricane.

I exited in a dark hallway on the first floor. The light streaking through the door in the gymnasium cast a dim glow down the hallway.

The door that led outside the building was about fifty yards down the passageway on my left. Nathan and myself had often used that exit when cutting out of classes.

I found the door and shuffled clumsily down a flight of stairs hoping the heavy iron doors at the foot of the stairs weren't locked. There was total darkness in the foyer as I searched for the exit to freedom.

Pattering feet in hot pursuit hurried along the hallway. Several flashlights brightened the way for my eager pursuers as they searched diligently for their prey.

The four doors at the bottom of the stairs were positioned

side by side, each having an independent locking system. The first door wouldn't open. Neither would the second.

The door at the top of the stairs flew open and Super Dice found me with a single beam of light. Darkness shrouded my mind and numbed the activity in my brain.

Super Dice was joined at the top of the stairs by his pack of hungry wolves. Flashlights beamed down on my frightened body. Warm tears welled up in my eyes.

The cold, unfeeling voice of my executioner registered death in my brain. "Nigger, you one slippery motherfucker. Don't try getting through those doors. They shut."

The excited crowd behind him clawed at each other, hungry, wanting to witness the slaying.

"Sucker, you gonna die," Super Dice said harshly.

Frightened, I turned around and tried the third door. It, too, was sealed—like my fate. I turned and faced my executioners, flashlights blinding my eyes.

Super Dice was content to watch me suffer. He had all the time in the world. He barked: "This here's our country, we don't need no ass-licking Uncle Toms and black Jews." He pulled a long switchblade from his back pocket. Stars bounced off the stainless-steel blade. "Kiss the world goodbye, boy."

I looked up with tears in my eyes. "Nathan, please, man, help me."

Nathan shrugged. "Sorry, Homes. The boss says you got to go, you got to go."

"Why, Nathan?" I pleaded. "I never done anything to you. I'm begging you for my life, man."

Nathan said bluntly: "I'm a Stomper now and the boss says we taking no prisoners." He shook his head from side to side and concluded: "This is no joke, Danny. You West Indians got to know we mean business."

Nathan's blunt refusal sent my mind cartwheeling backwards to my first day on the block. Nathan had sought my friendship and was only too glad for the black company. His family were the only blacks on the block at the time. He'd stood up for me in school and shown me how to move around the streets. But then things changed when Super Dice started hanging around the school. Nathan was infatuated by his notoriety and now it was his company he sought.

Super Dice taunted: "Well, ain't that a good boy! Saying your prayers. Well, that ain't gonna help you." He started his move down the stairs, followed by the hungry mob. "I'm gonna rip your little heart out and have a bite, boy."

I screamed, knowing there was no way out. Quickly I turned and tried the last door. A feeling of exhilaration electrified me as the door smoothly gave way, letting me out into the coolness of the night. There was hope. My only obstacle was a low iron gate with sharp Gothic spikes along the top. The fence was slightly taller than I. I quickly climbed up and jumped, catching the ends of my pants in the spikes and ripping them all the way up to my ass.

"He getting away!" an excited girl shouted.

I sprinted like a gazelle pursued by a hungry lion. Either they weren't interested or I was too fast, but the chase didn't continue outside the building. The streets were deserted, taking on an inauspicious look under the dim night lights. Sirens whined in a faraway distance. I felt like a fish out of water, running and looking behind me, suspecting the slightest nuance of movement to be dangerous. A bright-eyed cat scavenging through the refuse in an overturned garbage pan looked me in the eye and scampered down a driveway.

Home was only a few blocks away but it seemed like miles. I burst into hysterical laughter when finally I collapsed on the concrete steps of my house. Someone must have dropped an acid tab in my drink, I thought, unable to hold back the tears flooding my eyes. Nathan had once told me that acid made him see strange things, like angels falling out of the sky.

"Sure, that's it," I comforted myself. I smiled, actually believing it was a dream. Paul would be right there in the morning, running beside me.

A slow-moving vehicle with dipped headlights crossed over Linden Boulevard and headed down the block. I ran into the house and stood behind the door, peeping through the glass until the car passed. I slipped further into the house and stood under the fluorescent light directly beside apartment number one. My hands were caked with blood. I blinked, hoping the stain would disappear. Panic ran through my distraught body. Paul was dead. It wasn't a dream and I wasn't tripping out.

This was the real world, the world of hate and torture that had eluded me in my few years of existence. Suddenly I was alone, with no one to take my troubles to.

The lights blinked and then went out, plunging the hallway into total darkness. The yellow hue from the outside street light cast a glow through the glass in the front door. The dark frightened me for the first time in my life. The lights were controled by a timing system and weren't due to come back on until six in the morning.

Swiftly I felt my way up the stairs and stopped in front of Max's door. A beam of light peeped from under the door and the radio was on, tuned in to the informative talk show that kept me awake on so many nights. My room was directly above Max's apartment, facing the front of the house.

The stuffy, ancient smell of his lightly furnished apartment was calling me within an inch of knocking on the door with my clenched fist.

He shifted about inside as if he felt the presence of someone at the door. I needed the support of a grownup, someone wise and learned like Max. He was a man of the world and had a quality in his hoarse voice that would somehow bring me comfort. But any thoughts of seeking Max's counsel vanished when I remembered the farce earlier in the day when his hat was plucked from his head.

I tiptoed backward away from the door and made my way up the next flight of marble stairs, fumbling in my pocket to find the doorkeys. Locating the key socket was like pinning the tail on the donkey in the dark.

I rushed straight to the bathroom as soon as I entered the apartment. My hands turned foamy red as the dark, clotted blood dissolved and escaped down the drain. It took several scrubs to remove the stain from my hands and fingernails.

The little apartment had suddenly acquired extra rooms and dark chambers of horrors as I walked from the bathroom to my room.

The slightest movement in the streets caused me to rush to the window. Nathan knew where I lived and also knew that my mother worked nights and my father was on holiday in Jamaica. My mind raced, hurdling over the many possibilities of horror that could befall me before the break of dawn. And daylight would bring fresh horrors. I was a marked man. My ticker roped up and down like a damaged yo-yo. Strange thoughts passed through my mind. I can't die. Other people died. But did every man believe in his own immortality? The answer seemed to whistle in my brain. I was only a minor thread in the major tapestry of life.

The smiling faces of all-American basketball stars stared at me from the posters on the wall. They seemed to be laughing at me. I covered my ears and could hear them shouting "Blood!" In a frenzy I attacked the walls, tearing off the posters and screwing them up. The faces of Willis Reed, Wilt Chamberlain, Jullias Erving, and Kareem Abdul Jabar withered in an untidy heap on the floor.

I switched off the light and stood to one side of the window. The street lights outside shone in my face and cast reflections of tree branches in the room. I was safe by the window. There I could spot Stompers if they came. That would allow me enough time to climb the fire escape to the roof, and if I was lucky I could jump across to the neighbor's house and escape. Nathan had once dared me to make the Grand Canyon jump. I had taken the dare and almost fell to a crushing death below in the driveway, littered with the neighbors' old cars. Nathan had turned yellow and run from the roof laughing.

At some unknown stage during the night I fell into a troubled sleep, harassed by heinous nightmares. A glistening blade was a breeze away from my throat. The distorted faces of Nathan, Super Dice, and Charmane beamed down on me like microsurgeons.

"No, no! Please. I don't want to die!"

"Danny, take it easy, boy." Warm comforting hands shook my sweat-drenched body to a conscious awakening.

I blinked and rubbed the rocks from my eyes.

"Boy, your sins finally catch up with you. All that running up and down the streets during the days."

"Mom!" I wanted to throw myself in her arms and give her a big hug.

She looked around the room at the untidy mess. Her eyes rested on my bloodstained rags thrown on the floor. Stunned, she peeled the sheets from the bed in a quick sweeping motion and gave a long troubled sigh of relief.

"Danny, where all that blood come from?" she asked worriedly.

I turned in the bed and looked at the bloodstained clothes as if they were alien to me. Mom had seen blood on my clothing before when I dissected her pet kitten in the basement.

"For Heaven's sake, talk to me." She shook my body and moved briskly around the bed and stood over the clothing.

I sat up in the bed and was about to tell her what happened when there was a desperate hammering at the front door.

Mom gave a start and looked at me quizzically. The knocking got louder and louder as though someone was trying to kick off the door.

Fear struck a match to my nerves once more. The end, I thought.

Mom rushed from the room before I could warn her. She cursed as she skipped across the over-furnished living room.

I jumped out of bed dressed only in underclothes and rushed into the living room. In a flash I had the window open ready to climb on the fire escape.

Chapter 3

I was halfway through the window when a deep baritone voice declared, "Sergeant Polaski and Officer McCarthy."

Cops, I thought, halting my flight. The muscles in my body relaxed and a feeling of security replaced my paranoia.

"We would like to have a word with your son if possible."

"Why, what's he done now?" Mother asked wearily.

"Nothing of any great importance. He might be of some help in our inquiries," the cop answered.

"Officers, would you like to come in and have a cup of tea while I get him up?" Mother asked obligingly.

"No thank you very much. We'll wait here," the cop answered firmly.

The two officers stood to attention as I approached the front door. They flashed their silver NYPD badges.

"Officer McCarthy. Take it you're Danny Palmer?" said the taller and stockier of the two. His deep voice was labored, as if stuck in his throat.

"Yeah, I'm Danny. What's the deal?"

"That's no way to talk to the gentlemen." Mom slapped my back.

McCarthy gave me a wry serpentine smile, his pale, round face and hungry, grey eyes lit up like tongues of flames rising from an inferno.

The other officer, Polaski, cleared his throat and said formally: "No need to get uptight, Danny." His voice was cool and quiet like the calm before the storm. He was dressed more to the fashion than his partner whose blue suit under a long untidy raincoat seemed to have been tailored for a watermelon.

"Danny, we just want to ask you a few questions about last

night." His pencil-line moustache twitched. He had a big gun stuck in a holster under his black bomber jacket.

"What questions?" I asked suspiciously.

"We can discuss that down at the station," Polaski said bluntly. He combed his fingers through his sandy colored hair that receded from his pig-like forehead.

"Officer, could you please inform me what's going on? I work all night and just got in." Mom's voice was heavily accented. She stood shoulder to shoulder with me. She had a finely chiseled face and was in her mid-forties with brown, smoldering eyes. Her complexion was light and her thick shimmering hair was tied back in a ponytail.

"A boy was hurt at a party last night. We just want to show Danny a few pictures, see if he can identify any of the people that were there," said Polaski.

"Will he be needing a lawyer?" Mom asked anxiously.

"No, no," he replied emphatically. "He'll be out of the station within the hour."

"Where's your warrant?" I barked.

"Warrant!" exclaimed Polaski as if it were a forbidden word. "Warrants are only necessary when we want to arrest someone." He smiled as if trying to convince me that their actions were strictly aboveboard. "You're in the clear, kid, we just want a little help with our inquiries."

"No warrant, then I ain't going nowhere," I protested.

McCarthy's face hardened. He was pissed. "If you want us to get a warrant then that can be arranged." His eyes rolled and he rubbed his hairy, freckled paws along the framework of the door. "A warrant means we got to bring in the squad, rip this door off the hinges, smash up furniture inside, dig down a few walls, and if that's not enough arrest both of you for assault with intent." All that was said in one breath, causing Mom to cringe at the thought of the devastation.

"Danny, go with the police, son. They won't hurt you. I wouldn't like them to ransack my house," Mom said.

I drew back behind the door and shook my head disapprovingly.

"I'll come with you if you like," Mom said supportively.

Polaski quickly interrupted her chain of thought. "Sorry, Mrs Palmer, there isn't enough room in the car for anyone else. Regulations," he smirked.

The two officers stood outside the open door as I got dressed, hurried along by a frightened mother. She waved me on with an encouraging smile as the two officers followed me down the stairs. I was wearing a new T-shirt, jeans, and sneakers.

The cops' heavy footsteps tramped behind me as we shuffled along the first floor. A vicelike grip tore into my shoulderblades as we neared the front door. The light from outside streaked through the glass in the door.

"Hey, what the fuck is going on?" I yelled.

"Shut your goddamn mouth and move on," replied McCarthy's coarse, impatient voice.

A black unmarked police Ford was parked in the driveway. Slumped around the steering-wheel was a scruffy, untidy, undercover cop with a toothpick stuck in the side of his mouth. His slim face sprouted a week's growth of ginger stubble. The oversized hat perched on his head slumped to one side as he nodded approvingly as my two captors led me to the car.

The old battered Ford with the names Batman and Robin sprayed inartistically on the side pulled out of the driveway and away from the line of garbage pans so we could get in.

McCarthy gave me a hard shove as I climbed into the back of the car. They took a seat on either side of me. A mesh screen separated us from the driver. The engine caught and roared into action. The driver, with one arm hanging out the window, steered effortlessly out the driveway and along the quiet street. He took a left on Lenox Avenue and cruised slowly.

Polaski moved his left hand over and rested it on my leg. I tried to shake him off but his hand gripped me like crazy glue.

"Ever been fucked in the ass, kid?" he asked casually. The driver smiled and nodded his head.

McCarthy turned his head and tucked in his chin. "The officer is talking to you, boy."

"I ain't no faggot. Satisfied?"

McCarthy gave me a crisp backhand slap across the face. "Don't ever refer to me like one of your street buddies, nigger.

From now on you call me sir or Mr McCarthy. Now try answering that question."

"Fuck you!" I shouted.

"Boy, seems like we gonna have to teach you some manners. Ain't that right, Polak?"

"Sure the hell is, and if he don't cooperate I'm gonna put this here Polak dick right between his butt cheeks." He tried to get a handful of my nuts.

My fingernails dug into his hand and removed a piece of ivory flesh that slowly turned red.

"Son of a bitch," he yelled, shaking off his hand as the pain surged through his body.

The car pulled up behind three other vehicles at the intersection of Utica and Lenox. Early morning work zombies scampered between cars before the lights changed to green.

A sudden rain of blows bombarded me from both sides. McCarthy landed the heavier blows, concentrating on my ribs and middle section. Blood trickled from the corner of my swollen right eye as they pulled up outside the 71st Precinct on Empire Boulevard.

I had heard many chilling stories about the towering white chamber of horror. It now seemed I was about to witness those horrors firsthand. The two skunks, one on either side, dragged my screaming body up the stairs. Police with gun holsters on their hips ushered their catch through a green gate in front of me.

They booked me in hastily at the front desk, avoiding a line of foul-smelling hookers and transvestites scooped up from Buffalo Park during the night. Black people were begging and screaming for their rights. Literally every conceivable area of the station was swarming with people. They were handcuffed to steaming radiators and stairwells. A junkie was handcuffed at the foot of the stairs, left to cold turkey, and wallowing in his vomit on the ground. Young juveniles shouted obscenities as angry rednecks led them away to detention centers and Schimmerhorn Street for processing.

I was dragged up three flights of stairs to the fourth floor. A glamorous girl with a tall Afro and long shapely legs barged through a set of swinging doors. Her lips were red, like Marilyn Monroe's, her complexion high yella. She stopped dead in front of the two officers, blocking their path. "Polak, baby," it whined. She sounded like a lion in heat. "Come give sugar a kiss."

"Out of the way." Polaski's face flushed red with embarrassment.

"Jive son of a bitch, you been up my shit-pan so many times it still hurts," said the pansy.

This Polaski was really a faggot, I thought, fearing for my safety. McCarthy intercepted to save his partner any further embarrassment from the speeding tongue of the transvestite.

"How'd you like to be brought up on a charge of obstruction and spend a few days in the basement while we interrogate you?"

The rowdy transvestite snuffed in his breath and straightened the strap of the long pocketbook hanging from his neck. He gave McCarthy a quick, crocodile stare then stretched out an effeminate hand. His long, red fingernails cupped Polaski's chin. He pouted his lips mockingly. "Coochey, baby, you know where to find me when you need me."

Polaski gave him a silent *please not here you're embarrassing me* look.

The pansy sniggered, wheeled on his heels, and skipped off down the stairs like a ballet dancer. I was dragged into a bright, spacious room on the fourth floor. Plainclothes detectives with shoulder holsters danced around with sheets of paper swinging in their hands. Typewriters clicked noisily from the too many desks and telephones rang nonstop. Excited prisoners screamed and wailed as interrogating police laid siege on their brains. The whole scene was like a cattle auction. I was just another face in the vast chamber of horrors.

They threaded me through the mass of confusion and into a small room with bars on the window. In the center of the room was a wooden chair with straps to restrain the hands and feet. Directly opposite was a desk and chair. A bright bulb hung from the ceiling. The walls looked like the inside of a slaughter-house. I was made to sit down. McCarthy eased himself into the chair behind the desk.

Polaski had one leg on the ground and the other jackknifed over the top of the abused piece of furniture, bearing scars inflicted by lighted cigarette ends. He pulled a crumpled pack of lung-dusters from his pocket. There was one cigarette inside. He straightened it out and sparked a flame. His head pivoted and he looked into the ceiling and blew out a contented whirl of smoke.

"We got a nice treat lined up for you, boy. Knowing how you niggers like to cry racial harassment, you should have no complaints." McCarthy rocked in the chair, his fingers knotted in front of him. He landed the chair squarely on the ground and looked into my eyes. "There's a black enamel spade in here, thinks he's the station ace. He'll have a hell of a ball beating the shit out of you. But mind you," he paused as if offering me a deal I couldn't refuse, "he's not as nice as me and Polaski here. Save yourself some trouble and tell us what happened at the party last night."

"Go ask your mother," I said rebelliously.

"Oh, yeah," he smirked. "That's the way you want it. I'm gonna enjoy this more than I thought." He slapped the desk with an open palm. "Polak, give Riley a shout."

"My pleasure," said the foul buzzer-head, climbing from his perch and marching to the door.

Five minutes later, a tall, athletically built black officer strolled into the room looking like the world was his stage. He stared me up and down. His beady dark eyes weighed me up like a prized game cockerel after it had been spurred by his opponent. He brushed his lower hand over his low skiffle haircut and gritted his pearly-white teeth. "So you the man, or should I say the punk, that killed the Haitian boy." He spoke with a deep nasal twang and sounded like a ghetto pimp.

"Let me warn you, he's one hell of a ball buster. Looks like you gonna have to give him some of the same treatment that you gave that white juvenile last week."

"What you getting at, Polak? White or black doesn't matter one fuck to me, dig."

Polaski nodded and smiled reservedly, raising his hands in mock surrender. Riley stood in front of me and placed a firm hand on my shoulder, his eyes penetrating mine intensely.

"Now, punk, I sure hope you ain't fixing to bust my balls because you gonna be one sorry nigger."

Polak shifted around on the desk, his face showing his desire to witness a sadistic beating.

Riley waved a sheet of white paper in front of my face. "Right, here's a confession. Sign it so we can get the fuck out of here. All it states is that you killed Paul Semere by self-defence."

"Mister, you got the wrong person. Wasn't me that killed Paul. He was my best friend. Ask anyone at the party they'll tell you."

"They already have. We had Nathan and a few of the party organizers in here last night and they all said they saw you kill the kid then run away."

"They're lying, mister. When the lights came on he was bleeding on the ground."

Riley pounced on me ferociously, grabbing me by both shoulders and shaking me like a rag doll. "Yo, Homes, maybe you missed the point. I ain't asking what you did or didn't do, all I want you to do is sign this here paper."

"It's no use, Riley," McCarthy said wearily.

Still holding my shoulders, Riley turned to face the grotesque hulk swinging in the chair. "I think he needs to be left alone with Polak here for a while," he said.

A smile brightened Polaski's face as he climbed from the desk. He walked over to me and waved his cigarette effeminately. "These officers think you're a ball buster but I say different."

Riley placed his hands on his hips and looked on, seemingly outraged at Polaski's line of speech.

"What you say, kid. Just give the word and we can be left alone for a spell. I'll be nice and gentle with you because when those budi-bandits on Rikers Island get hold of you it's lights. How you boys say it in the ghetto? Homes, yeah. That's it. I sure hope you a virgin, Homes. You are a virgin, ain't you?" he asked, as if a "no" would actually disappoint him. His ice-blue eyes stared into mine.

"Cut the shit," Riley growled. He looked at Polaski with utter revulsion.

Polaski patted my shoulder with regret and returned to his

perch. Riley gripped my shoulder once more, this time with a vengeance. "How old are you, kid?"

"Fourteen and a half." I prayed my age would earn me a sympathetic reprieve.

"Fourteen," he reiterated. "The most you'll get for this is one year youth custody. And if we put in a word to the DA you could even get probation. Not like you killed anyone special. He was only another jungle bunny."

"He was more than you or your partners will ever be. Fucking house nigger, living to please the white man." The words just seemed to roll off my tongue, unchecked, uncensored. They were like a double-edged sword that sliced into Riley, stunning him momentarily.

Riley scowled at the two white officers as they exploded in a fit of derisive laughter. He was hell-bent on proving his impartiality in dealing with black prisoners. I was only too aware of the mental see-saw that was tilted away from Riley. I learned one important lesson that day, one that was to follow me for the rest of my life. Black cops meant bad news for black people. A black man stood more chances being arrested by a racist white cop.

I made up my mind to die at the hands of these rogues, and if the faggot Polaski wanted my ass it would be over my dead body.

Polaski and McCarthy held my arms while Riley fixed my hands and feet to the restraining straps on the chair. Riley's heavy hands delivered a series of crippling blows to my body.

"Is that the best you can do?" Polaski taunted.

Riley ignored the sarcasm and landed a few more punches.

"Sign the paper," he demanded. Sweat poured from his body like the Niagara Falls.

Blood trickled down my face. My body ached. I felt nauseated. I was about to pass out.

"Looks like you done gone too far," McCarthy said as my head slumped to one side.

I regained consciousness underwater. My mind raced backward to my earliest childhood memories. I was drowning. Water rushed into my mouth and nostrils. The smell of defecation and urine reeked in the frothing water that bubbled and roared around my head. Suddenly I was plucked from the water. I gasped hungrily for air.

"Boy, you got as many lives as a cat," said the unmistakable voice of Riley.

My spinning head slowly adjusted to the environment. They were holding me upside down over a toilet bowl.

"Ready to sign the paper?" Riley shouted impatiently.

With my last burst of strength I tried to kick at the other two officers holding my legs.

"Lower him again," Riley said.

"If he dies we got no choice but to charge you for murder," McCarthy said.

Riley looked at him sourly. "Why, you honky son of a bitch," he growled.

"Have it your way," McCarthy said resignedly.

They dipped me repeatedly into the water and held me under until I thought my lungs would burst. Riley made a point of flushing the toilet as soon as the water had gathered in the overhead bowl.

"The telephone book treatment never fails," suggested McCarthy as they pulled me from the bowl and supported me with their bodies.

They dragged me over to some stained washbasins where two telephone books were soaking in separate bowls. Leaning beside the bowl was a long police night stick.

The telephone book was placed across my midsection and secured by Polaski while McCarthy had me in a yoke around the neck.

Riley stepped backwards and took aim at the target. He made a strike, delighting himself and the other two officers as my body wheeled around like a spinning top.

I was in agony. It was a more intense pain than I had ever encountered in my life. Every nerve in my body was alive and pulsating. A surge of electricity passed through me. I started entertaining thoughts of signing the paper but their sardonic smiles and contemptuous behavior gave me the necessary boost of strength to resist them.

"Looks like you just about ready to sign the confession,"

Riley grabbed my chin and pivoted it towards his face. "House nigger, you nothing but a failure. This is as far as you will ever go." I spat in his face.

Riley stepped back, pointed the night stick at Polaski, and barked: "Get the other book. I'll show this little West Indian creep who's a failure."

"One more hit and he won't make it. He's only a kid, for Christ's sake," McCarthy warned.

"Do as I say, goddamn it, before I lose my temper and bust his head wide open with this here club."

Polaski removed the book from the sink. It was dripping with water. I closed my eyes thinking this was my last day on this miserable planet. I was going to join Paul and quite welcomed the idea. The devastating blow was landed. My bowels emptied immediately. My nerves pulsated as if each one was set alight by an open flame. After the pain had reached every part in my body only then did I pass out once more.

They forced me back to consciousness with a bright light that burned through my eyes and hit me at the back of the head like the blow from a sledgehammer. The bitter taste of bile erupted in my mouth.

They'd returned me to the little room in the back. Riley stood over me holding the interrogating light.

"Enough!" McCarthy yelled. He jumped up from behind the desk and strolled over. "Know something? This kid is right. You're nothing but a failure and your days around this station is just about coming to an end."

"Listen, McCarthy, I don't need no two-bit cop predicting my future. Honky motherfucker," Riley cursed ruefully.

"Ain't that just like a nigger. Put you under some pressure and your true colors come out," McCarthy said.

Riley quicky switched the light to his left hand and landed McCarthy a punch squarely to the jaw. McCarthy staggered backwards and drew his gun.

Polaski quickly jumped between his partner and a steaming Riley. "No, John, for God's sake, no," he pleaded.

McCarthy had one hand on the butt of his gun inside his shoulder holster, the other rubbed the hurt on his jaw. "Nigger, your days are numbered. It might not happen in a day but it's coming, as sure as the sun shines you can bet your sweet life it's coming." His eyes burned bright red, filled with a deep-seated yearning to get even.

"Come on, Riley. Get the fuck out of here before something happens." Polaski pushed him out of the room with his free hand.

Riley backed out of the room and slammed the door as he went. McCarthy slowly pulled his hand from the inside of his coat and walked behind the desk.

Chapter 4

McCarthy pulled a large grey file from an inside drawer and slung it on the floor, raising dust and scattering dog ends. "Pick it up," he barked in a gruff voice.

My hands unsteadily raised the file and placed it on my lap. Tentatively my fingers skipped through the pages, the contents holding my mind to ransom.

Drawing closer he asked: "Recognize any of those faces or seen any of them around the area?"

"No," I answered hastily, unable to suppress the twinkle in my eyes that suggested I was lying. The pictures quickly brought back to life the daily tortures that the people in the Kingston ghetto suffered under the hands of some of those men. As a young child I had spent many sleepless nights praying that these very same dreadlocked men wouldn't kick off the door to our house and take our lives. A new day would bring police and soldiers into the crowded tenement dwellings, ripping up the houses and accusing residents of hiding wanted men.

McCarthy interrupted my thoughts with a loud bark that frightened me back to the present. "I think you lying to me, boy. Those pictures were taken right there in your area, the Nineties and Fifties." He wrinkled his nose. The smell of shit drowned the damp air and apparently enticed Polaski.

"Help us nail some of those scumbags and we might just forget the murder."

Where was this nightmare going to end? I could take no more of their torture. "Leave me alone," I yelled hysterically. "I don't know any of those men and I didn't commit any murder." I threw the folder on the floor, scattering the contents. McCarthy looked down. The hard faces of dreadlocked gangsters stared at him as if in defiance and proclaimed their dedication to lawlessness. There was silence. A wounded look appeared on his face. He drew in his breath and walked slowly over to the window.

"For Christ's sake, kid! Do you think we like dragging you down here and beating the shit out of you?" He rubbed the hurt on his chin where Riley had socked him. "There's a bloody war going on out there. You brothers seem to think it's cool killing each other." He shook his head. "Life isn't about going to parties and wearing funny little hats. After the fun and games then you got to face me, so take a hard look because I'll be on you if you so much as sneeze."

He spat a foam of blood on the wall and watched it trickle down. "Paul Semere wasn't the only one to get killed as a result of gang violence last night. Eight! That's more than the amount of servicemen killed in two days of fighting in Vietnam." He turned around, braced his hands against the windowframe, and looked out, sighing heavily as if all the corruption in the city was there, bubbling under his nose like hot tar. He muttered spitefully, "I don't give a shit if you brothers slaughter each other." He spun around quickly and thumped his fists on the desk. "Not in my fucking area! Understand?" He whispered a low aside directed for Polaski's ear.

Polaski nodded and said doubtfully, "It's worth a try."

McCarthy walked to the center of the room and cleared his throat. "How'd you like to earn some extra money each week?"

"Fuck you," I hollered. "Stick your money up your ass."

Polaski sprang to his feet, relaxing only when his partner put out a hand, stopping him from delivering a blow to my head.

McCarthy placed a hand on my shoulder. His voice mellowed. "Stay on the right side of the law, kid. Start getting ideas and you'll be shoveled off the sidewalk in little pieces." He flung the door open, merging the noise from outside. "Get the fuck out of here."

I got up unsteadily and moved towards freedom, trying to get the fuck out of there before they changed their minds. Wondering eyes followed me through the crowded room. Shit seeped through the bottom of my trousers and left a trail where I walked.

"Whoo wee!" a blind man gasped, tapping his cane to seek some sanctuary.

"He one funky motherfucker," bellowed one of three Afro-headed tarts handcuffed together and sitting on a pew.

"Son of a bitch done shit himself," shouted a fly dude, dodging under a heap of cheap fur to get a whiff of his own armpits.

It was late afternoon when I staggered out of the precinct. The bright afternoon sun baked the slime that plastered my body. Flies gathered around and followed me along Empire Boulevard like bees round a honey pot. The battered gypsy cabs that roam the city for nickels and dimes spotting a passenger from a hundred yards on a crowded Fifth Avenue seemed to miss my salute to hitch a ride.

Bus drivers closed their doors in my face when I tried to get on. The passengers on board screamed for him to move on.

"Hey! Driver! Put your foot down, that motherfucker is stinking up the place!" yelled a brother near the front of the bus with a mute ghetto blaster sitting on his lap.

I was in pain and found difficulty walking. The telephone book treatment was now beginning to execute its full judgment. People side-stepped me and chanted abuse. They must have thought I was one of the whacked-out junkies that hung out on Union Street.

I fell to the ground and dragged myself along like a wounded fawn seeking the warmth of its mother. Hostile black folks passed me by, some discharging phlegm from the pits of their bellies and spitting at me with a twang. A middle-aged woman wearing a head wrap and carrying a Bible stopped and preached the gospel from St Paul. She rebuked me for being unruly and disobedient and said that Jesus loved me regardless of my sins. I felt relieved when she moved on, shaking a tambourine and shouting "Praise the Lawd."

I dragged myself to a phone box, but it was completely vandalized. How many times in the past had Nathan and I been the culprits of such acts? I tried a few more boxes along the way, finding them in the same burnt-out and smashed-up condition.

Mom was infuriated when finally I reached home. She was appalled at my revelations of torture and cried earnestly when she remembered how foolishly she'd allowed me to be taken by the two cops. "They won't get away with this," she said, dabbing at a lump above my right eye.

I stretched out in the tub, allowing the hot water to soothe away the many aches that afflicted my body.

Mom was hurt. Her face was drawn and her banana-skin complexion got darker as hot blood flowed through her veins. The only time I could ever remember seeing her in such a rage was when I shot dead the neighbor's dog with my uncle Fleego's gun. She was deeply moved by the news of Paul's barbaric slaughter. Pools of water welled up in her eyes. "Suppose those police come back? And what if those boys should hurt you?" Her voice was just above a whisper. She traced a line around my forehead with her long, slender fingers. "You're only a child. I would hate for anything to happen to you."

There was a brief silence when only the sound from a neighbor hammering in the driveway could be heard.

Mom's tear-filled eyes suddenly went aglow, sparkling like a prized jewel. "Danny!" she said softly but energetically. "Why don't you let me send you down to Jamaica with your father until all this blow over?"

I sat up in the tub as though a bolt of electricity had just passed through the water. "Mom, you know how I feel about him." I was daunted at the thought of having to set eyes on my father so soon after he had gone away.

Mom didn't try to hide her mounting agitation. "Nonsense," she said briskly. "Sonny would love to have you down there with him while he's repairing the old house."

Like hell he would, I thought. Without Mom around to stop him he would beat me to a frazzle. The thought of seeing my old neighborhood and friends did in some way sound enticing, but I felt I owed it to Paul and to myself to stick around. Head hanging down I said defiantly, "I'm no quitter, Mom."

She looked up as though she'd seen a ghost. "Boy, you're beginning to sound like your dead uncle Fleego." She rose to her feet and shook the soap from her hands into the tub, then gave me a condescending smile. One that was supposed to make me feel silly and green. "What do you know about trouble," she sighed, speaking as one that had truly seen some rough times, surviving as a woman in a Kingston shanty town.

"I had to hide you under the bed when gunmen threatened to root us from our little house." She stood with her arms on her ample hips and murmured, "Mixing with low life idle boys is not the way. Fleego had that same arrogant and no-quit attitude as yourself and he wouldn't rest until a policeman put a bullet in his brain." She quickly closed her eyes and crossed her chest.

I pulled myself from the tub and reached for the bathtowel hanging on the rack. Mom offered me a smile and shook her head pathetically.

"Wise up, Danny. Everything we have belongs to you. It might not be much but it's a damn sight more than some of those other boys have. Nathan don't even have his own bed to sleep on. His sisters are so dirty if you threw them on a wall they would stick."

Mom sure had a way with words. I smiled for the first time since Paul's death. She continued speaking as though trying to convince me of the poverty-stricken environment in which Nathan's family lived. "I had to lend Nathan's mother five dollars last week." She bowed her head and winked as if saying, "Think about that." She left the bathroom and closed the door behind her.

I returned to my room and slipped into bed. The aroma of a highly seasoned West Indian dish wafted in the air. This was a typical remedy of black eye peas and pigs' feet stewed and devoured hot. But there was a hurt that burned deep inside me; one that no amount of home cooking would ever cure.

That evening there was further panic when I passed blood in my urine. The rolypoly nurse on the ground floor was consulted. She allayed some of Mom's fears by assuming that I was experiencing a slight strain as a result of the beating. She advised Mom to seek a doctor for me if the symptoms continued.

Shadows of the evening crept through my window like uninvited guests. The Mets were five down to the Dodgers. A stream of orange sunset flowed through the window and blurred the vision on the little portable television sitting on the dresser.

I was on my back looking into the ceiling, falling victim to delusions of grandeur, thinking how I would overpower the might of the Stompers should they rise up against me.

A noisy ice-cream truck hammering the same hackneyed tune drew me to the window. The humidity of the evening had brought out an army of screaming kids. They played stick ball, paddle ball, and other games that black kids had devised over the years to amuse themselves.

Max was seated under the tree directly outside my window. He was alone and bored. He leaned forward in his chair and used a slippered foot to toy with a bottle stopper.

My father's car was parked in front of Max. It looked more like a birds' toilet every day. Dad loved his old Pontiac, and it gave me great pleasure to witness the acid that fell from the birds' asses and defaced the paintwork. The tree impaired my vision, blocking out Nathan's rundown shack at the end of the block.

The next few days I remained inside. A bag of nerves. At nights I kept vigilant guard by the window while Mom sweated away the hours cleaning floors in a tinning factory.

The Semere family came around. Grief had ambushed the heart of Mr Semere, a short, pleasant man. His wife was tall, stocky, and loud. She screamed for revenge and threatened death by witchcraft for all those responsible for her son's death.

"Let me prepare a bath for Danny," she appealed to Mom eerily, her voice a mixture of French patois and English.

"The Lawd is my spiritualist," Mom answered virtuously. "I leave everything in His hands."

Mrs Semere looked at her stupidly while her husband wept. "They killed my boy." He held a shaking hand over his heart and stuttered, "How will I ever fill the hurt I feel?"

Fueled by her husband's grief Mrs Semere danced around the room, brushing a crochet doll stiff with starch from the center table to the ground. She stopped in her tracks and looked around like there were spirits present only her eyes could see. Her eyes sparkled and she dipped into her bag for a strange phial. She opened the phial. A strange smell escaped into the air as she hastily dashed the contents to the four corners of the room mindless of where they fell. "Death and destruction!" she yelled.

On the morning of the fourth day I ventured outside, a stranger in my own neighborhood. Every moving thing seemed to be a potential threat on my life. Physically I was in good shape and I decided to run down to the milk stop on the corner of Church Avenue. I slowed up when I reached Nathan's house. The roses in his garden were in full bloom, carefully groomed by his mother, Matilda. I picked a fragrant petal and sniffed it while listening to the familiar uproar coming from inside the house.

Nathan's father was resigned to the bottle and constantly henpecked by his wife. He had long since given up the task of providing for seven children and a wife. The noise grew louder as a side door flew open and out staggered the inebriate himself. He looked lazily into the sky, lost to the world.

I ran off down the block testing my recovery with a full sprint all the way to the milk stop. I bought a cold egg-nog and sipped it slowly as I returned home. Passing Paul's house brought back bitter memories. I still had not come to terms with his death. I somehow expected to see his smiling face and bushy Don King Afro come rushing out of his house.

Cool Dave Green eyeballed me from across the street. He was washing his old Mustang. I moved cautiously, holding all Afro-Americans in contempt.

"Yo, Homes," he called out in a soulful voice.

The pavement gave way under my feet. I looked around nervously. He called out once more.

"Yeah, man, you. Come on over here." He looked mean but his voice was mellow and without malice. Water dripped from a piece of cloth held loosely in his hand and soaked into his old mashed-down sneakers. His legs resembled tree trunks. He would have no trouble catching me if I tried to run. He was bare chested and his muscles bulged, a towering stature well over six foot.

The morning was young. The residents had not yet taken to the streets in numbers. My body was geared up for the trucking.

"No need to worry. I ain't gonna eat you." He raised his hands in a welcoming gesture, then shuffled to the front of the car. He sat on the hood, causing rust and corrosion to trickle to the ground. "Heard those two bums Batman and Robin gave you a pretty good whopping."

"It was nothing," I shrugged, trying to look calm.

His deep brown eyes smiled, but still I kept my distance in case he was entertaining any way-out thoughts of capturing me for the Jolly Stompers.

"Man, what gives?" he asked, sounding slightly agitated. "I ain't got horns. Not that I know of anyway. Relax. I'm on your side." He looked me up and down. "Sulking ain't gonna get you nowhere. I mean it's a shame what happened to little Paulie. He was a nice kid." He wiped at his fingers with the rag and muttered philosophically, "There's an old saying that when your hand's in the tiger's mouth then you got to take your time and pull it out."

He sounded like an American version of my father whom I loathed but somehow wished was around. His hair was neatly cane-rowed with the ends tucked under conveniently. How I detested him, getting all the attention from Nathan's older sister, Nadine.

Lost in a tug of war battle of lust and hate, I forgot momentarily that I was on a gang's hit list.

Dave's long arms shot out, like a bolt of lightning. He one-a-catted me. The dirty rag in his hand dripped water down the front of my T-shirt. That wasn't the problem. I was caught by this towering giant. The carton of egg-nog fell from my hand and splattered in many directions on the ground. My heart stopped beating and my mouth went dry. His hands gripped me like a vice.

His belly laugh broke the quietness of the morning. "Take it easy, I know exactly what you're going through." He released me.

"What do you know about being a West Indian?" I barked, feeling a touch of self-pity. "I got hate coming out of my ears. In fact, hate is my middle name. I'm the black Jew. Plantain head. Uncle Tom. Name it. I ca—"

He raised his hand and cut me short. "There you go beefing like you the only immigrant being picked on. Wanna know about abuse, then stop in my school for a day. Imagine arriving from Jamaica and sounding like English was eaten with chop sticks, and hav—"

"Are you Jamaican?" I asked.

"That's right. I was born right there in the Kingston public hospital and grew up on Luke Lane. I was thirteen when I came here." He tilted his head towards the rays of golden sunlight that peeped through the trees. "Five years," he mused with a sense of pride. "That's the same year that Malcolm X died. If he was still alive these gangs wouldn't be killing each other in the streets." His face hardened and his brown eyes narrowed. "There was no doubt about brother Malcolm's love. He stood for all of us, not just Afro-Americans but Afro-Blacks all over the world. He taught us that we are all of one tree with many branches."

"Try telling that to some of these brothers around here," I said dismally. "Besides, it's all right for you. Everyone likes you." My words might have carried an element of grudge but it wasn't intentional.

He snorted. "Big deal. I'm a football hero. Everyone loves Dave Green. When I started Tilden High the handful of blacks in that school made my life a misery. My knuckles were forever sore from constant fighting." He made a tight fist and eyeballed his knuckles, searching for old scars. "My getting to play ball was a spot of luck. The coach for the football team saw me whopping one of his loudmouth players in the locker room. He waited until I nearly killed the sucker. I was prepared to get thrown out of school, but the coach just patted me on the back and said, 'That was some pretty skilful footwork.' He was referring to the way I had cleared my opponent's foot from underneath him with one sweeping motion of my right foot." He paused and pointed a finger. "That's one rule you must never forget—when fighting with Yankees always use your feet or they'll dance all over you because they've mastered the art of street boxing." He smiled.

"Yeah, the coach took me under his wing and taught me the game. I was keen to learn and here I am leading scorer in the high school football league. Come September got me a scholarship to play state ball. Girls are tripping over themselves just to date me, even the ones that had previously scorned me."

Slowly Dave was convincing me of his loyalty. I no longer held him in contempt. He scratched his broad forehead.

"Things sure are changing," he said regretfully. "In my day people only got beaten up. But now the youths are turning to murder to prove their point. They feel it's their duty to rid the country of the rising migration of West Indians. The Yankees have completely alienated themselves from the West Indian population. As a result the Jamaican youths are trading their once proud Afros for dreadlocks."

A car sped down the block and interrupted the conversation. He looked into my eyes intently and asked, "Why do you think you wasn't laid out beside Paulie?"

"They sure enough tried but I was too fast for them," I assured him, kicking at the dripping carton of egg-nog and crushing a few ants.

"Mean they tried to scare you. They chose the easier target," he said knowingly. "Haitians are quiet people. The most they do is babble about witchcraft. Jamaicans on the other hand are fighters. If word got around that a Jamaican got killed things would really start to heat up around here."

"Shit, ain't no Jamaican gonna come and save me. I got every psycho in the area wanting to put out my lights."

"Ever heard of the Rastafarians?"

"Sure, who hasn't? I would rather have all the gangs in the city on my back than those long-hair freaks."

Dave laughed. "Well, they are the ones that's giving the gangs a run for their money. They're armed and extremely dangerous. Many of them are murderers shipped out of Jamaica by the government." He clasped his hands in mock prayer and genuflected. "Behold, Satan comes bearing mighty powers," he said in a put-on voice. He stood up and stretched his legs, kicking out the cramp of sitting in one place too long. "Should be starting high school soon, right?" He stifled a yawn.

"After the holidays," I answered promptly.

"Try to get into Tilden High," he said.

"Too late! I'm already allocated to Wingate."

"Wingate!" he exclaimed. "That school is like a volcano just waiting to erupt. It's the headquarters for every gang in this city. They got more Rastas in that school than what exists on the island of Jamaica. The tension is thick when you walk down the hallways or venture out on the grounds." He shook his head in despair. "Make sure you got a bullet-proof vest before term starts. An innocent girl got shot last year when a

Rastafarian opened fire on a member of the X-Vandals gang in the hallway."

I stared at him hopelessly.

"That's no place for an academic mind. Don't let those guidance counselors lay that zone rap on you. Zoning is just another way of getting all the blacks and Hispanics in all the run-down schools around the city. Bro! You got to be diplomatic when dealing with the man. They be smiling in your face and kicking you up the can just as quick. Niggers as far afield as Brownsville and Bedford Stuyvesant are attending Tilden. And they are way out the zone."

"So what you saying? Tilden is the place to be at, huh?"

"They got their problems, but nowhere on the scale like Lane, Jefferson, Madison, and Wingate just to mention a few." Dave's pessimistic view of Wingate was enough for me to want an immediate change. The local papers were always highlighting the level of violence in the school. A police SWAT team was called in at one stage. They seized a quantity of arms and ammunition.

I was riding high when I left Dave's company. I had made a new friend. Someone who would possibly stand in my corner when the inevitable showdown occurred.

The sun came out in its full glory as the day aged. I must have been the only one inside. From my bedroom window I could hear the sound of cheerful kids playing in the sweltering heat. I was quite comfortable watching an old James Cagney rerun on the television, admiring his courage in the face of danger.

Disaster struck James Cagney only seconds before it swept into my world. An unprecedented silence fell on the children playing outside; the noise from the ice-cream truck ceased and was replaced by the sound of death in my ears. The war cry of Jolly Stompers summoned my quivering body to the window, my heart pounding against my ribcage: my executioners were at hand.

Max and the other old-timers clumsily made their way into the house, leaving behind their deck chairs in the rush.

The noise dropped as I stood in clear view for all to see. Super Dice looked me in the face. Nathan stood beside him waving a baseball bat in the air.

Super Dice spoke with a silky smooth voice. "I come to collect my debt, sucker."

Knowing full well what he demanded in payment, I considered the avenues for my escape. I counted fifteen heads, including a few girls from the school.

Charmane, the girl Deb known for her quickness with a knife, looked up tauntingly. She resembled a whore from Forty-Second Street. She wore a tank top with crotch-hugging cut-off jeans. Her legs were shapely and coffee-smooth. She was hot and looking for action. I had once seen her cut up a girl from South Shore High. Charmane had slashed the girl's face with a barber's razor just because the girl wouldn't get up and give her a seat at a basketball game.

Heads started popping through windows. The neighbors, frightened and confused, looked down at the menacing mob.

Accompanying the black warriors were a few Puerto-Ricans with bandannas around their heads. They wore vests and blue jeans with the name Jolly Stompers bleached down the side.

Super Dice shouted: "How's it gonna be, Homes? Either you come on down or we come up and get you. It's time for you to make a contribution to the soil like your Haitian friend."

Nathan laughed maliciously and turned on my father's car with the baseball bat. The front windshield went, then the back, followed by the side windows, and finally the bodywork. The crowd screamed with excitement.

I remembered what Dave said about Rastafarians and prayed one would march down the block with his head raised, pompous and proud. "My cousin is a Rastaman and he just came from Jamaica. He says if I have problems with you guys I should call him," I shouted.

Super Dice looked about arrogantly. "Nigger, did I hear your coward little ass fart or was it the wind?"

Nathan fell about the place with laughter.

Super Dice waved for quiet. "Punk. Ain't no nappy-head freaks can test my gang."

The bedroom door flew open and Mom rushed in, her face a mask of confusion. "What's all the noise?" She rushed to the window. "Jesus Christ!" she cried out, devastated by the sight that greeted her eyes. "Get away from my house before I call the police." She leaned out the window and waved them away angrily.

The sight of Mom and the sound of her deep, accented voice fuelled the gang's amusement. Super Dice brushed the tip of his nose with his thumb. He stood wide-legged with his hands folded across his chest in typical bad-boy pose. "Hey, bitch. It seems like you beefing for some of what your son's gonna get."

"She can get a mouthful of my buzzer too," shouted Mo Dean, making a provocative jerking off movement in front of his groin.

"She mine," declared Charmane. "I'll carve her up nice and slow."

"Why you little pissing tail good-for-nothing," cried Mom.

Charmane yelled. "Fuck that mumbo-jumbo shit. Why don't you come on down and make my day." She paused. "Guess you ain't got the nerve to. But when we come for your boy then I deal with you personally."

Mom was about to pull her head from the window when Charmane dipped behind a parked car and emerged with a stone. She quickly took aim and hit Mom above the eye. Spots of blood trickled on the steps below.

Incited by the blood, the gang sprang into action. Stones and missiles rained on the house, forcing us inside. The sound of glass shattering echoed around the house. The windows in my bedroom were shattered.

We rushed into the living room seeking cover, but none was to be found. The gang was in the driveway and around back, showering missiles at every window.

Mom rushed to the phone and dialed 911. Missiles were flying through the windows along with slithers of glass. The gang savagely plied their trade of destruction. We sought refuge in a spacious wall closet in the living room. Mom gave me a push inside and slid the door shut.

We were in there for what seemed like ages, uncertain of what the next minute of fate had in store.

The wailing of police sirens brought us out of hiding. Outside, neighbors had taken the place of the gang. A red-eyed police car was parked in the middle of the street. Two uniformed black officers dragged themselves from the car and parted the crowd.

The young kids danced and reveled in all the excitement.

I followed Mom as she stepped hastily from the apartment. She raised her skirts to avoid the splinters of glass that lined our path.

Max was outside in his short-sleeved summer shirt. Even Sophia, the old Jewish spinster confined to her room with acute agoraphobia, had been driven from her apartment. She stood supported by a walking frame, her jaw hanging and her eyes pleading to know what was going on.

The two cops met Mom on the stairs. She covered the cut on her eye with some tissue. "What took you so long?" she blurted angrily.

The taller of the two cops stopped chewing gum long enough to hiss, "Listen, lady, you not the only one got problems. Be thankful you still got a roof over your head."

Sweat stained the armpits of his shirt.

"To hell with you," Mom barked, apparently spotting the envy in his eyes that she owned such a property.

The other cop cleared his throat, and cocked his chin. He said arrogantly: "If that's the attitude you're going to take then we'll just leave you to solve your own problems."

"Officer," Max said in a deep baritone voice. Catching the cops' attention he commanded, "I suggest you address this fine lady with some more respect."

Both cops stood to immediate attention. It was as if they heard the voice of their superior officer. They knew a white face spelt caution. White folks knew people in high places and would normally take complaints to the areas where black people failed to tread.

"The boy responsible for this lives at the end of the block." Max paused to catch his breath. "He's making life difficult for many people around here. Not satisfied, he's brought his friends to help him accomplish this." He waved his hands over the destruction, his wrinkled face a mask of disgust.

The tall cop wiped his forehead. "I only hope when I apprehend this boy I'll have plenty of witnesses to stand up in court," he stressed sending fear through the shrinking black faces.

"I'm not afraid," declared Max.

The cop nodded. "Whoever wants to make a formal complaint, they are welcome to come down to the station. There's nothing more we can do until the complaint has been lodged under oath."

"Is that all?" Mom protested.

"That's all." The cop turned on his heels and walked away abruptly.

The angry crowd parted and gave them room as they swaggered back to their car and sped off down the block.

I decided to pay Nathan's house a visit. The Stompers had left behind a pile of stones. I chose twelve and strolled down the block. Nathan's younger sisters were playing on their spacious, threadbare lawn. They ran when they saw me coming. I walked around the house, smashing every window in sight. The neighbors nodded in agreement and returned to their houses. I returned home and awaited the repercussions.

Chapter 5

The double-glazing company was called in to replace the broken windows. Mom was forced to accept another one of their crippling payment schemes before they started the job. She was already up to her neck in debt to this very same company, having been conned eight months ago by one of the company's modestly pretentious agents. "With double glazing you can cut down on heating expenses," the balding agent had said. Eight months later the heating bills were still the same, if not higher. Mom had taken two night-cleaning jobs to help make the monthly payments.

Some of the neighbors chipped in and helped us clean up the broken glass. Mom was in tears when she weighed up the hard task ahead of her. "Sonny will have to come back from Jamaica to help me foot these bills." She threw some glass in the garbage pan.

The thought of my father returning so quickly sent shivers rippling up my spine. Dad had gone down to Jamaica to repair our old house and to throw out some squatters who had taken over the place.

Mom continued to complain as she worked. "The Amco oil truck will be around in two weeks. How will I be able to buy heating oil for the winter at this rate? With tenants like Max and Sofia it won't be long before the double-glazing company own shares in the house."

"I could always get a job," I suggested.

"The money would come in handy, but where are you going to find work at a time like this?" she asked dimly.

"The Big Apple supermarket on Church Avenue. They're always looking for people."

"We'll see." She looked apprehensive at the works truck that pulled up at the front of the house.

The double-glazing company brought out their full work force. Scaffolding climbed the sides of the house. Hammers echoed down the driveway. The workers raced against time to complete the job before nightfall.

The setting of the sun brought a look of contentment to Mom's face as she admired the workers adding the finishing touches. Her moment of relief was short lived when Nathan's mother and her eldest son Alphonso came strolling down the block. They looked like death. Nadine trailed behind them. She looked stunning even though she, like the rest of her family, was after my blood.

Mom stepped in front of me. She crossed her arms and stood firm. "Matilda! Let sleeping dogs lie," she warned.

Brimstone and fire flared from Matilda's nostrils. She was a tall, hefty woman with Indian ancestry. Her long unkept hair was bundled around her head. She spoke in a Deep Southern voice. "Bullshit. I ain't letting nothing lie. I want pay for my windows your boy broke."

"Oh, it's my boy now. When you have him running all over the place doing things your own kids refuse to do, then he's good old Danny."

Matilda gave a start as if her secret had been let out of the bag.

Mom nodded shrewdly and said: "Nathan broke my expensive windows and Danny broke some of yours. Some were already broken anyway."

Matilda barked: "What Nathan does is his business. If you bad enough to claim compensation then you welcome."

"So it's down to who's bad. Well, I'll tell you. The only thing bad is the way you bring up your children. Nadine has had every boy in the neighborhood."

"I ain't never had your ogle-eyed son," Nadine said unashamedly.

"Shut up," yelled Matilda, cutting Nadine short. "Talking about bringing up kids, guess you could do a better job. That's why your scavenging little ass upped and came to our country, because you couldn't afford a night's meal where you came from. I detest people like you sucking up to the white man and cleaning their shit. Doing domestic work and saying 'Yes massa, no massa.'"

"Don't mention night's meal to me, Matilda. Without me you wouldn't eat."

The neighbors laughed. Many were Haitians. They had heard about Paul's death and were expecting trouble.

Matilda looked around ruefully, challenging the very air she breathed. She took a mighty step toward us, silencing my mom.

"Don't fuck yourself," Mom warned sternly. She quickly unfolded her arms and pulled a long glistening kitchen knife from under the sleeve of her blue kitchen overalls.

Matilda was stunned. The varicose veins on her legs tightened. She huffed with a mixture of fright and vengeance.

Alphonso moved into action. His round, sleepy eyes narrowed.

"Don't get too close to her, Alphonso," Matilda warned. "She's mad like all those others that come off them there boats."

Alphonso's effeminate face looked dour. His neatly trimmed Afro boasted a brown streak down the left side. He carried his mother's height and vaunted a pair of gold studs in his ears. Being a gang member credited him with fine threads, a luxury denied his family.

Afraid of Alphonso's presence, I shrunk behind Mom. Alphonso was one of the leaders of the X-Vandals gang. He had a reputation for being extremely wicked.

"Don't run, Danny. Don't ever run from these people!" Mom shouted.

She was showing me a side I never knew existed, although my uncle Fleego had once told me that she was a bit of a tearaway in her younger days.

Alphonso pointed. "Back off, lady. My beef ain't with you, but if that knife so much as scrape my mother then you gonna be one dead woman."

"It would take more than you and that . . ." Mom stuttered and threw Matilda a sour look. She stood confident and announced: "Nathan and his friends killed the Semere boy. I'm not gonna. let anything happen to Danny. Not over my dead body."

Alphonso unexpectedly turned and gave Mom a double-handed push, throwing her off balance and pitching her backward. Matilda moved in for the kill.

Mom rocked around on her heels and recovered quickly. She eyed the danger and wiped the knife menacingly across the leg of her overalls. Her feet started to shuffle around like a street fighter. "Come on," she dared, poking at both her rivals. She gritted her teeth: "Matilda, if I push this knife inside you, then you gonna have to smile before I pull it out."

"That's it, you done gone too far." Alphonso prepared to pounce.

I was well out of his reach. "Mom, please." I squirmed, fearing for both our safety. "Please, Mom, let's go in the house." The tension had drawn a quiet murmur from the crowd who had previously cheered Mom on. The silence was broken by the heavy sound of a car engine racing down the block. The thundering of the Mustang's tired engine got louder as the car came to a stop in the street beside the action.

Dave Green gunned the engine, keeping it alive. He shoved his head out the window and shouted, "What's going on down here?" He removed his summer shades.

Alphonso smiled. "My main man! Come join the fun, Dave. This here's a double bill you about to witness." Dave allowed the car to tick over and stepped out, wearing a Yankees' baseball T-shirt, shorts, pro-keds, and knee-high tube socks.

Alphonso jigged around waving one hand like he was doing breast stroke, the other held on to his nuts. "This here coconut punk done broke all the windows in my house, Homeboy."

"Seems like someone been busy working on his house too." He observed the tense white faces on the scaffolding.

Alphonso was puzzled. "Hey, man, those things got to happen to let all these here immigrants know that they can't just roll into our country and take what's ours. As a brother you should know that."

Dave looked him up and down contemptuously. "What's yours, man? Since when a lowlife illiterate punk like you owned anything?"

Alphonso forced a smile. "Hey, Dave, chill out, slice. It's me you talking to, man."

"What the fuck about you?" Dave replied angrily.

"Man, since when you become a banana-boat lover?"

"When it sicks my stomach that you'd have the nerve to want to fight a grown woman and a boy."

Alphonso hissed. "The bitch got herself a knife. Ain't nobody pull no blade on me and get away with it."

Dave turned to Mom. "Give me the knife," he said softly.

Mom shook her head in defiance. "This is my security. The first one of them make a wrong move gets it."

Dave appealed to her once more. "Give me the knife, Mrs Palmer. No one is going to hurt you."

I tugged at Mom's overalls. "Do as he says, Mom. He's my friend."

She contemplated the decision, then twirled the knife around in her fingers before giving it to Dave. "Where I come from a soldier die with his weapon in hand." She bit her lip and rested a hand on her hip. Her hair was completely disheveled and fell about her face.

Dave threw the knife on the ground. "Make your move, punk." He kicked the knife within Alphonso's reach.

Alphonso sniggered. "Dave, you my brother. I can't fight you."

"Don't ever call me your brother again, punk. Make a move before I make one."

Alphonso looked around nervously at the hard faces that offered him no support.

Dave gave Nadine a quick, dismissive glance then looked arrogantly at Alphonso. "Just as I thought. You're all mouth. All you know how to do is mug little old ladies on the subway and snatch pocketbooks. Get the fuck out of here. Leave these people alone. Got any beef with them, then you take it up with me and my crew."

Alphonso took a few steps backward.

"Right on," shouted one of the white men on the scaffolding. Nathan's family was on the retreat. This brought applause from the onlookers.

"This isn't the end," babbled Matilda.

Mom continued to rub salt into the wounds and shouted, "Woman! Go and take a bath. You smell like rotten cabbages."

The neighbors gathered around to congratulate Dave. The applause was second only to when I saw him make a touchdown against Madison High in the finals.

"I hope this incident won't cause you any problems." Mom was concerned.

"These monkeys know what tree to climb," Dave said calmly.

"If there's ever anything I can do for you please don't hesitate to ring my bell," Mom said.

An elderly white couple sat patiently in an old, well-kept Chrysler behind Dave's car. They smiled cheerfully.

I followed Dave to his car, holding the door as he slipped behind the wheel. "Thanks again, Dave."

He looked confused. "Again?" he inquired.

"Yeah, man! For setting me straight this morning and now this."

"Think nothing of it, man. It's about time I did something to help anyway."

I bade him farewell and stood back as he injected some life into the Mustang and sped off down the block.

"Nice boy," Mom said as we made our way up the dimly lit stairs toward our apartment. She trailed behind me. "Some Americans can be so nice while others could be outright evil."

I knew Mom was talking about Dave, but I didn't let on that he was from the same country as us.

That evening my father made his weekly collect call from Jamaica. I could tell by Mom's words and actions that he held me responsible for all that went on. He was returning in two days.

The following day I went down to the Big Apple supermarket. The manager hired me as a stock clerk. The pay was sixty bucks a week and there was plenty of overtime. I wasn't expected to start until the weekend.

I was in an exuberant mood as I left the manager's untidy office and walked through the crowd-filled supermarket. The air conditioner was on full blast and the piped sound of melodic muzak poured from some overhead speakers. Young boys were at the cash-out desk packing customers' bags into trolleys. The security guard at the main doors eyed me suspiciously as I left the building.

I strolled lazily along Church Avenue. The heat had brought out a mass of bodies on the street. I ducked into the doorway of the Fruit of the Loom clothing store when I saw a group of mean-looking guys marching down the block. They were members of the Savage Skull gang. They were all dressed in sleeveless denim jackets with white skulls painted on the backs. The gang walked down the street, beating people at random and snatching chains from their necks.

A screaming police car with lights flashing turned off Utica Avenue and gave chase to the gang. I came out of hiding and decided to sneak into the Rugby Theater on Utica Avenue. There was a double-bill showing rated X.

Opposite the theater I caught sight of four of the Stompers standing by the underground bowling alley. I hid myself amongst the crowd and turned around. My heart raced as I weaved through the forest of bodies that milled around on the sidewalk. White faces on Church Avenue gave me a sense of security, halting my flight to freedom.

The old Jewish egg seller was sitting outside his shop on the corner of Church and Fifty-Second Street. The stalls were out with a variety of cheap eggs on display. Tempted and unable to resist the temptation I ran past the stall and knocked all the eggs to the ground.

"I'll have your mother know about this, Danny Palmer!" he shouted angrily.

I'd been wanting to do that ever since rumors started flying around the neighborhood that Nadine was giving him head in the back of his shop in exchange for free eggs.

This section of Church Avenue was still owned and operated by the Jews. Black people walking around were few and far between.

Out of breath and panting I strolled past Dave Green's house. He was standing on his porch with his head hanging down and a dismal look on his face. I stepped on the porch and took a seat on the wall. "How's it going, Dave?"

"They got me, Danny." His voice was harsh.

"Who, Dave? Who's got you?" I feared the worst.

"Uncle Sam. I am to report to the nearest recruiting office on receipt of this draft call-up." He produced a crumpled piece of paper.

"Tell me you joking, man."

"Wish I was, kid," he said sadly. "This looks like the end of my career."

I was about to lose the only person outside the family who would stand up for me in the face of danger. "There must be something you can do. Refuse to go, like Muhammad Ali."

"Refusal is sure prison and if I run away I'll be a fugitive for the rest of my life."

"Why you? There's so many other people they could choose."

"Politics," he answered hopelessly. "The whole purpose of this draft is to deposit a few brothers in the grave. This is the white man's answer to the rising population of blacks and Hispanics flooding this country." He snuffed in his breath and went on pessimistically: "They sending us to the land of no return. It just ain't fair. The whites in this country outnumber the blacks ten to one. That means that for every black that's drafted then ten whites should be taken but it's the other way round."

"Sorry," I said unhappily.

"Me too." He chucked the piece of paper on the ground and looked across the street where a short stubby man groomed his manicured lawn. "I need something to take my mind off this bullshit. Fancy coming for a ride?"

I shrugged. "No sweat. Got nothing better to do."

We got into his old boneshaker and sped along Church Avenue as if we were competing in a grand prix final. Carbon monoxide fumes escaped from a hole in the rubber that went around the base of the gear shift. It didn't bother me. I was enjoying the ride, sitting close to the window so the world could see that I was cruising with Cool Dave Green.

We rode along in silence. Dave was clearly taken back by the draft call-up. He pulled up at the lights on Church and Rockaway Parkway. The engine grunted as he prepared to sprint away from a group of smiling Puerto-Ricans in a red

Chevrolet who were challenging us to a drag. The lights changed. Tires squealed. The Puerto-Ricans left us in a trail of black exhaust fumes.

Bright sunlight spun around the car as we sped through the slum-infested streets of New Lots. The labyrinthine streets and derelict housing played host to poor and destitute blacks and Hispanics. The residents were out in their numbers. They milled about in their scanty summer threads. They hung from fire-escapes, in front of liquor shops, and on stoops. They were everywhere except in their rat- and roach-infested accommodations.

Graffiti slogans stained the walls. The white and black sign of the Tomahawks gang was everywhere. The names of some of their prominent gang leaders were also spray-painted on the walls. The streets and sidewalks were lined with broken bottles, empty beer cans, and over-spilled refuge from piled-high garbage pans. Hydrants were sprouting on every corner like the fountains in front of the Plaza Hotel. Half-naked children waded in the miniature pools created by the excess water and poor drainage system. I laughed at the total anarchy that ruled the area. The rising stink of poverty mugged the air of things pure and clean.

Dave checked his speed to a crawl as we approached a gang of slick-looking guys standing on the corner of Saratoga and New Port Street.

"What are you doing?" I stuttered.

"That's the Tomahawks gang over there. They get edgy when anyone speeds through their turf." He pulled up beside the curb.

The gang looked up from their game and shot us a quick scrutinizing glance. The circle of men separated. In the middle was a youth about my size but much older. He yelled to a clenched fist, "Roll baby roll." He let loose some dice and clicked his fingers anxiously.

The men's eyes left us and followed the rolling pair of dice to a stop.

"Shit." The short youth looked down at the dice with disgust. He handed over a handful of bills to the banker then picked up the dice. He walked with the rhythm of the ghetto towards the car. A long-handled gun stuck out from his waist. His dark complexion was moist with sweat. He wore a Robin Hood beaver hat with a long feather in the side. "Hey! All American, what brings you in this side of the jungle?" He shoved a hand through the window and gave Dave a lengthy soul brother handshake. He smiled as if showing off his many gold teeth, then drew back. "Kiss these here dice, Davie. They been rolling against me all day. I feel you just brought me a change of luck." He shook the dice around in his hand and offered them to Dave's willing lips. "Yeah! Now let's see them roll." He cool-shuffled his way back to the group who kept the action on ice, waiting for his return.

The banker smiled and held a stack of greenbacks above his head. "No name, no change." He rolled the dice.

The short, dapper youth rubbed his hands. Eyes shriveled, catcalls echoed. "Pay up, sucker," he yelled.

We sat in the car musing at Shorty's victory when a bundle of loose clothing came rushing through the window. The smell was unbearable. Dave gave a start as a sorry-looking face peeped through the window.

"Mister, youse ain't got a dime, has you?" said a smiling-gaped tooth bomb. His fetid breath poisoned the air. Spittle foamed at his mouth like a dog with rabies. His face was battered and chipped up.

"Beat it," Dave yelled. "I ain't got no dime."

The bum's face went sour like a rotten fruit. He barked: "Big black motherfucker. Driving this here expensive car and can't give a poor old man a dime." He made a grab for Dave who was halfway over my side trying to get away. The bum screamed: "I'll break your fucking neck."

"Pops. Take it easy," said the deep voice of the short youth.

The bum coughed up a whirlpool of stench from his guts and pulled himself from inside the car. "Gold Tooth," he scowled. "I'm telling you this sidewinder is one lucky son of a bitch. He's lucky I didn't rip his heart out. Talking 'bout he ain't got no dime."

"Here's a dollar, Pops, now shove off," said Gold Tooth.

The bum was all smiles. He held the dollar in his hands like it was worth ten times its value. He said politely: "Mr Gold

Tooth, man, you is the coolest cat out of all these here youngsters." He waved the dollar in the air and wobbled off towards the liquor shop, dragging a pile of rags behind him.

Gold Tooth stood a distance away from the car and crouched. He laughed out loud as he saw us gasping for air. His face suddenly went serious. "Be careful how you driving through, Homeboy. The Vandals are on the war path. Some joker wasted two of their men on the corner last night."

Dave's face showed deep concern. "I thought you guys had agreed to a temporary ceasefire." He was astonished.

Gold Tooth raised his eyebrows. "That shooting has blown the cover off the shit and it's getting stickier by the hour. The thing about the whole scene—wasn't us that done it. They ain't accepting our word, so fuck it. We go to war once more." The men behind Gold Tooth moved about quickly and their hands went for the weapons in their waist. They shuffled towards the car and shielded Shorty.

Across the road the object of their apprehension cruised slowly down the block.

"They circling again," said one of Gold Tooth's men.

"Don't move, Dave! Just sit still until they go by." Gold Tooth followed the car with his deep brown eyes.

Six disciples of death sat in the old battered Oldsmobile. Resting on the windows were their guns. Their faces, impregnated with hate, challenged the world.

Gold Tooth whispered: "Women and children walking around—they won't shoot." His eyes followed the car like a hawk as it passed and continued on its dark trail. "Let one of my boys escort you through this jungle, Dave."

"That won't be necessary. I'm friendly with everyone."

"Guess you right." Gold Tooth smiled.

The car's engine shuddered to a start. Dave shouted: "They done drafted me, Tooth."

"So what's new? Everyone in Brooklyn knows you're going to Ohio State." He slapped a sexy chick on her ass as she passed.

"There's been a change of plans. It's Cambodia Province now," Dave said.

"Shit!" exclaimed Gold Tooth removing his hat and rubbing his forehead. "No man's land."

"That's right, Homes. Just want to let you know before I slide out."

"Take it on the chin, blood. That there war ain't no different from the one we fighting right here on the streets."

His eyes were restless and his body was in motion. "Yo! Yo!" he shouted, deploying his men with quick movement of his hands.

"Freeze that motherfucker." He pointed to a red Cadillac cruising down the block with chromed headers and slick white-wall tires.

Men poured into the road from the four corners of the jungle, their presence frightening the very flies that fed on the ghetto stench.

He spoke hastily: "Chill out, Dave. I got to tax this free-riding sucker. They got to pay some dues if they want to drive through. Bullets cost money." He made his way across the road, leaning to one side and swinging his hands. Style was his god. His suede Pumas and sharkskin pants were the joint.

Dave drove slowly through the jungle of discontent. He was saluted on each corner by more of the Tomahawks gang who stood out among the throng of poverty-stricken black folks.

Slogans and graffiti-bright warnings stained the walls and outlined the Vandals' turf. ENTER AT YOUR OWN RISK. SPIES WILL BE EXECUTED.

Dave hitched up in front of a rundown semi-detached house. Five men and a woman were seated on broken slabs of concrete outside the shack. They were sipping cheap wine and cursing each other in drunken slurs. A young child dressed only in shit-heavy Pampers played at their feet, creeping among the filth that surrounded the house. The baby had a syringe in its mouth. The needle was missing.

The woman, resembling the scarecrow's wife, staggered to her feet. "Take that there thing out of your mouth, child," she yelled. One of the men filled her paper cup. She threw back the drink in one covetous gulp and drowned out her concern for the young child.

Dave hooted. The horn frightened and stunned the group of red-eye drunkards.

"Who you looking?" the woman slurred, exposing her stained teeth. Her complexion was losing the fight to stay black as the excess of alcohol in her blood turned her red.

The area was bubbling, shaking to the rhythm of black and poor, bad and ruthless. Black folks were fighting, laughing, playing basketball, swinging from fire escapes, dancing in the streets, shadow-boxing, wiggling under sprinklers, lying down in gutters, shooting dope and freaking out.

Dave was about to sound the horn when a cheerful round-faced girl emerged from inside the dingy house. Her broad smile faded as she made her way past the drunkards. She knelt down and snatched the syringe from the baby. "Is y'all blind or what?" she yelled, chucking the syringe into the heap of refuse that lined a little garden plot. The smile returned to her face as she rushed to the side of the car.

She pouted her brown-cushioned lips and looked into Dave's eyes.

"Hey, babes, thought you'd forgotten all about me." She pushed her arms through the window and circled Dave's neck. A pair of silver bracelets jingled on her hands.

Dave reached out and massaged her round buttocks through the fabric of her flimsy hot pants. She groaned ecstatically as her tongue snaked in and out of his mouth.

"Get in. We're going for a ride," he said smoothly.

She broke away and clasped her hands between where her crotch bulged. "Ah! Ah! Not so quick, honey. You look like you ain't been fucked in months."

"Could be," replied Dave.

She cast her alluring eyes to where I sat mesmerized by her beauty, looking down the cleavage of her chest, hoping one of her mammaries would drop out from her flimsy breastline sleeveless blouse.

"What's this? I didn't know you were into little boys, Dave."

"Why? Does it turn you on?" Dave asked.

She smiled, shifted her weight around on her feet and wiggled her ass. She moistened her lips, wiggling her tongue, rolling her eyes, and hijacking my emotions, causing a stirring in my young loins. The sensation was greater than sneaking into the Rugby Theater and watching *The Devil In Mrs Jones*.

Dave patted my leg. "This is my younger brother, Danny."

"Hi! Danny," she said in a trailing voice. "I sure hope you ain't nothing like your brother."

"He's exactly like me." Dave squinted: "Get what I mean?"

"Dave!" she sighed with a gleam in her eyes and a touch of innocence in her voice. "I hope you're not planning to abuse my poor little pussy."

"No more than necessary." He rubbed her crotch as she brought it into line with his hand, moving to give him clear access.

She groaned and jerked back. "OK, give me five minutes. I'm just gonna chuck some water on her."

Dave shot her a curious glance from the corner of his eye. She muttered, as if reading his mind, "Hey, babes, no need to be alarmed. How was I to know you'd show up? Just gonna make it nice and spicy the way you like it." She turned and wiggled like a worm towards the house.

Chapter 6

The girl was hotter than a sow for boar after a full moon. Her thighs and ass rolled like a ten-pin bowling ball as she disappeared inside the house.

Dave smiled. "One thing you got to learn is where to get the best pussy." He raised a black power fist at a group of guys passing on the sidewalk. "There's no pussy like ghetto pussy. Ever had none?"

"Sure, all the time."

"Don't jive me," he said. "If we going to be brothers then we got to level with each other. This broad right here is Bertha. She give the best head in all of Brooklyn. She got a tongue that can be as rough as sandpaper one minute then smooth as silk the next. The only other girl that come close is Nadine."

"What? Who?"

"No need to get excited. Nadine's the mattress for the whole football team. Don't tell me you got the hots for the little whore. She's bad news, got no respect for herself. In this man's town pussy is a dime a dozen if you know how to go about getting it. And just because a girl tells you no that don't make her no angel."

Dave was saving that punch ever since he saw the way I looked at him the day on the block when Nadine was braiding his hair. Nadine was a slut, but that didn't stop me from loving her. I still entertained sordid memories from two summers back when Paul called me discreetly into Dave's driveway. Through a crack in a little ground-level window we could see into the basement. Nadine was down there on an old mattress and the football team were having their way with her.

"She ain't that bad."

"Wanna know what she really like? Then offer her some money. After Bertha's finished with you then you'll be wanting every piece of ass that's available. You ain't scared, is ya?"

"I can handle it," I said, not really certain what was expected of me.

Dave shot a quick glance towards the steps where the drunkards were falling over each other and singing wino's blues.

"It's a shame, this Vietnam lark. A clean-up campaign. They sending me to my grave. Systematically taking me off the count." He brought his fist down hard on the dashboard, rattling some tools in the glove compartment. "I ain't gonna make it, man."

"Sure, you gonna make it," I said supportively. "There's been plenty of guys that's gone over there and come back."

"In little pieces," he said dully. "The media ain't focusing on the true horror taking place over there. Brothers are getting wasted left, right, and center."

"Ain't nothing gonna happen to you, Dave. Mark my words."

"Well, in case I don't I'm gonna get my full share of pussy before I go."

Bertha appeared at the door sporting a round Afro. She moved towards the car, wiggling past the winos like she was doing the hula-hoop.

The drunk woman tangled in the midst of the winos poked her head out from under the armpits of a wobbly kneed albino-looking nigger. "Take that nappy-head child with you." She looked sourly at Bertha, who bore a striking resemblance, then adjusted the strap on her dress where a withered breast had fallen out. She drained her paper cup hungrily.

Bertha kissed her teeth and skipped over the crying infant who reached out for her affection. She stood outside the car and hastily brushed a little red roach from her chest as it threatened to climb down her blouse.

Dave got out and pulled down the seat so she could jump in the back. She crept in carrying a smell of cheap perfume and sweaty flesh. "Damn! It's like an oven in here," she yelled. "My butt's roasting."

"Get you nice and warm for some action," Dave said. She shifted around on the torn leather upholstery like she was on hot bricks." "Hey, babes, you know what turns me on? A nice bag of Cheba Cheba and a Miller High Life, chilled."

"Who's dealing around here?" Dave asked.

Her voice carried a Billie Holiday lilt. "Them naughty Dreads in Herzl Park. They got some wicked Colombian Red. Redder than the insides of my you know what."

The car shuddered to a start and moved away from the curb, much to Bertha's delight. She sat wide-eyed, massaging both our necks intimately and waving at the curious faces on the sidewalk.

The park was a kid's nightmare. A school playground inhabited by drug pushers, junkies, liquor swiggers, and members of two different gangs. Graffiti slogans stained the walls of the handball courts, the back of the basketball rings, and the cracked-up asphalt. The only place free from the threat of the spray cans were the white fluffy clouds etched in the blue of the sky.

Dave hitched up beside the curb. Rastamen dressed in khaki fatigues swarmed around the car and besieged the windows with all variety of strong-smelling marijuana.

"Red, black, gold, or blonde?" one excited Dread asked. His breath smelt like marijuana was growing inside his belly. Sparkle-eyed, Bertha hollered, "The red." She covered her mouth, embarrassed, as Dave cleared his eardrums.

"Sell me a dime." He pushed $10 through the window.

The Rastaman sifted through a brown pouch strapped to his waist and pulled out a package while trying to keep off another peddler.

Bertha's hand shot from behind Dave's head like an arrow. She snatched the packet and eyeballed it. "Dread, I'm sure you can do better than this."

The Dread's ganga-red eyes fell on her intimately. He removed another smaller package from his bag and handed it to her. A silent message passed between the two.

The pigs were parked across the street in front of a rundown tenement. They looked nervous as whores tried to solicit them. Bums begged money, half-naked kids tried to screw off their aerials, and drunks staggered and fell on their car. The cops had their eyes set on the Mustang and the drug transaction.

No one was bothered by the two white cops. Rastamen were peddling grass, Yankees pushing tackle, and Puerto-Ricans hustling acid and mind-bending tabs.

The action in the park was like a circus. Rastamen blazed cone-shaped marijuana spliffs. They kicked around a soccer ball. Guns rested on their hips like the days of the Wild West.

Dave was uneasy as he drove off. The two white cops were giving him the shits. I was mesmerized by the band of Rastafarians as they tossed their dreadlocks in wild splendor.

We pulled up a block away beside a liquor shop where winos stood staring through the iron grill and licking their lips at the variety of cheap alcohol on display. I hopped out of the car and threaded my way through the army of beggars who were clawing at me and demanding a dime. Their sour breaths reeking of stale alcohol made me feel dizzy.

I bought a six-pack and two quart bottles of Night Train. Hungry eyes fell on me like the bullets from a machine gun as I walked out of the store.

"Hey, young blood. Gimme one of them there devil soups," shouted a short nappy-hair wino with thick, liver lips, wet with his dripping saliva.

"Get out of my face," I yelled, trying to keep his nimble fingers from plucking the beer from my hand. The winos closed in like ghouls in a horror movie.

Dave came to my rescue. His towering presence warded off the army of beggars.

Bertha was smiling like a Cheshire cat when I returned to the car. "I can see you ain't from no ghetto." She took a beer.

Tins were popping as the car wove a path out of the dilapidation and stench. "Ain't that a bitch," wailed Bertha. "We done forgot to get the Rizlas and matches."

"When we get out of the area we'll pick some up," Dave said.

"Don't blame you none. The jungle has turned into a fireball of action." She took a swig from her beer and wiped her lips with the back of her hand. "Heard what happened last night?"

"Sure did," Dave answered quickly.

Bertha frowned. "That's gonna start a lot of trouble around here. No one knows who done it." She cocked her eye and whispered, "I think it was those Naughty Dreads."

"Natty Dreads," Dave corrected.

She waved him away arrogantly. "Whatever their goddamn name is. They as mean as the devil himself. And they bold, too. Not even the cops fuck with them."

"They got their work cut out for them being right in the middle of the Tomahawks and Vandals," Dave said.

"Shit! They too stoned to give a fuck about any gangs. At nights they be in the park firing their guns and listening to that Rasta's music. The gangs don't bother with them because they crazy." She took a long swig of her beer.

Dave checked the rear-view mirror. A worried look appeared on his face. "Hide the gear good. I picked up a tail."

"What! The man?" exclaimed Bertha.

"None other." Dave was worried.

I turned around and looked over my shoulder to see what was generating such excitment.

"Don't do that," Dave barked. "The heat see us hawking them, then they know we got something to hide." He checked the speed and crossed over the Rockaway Parkway. "What's up with these dudes?" he said annoyed. "They about thirty yards behind me, just sitting there."

"Smart-ass, that's what they are," Bertha whined. "They ain't stopping no one in the jungle, they wait till you come out." New Lots was considered the jungle: a human jungle where gang warfare, prostitution, extortion, and poverty ruled like beasts in the wild.

Lights flashed through the car followed by a loud bark sounding much like an angry dog.

Dave double parked. The residents in the area quickly stopped what they were doing and gathered around. The tenement housings on either side of the street were in the initial stages of abuse. Garbage trucks were still making rounds. The sound of the trucks' hydraulic crushers added to the overture of the city's rhythm, the constant wailing of sirens.

"Dumb motherfuckers," protested Bertha. "Man, they just got to fuck around." She opened her mouth and shoved in the dime of grass. Her throat muscles went up and down as it disappeared down her gullet.

Two uniformed cops climbed from the squad car and waded

through the puddle of water escaping from between the legs of some young kids sitting on a hydrant across the street.

The cops adjusted their hip holsters and drew closer to the car, one on either side.

The cop on Dave's side rested a hand on the roof of the car. His snake eyes and pale face peered through the window. "Step outside nice and slow," he instructed in a big, gruff voice.

Dave got out, followed by me and then Bertha.

"Hands above your heads," the cop demanded.

"What the fuck you guys trying to do?" yelled Bertha belligerently. "My hand's staying right here on my beer."

"Take it easy, B.," Dave said cautiously.

The other cop, sporting a Miami tan and a Mexican moustache, turned his gaze to the wild black faces on the sidewalk. His fingers brushed the butt of his gun as if sending a silent message to anyone who opposed his authority.

"What's the charge?" Bertha grunted.

"You three fit the description of two men and a woman that just robbed a gas station in Brownsville," he answered dryly.

"Ha! Try another line, that one's out of tune. There ain't no gas stations in Brownsville." Bertha wiggled her ball-bearing hips in arrogance.

The cops sneered. "Well, try this one—soliciting the sale of a controlled substance." He turned to Dave. "Empty your pockets."

Dave did so without protest. The other cop, who was quite comfortable letting his partner do all the rapping, calmly instructed me to turn my pockets out also.

Bertha yelled: "Ain't no one searching me. I know my rights. You two one-suit motherfuckers better get one of your whores down here before anyone puts their hands on me."

"Tell it like it is, Mama," yelled a coarse male voice from the sidewalk.

The cop with the Mexican moustache ogled Bertha with a suggestive smile.

"What you looking at? Ain't no honky getting none of this nigger gal's pussy," Bertha said.

The cop smiled nervously, his eyes scrutinizing the crowd as if his tan would protect him from black hostility.

The other cop got on his knees and searched the car. He emerged with a disappointed look on his face. The crowd of bored, hot, and bothered blacks and Hispanics gathered around. Some looked down from roofs and fire escapes. A fat woman was propped up on some pillows and leaning through a window.

The pale-faced cop took Dave's driver's license and fed his details through the two-way radio in the squad car. He returned shortly afterwards.

Bertha's mouth was still babbling: "Man, y'all some jive cops. Ain't you got nothing better to do?"

"The motherfuckers looking to start a riot," shouted a slick-haired Puerto-Rican youth.

The cop handed back Dave's license. "Give you folks a little advice. Stay away from those Rastamen in the park. They're dangerous." His voice had lost its peppery sting, a clear indication that he was intimidated by the crowd's presence.

Bertha growled: "That ain't no advice. It's you pigs we got to stay away from."

The last word had barely left Bertha's mouth when the sound of glass shattering startled everyone. Someone had smashed the back screen in the police car. The crowd roared with laughter.

The cops rushed to the car but were further shocked when they saw that one of the back wheels was missing and the car was resting on cement blocks.

The kids sitting on the hydrant added to the cops' miseries when they got up and guided a stream of water across the street and drenched the two cops.

We got into the car and fell about the seat with laughter.

"I'm gonna be buzzing when this Cheba filters into my blood," said Bertha delightedly.

"I better drop you off at the hospital. That grass could be laced with angel dust," Dave said, concerned.

"Hospital!" exclaimed Bertha. "And lose my high? I would rather die. Besides, the Dreads don't use angel dust. That's why they got the most customers." She dipped into her knickers and produced the smaller package the Dread had given her.

"I should have known that you didn't get rid of everything," said Dave.

Bertha smiled like a naughty schoolgirl.

We drove out to Prospect Park and strolled along the bridle trails and tree-shaded drives. The summer had brought out a hive of people taking advantage of the park's expanse of woods and green meadows. Rowboats went up and down the dirty lake. Sunbathers lazed on the grass and lovers strolled hand in hand.

"Ow!" Bertha screamed. "I can feel this Colombian red taking me to cloud nine." She staggered, spilt her beer, and pulled on the fragrant joint.

Finding a spot behind some hedgerows and secluded from the rest of the park we sat on the grass passing the joint around and downing the beers. On the other side of the hedgerows was the vacant plot used for ice-skating in the winter.

The bright midday sun curtained down through the trees. I was high for the first time in my life. My thoughts floated lazily above the clouds, weaving through the letters that vapor-trailed from a jet's exhaust. "Use Copper Tone."

I closed my eyes and dawned in heaven. A giggle, and light fingers tugged at the zip of my trousers.

Bertha removed my young, inexperienced prick and slipped it into her mouth. My toes curled as pleasure unfolded its infinite delights. I held her to me with a new-found urgency. She broke away and spoke in a sweet, soft voice. "Take it easy, babes, it's a long afternoon." She stripped me naked from the waist down. Dave was no longer there. I was nervous in the presence of this hot woman. It was like being in a dream. Bertha rose to her feet like a snake from a charmer's basket. She wiggled slowly and provocatively out of her clothes.

There in front of me was the vision of the great whore that exists in the minds of all puritanical young boys abandoned to the inanimate pleasures of sex mags and jerking off.

Bertha descended lightly into my outstretched arms. She was soft. Our lips came together in a long, hot, passionate kiss, then she pulled away abruptly and allowed my eyes to feast on her dark nipple teats erect and quivering with desire.

I was aroused by the tangent smell of hot woman. A smell like no other. Sin, fornication, lust, hope, and danger were all in that uncaptured smell. God, was it sweet.

Bertha purred and rolled over on her back beckoning for me to take her. Sensing I was afraid she pulled me to her and guided me into her warmth. She knew I was a beginner. Her hips gyrated and controled me deep within her.

Beyond the blue of adolescence, manhood swung open its gates of wonder. From the pits of my belly an explosion occurred and shook my whole world. I growled like a young lion making its first kill.

Bertha wiggled underneath me like a snake and drained my body, twisting to the rhythm of experience, taking me to yet another height of pleasure.

Laughter broke the tranquility of everlasting lust as Dave's amusement gave me a start. He was looking on from behind a bush.

I rolled off of Bertha and rushed for my clothes. My penis was still erect, throbbing, and glistening with love juice.

Bertha wrestled away my clothes and pushed me on my back, intent on riding my pole until it submitted to a lifeless state. She got on top of me and impaled herself on my shaft. She was driven by lust and fueled by the Colombian red swimming in her brain.

Her muscles gripped me and kept me deep inside her. Her eyes were closed and her lips moved in silent and breathless murmurs. "Love your cock, babes. Much bigger than I thought." She squeezed her nipples until her long fingernails drew blood. She rode up and down my shaft circling the head before sliding down.

She was torturing me, making me pay for my inexperience. In a quick motion she rode my shaft to the hilt then jumped off and licked her tongue, excited by the juices that coated my manhood. She shot her tongue in and out of her mouth like a lizard then she devoured my tool once more.

Hot and cold flashes washed my body as her tongue tantalizingly drove me crazy. "Dave, Dave," I yelled. I wanted some release. My pleasures had long since worn off and my penis was hurting.

Dave allowed me to scream for a while, then came out of hiding with a broad smile on his face. His massive shoulders slouched as he put a "take it easy" hand on Bertha's head.

She shook him off and went for the kill. She swallowed me deep inside her throat where something tickled me to an explosion. She swallowed my juice with a look of satisfaction on her face. Still she wasn't finished. She squeezed my limp member and licked away the last remaining drop of fluid.

Dave waved me away discreetly as Bertha wrapped her lips around his prick, intent on deep-throating his entire twelve inches of solid meat.

I gathered my clothes and slipped out of sight, unable to keep my eyes off the battle that raged on the grass between the two experienced veterans. Bertha moaned and bucked but Dave was there to match her rhythm.

It was late afternoon when we left the park. The heat in the car was unbearable. The smell of stale sex kept alive the memories of the guilt-stricken afternoon.

Bertha puffed happily on the last remains of ganga, sperm running down her legs. I couldn't look her in the face. Friday afternoon the streets were crowded with Jews wanting to accomplish last-minute tasks before the setting of the sun.

Dave took a combination of back streets, avoiding the main roads wherever possible.

There was hysterics amid mass excitement as we descended the little grade that linked Church Avenue to East Ninety-Eighth Street. This was the gateway that led to New Lots and the teeming jungle of rundown houses and hostility. Bordering that jungle was Brownsville, the great whore of tenement high-rises and mass unemployment. A crowd had gathered. Police were directing traffic. Sirens were whining. Traffic had come to a standstill. In the distance arms of flames reached into the heavens, chased by the jet of firemen's hoses.

"The jungle is on fire," Bertha yelled. She sat up and peered open-eyed through the front screen.

"I'm gonna have to let you off here," Dave said. "There's no way I'm passing that crowd."

There was an explosion like bombs going off. The crowd stampeded. A white cop went for his gun and slapped the hood of Dave's car. "Come on, move it," he yelled.

Destruction was excitement in the ghetto. The more heinous the situation the more the black folks revelled in the frenzy. The crowd made a dash past the police and headed for the direction of the fire.

Dave pulled up by a nearby curb to let Bertha out.

Mindless of the chaos taking place outside she rubbed his shoulder. "Hey, babes, how's about a little candy?" She rolled her eyes and patted his pockets. "You know how it is bringing up a young child."

Dave pulled three crumpled one-dollar bills from his pocket and handed them to her. "Sorry, babes, but that's all I got on me right now," he apologized.

Bertha shrugged. "It's better than nothing," she said crabbily. She took the money and shoved it down in the warmth of her bosom.

Dave got out of the car and folded down the seat to let her out.

Bertha immediately spotted someone she knew in the rushing crowd. With half of her body outside the car she yelled out, "Billy! Yo, Billy!"

"Bertha!" exclaimed a shabbily dressed middle-aged man wearing a pair of sandals on his dirty feet.

"What's going on?" Bertha asked. She eased out of the car and plucked her knickers from out of the crack of her ass.

Billy spoke with a hasty Southern drawl. "Shit, all hell's breaking loose, child. Some crazy motherfucker done shot up Shorty Gold Tooth and they bombed the Tomahawks' headquarters, too. Niggers are going wild and looting everything in sight."

"Is Shorty dead?" Bertha asked, seemingly concerned.

Billy looked around quickly like he was being chased. "So many shots firing. It's hard to know who's dead. I just saw bodies hitting the dust and chipped. I'll tell you one thing—whoever started this shooting better wish he dead. That Gold Tooth is mean."

New York City housed three hundred gangs. Many of these gangs started out as peacemakers to protect their neighborhood and communities from the heroin addicts committing petty crimes and the wave of violence associated with the smoking of angel dust. The numbers runners, shylocks, pimps, and petty hustlers sought protection from the gangs and paid them handsomely to protect their interests. The Jews fleeing from the black and Hispanic neighborhoods paid the gangs to burn down their premises so they could collect on their insurance policies. The black politicians used the influence of the gangs to threaten people in their communities to ensure that they retained their seats. Eventually the gangs grew hungry for power and started invading each other's turf. This led to bitter clashes and more gangs being formed to protect their communities and remain in control of the action.

A group of girls came rushing down the street. One stopped beside Bertha. She was a shade smaller, with a brown streak at the front of her fried hair. "Bertha, you missing all the fun, child. Come on, get your ass in gear." She grabbed Bertha by the arm and wheeled her away at a trot.

"Wait for me." Billy jumped up like an old crank engine. "I want my share of looting, too." He was quickly caught up in the excited whirlpool of bodies that ran down the block screaming and breaking windows.

Dave was bitter as we made our way out of the sea of confusion. He rammed the car into gear with vengeance and cursed under his breath. "The fucking system is slowly killing everybody off. One way or the other they always win." His voice became choked. "Shorty's like my brother. He took me under his wing when everyone else rejected me. He's the only one other than the coach who encouraged me to play ball."

Home was less than five minutes' drive from where Dave pulled up at the lights on Church Avenue and Ninety-Third Street. Through the side-view mirror I could still see the dark smoke rising from the fire down in the jungle. As I sat there waiting for the light to change I realized why the Jews were moving out of the surrounding areas. They were afraid that the hostility would rise up from New Lots and Brownsville, sweep through the Nineties, and descend upon them like God's wrath against Solomon.

The lights were changing and cars continued to race along Linden Boulevard like roaring demons were in hot pursuit. Instead of taking the right for home Dave turned left on Linden Boulevard. Brookdale Hospital was at the next set of lights.

"I can't leave the area without knowing what happened to Shorty. I owe him that much."

Dave went silent, his mind wandered into a valley of thorns where disaster festered. He was so far rooted in that desolate land that he never heard the wailing fire engine tearing down behind with lights flashing.

Snapped from out of his stupor, he pulled over, narrowly missing a car coming down the inside lane. The fire engine raced past, shaking the car with its force.

Outside the casualty department of Brookdale Hospital was like Grand Central Station in the rush hour. The front of the hospital was on the corner of Linden Boulevard and Rockaway Parkway, the back overlooked News Lots and Brownsville. The acrid smell of the fire rose over the top of the building stifling the already hot, sticky air. Ambulances were arriving with bodies from the jungle. Porters and medics were on their toes wheeling the dead and injured through the swinging black doors. Police and security guards battled with a screaming crowd as they threatened to storm the hospital.

Brookdale is a modern hospital intended for the affluent Jews of the community. Security guards patrolled the main gates twenty-four hours a day, seven days a week, to keep out the poor blacks and Hispanics who were on Medicare and Medicaid. Each day the guards battled with the throng of afflicted people turning up from the surrounding areas: New Lots, Nineties, Brownsville . . . These people demanded treatment for their children suffering from so many poverty related complaints, from things as simple as lead poisoning and rat bites to the injuries and the diseases that accompany malnutrition and the poor sanitation of the ghettos. To add to all that confusion were the army of dope fiends turning up at the hospital for Methadone treatments. The looters who had raced the few blocks from the jungle were also caught up in the chaotic scene.

"Back up." A black security guard steadied his hat and reached for his night stick. "Ain't no one passing me unless they dead or dying." He waved his night stick menacingly at the crowd.

Caught up in the screaming rebellion of fierce black folks, I suggested we go through the delivery bay. Nathan and I had often used that entrance to slip into the hospital's stores on hot summer nights to steal ice-cream from the giant freezers.

We gained entrance and made our way to the emergency lobby. A sea of sick and afflicted black people overran the area. They were screaming and shouting. The seating area was packed. People were leaning against walls and sitting on the floor. A press of people forty deep led to an untidy desk where a frosty-faced nurse took down complaints.

Dave muscled his way to the front of the crowd and stood behind a woman holding a screaming child.

"Ain't you got no respect for your elders?" a woman barked, giving Dave a push from behind.

"He must be one of them there hoodlums," shouted a sorry-looking man with his arm in a sling.

The woman with the screaming child exploded: "What you mean? My child don't look like he been poisoned?"

"The doctor can't see you before your number has been called so you just have to wait your turn." The nurse spoke with an arrogant tone of superiority.

"Fucking West Indian whore." The woman snatched the waiting ticket and walked away.

"Nurse, is there a Michael Baxter here? He was wounded in the New Lots shootout."

The nurse looked up wearily. "Can't attend to you now, I'm busy with other matters. Can't you see?"

"Dog, done pushed in front of everyone." The old woman pushed Dave once more.

"Nurse!" Dave barked impatiently.

"Next!" the nurse shouted with a Jamaican lilt to her voice. She made quick notes on a pad.

Dave reached behind the desk and collared the nurse, lifting her out of her chair by the fabric of her uniform. Her arrogant world disappeared and was replaced by fright and submission.

"Where is he?" Dave drew her close until the bridges of their noses touched.

"Told you he was one of them hoodlums," said the man with his hand in the sling.

"He's on the second floor, waiting to go into surgery," the nurse said quickly. Her eyes danced worriedly around the room.

"Guards, guards!" she shouted as Dave slung her back into the chair. The noise and confusion in the lobby drowned out her voice.

The crowd cleared our path as we made our way to the exit. Outside the surgery on the second floor was like a scene from a war movie. The dead and injured were laid out on stretchers. Their bodies were covered with bloodstained sheets. Nurses in white uniforms moved from stretcher to stretcher, taking stock and making the difficult decision of who should be wheeled into the surgery next.

Four police stood over the bloodstained body of a black man strapped to a stretcher. One cop was handcuffed to the man.

We moved from stretcher to stretcher, horrified at the level of treachery that black folks inflicted on each other.

An old woman leaned over a shotgun-blasted corpse of a boy and screamed hysterically.

Shorty Gold Tooth was on his back, breathing heavily. The gold in his mouth was stained with blood. A white sheet covered his body. His eyes opened slowly as Dave stood over him. "Dave! Dave!" His voice was faint.

There was movement in the lobby as we attended to Shorty. It was as if we'd disturbed a hornets' nest. Dave bent down and put an ear to Shorty's mouth.

Shorty whispered: "Get me out of here, they're all over the place. Had it not been for those cops I'd be dead." Blood drained from the corner of his mouth.

Dave peeled back the sheet and sighed heavily. "It's a wonder he's still alive," he mumbled quietly.

Shorty's belly was all shot up. Blown apart by buck shot. He coughed feebly and pulled Dave to him with a bloodstained hand.

"Take it easy, you'll be all right." Dave's eyes ranged suspiciously over the healthy faces lurking amongst the afflicted.

There were obviously grounds for Shorty's fear. Among the crowd were a few desperate-looking men who didn't seem to be there because of any injuries.

Shorty pulled Dave to him and whispered: "I know who started the shooting. It was that punk Super Dice and his gang, the Stompers. They the same men that shot the two Vandals last night, tryin' to frame the Tomahawks. The punk's here in the hospital. He stood over me seconds before the cops arrived. Must have thought I was dead."

A nurse examined the handcuffed body on the stretcher.

"He's dead," she said indifferently. She pulled a bloodstained sheet over the man's head.

"The cops are about to leave," Dave whispered as the cop unlocked the handcuff and let the dead hand fall.

"Make your move now," Shorty stammered.

"Man, you gonna bleed to death if I move you," Dave said.

Shorty's mouth moved up and down, pain strangling the words in his throat.

"Porter," a nurse shouted. "Wheel this man into surgery." She indicated to a bloodstained body beside Shorty.

The four cops disappeared down the lobby and around a corner by the elevators. There was movement in the crowd to the right of where we were. A man with medium build stepped from behind a little girl tugging at her mother's skirts. He quickly peeled back his windbreaker and shuffled in his waist.

"A gun," Dave screamed.

The man in his late teens smoothly selected a bullet into the breech of the gun. The crowd screamed, the whites of their frightened black eyes rolled over.

The man pointed the gun at Shorty's body and pulled the trigger. There was silence as everyone waited for the explosion. There was none. Confused, the gun man jerked the slide of the gun, intent on selecting another round.

"You bastard," Dave shouted as we both dived on the man and wrestled him to the ground. Dave hammered him in the mouth. His head slumped into oblivion.

I yanked the weapon from his hand and gave it to Dave. The emergency area was in total disarray. Black people were running up and down in all directions, screaming and trying to get out of the way.

The gun dangled in Dave's hand as he stood over Shorty's body.

"Give me the gun," Shorty groaned. He curled his stubby

fingers around the trigger as Dave rested the gun firmly in his right hand. "The bullet is stuck in the chamber. Put some strength on the slide and pull it back."

Dave took the gun and his face wrinkled as he used his strength to ply back the jammed mechanism. Finally there was a click and the bullet ejected from the gun.

There was a faint smile on Shorty's face as Dave handed him the gun.

The door directly beside the lobby where we were standing suddenly flew open. A mass of frantic people came streaming inside crying for mercy and wailing "Murder."

"They shooting up on the third floor," shouted a morphine freak. "Two men are dead and they done shot up a nurse, too." Super Dice and his mob were combing the casualty area on the third floor, searching for more of the wounded Tomahawks soldiers.

"What about security?" an elderly woman asked.

"Shit, they firing at them, too." His eyes darted around the lobby as if looking for something to steal. The security guards in the hospital were auxiliary New York cops. They wore the same uniform but were forbidden to carry guns. They were often the victims of gun attacks to which they had no response. On these occasions they would have to radio for backup from the NYPD who took their time in responding.

"They'll be coming here next," Dave said excitedly.

"Let's get out of here while we still have a chance," I said.

"I'm not leaving without Shorty," Dave replied sternly.

Chapter 7

Dave ran down the corridors pulling the stretcher whilst I pushed from behind. People melted out of the way as we dashed for the elevator. The yellow lights above the elevator doors flashed rapidly as the carriage skipped floors like an express train burning through stations. Dave thumped the call button frantically when the lights stopped at the eighth floor. Our eyes were transfixed by the stagnant illumination when a chilling voice barked from behind.

"Stan' right where you are. Ain't no one going nowhere."

We turned slowly to find ourselves face to face with Super Dice. He had a pump-action shotgun leveled at us. I stared at the two dark holes of oblivion. He wrenched the pump back and slammed a shell into the breach.

"I want to see your blood spurt when I blow off your fuckin' head." He jabbed the gun at my temples. My mouth was dry and the pit of my stomach churned down to my knees. My eyes stared big and white, I slammed them shut, but my teeth trembled together and I could feel the well of water building beneath my closed eyelids. My breath pumped in small erratic bursts until a loud bang terminated it. It seemed to terminate the world . . . I was on the floor when I realized I was still alive. I didn't dare to move but my mind ran a check over my body and I could locate no injury. Nervously my eyes opened.

There was another deafening report as fire and smoke erupted from the gun in Shorty's hand. Super Dice dived for cover in a nearby exit; Shorty lay stock-still, his finger on the trigger. Shots lodged into the ceiling, puncturing the plastic casing on a flickering fluorescent tube and ricocheting off the walls. Shorty clicked the gun until it failed to answer.

Dave hurriedly picked himself up from the ground and looked

down at Shorty's bloodstained body. "There's only one way out. We got to carry him down the stairs. Take the gun."

I took the bloodstained weapon from Shorty's hand and pushed it down the back of my jeans. Dave carefully picked up Shorty while I held the exit door open. There was movement on the stairs as we entered. Police with guns drawn were swept back by a tide of frightened civilians making a rush for the first-floor lobby.

The ground floor offered no escape from the mutiny taking place on the upper floors. A wave of bodies chased down the hallway and away from the main lobby doors.

Shorty had stopped groaning and his body went limp in Dave's hands. "He's either dead or unconscious." Dave looked worriedly at the group of thugs coming down the lobby.

The paging system was set alive with an excited voice calling for police and security to report to the lobby and second floor. Members of the Black Pearls gang chanted a war cry as they stormed the hospital. They were out of Bedford Stuyvesant and had a full thousand following. They were long-standing enemies of Shorty Gold Tooth and the Tomahawks gang. This was a good opportunity for them to get even with the general. The might of his army was down in the jungle, locked in a bitter gun-battle with the Vandals gang. The gang were wielding chains and swinging baseball bats. Their presence caused us to seek a side exit to avoid being caught up in any further acts of violence. Dave cradled Shorty in his arms as we emptied out through a side door in the hospital's parking lot. The humid breath of the city embraced the evening air. Sirens were screaming. The music of legal rebellion filled the air.

We made our way towards the car where Dave laid Shorty down on the back seat. The engine ticked over after a few no-starts. The evening rush hour was on. Screaming police cars wove through the traffic like crochet needles. Rockaway Parkway was not yet at a standstill. Dave cut through the cars in a desperate bid to leave the area fast. He was making a series of maneuvers when we were rammed from behind by a blue Buick Skylark. The force that hit the Mustang pushed it into the back of a van. Dave quickly found the reverse. Shorty Gold Tooth stirred.

"He's alive."

"Thank heavens." Dave put the car into gear and moved around the van as an angry driver came out waving a claw hammer in the air.

The Buick was hot on our trail. Dave tried a few Russian roulette passes in the path of oncoming cars before returning safely into the main flow of traffic.

"Can't we go any faster?" I asked as the Skylark drew closer. They were three cars behind and looked menacing. Four men including the driver were inside and they had shotguns positioned on the windows. They were trying their utmost to come beside us.

Dave used all his driving skills to keep them at bay. "If I can turn off at the intersection of Church and Rockaway then I might be able to lose them. The short blocks in the Nineties will enable me to shake them off."

"They sure desperate to put Shorty in the boneyard."

"If they catch up with us then we gonna join him as sure as day," said Dave as he wove around a Monte Carlo. The Buick lost some ground. "I should have known. That Skylark is driven by Super Dice' ace honcho Mo Dean." He checked the rear-view mirror once more. "The race is on. The crazy motherfucker is coming like a bulldozer."

A Puerto-Rican member of the Stompers gang leaned out the front window of the Skylark with a pump-action shotgun.

"He looking for a shot." Dave swerved into the path of the oncoming traffic. The Puerto Rican let loose a burst of fire from the muzzle of the gun. The back windshield shattered and pieces of glass covered Shorty's body.

"Christ!" Dave swerved into the approaching lane, narrowly missing a highly chromed Mack truck which powered straight on past with a blare of a horn like a locomotive. The sound of metal crunched as the Mustang scraped the side of a car to gain access back into the flow of traffic.

Mo Dean had spotted the Mack and swerved even further into the path of the oncoming traffic. He was in the middle lane facing the cars coming towards them. The shotguns exploded repeatedly, clearing their path with rounds of buckshot. Cars stopped dead. Some crashed. Drivers abandoned their vehicles and ran to the sidewalk for cover.

"I've got to make these lights," Dave said as Mo Dean miraculously forced his way back into the main flow of traffic. The car was battered. Two more bursts of shotgun fire erupted. Cordite burnt in the air and settled at the back of my throat.

"Here goes." The car seemed to find a new burst of life as it railed up and around the car in front that had sighted the danger at the intersection and stopped.

"No," I screamed as we did a ninety-degree turn on Church Avenue in front of approaching cars. The car was hit and spun around in a whirlpool of confusion. A bus had winged the back of the car and knocked it on the sidewalk. Some old men seated around a table playing dominoes hurriedly shuffled out of the way.

Shaken and confused, Dave fiddled with the ignition. The engine roared into action as if by will alone. The Skylark had caused a major pileup at the lights and was rapidly approaching. To create panic the Puerto-Rican fired a few shots at the pedestrians on the sidewalk.

Dave used the sidewalk as a runway to pick up speed. The Skylark ran line in line with the Mustang. The shotgun popped up between gaps of parked cars. Lines of Caribbean and Hispanic makeshift stalls went up in the air as the Mustang sped along the sidewalk. People dived for cover. There was a gap near the curb on the corner of Ninety-Second and Church. The Mustang landed with a bang and raced down the block. The engine roared like a dinosaur, filling the narrow street with the sound of a tired engine and loud exhaust. Frightened eyes turned and stared. Women shuffled little children into houses and driveways.

The teeming streets of the Nineties were alive. Black people were out in their numbers. Junkies, winos, hookers, robbers, and other social misfits in the area dived for cover as the two speeding cars raced down the blocks. Shotguns were blazing from the windows of the Skylark. Finally the old Skylark could take no more. White vapor streaked from beneath the hood as the car came to a stop beside the Holy Roller Baptist Church.

"We lost them," Dave rejoiced, looking over his shoulder through the back windshield that wasn't there. He looked down at Shorty's body which remained silent. "Don't die, Homeboy. Just a few more blocks and we'll be at the slaughterhouse."

Shorty groaned. I turned around and brushed the glass from his face.

Brookdale was a paradise haven even on the worst of days compared to Kings County Hospital. Inside the emergency area the victims of a warped society clustered. Black people were nursing wounds inflicted by each other. They suffered from gunshot wounds, acid burns, drugs overdose, stab and chop-up wounds, toothaches. The list of ailments was infinite. The faces of the afflicted looked sour. They didn't like waiting in lines.

Dave cradled Shorty and carried him to the emergency desk.

"Put him down on any available stretcher and fill out this paper," instructed a Farrah Fawcett-looking nurse. She tossed a white piece of paper over the desk.

"This will take ages to complete," protested Dave. "He's dying. Can't you see?"

"He ain't the only one dying. Look around. He has to wait his turn like everyone else." She picked up a ringing phone and smiled softly into the mouthpiece. The paging system echoed around the room. A high-pitched voice urgently summoned a Dr Watson to surgery.

We found a stretcher and laid Shorty down beside a group of angry-looking black folks waiting their turn on plastic chairs. Children ran around the place. Spilt coffee and tea stained the floor. Paper cups and McDonald's wrappers fell about the place. Tramps sifted among pieces of paper for cigarette ends.

"It will take at least four hours before we're seen to," Dave said. "Some of these people are in pretty bad shape." Shorty's parched lips moved. "Dave, Dave," he muttered feebly.

"Take it easy," Dave said.

"Call this number in the Bronx. Just say Gold Tooth and where I'm at." He whispered some digits.

"Got it?" Dave asked. I nodded.

"Give it a ring while I keep an eye on him."

Finding a telephone box was like locating a needle in a haystack. I had to leave the building and walk a short distance along Clarkson Avenue before I found one.

"Yeah," a coarse voice answered after the fourth ring.

I quickly relayed Shorty's message. Then the phone went dead, leaving me gaping down the receiver.

Dave stood protectively over Shorty's body when I returned to the lobby. "Did you get through?" he asked anxiously.

"Yeah, but the phone went dead as soon as I delivered the message."

"They'll be here pretty soon." Dave was confident.

"The nurse that lives in my house works here. If I could see her then she might be able to help." I walked over to the reception desk and asked for a Nurse Johnson. Minutes later the frightened-looking rolypoly nurse arrived in response to the paging.

"Danny, what are you doing here?" she inquired curiously.

"My friend's been shot and he's over there dying."

Her eyes lit up like sparklers. She took my hand in alarm and trotted over to the stretcher. "He's in pretty bad shape." She replaced the sheet and made a dash for the emergency desk where she whispered a few words to the other nurse.

She returned and said, "They're going to wheel him into surgery as soon as the porters arrive. Does this have anything to do with the incident at the party?"

"No, I was in the New Lots area when someone shot him from a car."

The nurse's warm, gray eyes scrutinized me accusingly. "Why didn't you take him to Brookdale? He might have stood a better chance of surviving."

"It's a long story, Nurse," I said, exhausted.

"Take it easy, Danny. You're a nice boy. Every day I see kids like yourself coming in here on stretchers. It's sickening. Don't get yourself involved."

"I'm not involved in anything, Nurse. Come tomorrow I'll be off the streets because I start a new job at the supermarket."

"Very nice, Danny. Mom should be very proud of you."

"Shucks, I ain't been home all day."

"Mrs Palmer must be worried sick about you. Give her a call and let her know that you're all right." The porters arrived and wheeled the stretcher away, ignoring the angry crowd cursing them for being selective. The paging system called for Nurse Johnson to report to the dispensary.

"See you later. There's plenty to do around here." She shuffled off, waving her fingers.

"I sure hope Shorty's men hurry up and get here." Dave was agitated.

"That's if he lives."

"It takes a lot to kill niggers like Shorty. They got all the luck in the wind."

"What we gonna do now?"

"Stick around until his boys arrive. I'll feel much better because it won't take the gangs long to figure out where he at."

Gang warfare was a thriving business throughout the five boroughs of New York City. It was the focus for unemployed youths who thrived on dope peddling, extortion, gambling, armed robbery, and contract killing and in some cases the taxation of high school and junior high school kids. The Tomahawks were the largest gang in the city. Their policy of infringing on the turf of other gangs had earned them a lot of enemies. Enemies who would take advantage of the slightest weakness just to even the score.

"My life ain't worth a dime after what happened with Super Dice in the hospital," I said.

"More reason for us to stick around. The Tomahawks might be able to offer us some protection, too," Dave answered.

"I'm sure gonna need it."

We kept a low profile near the main doors. Two hours later an army of vicious-looking men stormed into the hospital, their eyes devouring the surroundings. Emblazoned on the back of their denim jackets was the double axe insignia of the Tomahawks. The gang spread out in groups of four and walked through the crowd. They petulantly scanned the horrified faces.

"That's our man over there. The tall, hefty motherfucker," said Dave.

"Man, he built like Hulk and black as night."

"Hulk ain't the word. That's the leader of the Tomahawks and his name's Sugar Bear."

Fear washed the faces in the emergency area. The presence of the gang brought to mind the horrors it was capable of inflicting. Two security guards stood poised near the reception desk. Sugar

Bear stood menacingly, confident, with his hands crossed and his legs spread.

Members of the gang reached into the pockets of their denims as we drew closer. Dave stood shoulder to shoulder with the Bear. He handed over the crumpled piece of paper that I had written the phone number on.

The Bear searched Dave's eyes. His hand went up in the air and he relayed a finger message to his men. "They cool." He actually sounded like a bear and smelt like one too. "What gives? My cousin dead or what?" he growled.

"He went into surgery two hours ago," Dave said.

"You ain't heard nothing more?"

"The nurse said he's in bad shape. That's about all, besides she's a friend of Danny here. That's why he got through so quickly."

"We heard he was kidnapped from the Brookdale by members of the Black Pearls gang," the Bear said.

Dave brought him up to date as to what took place at the hospital.

"There were at least three different gangs in the hospital trying to get to Shorty because they knew the might of the Tomahawks was locked in a bitter gunbattle with the Vandals down in the jungle."

"Man! I tried to warn him about that ceasefire. It looks like wanting peace done cost him his life." He paused and rubbed his chin thoughtfully. "Seems to me Super Dice was the one who started the shooting last night to make it look like the Tomahawks. Then he joined forces with the Vandals today and carried out the attack." His hands suddenly went above his head once more and his fingers did a sign language to his men. He took a deep breath and sighed heavily.

Two cops emerged from around the corner at the far end of the lobby. One was white, the other black. The white cop walked directly up to the Bear. "Far away from home ain't you, Wallace?"

"No further than you are," the Bear answered sarcastically.

"This is my area." The cop shuffled his hat on his head, rumpling curls of ginger tresses. He was in his late thirties with green street eyes. His uniform was draped carelessly on his body. His gun swung in his holster, like it would fall out.

"You beefing or what, Sullivan?" the Bear growled.

"Just one fuck-up, Wallace, and I'll have your ass."

"Like how you raped that little Puerto-Rican girl on the roof in the Bronx three years ago!" the Bear sneered.

"Fucking piece of shit. Up against the wall and spread-eagle." He stepped back and brushed the butt of his gun.

"Bullshit," the Bear growled. He pulled back his jacket and showed a gun swinging in a shoulder holster. The other members of the Tomahawks gang followed suit. He looked at the cop and said calmly, "Don't go trying to make a name for yourself, Sullivan. Nothing is going to erase the scum that you are. There's a war going on. Get in the way and you get wasted. It's as simple as that."

Sullivan's face flushed red. "Dumb son of a bitch. I should have done something about you a long time ago." He went for his gun.

Sugar Bear was faster to the draw. His speed and precision was matched by his men. The sound of bullets selecting in the chambers of automatic weapons sang out in the tension-filled atmosphere.

Sullivan raised his hands level with his chest. "Gone too far this time, Wallace. Pulling a gun on an officer of the state. This is a sure enough ticket to Sing-Sing." He tried to sound calm.

"Guess you going to escort me there?"

"You ain't crazy enough to shoot a cop. The whole of the fifty states would be on your back the minute the bullet leaves that gun." He shifted around nervously.

"Don't be too certain what I can or can't do these days, Sullivan. Get the fuck out of my face before I rip your honky ass apart with my bare hands."

Sullivan's colleague placed a hand on his shoulder.

"Listen, Harry. They ain't doing anything wrong. Leave them for someone else. We're on a different mission."

Sullivan flinched under the restraining arm. His eyes locked heatedly with the Bear's.

"Punk!" A spray of saliva covered Sullivan's face. "Just say one more word an' your family will be collecting that well-overdue compensation," said Sugar Bear.

"Come on, Harry," his partner coaxed. Sullivan eyed the

Bear sourly as his partner carefully edged him past the Tomahawk gangsters.

Sugar Bear shouted as Sullivan neared the doors. "Next time you got anything to say make sure the SWAT team is with you." The crowd whispered in fear as the cops disappeared through the doors.

"Jive motherfucker." The Bear holstered his weapon. He pulled a small brown package from his inside pocket and used the long fingernail of his left little finger to scoop out some white powder. He drew the powder into his nose. "Yeah." He sniffed contentedly and rubbed his nose. "Whichever way this goes both of you have my respect. I've seen better men desert in the face of danger. I can assure you guys that there'll be no repercussions. From today I am waging a full-scale war on the Stompers and the Vandals."

The Bear must have crept into my mind and back out. He put a firm hand on my shoulder. "My man, if the Bear says you got protection then you got it. My men will be watching you like guardian angels. Just get on with your life."

"Much appreciated," I said.

"How about you, man? I can provide some protection for you, too. There ain't no muscle can stand up to firepower at the end of the day. Even an all-American can do with some protection." He smiled. "Seen you play on many occasions. My cousin also hold you in high esteem."

"Only protection I'm gonna need is in Nam."

"What!" the Bear exclaimed.

"Yep! They done drafted me," said Dave.

"Ain't that a bitch, man! Seems like they only interested in vacuuming the young and athletic-inclined. Shit! I was even thinking of making you a proposition. I know you'll be needing a manager." He looked around conspiratorially and whispered, "I'm not just into gang warfare. I got some legitimate business running too, kind of security like."

Dave smiled faintly as if weighing up the possibility of life in the Vietnamese jungle compared to one hitched on the tails of ruthless gangsters.

The Bear returned the piece of paper with the phone number to Dave. "This here's my personal number. My cousin saw fit to give it to you. That makes you one of us. Any problems, just get on the blower."

Nurse Johnson's sweet voice beckoned for me to leave the crowd and come over to her. "Danny, who are those boys? They look like they've been chartered from hell."

"They're friends of the guy that got shot."

She gave them a quick, dismissive glance. "He's going to be all right."

"Yeah!" I yelled, throwing a fist in the air.

Sugar Bear rushed over quicker than a bat out of hell. Nurse Johnson put a hand over her chest and sighed as he growled, "What's the news?"

"He's gonna be all right," I said excitedly.

The Bear shouted for joy and slapped hands with his men. Their shouts reverberated in the lobby. The agitated crowd seemed to draw pleasure from their delight.

"See you later," the nurse said in an apparent rush to get away from the Bear and his clan.

"I knew they couldn't kill that nigger. He the luckiest mother ever did walk." The Bear was overwhelmed with joy.

Shorty and six members of the Tomahawks gang had once been ambushed down at Coney Island by members of a rival gang. The gang had led them under the boardwalk and gunned them down. To make certain they were dead their leader fired a bullet into each man's head, but the bullet intended for Shorty's brain only grazed his skull. He spent nine months in a coma before recovering.

The gang escorted us to the car when we left the hospital. Sugar Bear personally saw us off. "Neither of you guys worry, dig? The main man got y'all under the wing." He slapped the roof of the car as we drove off. The Tomahawks' insignia were silhouetted in the evening twilight as the car pulled away.

Chapter 8

The first day of work was spent unloading the Big Apple delivery truck parked in front of the supermarket. I worked nonstop from eight in the morning until twelve when we knocked off for lunch.

The afternoon was hot. White fluffy clouds floated lazily across the sky. The smell of burnt oil, exhaust fumes, and fast foods from vendors' carts filled the air. Crowds of people had taken to the streets. Stalls were out along Church Avenue. I saw many familiar faces from the area. Some looked at me with awe and astonishment.

Groups of black men moved like snakes amongst the scantily dressed white folks, clipping their money, cutting the straps from their bags, and robbing the very shoes that they were wearing.

I kept a watchful eye for danger at all times, shielding behind the boxes that I carried on my shoulder from the truck to the roller track. The track ran along the sidewalk and down to the basement. There was no sight of the Bear's men among the forest of faces that moved along the sidewalk.

Entertainment through the long laborious day was supplied by a loudmouth who worked beside me. He talked of his affiliation with the gangs and the many horrors he had personally witnessed. He was quite well informed but proved to be nothing more than a mouthpiece. He wore a pair of jeans that boasted the name of the Jolly Stompers down the side.

Every muscle in my body ached as I lay on my bed that night. I was even too tired to remove my clothes. The following day Dad returned from Jamaica. He was hell bent on busting my ass. Had it not been for Mom's pleas and ability to calm him down in the bedroom my butt would have been roasting like the burning sensation in my prick. Taking a piss was a nightmare. The burning sensation got worse as the days passed. Mom sussed on that something was wrong after a week.

I was getting ready for bed when she entered the room. Flashes of light from the portable television danced across the ceiling. A fresh perfume odor from the bath preceded her into the room. She wore a pink nightie that fell loosely to her knees. She sat on the edge of the bed and crossed her legs, then looked into my face and gave me one of her sly "You brute" looks. "Danny, is something wrong with you?" she asked. It sounded more like a statement than a question.

I forced a smile. "No, Mom, just feeling tired from work."

"And it's because you're tired you groan when you take a pee?"

Embarrassment gripped me as I could detect an undercurrent of chiding in her voice.

She nodded her head knowingly and said calmly, "Seems like you've finally turned into a man. Getting involved in things you know nothing about." She stared into my eyes in another buildup to one of her grand slams. The ones that usually finished up with a loud bang. Her voice took on an aggressive tone. "Some nasty girl has given you a disease and you better have it seen to before it get into your blood and drive you mad."

"But, Mom." My voice was low. "I haven't been with any girls." I forced another smile, fighting hard not to scratch the niggling irritation in my penis.

She snapped impatiently: "Boy, you think I was born big, don't you? One thing to learn in life is that you can't trick a trickster. Tomorrow morning I'm taking you down to Kings County Hospital to let a doctor have a look at you. And if it's what I think it is then you can expect two long needles for your sins." She got up and swept out of the room leaving me to brew over the thought of the needles until morning.

Early next morning, at Mom's insistence, we joined a waiting room of people in the Kings County Hospital. We spent the whole day in the crowded lobby waiting to be served. It was after four when my number was called. Mom accompanied me into the doctor's office.

The smell of antibiotics and medicine increased my fear as I entered the spacious room. Sitting behind a well-kept desk was the doctor, dressed in a white coat with a stethoscope around his neck. He had a full head of hair that glistened at the temples. Mom coughed politely into a fist to let him know we were in the room.

"Have a seat," he said dryly, keeping his eyes glued to a grey card held firmly in his hands.

Beside the window a mass of surgical equipment sat menacingly on a trolley. Mom motioned me to take the only available seat opposite the doctor. He removed his spectacles and stared at me with wide blue eyes. He was white as snow and looked evil.

"How long ago since you passed water?" he asked.

"About twenty minutes, sir," I said innocently.

He growled. "Next time don't pass water until you're seen by a doctor. Is that clear?"

The voice of authority sparked a flame in my brain. I was on the defence, ready to match fire with fire. "There won't be no next time," I answered.

His eyes narrowed and he got on his feet. "Step behind that screen over there." He slipped on a pair of surgical gloves. "I don't have all day, so make it fast or leave the office."

Mom squeezed my shoulder silently, commanding me to calm down and not give the doctor any trouble. He followed me behind the screen.

"Drop your trousers," he said.

Not wishing to cause any more friction, I complied. He took my penis with one hand and pulled it five times like he was milking a cow. "Hmm," he hummed with a mixture of rebuff and speculation as the yellow discharge oozed out. "Looks like the clap." He took a sample and wiped it on a slide. Then he ordered me to urinate into two glasses.

We were asked to leave the room for another forty-five minutes while he cultured the results. On our return he had the object of my fears sitting on the table.

"Gonorrhoea," he announced as if passing sentence. "I would like the name and address of anyone you have been with in the past two weeks. You do know the name of the young lady that you were involved with, don't you?"

There was no more secret about my sexual encounter. The cat was out of the bag. Head hanging down I answered: "Bertha. She live in the New Lots area."

"New Lots!" Mom shouted, momentarily forgetting where she was. "How did you find your way over there?" She sighed heavily and shook her head in disgust.

The doctor scribbled on a piece of paper. "Was there anyone else apart from this Bertha?"

"Yes! My friend Dave Green," I answered sharply.

Mom was outraged. "What nastiness have you been up to?" she shrieked.

The doctor sat back in his chair and folded his arms across his chest. He seemed to take pleasure from Mom's fit of hysterics. "I think you misunderstood my question. Was there any other woman apart from Bertha?"

"She was the only one," I said freely.

"Two shots for the clap." He prepared the needle, allowing Mom the pleasure of watching me suffer. His eyes glowed with a hint of sadism as the penicillin filled up in the syringe.

Mom squinted and said mercilessly, "Want to play man— now take man treatment."

The doctor rubbed one side of my butt cheek with a piece of cottonwool then administered the first needle. It hurt like hell. It hurt so much that I welcomed the second jab as it kind of leveled me off.

The ride home in the taxi proved to be quite painful. I found great difficulty sitting down. I hated all women and the thought of going near Bertha again sent shivers up my spine. There had been no sign of Dave since the day he dropped me home. I started entertaining thoughts that he was musing somewhere over the great stress he had caused me.

Paul's body was released from the morgue. Two days later members of the Tomahawks gang gunned down three of the Jolly Stompers on Clarkson Avenue. Prayer was held for Paul in the basement of his parents' house. The body was then flown to Haiti for burial.

The loudmouth at work kept me well informed as to what was happening with the gangs. The Tomahawks and its ten thousand strong membership had waged an all-out war against the Jolly Stompers and the Vandals. My neighborhood had suddenly become deserted as many of the youths got drawn into street wars. There was no sign of Nathan, Super Dice, or Alphonso, not to mention Dave Green. The Nineties and New Lots were declared no-go areas. The local newspapers carried day-to-day accounts of the war taking place in the ghetto.

In anticipation of school re-opening the boss laid me off with a pat on the back. My father practically placed me under house arrest. His philosophy was, "Don't spare the whip and spoil the child." Licks were my daily bread. When he couldn't find anything to beat me for he would whop me for something he had already thrashed me for some time back. While he was in the house I confined myself to the bedroom as much as possible.

It was early morning the front door slammed. This was the happiest part of the day. My worst enemy had just left for work. The upkeep of the house was my job. I had to make sure the flights of stairs were swept and mopped. The driveway and front of the house had to be swept and kept clean, no thanks to the leaves that had started to fall from the trees. The gap between my father and me had widened since his return from Jamaica. He was more hostile toward me both mentally and physically. I was reaching the end of my tether and entertained thoughts of running away.

As I walked around the room in deep thought there was a knock at the door.

Danger. There was another knock. Batman and Robin. The Stompers. Alphonso. Who? The big race at Belmont was on. My brain was running hurdles once more. Creeping on my toes I slid across the living room and up to the front door.

"Danny!" a familiar voice shouted.

I quickly turned the lock. "Dave." My hand went out to him in a long black power handshake.

He drew back. "Hey! You act as if I just won an Oscar or something."

"Shit. I'm just glad to see you, that's all. What's up with the bald head?"

"Today I leave for boot camp. Just wanted to let you know that I was leaving and to explain about the clap."

"It was nothing."

"Nothing!" he screamed. "That was the worse case of clap I ever caught."

"What? You caught it before?"

He chuckled. "A man ain't a man unless he catches a dose," he proclaimed.

"If that's the price for some pussy I sure don't want no more. To think I used to worry that I would never get laid."

"Nonsense. They ain't all like that, but go messing with broads like Nadine and you might just get shot. Gon-o-rrhea shot. From now on she's nothing but a bag of germs." Dave's eyes sparkled. "Come on downstairs. I got a surprise for you."

"Please, not another Bertha."

"Well, she's shaped like Bertha but this one is a little more loyal."

"But . . ."

"No buts, man. Don't refuse my last wish." He took my arm and pulled me through the door. The morning was bright. There was a freshness in the air. From a defensive position on the steps I looked about cautiously. There was no sign of Dave's surprise.

"There she is," he said excitedly. "The finest beauty in all of New York."

"Stop joshing," I said seriously. "Where she at?"

"Over there. The green one. She's all yours."

It took some time for me to recognize the old Mustang.

Dave said proudly, "Had it done up—engine and all."

"She's beautiful." I crossed the street. "I don't even know how to drive." My hands moved smoothly over the well-polished bodywork. "She'll be right here when you get back."

"She's yours and that's all there is to it." His face tightened. He handed me the keys and instructed me to have a seat behind the wheel. The interior of the car had also been upholstered. The smell of the leather was still fragrant.

Dave entered from the passenger's side and took a seat beside me. "The reason I ain't been around is because I was in Florida saying my goodbyes to family and friends," he said apologetically.

"You ain't got to feel no guilt about me catching the curse."

"Just want to set things straight, that's all. It must have

looked real strange—me disappearing right after the affair with Bertha."

"We brothers for life. There's no need to apologize. It was an experience."

He squeezed my shoulder. "Take it easy, Danny. I will be praying for you."

"I'll be fine—just drop me a line. Let me know what's going on. If I was old enough wild horses couldn't stop me from coming with you."

"No way," he protested. "This ain't no war. It's a hari kiri slaughter. A sacrifice. Uncle Sam is thirsty. His thirst ain't gonna be quenched until a few thousand brothers have lost their lives. Once this hungry beast has been fed by our blood, then they might ease up for a while."

"Man, you ain't gonna die. You going to dazzle those Chinks like how you dazzled the might of the Jefferson defense in the finals."

"The old rope-a-dope trick. Only then I weren't dodging weapons of war. That was a game. This is reality. The US got the technology to finish this war without drafting so many men. This alone convinces me it's a hopeless cause. We're going in with one hand tied behind our backs."

The many sit-ins and public demonstrations against the war were proof of what Dave was saying.

"In years to come don't feel that I was a defeatist."

"Never," I said, with maximum respect.

"Danny, I'm going in there to fight as hard as any man in that war even though, like all the others, I don't know why or what reason we are fighting for."

The minutes leading up to Dave's departure were emotion filled. He left with a broken heart. He also left me a present— one that was to change my life.

The gun taken from the assassin in Brookdale Hospital.

Chapter 9

The long, hot summer of discontent passed on, leaving memorable scars. The breath of revolution swept mercilessly throughout the United States. In the ghettos young blacks and Puerto-Ricans fought a bloody war to the bitter end. The near assassination of Shorty Gold Tooth triggered a war that now involved every gang in the city. The Tomahawks, who were by far the strongest gang, sought to dominate all the weaker gangs. Sugar Bear swore to gain control of all five boroughs.

The rich and affluent white areas experienced the opposite of what was taking place in the ghettos. Jewish, Italian, and Irish parents looked on with disgust as their once proud children willingly embraced the hippie movement and reveled in a life of anarchy fueled by sex, drugs, and rock and roll.

School officially opened on the ninth of September 1970. Mom had managed to secure a place for me in Samuel J. Tilden High School. Outside the school I checked my watch anxiously, awaiting the bell that would signal my entry into the belly of the proud stone structure. The smell of marijuana hung in the autumn air. Young hippie followers sat with their legs tucked under on the freshly cut lawn, mown to a precise three-quarters of an inch. The lawn went round the perimeter of the school. Curls of marijuana smoke crept from the hippies' nostrils and floated above their heads like thick fog in winter.

The bell finally rang and a wave of bodies swept along the stone pathway leading up to the stairs. On either side of the walkway low privet bushes, trimmed and groomed, set off small gardens of roses and marigolds. The bronze statue of Samuel J. Tilden seemed to welcome us into the building as we passed through the green iron doors. The hallways were brightly polished. Fluorescent lighting reflected from the silky sheen of mosaic tiles that decorated the floors. There was an aroma of newness mixed with the ancient smell of schools and moth-infested books drying out on the shelves.

Students rushed around hastily, trying to find their way inside the maze-like establishment. Twenty minutes after wandering around the labyrinthine hallways and stairwells I found my destination, room 306 on the third floor.

"Good morning. You must be . . .?'

"Danny Palmer," I informed the balding master who greeted me with a smile and a warm handshake as I entered the classroom.

"Very nice of you to join us, Mr Palmer," he said jovially. A chorus of discreet laughter filled the room. "My name is Spielberg. I am to be your home teacher. Find yourself any available seat for now."

The tops of the wooden desks were freshly varnished and were now laden with bright, colorful notepads and folders. I found a spot in the fourth row back near the window. The students continued to trickle in. Spielberg greeted each one with a smile and a friendly handshake. He was in his late forties and medium built. "Would someone like to open the windows?" Spielberg asked politely.

I willingly accepted the chore. The cool Indian summer breeze charged through the open window, carrying the smell of fresh grass and the initial breath of fall.

Spielberg wrestled with the tie around his neck and took a seat behind his desk. His gray tweed jacket was clearly too hot for that time of year. He resembled a lizard trying to get out of its skin. "Excuse me for starting out late but students usually find it hard locating their rooms on the first day. Many of you students are new to Tilden. A few students I recognize from last year. Sad to say you're still sophomores."

Mocking laughter filled the room. A few hard faces of the guilty left-backs didn't share the joke with the rest of the class. Spielberg rose to his feet and rocked on his heels as he delivered a proud prologue on the great wonders of the school. He took a deep breath and molded his fingers thoughtfully. He began: "Tilden, the great and noble father of our school. Had it not been for a minor twist of fate this man might have defeated

Jefferson to become President of the United States. The excellence of his name is to be maintained throughout this school. We pride ourselves on turning out top quality students who can find meaningful places in our society."

He finished speaking and handed out prearranged program cards. The guidance counselors had sat with each student prior to the opening of the school to discuss classes best suited for their academic achievement.

The door breezed open. A tall, dark Rastaman walked into the room. He wore a red spitfire hat perched on his head like a stuffed pillow. He was dressed in a full suit of khaki fatigues. Buttons of Haile Selassie and Marcus Garvey were strung across his chest like medals. In his back pocket hung a pink face flannel. On his feet, brown polished revolutionary steppers.

"And who might you be?" Spielberg asked.

"Jerome Spence," replied a heavily accented Jamaican voice.

Spielberg stretched out a hand. "Pleased to see you could join us, Mr Spence."

Spence stared at the teacher's outstretched hand with disgust. He avoided the handshake and bopped over to a seat in the middle of the first row. Behind him a Yankee girl with a tall Afro blew a chewing-gum bubble until it popped. She screwed up her face and moved to another chair across the room, fanning her nose as if she had just had a whiff of a very unpleasant odor.

Spielberg's eyes narrowed. He stood at the front of the room and looked ruefully down the aisle. Spence returned his stare with a more intense screw.

"Mr Spence, would you mind removing your hat? The law of this school is that hats are not to be worn in the classrooms."

"Religion, boss, can't remove my crown in public," Spence answered in a deep, arrogant tone.

Spielberg's face flushed red. His authority was being openly challenged. "Mr Spence," he said diplomatically, "from now on I suggest you refer to me as Mr Spielberg or teacher, not boss. I will allow you to wear your hat today, but if you wish to do so in the future then I suggest you get a note from the Dean giving you permission."

"Cool runnings, boss." His face was stern and militantly handsome. The class erupted in reckless laughter.

Spielberg allowed the merriment to continue for a short while, then waved for silence. He said softly: "Every year a class clown emerges. He's made us laugh so now we can all get on with some work."

Each student was asked in turn to stand up and talk a little about themselves. A few smiling girls stood up and ranted on about what a nice summer they had had. They sounded like runners-up in an amateur beauty contest.

The object of my fascination, a short, delicately beautiful girl, stood up. Her bushy Afro glowed with sheen. Her complexion was Demerara brown. Laughter filled the room as she opened her mouth. The laughter started with the Yankees and Puerto-Ricans and ended with the whites, who were always suspicious of black hostility. The girl spoke as though she just got off the plane from Jamaica. She made no attempt to sound even the least bit like an American.

Spielberg cleared his throat. "Thank you, Miss White, you may sit down," he said in a dismissive tone.

"But A don't finish talking yet," protested Sheron, apparently unperturbed by the sight of students falling out of their seats wildly entertained by her outlandish accent.

"Time is running out, I would like to cover as many students as possible," said Spielberg.

There were a few hard faces who didn't share the joke with the rest of the class.

"Damn. She just ought to get her shit together," said a girl in the front row.

"Boat people. What'd you expect?" said a grubby-looking youth.

"Monkey chasers. That's what they call them," said another youth.

"Mr Williams," Spielberg reprimanded. "Would you mind removing your foot from the desk?"

"Hey! Teach, with all this here excitement there should be some popcorn and peanuts to munch on," Williams laughed.

"Maybe I should offer you a medal instead. Seems like you'll be the only student to repeat the tenth grade three times."

Williams, embarrassed by the laughter, slowly removed his foot from the desk and shrank into the seat like a frightened cur.

"This is no way to start a new year." Spielberg looked down the aisles and sniffed suspiciously. The smell of marijuana wafted strongly in the air. He strolled down the outside of the first aisle. "So this is what this proud school has deteriorated to?" He spun around quickly in the hope of catching the guilty party.

The joint moved around under the desks with no problem, finding eager recipients.

Four years in the States had not rid me completely of my Jamaican accent. West Indians couldn't detect it in my speech, but Yankees picked it up quicker than a seismograph.

"Shit, they even trying to sound like us," remarked a short, squat girl from behind her hands.

"Looks like he just come off the boat," jeered a Puerto-Rican as I sat down.

The Puerto-Ricans spoke with a Latin accent but no one laughed at the way they juggled words around under their tongues. They shared the streets with the Yankees and were feared for their quick tempers and swiftness with a knife.

Eyes opened wide and jaws dropped a few notches. "Wows!" and "Damn!" sounded in the room. Jerome Spence was on his feet. He removed his hat and gave an arrogant toss to his heavy mane of waist-length dreadlocks. His hair fell about his body like exposed tree roots. Each individual lock seemed to quiver with satisfaction, reveling in the others' shocked response. To wear dreadlocks in those days was as frightening as if the devil walked down the street stark naked and wielding a pitchfork.

"Jah Rastafari," Jerome roared. He shook his locks.

Spielberg stroked his smooth chin, gasping in awe at what seemed to be his first encounter with a Rastafarian.

Jerome began: "I know my appearance may seem strange to many of you. I offer no apologies." His fingers were knotted in front of him making a peace sign, one commonly associated with Haile Selassie. He declared: "I reflect the face of oppression, the unconquerable and undefeated."

Spielberg interrupted: "This is neither the time nor place to profess your revolutionary ideas." His voice was harsh.

Jerome protested: "Four hundred years of keeping my people down and now you want to silence me. Rasta can never be silenced. This is the only religion to father the poor and give insight to the blacks coming out of colonial oppression."

"The first rule of any religion is respect for your fellow man," chided Spielberg.

Jerome spat: "Respect doesn't come about with pretty smiles and false handshakes from Babylon. Rastas don't stretch forth their hands unto iniquity." He stood proud.

"Babylon!" Spielberg knit his brow. He rose to his feet, outraged. "I hardly see that I am Babylon when my people have been persecuted for years."

"Your people?" replied Jerome, looking sourly into Spielberg's eyes. "Not your people, Rastaman. We are the original Jews."

"Complete and utter rubbish." Spielberg's voice hardened with resentment. "I am sure you'll find that the Jews are the original Israelites. This Rastafarian movement originated in the slums of Kingston, Jamaica, taking their teachings from Marcus Garvey, whom they hail as prophet, and Haile Selassie, whom they claim is God."

Jerome flailed his hands in the air in protest. "Blood, Babylon. Fire and brimstone burn the wicked." The class roared with laughter.

Spielberg waited patiently for things to settle down. He walked to the center of the room and traded heated glances with Spence, who had taken his seat and was pushing a lock of his hair under his hat.

"You're a very impertinent and ill-mannered young man, and further to your misguided teachings I can assure you that the Jews can trace their history over a period of five thousand years," he said.

"Propaganda," shouted Spence. 'The black man is the original Jew. Abraham, Moses, David, and Jesus Christ. They were all black men."

The bell rang in the middle of what promised to be a red-hot discussion. The students bolted for the door as if an air-raid warning had just gone off.

"Mr Spence," shouted Spielberg, "I would appreciate it if you remained behind for a few minutes."

Spence had his hand on the doorknob and contemplated whether he should go on his way or stay behind. He breathed deeply and walked back a little way towards the teacher's desk.

As if drawn against my will, my body remained frozen to the chair I was sitting on. I wanted to witness the fate of my countryman, one so outspoken and rebellious.

Spielberg was so worked up he hardly noticed the four students that remained behind, occupied with shuffling a few books on their desks.

"I don't want you back in my class," Spielberg said harshly. "I will arrange for you to be assigned to another home room." He sat back in his chair with a meddlesome look on his face. His fingers were knotted in front of him and twitched agitatedly.

"The truth is a hurting thing," said Jerome.

Spielberg leaned forward and chucked some papers into his briefcase. "You wouldn't know the truth if it was staring you in the face." He stood up and closed the briefcase. "The trouble with people like you is that you feel the world owes you a favor."

"Sure right," said Jerome. "Only Rasta isn't waiting for it to be handed down on a plate. We've come to conquer. The wicked is going to scream like how you are screaming."

"Get out of my sight."

"My pleasure." Jerome smiled provocatively. "Don't feel that you're a bad man or anyone is afraid of you."

"Preposterous." Spielberg wheeled around and rushed to the door as if there were lightning on his tail. He held the door open and huffed. His eyes burned with fury.

Jerome walked towards the door and stopped dead in front of the slightly taller teacher. Their eyes locked. "Consider yourself lucky. Where I come from teachers like you wouldn't last a day." He took a few steps closer to Spielberg.

Bug-eyed, Spielberg growled: "Should I take that as a threat?"

"Take it any way you want. The next time you disrespect me will surely be your last."

Spielberg clenched his fists and gritted his teeth. His breathing was loud and irregular. For a moment I thought Jerome was going to land a punch. He stormed past Spielberg, deliberately brushing him as he went through the door.

I slipped through the back door followed by the other three students. The scuffing of feet on the brightly finished mosaic tiles echoed down the length of the hallway.

Jerome took long strides down the hallway followed by me, Sheron White, a tall black youth who had introduced himself as Patrick Bailey, and a scraggy-looking white youth with long, uncombed shoulder-length hair.

"Jerome," I shouted, bringing him to a stop near some billboards not yet clothed with posters.

He turned around: "Yo!"

I made quick steps to where he was standing. "Danny Palmer," I introduced myself. "That was some way you handled that teacher."

"More than I can say for you." His voice had a coarse edge. He was still fired up from his run-in with the teacher. "Jamaican?"

"Yes."

"Can't let those Yankees cause you to lose identity."

"They don't bother me." I shrugged.

"Man, I could see the way you drew into a shell when they started laughing." His eyes followed Patrick's movement as he limped closer.

Patrick was much taller than Jerome, with thick, bushy hair combed backwards. He had a slim face, dark complexion, and big, sleepy eyes. "Rastaman, it's people like you that make me feel proud to be a Jamaican. As a youth I grew up to be afraid of Rastamen. My parents referred to them as Black Heart men. You've just made up my mind that the Rasta movement is where I belong."

"Praises," said Jerome. "The Father is calling his children home from the four corners of the Earth."

Sheron held a red folder to her bosom and smiled warmly as she edged closer to the circle. She was petite, had a round, curly Afro, and wore platform shoes to make up her height. She wore a pair of hip-hugging gray pants flared at the feet.

A conversation developed between the four of us and a bond was sealed that hour. Sheron and I turned out to be from the same area in Jamaica. She had recently arrived in the United States. She confessed that she had left behind in Jamaica a boyfriend who was a Rastafarian.

"The Rasta movement is taking over the country," she said, unable to take her eyes from Jerome, who saw the amorous glow in her warm, brown eyes.

He pulled a lock of hair from under its nest and curled it around his fingers. "Looks like you're in pain." He noticed the painful look on Patrick's face.

"It's getting better." Patrick unbuttoned his shirt.

"Oh! My God!" Sheron raised a hand to her mouth.

"Those are some pretty nasty scars. You're lucky to be alive," said Jerome.

"Who done it?" I asked, horror struck.

"Nothing more than I was playing basketball when a group of guys with the name Jolly Stompers bleached on their jeans stormed into the court and singled me out. One of them drew a gun and pointed it at me. About ten of them pinned me to the ground. The guy with the gun said: 'This one belongs to Nathan.' Then this Nathan pulled a switchblade and carved into me."

"Nathan done that?" I was shocked. Scars ripped across Patrick's belly and up to his ribcage. It was as if those very scars were inflicted on me.

"Nathan was the one," he said vengefully. "I live for the day when I set eyes on him again. I've spent days walking the streets looking for him."

Spielberg walked out of the classroom, stopped at the door, and looked up and down the deserted hallway. He seemed to be contemplating whether we were hostile or friendly. His mind made up, he clutched his briefcase and started walking. He made a mental note of all the faces as he passed, headed for the down exit. He turned around and took one last look in our direction before disappearing down the stairs.

"Hey! Long nose, you a spy or what?" Jerome barked at the white youth who kept a safe distance.

"I?" The hippie youth turned a thumb towards his chest and looked around like Mr Cool.

"Yes, you." Jerome's voice was deep and intimidating.

The hippie smiled and walked over, sweeping the foot of his flared denims on the floor. He looked dirty. "Call me a spy if you like but I got my eyes on you guys."

"Guys!" Jerome protested. "Never, ever refer to any Rasta-man as a guy."

"No offence, man. My name is Billy Weinstein. I might be able to help you gu . . . Oops! Sorry."

Jerome grabbed him by the lapels of his soiled suede jacket. "What help can you offer us and who told you we needed any help?" He threw the frail body with such force that he whirled around in front of us like a ballet dancer.

The hippie sneered: "I got drugs?" His blue eyes sparkled. Looking for a favorable reaction. The smile vanished from his face when his bait failed to bring in a catch. He searched his mind to find a more subtle way of foisting his wares. Then, as if whetting our appetites, he continued: "I got reds, blues, greens, ups, downs, morphine, acid, horse. I'm a drugs smorgasbord." Pleased, his willowy body did a little dance like old Fagin in the movie *Oliver Twist*.

"With so much shit it ain't no wonder you was left back," I said.

He was unable to comprehend why he didn't have us under his spell on account of his assortment of dope.

"Go find some Yankees to supply. Jamaicans don't fuck with that shit," Patrick said.

"Far out," Billy yelled. "I've made the right choice. How'd guy—?" He jumped back out of Jerome's reach and apologized. "Sorry, I really am. How'd you people like to be my protectors?"

"Back off," Jerome warned.

"Please! Please," he said earnestly. "I can make each of you rich." He looked nervously over his shoulder as if he was under surveillance. His blue eyes were wet and dripping with anxiety. "There's strength in you people. I can feel it, strong like electric. No one would bother me if I was allowed to hang out with you guys."

Jerome was about to boot him up the can when the exit doors that divided the hallway on either side flew open. Three black men, out of breath, looked about with ravenous intentions.

"They're on me." Billy's wonky frame turned around on a dime. He bolted down the hallway towards the exit at the other end of the building.

"He getting away," shouted one of the men. Sneakers and rubber soles on Playboy shoes scuffed down the hallway. The men breezed past us like a tornado.

"No wonder they have segregated schools," Sheron said.

"Serve him right," Patrick said. "He's looking for trouble talking about all them drugs. I feel sorry for no one since them Yankees near took my life in the park."

Curiosity led us along the same exit path as the hippie. We entered the down exit and were on the second flight of descent when a faint, agonizing groan crept up the stairs.

"Sound like someone's hurt pretty badly." Sheron froze in her tracks and lent her ear to the cry of anguish.

Our feet made haste down the stairs, leaving Patrick lagging behind because of his injury. The stairwell was slightly damp and the lighting was not as bright as in the hallway. The walls were freshly painted in an attempt to cover scrawls of graffiti.

Billy was lying in a corner of the stairwell curled up in a protective ball. Beside him were a few teeth that were still bleeding. Blood oozed out of the corner of his mouth. He drew up as he felt our presence drawing nearer. "No more. I can't take no more." He covered his battered face to shield himself from any further blows.

"We ain't gonna hurt you," I assured him.

His frightened blue eyes opened wide like he'd seen a ghost. "Why me? I want to die," he sobbed.

"We better take him out in the hallway," suggested Jerome.

Sheron held the exit door open while Jerome and myself carried the fear-bitten Weinstein into the brightly lit hallway on the main floor.

"Don't leave me," he moaned as we laid his body down. He held onto my arm with an urgency.

Sheron looked quizzically towards the intersection where the hallways crossed and students were leaving the building.

Patrick, as if reading her mind, said wearily: "The Dean's office is down that way. By the girls' gym."

She strutted off towards the Deanery fifty yards down the hall on the right. Her platform shoes beat rhythmically against the tiles. She returned shortly afterwards trailing behind a ginger-haired man of medium height in his late thirties. He jingled a set of keys hanging on a chain from the loop of his broad leather belt.

He knelt down beside Billy and groomed his crooked Mexican moustache which seemed to be glued above his top lip. The sight of Billy didn't seem to shock him. "Weinstein! Starting the term early," he said with a hint of satisfaction.

"Fuck you," Weinstein groaned.

"That's no way to talk," the Dean said mockingly. He prodded Weinstein with a few fingers. "One of these days you're going to go too far. Who's responsible for this?"

Weinstein slowly raised himself to a sitting position. He fingered away some blood that ran down the side of his mouth.

"You're nothing but a hypocrite," he muttered.

The Dean stood up and drew a pen from the breast pocket of his red and black checkered shirt. He was a typical white-collar stiff with brown polyester slacks flared at the foot and a Farah tag on the back pocket. "He'll be all right," he said flippantly. "Anyone see what happened?" He looked at us in turn and smiled at the absurdity of such a question. His eyes rested heavily on Jerome. "Rush along. I will take care of Mr Weinstein." He gave Jerome an at-a-boy pat on his shoulder to dismiss him.

Jerome shifted his body abruptly. The Dean's eyes narrowed like a polecat. He seemed to be a man destined to have the last word.

"Don't go, you guys. Come back!" cried Weinstein as we walked off.

The sun was high in the sky when we exited from the green doors on to the stone platform. The smell of an early fall hung sweet in the air. All around was green from the many evergreen trees and privets that set off the neat rows of houses opposite the school. Students milled about, drinking and smoking dope on the sidewalk. Tilden Avenue was like a grand prix circuit. Motorbikes and souped-up jalopies were impressing smiling long-haired girls wiggling their asses and leaning on car windows.

The walkway leading to the main gates was littered with hippies sitting on the ground with their legs tucked under, blowing weed and strumming guitars. Smoke rose from their nostrils.

Students were seated on the cars that were parked along both sides of Tilden Avenue. Ghetto blasters were resting on cars and music was blaring out. Blacks and Puerto-Ricans were getting down to the sound of James Brown.

"Sex machine," shouted a dark-skinned girl wiggling and getting flat like a belly dancer. She was dressed in jeans and a blouse that barely covered a pair of bouncing breasts.

"Get down, Mama," shouted a coffee-colored youth, clapping his hands and gyrating towards her. The smell of marijuana laced with angel dust and embalming fluid filled the air. Some spaced-out hippies were seated a few yards away from the group of blacks and Puerto-Ricans. One of the hippies strummed a guitar while another sang a flower power song.

Further down the block an isolated group of West Indians gathered in a mass. The Jamaican men were easily distinguishable. They wore drainpipe trousers with shirts hanging out and a rag waving from their back pockets, and woolen hats perched on their heads.

We threaded our way through the tide of human flesh spread out along the sidewalk. The atmosphere was like a ritual proclaiming the last day of freedom before school actually started.

"Look up," shouted one of the Jamaican men spotting Jerome and passing him a ball that was being kicked around in a game of Keep Up.

Jerome's lithe body advanced. He caught the ball on his chest and danced it around his body, entertaining the crowd who cheered and catcalled. Even a few Yankees turned and stared. He passed the ball back to the group then swaggered to where we were leaning against a car.

"Getting old," he said breathlessly, throwing a starry-eyed Sheron a soft smile.

"Too much ganga smoking." Sheron moved over so he could take a seat beside her on the hood of the car.

"Ganga is the healing of the nation. Ever tried it?" He removed his hat and shook his locks vigorously.

Sheron grimaced. "I tried it once and it made me dizzy."

Jerome checked his watch that had a red, green, and yellow strap. "Some girls from South Shore High is keeping a day party in the New Lots area. Should be starting about now."

"How about the war taking place over there? Everyone says it's a no-go area," I said.

He looked at me, disappointed. "That's Yankee war. Got nothing to do with Rastaman. In Rasta's house there are many mansions with no barriers."

Patrick sighed. "I would come along but this cut in my belly is giving me hell."

"Some Rastamen will be there. Elders, men who will inspire you if Jah is what you really seek." He dried his face with the flannel from his back pocket.

The invitation was accepted by one and all.

Chapter 10

Gangs of young warriors were on each corner guarding their turf with fearsome weapons. The residents of the New Lots area knew the horror of the guns. They bore the scars of violence. Tension was heavy in the area like the stench of poverty, creeping from the rat- and roach-infested houses. Graffiti slogans streaked in bright, lively colors marked the areas. Cats and dogs fought in the alleyways over man-gnawed bones.

The party was kept in a rundown tenement directly across the street from Herzl Park. Noisy children had taken the place of the Rastafarian drug peddlers that occupied the park during the summer. In the distance the chimneys of Brookdale Hospital were spewing whirls of smoke into the sky. The sound of reggae music could be heard from outside on the sidewalk four floors down.

Rastamen armed with pump-action shotguns under their green army coats stood outside the building like soldiers on the Russian army front. Black folks condemned to the hell of their own making walked up and down the sidewalk showing sour faces. The sun was high above dark clouds that set over the area like a curse. Drug addicts with creepy, watery eyes staggered out of the building. Cops were near, sitting, waiting, parked in front of the park like carrion birds sniffing for dead meat.

The music grew louder as we climbed the dirty stairs. The walls were stained with all manner of graffiti slogans and grime. Maggots and roaches crept from the garbage that was thrown about the place as if deliberately. The smell of hog maws, collard greens, and soul food crept from behind apartment doors. The dirt and stink was alive, infectious.

The door to the apartment was open and fierce-looking

Rastamen and high school girls were outside on the landing burning marijuana.

There was a large crowd inside the dark apartment. The smell of marijuana was strong. A small tube amplifier with a fan behind it produced the music that tore through my body like a power drill breaking up a concrete slab. I was sucked into the crowd like a stone thrown into quicksand, tossed about among sweaty bodies.

Jerome, Patrick, Sheron—they'd all drowned in the heavy waves of human flesh and thick, noxious smoke. My eyes slowly adjusted to the dark. The faces that surrounded me weren't strange. Many I had seen in the police surveilance book. I had no idea at the time that many of the men and women present were one day to become my bitter enemies and go on to form some of the most ruthless posses to terrorize the streets of the USA.

Jerome rescued me from the sea of moving flesh and led me into a little room where a group of Rastamen sat in a circle on the ground burning a chalice. Entering that room was like stepping into the past. Back to the seedy squalor of the tenements where Rastamen burnt the chalice under the stars, charging their brains with enough dope to transport them through a night of violence, robbing, raping, and murdering. Jerome had brought me to my death, to die at the hands of some of Jamaica's most wanted men. Here they were, eyes glazed and crimson. Arms of dreadlocks sprung from their heads and ropes of hair hung below their chins. They resembled lions relaxing under a canopy of trees. Somehow they'd managed to escape the Spanish Town gallows and the violent deaths they'd inflicted on innocent people.

The faces took shape in my brain as Jerome drew me closer to the group, much against my will. The wanted posters on the walls throughout Kingston suddenly came alive. There was the bitter and scarred face of Chico Red, a convicted murderer wanted in Jamaica for the death of a preacher. Loraine White, alias Joe Brown, wanted for executing the Boys Town Massacre. Alton Williams, alias Doc Holiday, a hit man for the Phoenix gang. Mahoney Brown from the notorious Warika Hill gang who thrived on killing police and raping young girls. Baby Face

Dillinger, a cold, ruthless murderer second in command to Coppa, the leader of the Warika Hills gang. Natty Joe, who moved around the gangs, never finding a home because of his passion for executing his own men for the slightest mistake. These men were known to the smallest of Jamaican youths like the national anthem that we were forced to recite in class each day.

"Brother Jerome," said a squeaky castrato voice.

"Peace and love, Brother Screaming," answered Jerome.

Screaming was a brown-complexioned man in his early twenties. His dreadlocks were longer than any I had ever seen. He had a speech impediment that caused him to speak from the back of his throat. "You've brought one of Jah lost sheep."

"This is Danny." Jerome led me closer to the group of men and stood me beside Screaming. In front of each man was a gun.

"I think he have the making of a good soldier. His eyes are like a burning fire."

"Yes." Screaming groomed the twines of locks below his chin. "His eyes are like Zakies', the high priest who once controlled the Phoenix gang." He eased me down beside him on his right.

Jerome pulled a Colt .38 from his waist and sat on the left side of Screaming.

There was silence in the room. Each man seemed to be in a daze. Their eyes were half closed. Ganga was swimming in their brains. Screaming took a handful of potent weed from a little cuttingboard sitting in the center of the men. He prepared the chalice like a priest performing his sacred duties. "Jah Rastafari." He held up the chalice towards the beam of light from a shaded bulb. Lingering smoke, thick and noxious, swam below the light like early morning fog over a river.

The chalice was lit. It crackled and blazed like the sound of twigs burning. As the smoke filled the room and the beat of the music ripped through the walls Screaming's shrill voice delivered a catechism in the doctrine of the Rastafarian religion. "Rastafari is the religion our parents tried to poison our hearts against. They told us beware of the Black Heart man. But the Black Heart man never troubled anyone." He took the chalice from

Jerome and prepared it once more. This time it was intended for me. "Danny, to be in this room is to witness the great powers of the Almighty." He carefully stuffed some weed into the mouth of the chalice. "Every man in this room, including myself, was once a part of the ruthless gangs that erupted in Jamaica after the 1962 elections." He continued to speak of the injustices that the British colonizers had inflicted on the islanders and how they left the island in a state of political turmoil before giving them their independence. The new politicians had used the poor and hungry men in the ghettos as stepping stones to get into power. Political violence led to gang violence. The men in the Kingston ghettos embraced the Rastafarian religion as opposed to Christianity which they claimed belonged to the evil colonizers.

Screaming waved his hands over the awesome weapons in front of each man. "We're forced to bear arms because the Yankees are making life difficult for us. These arms we had laid down when given a chance to cross the ocean. The voice of the Jamaican people in this country is crying out for us to deliver them from the threat of the gangs." He handed me the chalice.

"Danny, you are now one of us. Soon your dreadlocks will flourish like ours. Jah has brought you to us. Who God bless no man curse." He struck some matches and put flame to the mouth of the chalice.

The chalice shook in my hand. I was afraid, expecting any minute that one of those men would waste my life. I drew on the stem of the pipe and my lungs were filled with the thick, white smoke that caused me to choke.

Screaming took the chalice as I coughed. A burning sensation stung the back of my throat but my chest suddenly felt clear, like night giving way to daylight. Water welled up in my eyes as the smoke tore through my body.

Screaming patted my back. "Doing well." He raised the remainder to his mouth and sucked long and hard. The weed blazed like a forest fire.

The ritual of the chalice repeated itself at least six more times. The third time around I had got the hang of what was expected of me. I was no longer afraid. These men had accepted me as their brother. I was higher than a kite on a summer's day. My feet never touched the ground as I returned to the main body of the party. School girls of my own age hugged and danced warmly, arousing my passion to a live wire edge. Jerome found Sheron. Patrick scored one of the chicks from South Shore High. The party lasted until late into the evening.

That night I lay awake, twining the ends of my hair and swearing never again to use a comb. My mind flooded with the weird and wonderful things that happened to me through the day. The portable television flashed ghosts around the room. The weed was still stuck in my brain, allowing me to dream freely.

Mom rapped lightly on the door and came into the room, then took a seat on the edge of the bed. There wasn't a night that she didn't come in to have a little chat with me. Her hair was piled up on top of her head. "How was school?" The lighting prevented her from seeing the red in my eyes.

I turned lazily, still dressed in the clothes I had been wearing all day.

"It's a fine school, Mom. The kids are really friendly." My voice was hoarse from the chalice-smoking.

"Sounds like you're catching a cold." She felt my forehead to see if I was running a temperature.

"Where is he?" I whispered.

"Danny, you must stop this foolish behavior. Don't lock yourself away every time he's around. No matter what he is your father. Maybe if you tried a little harder things could work out between both of you."

"Never," I protested.

Dad suddenly shouted out from the adjoining bedroom. "Mavis! Mavis!"

Mom jumped up and swept out of the room, carried by the fright of Dad's deep, gruff voice. I followed her through the living-room and into her bedroom where Dad's eyes were glued to the television. The bedroom was neatly furnished with red plush carpeting. There was a double bed with dark-polished wood frames and matching side tables. There was an eight-track radiogram set between the two outside windows. Directly opposite the bed was a wall-length dresser stacked with women's perfumes, powders, and crochet ornaments.

"What's the matter?" Mom asked apprehensively.

"Shh . . ." He flailed his long, muscular arms in the air. He was a tall, hefty man in his late forties with receding hair and a pitch-black complexion that shone.

The object of his curiosity was a beautiful female newscaster reporting on an incident that happened in the New Lots area an hour ago. "Members of the Militant Rastafarian sect opened fire on police, seriously wounding one. Unconfirmed reports are coming in that a mother and her two-year-old daughter were gunned down in the exchange of fire between police and the Militant sect. The police, acting on information, approached the men as they walked along Herzl Street. The men turned and opened fire. Many of these men are known to the police as being wanted in Jamaica in connection with gangland and police murders."

Pictures of some of the men I sat with earlier came up on the screen, along with their names and aliases.

Dad jumped up from the bed and switched off the television. "Imagine that. The government allowed dogs like those to leave the country and they come over here with that Rastafarian nastiness."

"But how could the government allow someone like Natty Joe to leave the island?" Mom was amazed.

"I don't know, but America is in for trouble. How many nights we had to sleep with the windows of our house barricaded because of that man and his gang running wild?"

"He's wearing dreadlocks now," Mom said.

Dad sighed. "This country seem to be a breeding ground for worthless people. All the young Jamaican boys are following this Black Heart religion, smoking ganga and teaming up with murderers like they were decent people." His gray eyes regarded me bitterly. His broad forehead wrinkled. "Looks like you're turning Rasta as well." His eyes rested on the twines at the end of my hair.

"Oh, Sonny." Mom breathed at the absurdity. "Danny a Rasta!"

"Saturday morning I am taking you down to Nostrand Avenue, have all that shit cut off your head. Hear me, boy?"

"Now, Sonny," Mom said reasonably. "All the other kids have Afros. Danny would look out of place with a haircut."

"Mavis, you're spoiling that boy." He chewed on his bottom lip, a strong indication that he wanted to tear ass. "I'm not going to close my eyes to reality. The Mathews didn't believe their boy would turn Rasta here in this country and it happened." He paused long enough to intimidate me with his tight face, muscles bulging under a white vest. He pointed.

"Any day you have any ideas of turning Rastaman or any man, you can start looking for somewhere to live."

"Go to your room." Mom gave me a light shove. It was as if she was reading Dad's mind and knew what would happen next.

Relieved, I backed up out of the room and closed the door behind me. My ear was cocked to the door.

"Was that necessary?" Mom asked.

"Everything I say to that boy is necessary."

"Children these days are different than in our times."

"That's why I'm not sparing the whip."

"Sonny, Danny is getting so much beating it's making him hardened. I fear the worst."

"You're the one that's making that damn boy feel important around here."

"'Damn boy'! He's my only child. For you it's different."

"What you talking about, woman?"

"I know about the two bastard children you have in Jamaica. Children you don't even care about. I send them a little money sometime when I can spare it." There was silence, then Mom screamed. Things were flying around the room. I rushed inside.

"Mom! Mom!" I threw myself at my father as he was about to hit Mom once more. She was on her knees, weeping.

"Boy, you turned man." He threw me against the wall and tugged impatiently at his broad leather belt. It was caught up in the loops of his trousers as he tried to pull it out fast. I went down when he kicked me in the belly, cramping all the muscles in my body. Hatred breathed heavily in my brain. I saw red. One more kick and I was near unconscious. He was still struggling with the belt.

"Sonny! No more!" Mom pleaded, her mouth bleeding. "What did we ever do to deserve all this?" she cried.

Mercilessly, he tried to shake her off as she held onto his knees, concerned only about my safety.

While she stalled him I was able to slip out of the room and into my room. The keys for the Mustang were on the dresser. Mom's shouts of anguish quickened my feet. I slipped through the front door, out of the apartment, and down the stairs, guided by a desire for revenge. Revenge for Paul, Mom, myself. Bloody revenge.

The cold steel of the .45 felt heavy as I raised the black death from the trunk of the car. A chill ripped through my body which was similar to the night at the party when Paul died. I rushed back into the house and took the stairs with the same speed as I had come down them.

Fright cocked my father's whole black being as he stared at the gun in my hand. He smiled like he didn't think the gun was real. Mom writhed on the floor, her face battered like a squashed tomato. Silence reigned.

"Boy, I'm going to whop you like you never been whopped, running in here with a toy gun." He raised the belt that he had just used to thrash Mom.

"This is where you die." I raised the gun and selected a shot into the chamber like Dave had shown me. He wrapped the belt slowly around his knuckles. His eyes sparkled. My finger curled around the trigger and boom! Fire and smoke jumped from the muzzle of the gun. There was confusion. My body trembled from the force and the kickback of the explosion. I was afraid. Mom screamed. The gun almost fell from my hand. A blunt, metallic taste stung the air. The smoke and fire that dazzled my eyes was just temporary. I was in control once more. The awesome tower of strength that had plagued me all my life dissolved in front of my eyes like snow on a hot pavement. His jaw dropped a few notches. Plaster and dust disturbed by the bullet fell from the ceiling and trickled on his head.

"Didn't believe me when I said you was going to die. Ha!" I could taste his fear. It was sweet. He looked at me like he was shot between the eyes.

"Oh God! Oh God! My sweet Jesus." Mom held her belly. "Please, son," she wept.

"If I don't kill him we'll never have any peace. He has to die. On your knees. That's right, now open your mouth." He got down and raised his hands like he was praying. "Yes." He was praying to me. This was power, real power. Super Dice, Sugar Bear, Shorty the general, the Dreads—they all had this power, then why shouldn't I?

I stood over him, pushed the muzzle of the gun into his mouth. The gun gnashed against his dentures. His teeth clicked like miniature tap dancers. "Not so big now, are you?" The power was inspiring. I wanted to hold onto this new-found glory as long as possible.

"Danny," Mom's trembling voice pleaded. "Put down the gun, son."

Pull the trigger, a voice inside my head demanded. Why not? I asked myself. This pathetic lump of shit deserved every bullet that the gun carried.

The whites of Dad's eyes rolled over and pleaded to my sanity. He owned a gun and he no doubt was aware of their temperament, especially automatics.

"Son, if you love your mother please put down the gun. Life will never be the same if you kill your father." Tears rolled down Mom's cheeks. She got on her feet and walked towards me with outstretched hands. Her head turned, angling my eyes in slow, staid movements. The undisputed love I had for her touched a cord inside me. The strain of losing her husband would surely be too much for her to bear.

A streak of saliva stretched across the barrel of the firestick as I yanked it from his mouth. "Ever lay your hands on me again, you're a dead man. You may come at me unaware or in my sleep, but make sure you kill me because when you've had your fun I'll have mine. I'm a Rastaman. Come to eat of my flesh, you shall stumble and fall."

"Jesus! You've finally gone mad." Mom bit hopelessly at her fingers.

The gun dropped to my side. "From now on I'm my own boss. I do whatever I want."

Dad's frightened eyes followed me as I left the room. He realized how close he had come to death. The incident would haunt him for a long time. He had been humiliated in front of his wife. The fear and cowardice that had led him to turn on his family had finally been exposed. He had come to the end of his reign.

Firing that bullet into the ceiling and commanding respect by the use of the gun changed my life. I craved power and a chance to exercise the weapon that was my strength. I wasn't afraid of dying. Dave Green had sacrificed himself to the dark jungles of Vietnam. Paul had faced death courageously.

That night the weapon never left my side. I waited for Dad to make a false move, one that would surely signal the end of his existence. Silence reigned throughout the house. Not even the sound of a television or a whisper could be heard through the paper-thin walls. At the crack of dawn I closed my eyes. There was no longer any need for concern. The black instrument of death lay openly beside me as I slept.

Mom's sour face shunned me as I dressed for school. The warmth from her eyes and her gentle smile had disappeared. A slight groan escaped her mouth as I went through the front door with my thick bushy Afro stuffed under one of her old woolen tams.

I stepped out into the morning, my head raised pompous and proud. I was now a Rastafarian, a prince in Babylon without fear. My Tilden duffel bag was slung over my shoulder. Inside was the .45 caliber of strength. The visions of my brethren sitting in unity and smoking the chalice flooded my brain. I felt older, like I had been robbed of my boyhood and shunted into the paws of manhood.

Classes started at seven thirty. Pill-poppers, needle-stickers, weed-blowers, and dragon-chasers were on the steps getting a final early morning fix before tackling the day.

I met immediate opposition from a history teacher, a liberal who allowed me to wear my hat after a debate. The other teachers weren't so understanding.

Jerome and Patrick were in my ten o'clock gym class. We were seated in three rows of seven on a polished formica basketball court. Upstairs, around the perimeter of the court, was an indoor track. At one end of the court was an electric scoreboard suspended from the ceiling.

The instructor was a short, muscular man in his late forties, with sandy, receding hair. He was dressed in a tracksuit with a whistle around his neck. "Tilden has many sports facilities." His voice was hoarse. "The girls' gym is on the other side of the building."

"Shit, Coach, what's up with the co-ed rap, man?" said a dark youth.

"Not for some time yet. Last year we graduated one of our finest ballers. The football team will be at a great loss without him. Anyone wishing to sign up for varsity or junior varsity teams can do so."

"What's the deal on the basketball team?" asked a white student.

"Our weak link," the coach answered disappointedly. "For some reason the basketball team failed to complete the year with the punch they started out with at the beginning of the year."

"That's because they all on drugs," said a Puerto-Rican.

"There's no doubt in my mind who supplied those drugs, Mr Fernandez." He waited patiently until the students had finished laughing. "There are a few up-and-coming players here from the junior high schools. I have had the pleasure of watching them play." He walked slowly down the rows of men and stopped beside Patrick. "Sorry you won't be playing for Tilden this year. How is your injury coming along?"

"Still hurts when I move around. Other than that it's healing up quite nicely," Patrick said.

"There's a remedial gym instead of attending this class. I will have you placed on it."

"Thank you very much." Patrick smiled.

The coach walked back to the front of the class and stood under a basketball hoop. "A soccer team was requested by our rising number of West Indian students. Through no fault of their own they find it hard to compete in our traditional sports. The Principal has given his permission to host a team. Anyone interested can give their names after the class."

Chapter 11

The bell rang and sounded throughout the building. The coach jotted names down hastily on a piece of memo paper. The class poured out into the teeming hallway.

Jerome stood beside me as I placed a combination lock on one of the many lockers against the wall near the gym. "What class you got?" He took the program card that was in my mouth. "Math." He was delighted. "Sheron is in that class. This will give me a chance to see her."

We walked along the hallway and entered the stairwell behind a group of students and followed them up the stairs. Suddenly Charmane's body pushed through the crowd on her way down the wrong set of stairs, which was a violation of the school rules. She stopped and looked at me bitterly. Her hair was still in the Mohican style. She wore a blue windbreaker and jeans. "Out the way," she screamed. There was plenty of room for her to pass but she just wanted to be bad.

"Where's your manners? The down stairway is on the other side," Jerome said.

She pushed out her chest and yelled: "This here's our country. I got a right to walk wherever I please." Her voice dropped to a deep drawl. "Telling me which side of the stairs to walk on. Get the fuck out of my face." She pushed Jerome out the way as if he was invisible.

"Hey, gal! You mad or what!" Jerome slapped her face. The sound echoed up the stairwell.

She dropped her books. Pages of A4 paper slid down the stairs followed by an American history text. "Sucker, you bad. Huh?" She stepped back and whipped a razor from the side pocket of her coat. The blade glistened as it sliced through the air.

Charmane moved with the grace of a professional. A street fighter, swift and light on the feet. The knife breezed through the air, dropped and sliced across my chest, cutting the fabric on my bomber jacket and exposing the fluffy white padding. In the same quick motion she cut Jerome across the forehead and drew blood. Her brown eyes sparkled with astonishment. She jumped back to admire her work before launching another attack. Her speed had failed her as she'd gone for Jerome's throat.

A mass of excited students had gathered at the foot of the stairs. The white students, fearful and apprehensive, stood near the exit doors.

Charmane threw the knife from one hand to the other, then stared into my eyes with bitter vengeance. "Had my way you would have died alongside your friend the night of the party. But now I get two for the price of one." She twirled the knife around her fingers like a baton. Cheered on by the thrill-seeking students at the bottom of the stairs, she poked at the air, descending on the stairs slowly, following us as we backed out of the reach of the knife and the menacing look in her eyes.

She stabbed after Jerome once more, but this time his long willowy leg went out and kicked her in the solar plexus. She went down groaning in agony. The knife dropped from her hand and fell down the stairs.

Jerome took her by the hair and dragged her down to the bottom of the stairs. He kicked her in the guts, up her ass, and anywhere he could get his size nines.

"Cool it." I threw myself at him and held him with all my might.

He breathed like an old steam engine.

"Motherfucker. You dead!" Charmane screamed.

Jerome tore away from me. The cut on his forehead had widened. Blood dripped on the fiery woman as she rolled up in a protective ball on the ground. He kicked her repeatedly about the body. "This one's for you. The other's for the Stompers."

The Dean rushed through the open exit door, throwing students aside. "Let's have everyone away from here and in your classes," he barked in a big voice.

"Them the ones," Charmane sobbed. She feebly pointed in our direction. "They tried to rape me."

The Dean looked down at the knife still stained with Jerome's blood. "Get yourself down to the sick bay and both of you report to my office." He taxied over and helped Charmane from the floor.

The sick bay was downstairs near the lunch room. I waited outside while the nurse took care of Jerome's wound. It didn't require any stitches, just a bandage.

He swore to kill Charmane as we walked back up to the second floor. The Deanery was actually two rooms in one. The smaller room was partitioned off and stood in the right-hand corner overlooking the football field. The larger room had pews against the walls and a desk in one corner for the Assistant Dean.

The Dean had Charmane in the little room. The knife rested on a green pad beside the telephone. She swiveled around on a chair and cast her evil eyes through the panes of the glass partition that separated the two rooms. She turned around and cursed the Dean loudly. She was giving him a hard time. After one of her loud outbursts she stormed out of the room and stopped bravely in front of where we were sitting. "Nigger, you dead." She stared venomously into Jerome's eyes.

He leapt up like he was on springs.

The Dean quickly rushed from the office and threw himself between the two.

"Yeah! You try it, sucker." She faced the Dean, intent on getting to Jerome. Her fingers went up above her head in the gang street code meaning death.

"Fuck off, you little tramp. You're nothing but the Stompers' worn-out mattress. They ride you like the express train." I jumped to my feet, sickened by her behavior.

She yelled like the cheap slut she was: "That's right, punk. I fuck who I goddamn please. That's more than you'll be doing when we take your funky ass off the count."

"Miss Freeman, those are no words for a young lady to use," the Dean protested.

"They just called me a Yankee whore. Tell me you never heard that neither."

"That late pass only lasts for five minutes. I suggest you find your class immediately."

"I dig your rap," she said nastily. "Make sure you call me when the heat gets here because I'm pressing full charges."

The Dean escorted her through the main doors and gave a long sigh of relief as her feet pattered down the hallway. He paused momentarily. "Which one of you's going to tell me what happened?" His eyes rested on the buttons of Jerome's chest.

"Ain't no one raped her. She disrespected us on the stairs," I said.

"So both of you decided to give her a good hiding," he said conclusively.

"Something like that," Jerome said ruefully.

"I can see we're going to have another year of discontent. The close of the summer semester witnessed some very nasty incidents between the West Indians and the Afro-Americans. Why? I thought the white man was the devil and you brothers stuck together."

"Yankees giving us a hard fight," I answered.

"At this rate it won't be long before someone gets killed." He stared at the bandage on Jerome's forehead, then the cut on my jacket. "Consider yourselves lucky. Miss Freeman has a reputation of being very handy with a knife. She has a list of convictions longer than my arm. How she ever got into this school is beyond me. She wants the police brought in but I'm going to investigate the matter thoroughly first. After all, she was carrying a knife."

He seemed fascinated by Jerome's appearance. "Why is it that most of the Jamaican students are turning to this Rastafarian religion?"

"It's the will of the Father," Jerome answered.

"This religion is too serious for high school students. It's as if growing dreadlocks has put them on a road destined for doom."

"This is serious times," Jerome said.

"Does that give you the right to pick up a weapon and slaughter anyone who doesn't go along with your religion?"

"If need be," Jerome answered.

The Dean's eyes narrowed. "Thank you very much for answering my questions." His voice was on edge. "I want both of you to stay away from Miss Freeman. Any further disturbances and both of you can find another high school." He dismissed us with a late pass.

We headed straight for the main doors and into the balmy morning air. Outside the school was ripe with activity. There were the usual layabouts blowing weed and getting high. Puerto-Ricans were playing Chinese handball on the sidewalk. The beat cop marched up and down the block, his chest high from inhaling too much marijuana smoke. Hippies were on the grass and sitting around on the sidewalk. The smell of hot dogs and pretzels escaped from the handcart pushed around by the old Jewish vendor.

We sat on a car under the shade of a tree and lit up two giant-size spliffs. Within seconds my lungs were filled with the thick, noxious smoke. "What we gonna do about the Stompers?" I asked, expecting them to come rushing out from the side streets that led off the avenue.

"My gun carries nine Stompers, so I ain't worried." Jerome blew a gust of white smoke from his nostrils. His glazed eyes met mine. "Danny, I've killed many times before and would kill again if necessary. In Jamaica I used to run with the Little Spanglers gang. I was nine when I took my first life. Jamaica is the guerrilla warfare capital of the world. These Yankees don't know how to fight war. They make a lot of noise and are bad when they are in gangs. With us it's different. Our whole life is structured around war. The music, the forces in nature. For us it's all war. We're a strong, rebellious nation. It only take a handful of us to turn over any system."

The beat cop passed and saluted with a wry smile on his face.

"Those brethren we sat with yesterday. They're all wanted men, murderers," I said.

"They're political refugees," Jerome said sharply. "When the time is right they'll return to Jamaica."

"But they're walking mines, ruthless."

"Rastamen," he growled. "All of those men are committed to serving Jah, whose will has brought them together. Governments crumble at the knees when they consider the great power that has brought so many enemies together."

"I can see some very hard times ahead. The Yankees are in for the fight of their lives. They don't think wicked like Jamaicans."

He pulled hungrily on his spliff. "Regardless of all that's taking place the Yankees are still our brothers. Slavery is responsible for all that is happening now."

He went on to speak of his bitter poverty in the ghettos of Kingston, Jamaica: the hunger that made men angry, turning brother against brother and father against son, the deprivation of living in squalor, where politicians offered guns instead of food, the blood money received from the politicians in exchange for killing people, just to secure their seats. He spoke of how as a child he had longed to become a man so he could fire a gun. To kill and be feared. Respected! He told how the elder men in the ghetto taught him badness because badness was a temporary escape from poverty.

The bell sounded. Students rushed up the stairs for the main doors. The activity outside the school never ceased. There were at least three different gangs that hung out around the building. Members of the Devil Rebels gang strolled down the sidewalk and headed towards Ralph Avenue where a group of Ban the Vietnam War protesters were marching. The insignia of the little devil wielding a pitchfork was emblazoned on the backs of their jackets. They snatched a few guitars from some hippies on the sidewalk and smashed them before passing on.

Tension was high, riding on the light breeze that sweetened the breath of the morning. We kicked around a soccer ball on the sidewalk, joined by a few elder Rastamen who hung around outside the school to pick up girls.

The afternoon was spent in Ninety-Fourth Street park where Rastamen sat around beating dominoes on the concrete tables and burning weed. This was the hangout for the Dreads who lived in the Nineties area. The Nineties was an abused work of art that was never appreciated by the new residents. There were beautiful limestone and solid-brick houses erected by the eastern Europeans, Jews who had settled in this area just after the First World War. They were built to reflect the old-world charm of Prague, Budapest, and Berlin. The area earned the name

"Nineties" from the blacks and Puerto-Ricans who now control it, because it started at Ninety-First Street and ended at Ninety-Eighth.

Screaming was delighted to see me and introduced me to the Bible on the steps of a primary school that overlooked the park.

That evening we ended up in Screaming's basement two blocks away, on Ninety-Second Street. The ceiling was low and light crept in through four street-level windows. Wood paneling went around the side of the walls. Most of the men from the park had also found their way down to the basement. Ganga smoke drowned the damp air.

The front room in the basement was slowly overrun by men coming in from off the street. Screaming led us into a little back room to the rear of the basement. The lighting was dim and the floor stained by the soot from a furnace burning in a little security room. We sat on some milk crates under the glow of an overhead bulb. Screaming blessed a chalice and we filled our lungs with smoke.

Light footsteps broke the silence of our meditation. Chico Red appeared, carrying an aura of doom. He was medium built and had a light-brown complexion. His deep voice boomed: "One of the men cooked up some food."

"Tell Tenge and Larry to bring enough back here for three men." Screaming sensed his disapproval. He was not the type for taking orders.

Chico gloated at the chalice held in Jerome's hand.

"There's still enough weed on the board if you care for a smoke, my brother," Screaming said.

"Joke!" he spat in disgust. "These youths shouldn't be smoking the herb that we have to scrape together to buy!"

"The weed is necessary for their cultivation. They're being trained as soldiers, loyal to our cause."

"What cause?" he exclaimed. "It's about time you realized that we can't keep living like this. We came to this country to make money, not sit around nursing little high school boys."

"What d'you suggest?" Screaming asked heatedly.

"I don't need to repeat myself."

"Yes," Screaming mused. "Killing innocent people and robbing their earthly possessions."

"Those were the acts that put food in your hungry belly when you was starving in Jamaica, or don't you remember those days?"

"Days I would rather forget. I'm a Rastaman dedicated to righteousness."

Chico was vexed: "Our numbers are increasing by the day. More and more men are arriving from Jamaica. They need food, clothes, and shelter. We have nothing to offer them but a place in this sweaty basement. We got to steal from the shops to eat. The men are growing restless. Something has to be done."

"What you say is gospel. But we have to be careful. The police are hot on our trails. If we're caught it's deportation to swing on the Spanish Town gallows. Without our dreadlocks we'd have been picked up a long time ago. That shoot-out in Herzl Park by Nine Fingers and his followers is only making things worse for all of us."

"Heat I can live with. Living like a bum is not my style. If our fate is the gallows, then what have we to lose? Better to die on our feet than keep living on our knees. The men respect you for stopping the war and bringing us all together but—"

Screaming interrupted him with a loud bark. "But now you and the others want to show America what manner of evil lies beneath our crowns."

"Why not?" he yelled. "The gangs are doing it. A little idiot gang called the Stompers has moved in right here in the Nineties. They've set up a drugs house in the tenement block."

"Our time is coming," Screaming said reassuringly. "The next Prime Minister of Jamaica is our man. Once he's in power we'll have no problems exporting drugs."

Chico Red breathed heavily and pushed back the brim of his crown. "If you seriously believe that the government of Jamaica will come to our aid then you have another think coming. They're only interested in getting into power. Once there we're history. That same government is setting up a new prison called the gun court, where it's life sentence just to have a bullet in your possession."

Screaming looked up with red eyes. "We give them another

year. If they don't come up with a solution to our problems then we seek other alternatives."

"Herb talk," Chico protested. "In one year the gangs will have complete control of the streets. We'll be under their thumbs."

While Chico was speaking, the dark stature of Natty Joe swept into the light. He crept up through the basement like a thief in the night. The violent waves of his past came rushing into shore, filling my brain with the screams of his victims that cried out in the night. Held captive in the human slaughterhouse that had been set up by him and his men. The break of dawn would give rise to the chilling stench of bodies rotting in the early morning sun. He'd killed his own girlfriend and thrown her in the concrete gully that ran through the entire Rema area. Carrion birds flew overhead, drunk on the smell of human flesh. Three excited pigs fed on the naked corpse. One pig got a mouthful of intestines. Thrilled by the taste of human shit and flesh, it dashed off screaming down the gully, dragging yards of belly.

"What's this? A party?" He had a deep commanding tone that so frightened the residents of the Rema area, especially the young girls and their parents who were compelled to offer him their daughters whenever his sexual appetite ran high. Limbs of dreadlocks sprang from his head. He had a big nose, a broad forehead, and was black as the edge of night. His face was rough like the grains on sandpaper. "One of your Yankee spies is here to see you. He says it's urgent."

"Bring him in." Chico's voice was coarse. He looked about the room then turned to the slightly taller Natty Joe. "What's there to hide? Bring him forward." He peeled back the hem of his pinstripe-arrows shirt and rested a hand on his hip where he carried his gun.

Natty Joe slipped away with the ease of a cat. He returned shortly afterwards leading a pint-size rogue with shifty no-good eyes. The man was shabbily dressed and twitched around like a junkie. He was in his thirties but looked like fifty.

"Better have something important to say or I'll have to discipline you for wasting my time," Chico said.

The scruffy man spoke with a slurred Southern drawl. "Mr

Red, I sure ain't gonna waste your time none. Just that you done told me to keep an ear out to what's happening with the gangs. Well, I got some news fresher than that herb I'm selling." He showed some dirty teeth.

"There's plenty of herb, but first news."

The scrawny body under an oversized short-sleeved shirt and dirty oil-stained dungarees lapsed into what appeared to be an ignorant silence. He was simply not there while he weighed up the possibilities of gain.

"Well, speak up before I lose my patience." Chico feigned a shuffle for his gun.

"OK, Rass, but you got to take care of me. Four of them Stomper fellers was gunned down this afternoon, right in front of everybody."

"That ain't no news," Chico said.

"It sure is. Them the same ones set up that there drugs house on the corner. Some Suni Gods from Buffalo area blasted them when they were rolling down the subway station on Saratoga Avenue. Blew them away with buckshot."

The Suni Gods were an Islamic sect. They claimed they were gods of the universe and that they were the givers and takers of life. They were opposed to gang warfare and black men killing each other. Their sect started in Attica Prison where they took their teachings from Clarence 13 X.

"But I thought the Suni Gods were neutral." Chico rubbed his chin thoughtfully.

"They were, until the Stompers stabbed up one of their young gods at a party a few nights ago. Now, Rass, this here's gonna change the whole face of this war. The Sunis are strong, they threatening to shoot up all drugs houses and stamp out prostitution in Buffalo Park."

Chico nodded approvingly. "That means the Nineties will fall under the leadership of the Sunis."

"Yep! Until that madman the Bear move in with them Tomahawks."

Chico looked anxiously at Screaming, then Natty Joe. "We could be in business very soon if what this man says is true."

Screaming, tall and willowy, jumped to his feet in a huff. "We agreed to give it a year."

"No. That was your decision. I say we move in now and take over that Stompers base on the corner."

The informer scratched his groin. "Rass, best you leave that there base alone. Them Stompers got Mafia connections."

"Get this bum out of here!" Screaming shouted. "He's a junkie selling information to the highest bidder."

Chico pulled a small joint from the breast pocket of his shirt and offered it to the junkie. "As soon as you hear any more news let me know."

The informer gazed angrily at the joint like it was an insult. He shook his nappy head. "Rass, you know that ain't gonna do me no good. All you got to do is tell that there Rodriguez on the corner to give me a bail until I get some swag later. He shit scared of you Rastis."

"I'm busy right now. Leave it till later," Chico said.

"I'm kicking, man. The quicker I get that there fix then I can be on the street looking some money." He rubbed his index finger across the bridge of his nose and sniffed, sickly.

"Have I ever let you down?" Chico asked.

"No, I ain't doubting you none. Gotta lot of respect for you Rastis. My grandmother came from them islands too. Yes sir-ree, she shaw enough did, and she can talk that there Rastis talk just as good as if she was one."

"Joe, take him on the corner and tell Rodriguez to sort him out for me," Chico said.

The informer's eyes lit up like the neons on the Nevada strip, mindless of the heavy hand that Joe placed on the nape of his neck.

Screaming burst into a fit as they disappeared. "What d'you think you're doing? Only a fool would talk business in front of a junkie."

"That junkie as you call him is going to be the one that opens the way for us," said Chico.

"Speak for yourself. I guarantee you he'll be trading secrets with one of the gangs by nightfall."

Chico quickly and deviously switched the tone of the conversation. "You're getting soft. The men look to you as a leader and all you do is fill their heads with promises and excuses."

"There's no leaders among us. We're one. Every man is as independent as the hair on his head."

"Well, the men are getting restless. They want some action."

"I can't give the word for my brethren to start a war here on our doorstep. It would be suicide. The Suni Gods and the Stompers would wipe us out. Just give them time and they will wipe themselves out. No one is winning the gang wars. They are just pumping shots into each other."

Chico shook his head. "I don't want to go against you, Screaming, but if things continue at this rate then I'll have no choice."

Screaming stared deeply into his eyes. "I knew it wouldn't last. Disunity has been floating in the air like pollen. A house divided amongst itself can't stand, neither can a man alone."

"I don't intend to be alone," Chico said threateningly.

Screaming eyed him bitterly. "Of course. I should have known. Rano Dread in the Bronx and his band of cutthroats. They would support you."

"I make no secret of the fact. Rano has proven that with a handful of men he can function on the same turf as the gangs."

"Rano is a disgrace to the name of Rastafari. He fail to recognize Selassie and Garvey." Screaming was outraged.

"Getting the rest of us to help you chase Rano out of Brooklyn wasn't such a good idea."

"That's where I made my mistake. He should be floating at the bottom of the Hudson along with the others. Just the sound of his name cause my blood to boil. I should lead a posse of men up there to carry out his execution."

"He's no threat to you."

"Any man who sells heroin is a threat to me. No Rastaman in this town will agree to what he's doing. Chico, you surprise me. Is that what you have in mind for that Stompers drugs house? To sell heroin?"

"Fuck the rap. Either we take this Stompers drugs house or I pull away." Chico had Screaming in a catch-22 situation.

Screaming clearly didn't want to lose the loyalty of such a dangerous man. "Trust me and give things one more year," he entreated.

Chico sucked in his breath. He was like a keg of gelignite ready to explode. "Six months."

"Nine, the least," Screaming bargained. His hands braced the pockets of his trousers.

"Nine, and the safe return of Rano Dread to Brooklyn," Chico said sternly.

Screaming gave a start. Vapors of fury seeped from his pores. "We have fought on different sides of the fence. This I can live with. My mother and two sisters were raped by this same Rano Dread and the Vikings gang. This I have also learned to live with. But Rano Dread I can't live with. He threatens to break up the bond of unity we have formed. He believes money can only be made if we are at each other's throats."

"Banning him from Brooklyn won't solve the problem. At least here we can keep an eye on him."

"Madness!" Screaming raised his fingers as if he were holding a gun and held them just a breeze away from Chico's nose. The veins along his neck stood out in protest.

Chico Red smiled on the right side of his face. "There would be no need for him to deal in powders if your plan work," he said snidely.

"Not my plan," Screaming protested. He dropped his hand and paced around the floor. His voice became strained. "We're all the victims of the same establishment. The opposition and Prime Minister of Jamaica promised us in strict confidence to make our way clear once settled in the United States."

"That was all a sham. They didn't do us any favors by shipping us off the island. The only way Jamaica could avoid a civil war was to send us here. They satisfied the private sectors who were crying out for our blood, and quiet the youths who were willing to die for us."

"Patience," Screaming said earnestly. "It's no secret. We were used by the system. The government of Jamaica can't draw any more bad cards. The youths in the ghettos would turn the island upside-down if we so much as give the word. They've asked for time. Let's give them their wish and sit back and reap the fruits of our labor."

Screaming, like so many youths from the ghettos of Kingston, believed in the integrity of politicians. Men who promised vast riches once they got into power. In the case of Screaming and the other men's exodus from Jamaica, they were promised vast amounts of money so they could live comfortably in the States. The men also took one step further in believing that the politicians would open a magic door through Customs and supply them with endless amounts of marijuana.

The motor from the furnace chipped in and drew on the electric supply. The light above their heads dimmed. An omen. Their shadows stretched across the floor.

"If after nine months they don't deliver, then we paint the streets of this city red with blood. Rastamen have to stake a claim in at least one of the five boroughs. We're all professional guns. No Mafia, Black Panthers, or gangs can use a gun as efficient as ourselves. Why should we let some overnight gangsters control all the wealth? We got to start commanding some respect and only with a gun and big bucks will we do so." He placed both hands on Screaming's shoulders. Their eyes locked. "I love you, my brother. Whatever course we follow is the will of Jah Almighty himself." There was an undercurrent of insincerity in Chico's voice.

Under the glow of the overhead light and the humming furnace Chico and Screaming agreed to allow Rano Dread back into Brooklyn and also to use the gun to make their mark on the city if the Jamaican government did not come to their aid in nine months.

Chapter 12

Cold winds swept down from beyond the Canadian border. Winter for 1971 was predicted to be the worst since '65. The cold weather had sent many of the gangs underground. Subway stations, parties, trains, and crowded areas became battle-grounds whenever the gangs met.

The Suni Gods now patrolled the streets of the Nineties and Buffalo Park. Prostitutes using Buffalo Park for their brothel fell victim to sniper fire from the Gods. Drug peddlers and junkies in the Nineties were chased off the streets by the sword-wielding Gods.

The Jolly Stompers continued to move from strength to strength even though they'd been chased out of the Nineties by the might of the Gods and had the heavy breath of Sugar Bear breathing down their backs. They controlled Crown Heights, Clarkson, Rugby, and some parts of the Flatbush region. The whores, pimps, gamblers, and drug pushers had to pay their turf dues directly to Super Dice.

Screaming taught me how to use the gun. Shooting ranges were derelict houses in the New Lots area. I celebrated my fifteenth birthday tossing young dreadlocks and blazing the chalice. My mentor's red eyes sparkled with delight. I was now a soldier ready for any tasks set before me. The basement in the Nineties among the growing number of Rastamen was where I spent most of my spare time. On the streets I was given maximum respect for saving Shorty Gold Tooth's life. For the first time in my life I had the might of an army behind me. I was no longer the hunted.

Home life was somewhat nonexistent. I was staying away for days on end. Occasionally I would follow Natty Joe and Baby Face Dillinger on some armed robberies. I was also getting a name for myself on the streets. This led to me being propositioned by Nine Fingers, a small-time hood who controlled a handful of Rastamen opposed to Screaming. The Nine Finger clan hung out in the New Lots area.

Screaming was outraged at the proposition and also the audacity of Nine Fingers in trying to recruit one of his soldiers. He advised me against seeking their company, realizing that I would be used for my vulnerability and ability to handle a gun.

Mom became increasingly suspicious of my activities. She was very concerned. On the occasional nights that I went home, tired and bombed out, her tear-filled eyes would follow me as I moved about the kitchen, hungry and searching for food. She seemed to have aged rapidly since the night I pulled the gun on my father. But what really sealed her lips and her heart were the dreadlocks on my head. She would retire to her room only when she was certain I was in bed. Before leaving for work in the mornings she would leave $1.50 on the kitchen table for my school.

My father kept his distance from me. The warning I gave him the night I pulled the gun on him was sufficient. If he came to eat of my flesh he was going to fall. He knew there was no half stepping, either he killed me or he left me alone. He chose the latter.

The Tilden Booters were taking a beating in the soccer league, so too were my grades, which fell below the 65 average for an academic student. The Dean summoned me to his office during the lunch period the day after I had returned my report card with only one pass.

I stood outside the Deanery admiring some of the young girls in leotards as they skipped to and fro from the gym. Billy Weinstein stormed out of the office sporting a shiner. He cursed under his breath and raised his fingers. He stopped in front of me looking scruffier than the first time I set eyes on him.

"It's easier for a camel to pass through the eye of a needle than a rich man to pass through the gates of heaven."

"What do you mean by that?" I asked.

"Nothing," he said wearily. "Only every time you see me you act as if I got the plague or something."

"That's because you a creep."

A crestfallen look blanketed his face. His voice erupted in a baritone of self-pity. "Why'd you pick me up on the stairwell if I'm a creep?" His eyes widened. "Can't answer, can you?" He spat on the ground. "You're no different from the rest of them, and to think I thought you was special."

"Danny Palmer," the Dean screamed for the second time.

I shoved a finger on the bridge of Billy's nose, standing on tiptoe to do so. "If I wasn't going inside I would bust your face wide open."

"Go ahead, sock me. Everyone's having a bash, take yours." He offered me his chin. "Can't do it, can you?"

Temptation was biting, fists were clenched, but I couldn't deliver the blow. "Get the fuck out of my sight, junkie."

His eyes narrowed. "There ain't no getting away from me. I'm gonna be right behind you wherever you go." He smiled and said smoothly: "I want to be your friend, man."

The Dean bellowed my name once more. Billy took a few steps, then turned around. "Take care. He's nothing to worry about. All mouth . . . a paper tiger." He shuffled off down the hallway with his flared jeans sweeping the floor.

The door slammed as I entered the office, causing the Dean to look up angrily from his desk. He was seated in the larger room, where his assistant normally worked. He flexed a pencil in his fingers and indicated a swivel chair beside his well-kept desk. He waited until I was seated then picked up a copy of my report card from his desk. "Not doing so well, are you?" His eyes were alert and quickly picked up on my agitation. "Perhaps you'd be better off taking commercial subjects?"

I winced at the offer. The thought of descending the academic ladder shook my whole world.

"I have your records from Winthrop Junior High. Up until your graduation you were maintaining a ninety average. What has brought on this drastic change?" His eyes rested accusingly on the woolen tam that covered my young, budding dreadlocks. "There are no doubts in my mind that if you settled down you could make vast progress. Passes in academic courses are not achieved by fluke. These courses require a lot of reading, as you may no doubt have discovered. I suggest you find some time to dedicate to your studies." He sat back comfortably in his chair. "The coach for the soccer team has been advised to drop any students lagging behind in their schoolwork."

There was a hint of satisfaction on his face when he saw that his carrot had taken root. There was no hiding the disappointment. I enjoyed playing for the soccer team even though I lacked the skills.

"Can I expect to see some improvement by the next issuing of report cards?" he asked wryly.

I nodded my head in resigned silence.

"And next time, if you're going to sign your mother's signature have the initiative to ask one of your friends to do so for you." He paused for a moment to move up into gear. "The Booters are playing Wingate next week," he stated regretfully, his eyes meeting mine. "There seems to be quite a large following that attend the matches."

I shrugged, trying to avoid his accusing eyes.

"Is there a problem among the Jamaicans and the other West Indians?"

"Not that I know of."

He smiled knowingly. "There seems to be some discontent. A Haitian boy was stabbed in the back during the last game played on the Erasmus' away ground."

My body froze, warning signals whistled in my brain. He was wading into my solemn and quiet forbearance with the hope that I would leak information. Fortification barriers stood up in my brain. He hurdled them quicker than a stallion in the Kentucky Derby.

"Been around longer than my body suggests, kid. I appreciate the code of silence among you Jamaicans but I must warn you."

I took a deep breath and sat back in the chair, holding my Tilden duffel bag securely on my lap.

"Are you ready for what I have to say?"

"Shoot."

He nodded. "I think you brothers should rewrite the English language." He slapped the desk authoritatively then leaned forward. "There's trouble brewing for you and your Rastafarian brothers."

The shot couldn't have had more impact than if it had come from a cannon. "Sorry, I don't know what you're talking about," I said hesitantly.

He picked up my report card and tore it in half, then spoke softly as though I was not in the room. "It's a shame. You're a brilliant kid, but associating with armed terrorists and carrying weapons will only lead you to the Tilden cemetery or Rikers Island."

"I ain't . . ."

He raised his hand. "Save it. Want to be a wise guy? Then you're going to find yourself in a lot of trouble."

Relieved he'd finished his mind-bending arguments, I stood up quickly, forgetting my duffel bag was on my lap. It thumped on the floor. Quickly I got down to retrieve it. The Dean was down there just as quick. His green eyes stared alarmingly into mine as we struggled for possession of the bag. Slowly he released his hold and stood over me.

"Is there something in that bag that you don't want me to see?"

"No," I answered hastily and out of breath. I got up and clutched the bag to my chest.

"If necessary, I have the power to search you," he said threateningly.

I started a slow backward march out of the room, eyes frightened and wide. "There's nothing in there but books," I said, panic-stricken.

"How about the weapon?" His eyes sparked as he drew closer.

Sweat washed my whole body. Run! My instincts demanded. I couldn't let him find the gun. Music from the girls' gym was beating the same rhythm as my pounding heart.

"I know all you Jamaicans carry long kitchen knives." He stopped walking as my back edged up against the door. "I'm going to give you some advice. Leave it at home because it's automatic expulsion if I find it on you." He put a hand on my shoulder and escorted me out into the hallway.

I slung the bag over my shoulder and stepped away like Barabbas winning his reprieve. The clock on the wall at the intersection where the hallways crossed registered 12.15. I entered the stairwell for the cafeteria in the basement. The noise from utensils, music, and loud chatter echoed up the stairs. Light footsteps descended the stairs behind me. "What you trying to do?" I turned around and shouted arrogantly.

"Cool, man, I just want to rap with you a while." Billy's face was as pale as the white of rice.

"There's nothing to talk about." I took another step down the stairs.

"Shitbag. Stop and listen to me," he shouted desperately. Getting my attention, he said: "I ain't no scum. I got pride." He slapped his chest and gritted his teeth.

There was something in the way he said "pride" that hinted that behind the dirty exterior and hippie front there was a warm, innocent victim crying for release. He produced two healthy joints from the side pocket of his coat. "There's still enough time for a smoke before the next class."

After a session with the crafty Dean I welcomed the offer. We walked down the hallway and through a set of swing doors and into the auditorium.

The auditorium was like a movie house with rows of flip-up seats. There was a stage with blue velvet curtains. Below the stage was a piano where some black students gathered around, crooning a gospel hymn.

We took a seat near the back row, the smell of weed already strong in the air. Students cutting out of classes used the auditorium for sanctuary.

The aroma of Billy's weed caused a few heads to turn. "Hey! That there's some wicked motherfucking shit you smoking," said a smiling black youth sitting next to a girl two rows down.

"Colombian red," Billy said delightedly. He whispered a low aside in my ear: "There's a lot of imitation around, but this is the real thing. Got to be careful. They got some dealers putting embalming fluid on their grass to make it stronger. Get that inside your brain and it feeds on the cells like cancer."

"How d'you know the difference?" I asked worriedly.

"Smell, man. It's just got one of those smells you just can't explain, and the weed burns like it's got gasoline on it." He pulled on the joint for a while then drifted back into a state of gloom. "My life is all fucked up. I wouldn't mind shuffling off this mortal coil."

"Ain't no one to blame but yourself. Can't you see what's happening around here? People are dying of the heroin and pills you're dealing."

"Got no choice. If I don't supply the junkies in this school they gonna take me off the count."

"They busting your ass anyway."

"Only the brothers. They don't pay. When a certain drug is scarce, they get real nasty."

"Fuck that shit. Let them find some other supplier."

"If I had some protection I would quit right now." He looked pleadingly into my eyes. "Them brothers shit scared of you Rastas. They think you guys are crazy. Let me hang out. They would soon get the message and leave me alone."

"Easier you just move to another school."

He shook his head hopelessly. "I've been to four schools already. Just when I'm settling in, along comes someone that knows me and it's bingo."

The weed was good. The best I ever had. Caught on a lazy cloud, I accepted Billy's offer to let him hang out. In other words I was to be his minder. Curious, I inquired how he ever got involved in the drug trade.

He smiled and answered: "Some guys from junior high school found out that I was working part-time in my uncle's drugstore. They asked me to get them a few pills. I saw nothing wrong and agreed. Two months later they were beating me up and demanding more gear. My uncle finally caught on and laid me off. I paid my younger cousin to get me a set of keys made up. Things started rolling again until my uncle caught me creeping the shop. The sentence was a good Jewish whipping." He quivered at the mention of the word. "Tell ya, after that whipping I never went within a mile of his shop. The junkies team up on me. They weren't satisfied with pills any more. They wanted hard drugs, like charlie and the horse."

"How the fuck did you manage after that?"

"Burglaries," he said dryly. "Saturdays when the Jews down at the synagogue I crept their houses." He looked candidly into my eyes and entreated: "Don't mention what I said to anyone or it's prison, and from what I hear about those places I stand as much chance of surviving as an angel stranded in hell."

Billy had a string of problems. There was an Italian dealer on Beverley Road that he was in debt to. He was working off the debt by peddling smack. The dealer turned out to be his worst enemy. He didn't want to lose the service of the vulnerable Jew. The next few days Billy hung out with the West Indians. The Yankees thought the Rastas were taxing him, so they left him alone.

One Friday afternoon I took Billy home to help me with some homework. The city-wide exams were coming up and I was intent on getting some good marks.

Mom wasn't too pleased by the sight of a hippie coming into her house. She busied herself around the draining rack, drying and redrying the plates. Her eyes devoured Billy's unkept hair and soiled rags with relish. She winced at the sight of him sitting around the kitchen table draining a glass of milk. "Not satisfied with disgracing the family, you've managed to corrupt this boy as well," she grunted.

"His name's Billy, Mom, and I did not corrupt him. He's a hippie." I sifted through the piles of books on the kitchen table.

"Hippie, Rasta, and God knows what!" she exclaimed. "What in Heaven's name has gotten into you kids?" She stopped drying a china plate and looked Billy up and down. "I suppose you have needle marks up your arms as well."

"Mrs Palmer, I'm clean," Billy said politely.

She flinched as he got up and removed his coat to show her his arm.

"And what do your parents think about the way you carry yourself?"

Billy sat down. His heavy jacket fell from the back of the chair and dropped on the floor. "My mother feels if I get rid of this then half the problem is beat." He curled his finger around a lock of untidy tress.

Mom nodded. "How true," she said agreeably.

Billy looked admiringly around the neat kitchen. The spices were labeled and set out in a rack hanging on the wall. The cooker was spotless, so too were the washing machine and the refrigerator. The floor was polished and smelt of Pinesol. "Nice place," he complimented her.

"Thank you. It's a pity that you can't get yourself in the same order."

"I intend to," Billy answered sincerely.

"When it's too late?" Mom stepped closer to the table. "Son, take my advice. Don't follow Danny and worthless people. Pull yourself together and live a good life."

Billy turned around in his chair. "Mrs Palmer, I would like to take you up on your advice. Could you please do me the honors?" He held up a handful of his hair and snipped his fingers together like they were scissors.

Mom looked at me innocently as if seeking my advice. "I don't know, Billy." She wiped her hands nervously on her apron.

"There's no time like the present. If you could please cut it all off I'll be very grateful. One day I might be able to return the favor."

"Favor! To see you looking like a decent human being is more of a favor to me. I can't save Danny, but maybe I can help someone else."

"Then you will do it," Billy said delightedly.

"I'm no barber, but I will do my best." Mom was committed. She left the kitchen to get some scissors.

"Now you've really gone and done it."

There was a sparkle in his eyes. "Somehow I don't think so. I feel better already, Danny, you're looking at a new man. I'm gonna be a lawyer like my brother Jack. There's a lot of innocent people around, getting screwed up by the system. I want to reach out and help them."

Mom took Billy out on the landing and did a fair job on his hair. He checked himself in the bathroom mirror and thanked her repeatedly.

As he left the house that afternoon bursting with pride, I knew he was destined to achieve his goal.

Chapter 13

The March rain drizzled over the Wingate football field. The floodlights were blazing through the evening gloom. Wingate were the league champions. At half-time we were one-nil down. The uneven, threadbare pitch helped to offset our game. The second half witnessed a flash of brilliance from our star player, Jerome. He wormed through the defense twice to put the Booters ahead by one goal.

Screaming and a handful of his men were there to witness our triumph. The X-Vandals and the Stompers were at opposite ends, watching the game from the stands. The presence of the gangs was at all our games, but they never caused us any trouble. Today, however, there was some reason for concern because it was the first time the Stompers had attended one of our games. Wingate played host to most of the gangs in Brooklyn. The school was like an active volcano. Once in a while a life would be sacrificed to quell the flames.

The few spectators and teachers melted away before the full-time whistle blew. After the game the coach, uneasy about the presence of the gangs, congratulated us on the victory and raced for the safety of his car.

The captain, a tall Barbadian youth, led the way across the field towards the exit. There were no changing areas and we had to get dressed off the field on the sideline by the concrete stands.

Screaming, Natty Joe, Baby Face Dillinger, and Chico Red trailed behind, pushing their bicycles and chatting to a few umbrella-shaded girls from Wingate.

The Stompers, numbering about twenty, made their way from the terraces and headed past the rows of swings and graffiti-stained handball courts. They stopped against the wire fence that went around the perimeter of the park.

Super Dice, Mo Dean, and Nathan stepped from amongst the body of the Stompers. They quickly produced weapons and held us at gun point. Super Dice pushed his way through the members of the soccer team and stopped in front of Jerome. "We got a score to settle. Nobody, but nobody, hits my woman, sucker." He pointed a German Luger at Jerome's mid-section.

The members of the football team froze. Visions of gangs brutalizing helpless West Indians drowned their brains, causing their knees to buckle.

Super Dice threw back his head. "Think you some hotshot or something? I saw you out there on that field. Them the same fancy kicks you laid on Charmane."

Jerome had a look of arrogance on his face. His Tilden bag was slung over his shoulder with his gun inside. He hadn't bothered to change and was still dressed in his dirt-stained soccer garbs.

The rain-streaked faces of the Stompers, hungry for blood and eager to gain a name for themselves, beamed down waiting for the order from their boss before letting loose with hails of bullets.

Screaming and the other Rastafarians had seen the danger and walked up wheeling their bicycles.

"This here's got nothing to do with you guys. If y'all know what's good for you then turn around and head for the other exit like them rag-head tarts." Super Dice didn't take his eyes from Jerome.

Screaming slowly laid his bicycle down. "Maybe we don't know what's good for us."

Super Dice took his eyes from Jerome. "Dig this, the motherfucker sounds like a goddamn bitch."

"Sure does." Nathan picked at his fingernails with a long switch blade and stared challengingly into my eyes.

The Rastafarian Militants sat comfortably on their bicycles, showing no signs of being bothered by the might of the Stompers and their deadly weapons.

"These are my brothers," Screaming said.

"Call these punks brothers? They just about ready for the boneyard." Super Dice returned the stare Natty Joe was giving him. "How you guys want it? A bloodbath or a ticket out of here? Makes no difference to me."

Screaming groomed the ropes of locks below his chin. "Guess you right, they're hardly worth fighting over. We'll be on our way if it's all right with you." He bent down to pick up his bicycle.

"Not so fast, sucker. I got a better idea. Stick around and watch how I do my thing."

"Please! I don't like the sight of blood," Screaming entreated, rising slowly to his feet.

The stern looks on the other Rastafarian faces were unchanged. Jerome had an air of confidence in his manner, die-hard and fierce. He somehow knew he could defeat death. The members of the football team shook with fright. I wanted to reach for my gun but the odds were against us.

"Shit, what I tell you guys." Super Dice turned around confidently and faced his men. "These motherfuckers bleed like everyone else. All them other gangs got some phobia about fucking with dreads. They ain't nothing but long-hair freaks. Hippies."

The gang fell about the place with laughter. Screaming suddenly reached out and yoked Super Dice around the neck as he paraded in victory. The smiles on the Stompers' faces vanished.

Screaming tightened the yoke around Super Dice's neck and slipped a chrome Derringer from inside the sleeve of his coat. He pressed the Derringer against his temples and cocked it, breaking the stillness of the tension-filled atmosphere.

"Throw all your weapons on the ground and step back." The Stompers looked towards their leader with uncertainty. Scream-ing released Super Dice, giving him enough air to breathe. "Do as he says." His voice was three octaves lower. The clanging sound of weapons hitting the concrete slabs brought a sparkle to Natty Joe's eyes. The frightened members of the soccer team breathed with a sigh of relief.

"Back up," Screaming barked aggressively.

The gang put their backs against the fence. The street behind them was dark and cars were parked in silence. The atmosphere was right for a massacre.

The Militants dismounted from their bicycles and waded through the crowd of soccer players. Chico Red slowly unbuttoned his green army great coat and pulled his prized possession from his waist.

Screaming cast his eyes on Nathan. "Pick up the knife and walk over here." He gave Super Dice an aggressive push and lined him up with the frightened Nathan. "Cut this joker from ear to ear," Screaming said.

Nathan shook his head and looked fearfully at his captured leader.

Chico Red took quick steps over to Nathan and gun-butted him across the face, drawing blood from above his right eye. "You deaf or what? Didn't you hear what the man say?" He grabbed Nathan by the scruff of his neck and pushed him.

Nathan placed the knife on his master's face. "Sorry. They gonna take me out if I don't do it." The whites of Super Dice's eyes rolled over as the knife walked through his flesh. Red slabs of meat rolled over and blood gushed from his face like a waterfall. He dropped to his knees and screamed like a pig poled by a butcher's knife.

Chico Red turned towards the cowering members of the football team. "Get the fuck out of here. Cowards make good witnesses in court."

The men hastily dismissed themselves.

One of the Stompers tried to get away. Natty Joe allowed him to run for a few yards, then exploded a bullet into the back of his head. Marrow and brains nastied the area between the gate and the sidewalk. The Stompers gang, many witnessing death for the first time, shrunk into the innocence of submission.

"Four of you. Over here and hold him down," Screaming ordered. He kicked Super Dice backwards into a puddle of bloodstained water.

Chico Red walked over to the fence and chose four from the cowering bodies. The men tried to push each other in front in a desperate bid to escape the haunted eyes of death. The four men were ordered to hold down the screaming Super Dice while Nathan split the soles of his feet.

Nathan stood over his master, deafened by the scream, wanting to erase the wrong, his face pleading for forgiveness. Blood trickled from the tip of the knife held loosely in his hand.

Chico Red's coarse voice gave him a start. "Which of those youths is the closest to you?"

"That one," he said hesitantly and pointed to Mo Dean. Chico handed Nathan his gun. "Kill him."

Nathan stepped back and shook his head, the gun hanging loosely in his hands. "I can't," he cried.

"Either he dies or you." Chico's voice was cold. Thunder galloped and roared in the heavens.

Mo Dean pleaded: "Please Rass. I ain't no Yankee. My parents are Jamaican."

"More reasons for you to die. It's guys like you who have no mercy in dealing with your own people. You're about to witness the greatest gift of life. Death! That's why it's saved till last." He turned to Nathan: "Hurry and get it over with."

Nathan pleaded: "Danny, please. Help me."

I looked at him with burning hatred and the desire to see justice done. I wanted to see him suffer like how he made Patrick and Paul suffer. His heart-jerking pleas fell on deaf ears.

Death had crept into my body like heroin racing through the veins of a junkie. This was the unwritten law of the streets. It was the law of the Nazarene, the law of David who slew many Philistines and Judas Maccabeus who God rose up to crush the Babylonians. My daily chanting from the Bible taught me that these men were my enemies. They had come to eat my flesh; the law of Rastafarian Nazarene is that they should stumble and fall.

"Five seconds." Chico raised one of two guns he'd taken from the ground earlier and pointed it menacingly at Nathan's head.

Nathan panicked and pulled the trigger. The bullet exploded and ripped off Mo Dean's arm: it dropped to the ground and twitched. Fear suffocated the hearts of the other Stompers as they saw yet another of their confederates tortured. The gun barked once, the bullet destined for nowhere in particular.

Chico Red cocked his gun. "Two more bullets remaining. Make sure he's dead by the last one."

Nathan's eyes darted around nervously, his body shaking, terrified by Chico's voice, slowly counting from five backwards. He raised the gun unsteadily, realizing he had only seconds to live. His fingers curled around the trigger.

The fatal bullet exploded and hit Mo Dean in the center of the forehead, scattering his brains to the four corners of the cosmos. His body keeled over and lay still in death.

Nathan fell on his knees and dropped the gun like it was possessed. The gun hit the concrete beside the dead corpse and the blue steel sizzled in the water.

I walked over to Nathan, ready to eat my long-awaited revenge, the taste of sweat and rain salty in my mouth. He was in another world beyond his greatest imagination, eyes vacant as though he'd gone mad.

There was no sympathy in my heart for this youth that once accepted me as his brother. My heart had turned cold. Death was now a part of my life. I had witnessed the dark destroyer rising from the pits of eternity and executed by Natty Joe and Dillinger who drew strength from taking people's lives.

"Who killed Paul?" There was a coldness in my voice, foreign and deep. I rested my knife on his right ear.

"Charmane," he muttered.

The name had barely left his mouth when I presented him with his severed ear, dripping with blood. He screamed and put a hand to his wound.

"Eat it." The blade was at his throat, piercing his flesh, turning on his blood supply. The warmth of his blood filled me with excitement.

"Shame he's so young," Screaming said regretfully. "Any time I draw my gun I make a point of using it."

"Kill him and have one less enemy in the world," Chico urged, his words ringing with taunt.

"Let him live. After today he'll never be the same." Rapturously I watched as Nathan chewed on the ear. His Adam's apple went up and down as the gristly meat slithered down his throat.

He retched violently and the ear flew out of his mouth and

landed in a puddle of bloodstained water. I made him pick it up and swallow it once more.

Police sirens cried out in the distance beyond the towering chimneys of Kings County Hospital.

Troubled, Screaming weighed his gun in his hand, made heavy by an extra bullet. His gaze drifted towards the cowering Stompers. He moved over the clustered body of men and scrutinized them with a malevolent look in his eyes. He raised the gun and took aim at one of the young warriors. The gun barked angrily and ended a life.

The smell of fresh blood and the pain of suffering thrilled Chico Red. He thrived on having a notorious name, second to none. Whatever Screaming had done, he had to go one step further. He selected a shot into the breech of his gun, excited by the cowering Stompers as they dived for cover. He picked off three with straight shots to the heart before they could hit the concrete. He turned to Screaming and eyed him with a sense of superiority.

Chapter 14

The array of weapons was gathered and tied together in Screaming's coat. Quickly we left the area. I rode on the handlebar of Natty Joe's bicycle while Jerome rode with Dillinger. The rain and wind lashed our faces as we cut across Utica Avenue heading for the Nineties.

The men in the basement were amazed at the weapons. Blissfully, they looked down at what seemed to be an arsenal.

Chico Red took possession of a pair of chrome .45 Magnums with pearl handles. "These will suit me fine." He offered them to the overhead light.

"Man, you know that's not the way we do things." Screaming's voice was sharp.

"What you talking about?" Chico was cross.

"No man has the right to claim any weapon for themselves. The guns are for everyone to use."

Chico stepped away from the body of sweat-smelling men, standing over the guns. He spun around quickly. "Who's gonna stop me from claiming these?" His eyes rested on the men he knew were loyal to Screaming, then his manner changed. The numbers were still not in his favor. "That old nine-millimeter I've been swinging for the last year has killed too many people. If the police catch me with it I would never see the light of day. The hammer has been filed down so many times it's a wonder it still fires."

"Give me the guns." Screaming stretched out his hand.

"No Rass way," Chico protested.

"Seems like you're bent on breaking the peace that exists among us," Screaming said authoritatively.

"What peace! How can a poor man think of peace? All we do is smoke ganga and chant down the system. With these guns some serious money can be made. The days of Rastamen living in the hills without luxuries are over. I'm going to get a piece of this Big Apple whore."

Screaming shook his head hopelessly. "So this is what it all boils down to. Soon you'll be wanting to bear arms against your brothers like the bloody days of gang warfare."

"Man, you living in the Dark Ages. Here we are cursing the gangs and calling them Yankee bald heads. They're only youths, but they're more progressive than any one of us." He spread his arms out over the weapons on the floor. "Just look at these guns. They make what we carry look like peashooters." He paused momentarily and looked at the faces of the men. "There's a place for Rastamen in this city and it's not sitting around preaching peace and love and praising Jah."

Screaming was outraged. He threw his hands in the air and chanted a psalm of rebuke. Some of the men also uttered words of chastisement.

Chico was unmoved by the protests. He waited until the chanting had died down, then gave Screaming a long, hard look, one that would melt an iceberg. "Ten virgins tilled their lamps, five were wise and five were foolish. The foolish ones were shut out by their masters. I don't intend to be shut out."

"The trouble is you're obsessed with killing. Danger and gang warfare sweetens your blood."

"Yes! But there's something else more sweeter than blood— money! This town is rolling in wealth. The gangs know it, that's why they're dying in the streets. The gangs are selling the most ganga in this city. Rastaman should be in control of all ganga distribution. We walk around in all kind of weather with holes in our shoes. Some of the men in this room have nowhere to rest their heads at nights. This isn't the way, Screaming. Jah Almighty is my witness." He shook his head as though actually concerned about the men and their wellbeing.

There was silence as Screaming looked around at the sorry faces. Chico Red was right. Something had to be done without delay. The men were just surviving on hopes and their commitment to the Rastafarian religion.

Chico broke the silence: "Now's the time for change. Not six months or a year, but now. I know we made a deal to wait but in view of what happened at Wingate we better secure ourselves financially in case we have to run away. With these guns we can make our move. Strike while the iron's hot. It's time we start kicking off a few doors and chasing these punk gangs out of the area."

"Then what? We take over their trade of death and deal in hard drugs like Rano Dread," Screaming protested.

"Never. Only ganga," Chico specified. "Rastamen loyal to us will never handle hard drugs."

There was a doubtful look on Screaming's face.

Chico was determined. "Don't delay this move, my brother. If you pull five dollars from your pocket right now you can have these guns."

"We'll all live to regret this day." Screaming gave up the fight, much to the delight of the men who were slowly being poisoned by Chico's rebellion.

Chico raised the guns in the air. "Let all the blame rest on my shoulders. Future Jamaicans and Jamericans will know that it was I, Chico Red, who first led the charge to rape this Big Apple and put money in Rastaman's pockets."

Screaming mused: "Life is funny. One day we're righteous men, next we're switching to a crime network."

"Just taking what's ours," Chico said coolly. "Money is sitting in check-cashing joints, banks, security vans, stores. We're all robbers, and if all fails there's enough marijuana in Jamaica to make us all millionaires."

"What you have in mind will take careful planning so that every man can benefit," Screaming said thoughtfully.

Chico weighed the two guns in his hands. "From now on the Robin Hood style is in full effect." An evil look spread across his face, recalling the many lives he'd taken. "For starters we're going to hit the Tomahawks' drugs house in Brownsville."

"When do we strike?" asked Natty Joe excitedly.

"Ten o'clock tonight. They won't be expecting a dreadlocks assault."

Natty Joe rubbed his hands eagerly. "From the sound of things it looks like I'm about to be rich."

Chico stared at me and Jerome in turn. "Now is the time for you two youths to prove yourselves."

"They are fit and ready," Screaming said confidently.

Twelve men were selected to carry out the raid. The chalice was lit and psalms chanted amongst the gathering. The twelve men pleaded to the Almighty for guidance in the face of battle.

The eight o'clock news focused on the slaying in Wingate Park. The deaths were attributed to members of the X-Vandals gang.

The twelve-man assault team, armed and dangerous, embraced the cold breath of winter. We rode through the back streets of New Lots into the squalor of Brownsville. The rising stench of poverty seemed to make drunk the destitute black folks walking about in a poor state of confusion and trying to escape the jungles of seedy tenements. Neons, broken and dull, outlined the names of shops clothed in security netting. Men gathered around blazing drums on the sidewalk to keep warm.

Our target was a tenement block in the center of the projects. Donkey paths cut through threadbare grass that was once intended to add beauty to the towering giants. The bicycles were left at a strategic position eighteen floors below our target.

The rain had stopped and left in its wake the rising stench and rawness of uncollected refuse, dead cats, dogs, and rats that drowned in the river of water that flooded the streets.

The concrete walkway leading up to the tenement was slippery. Six members of the Tomahawks gang patroled the outside of the building. The men were clothed in long coats and fur-lined hats pulled down over their ears. They raised pump-action shotguns and stood to attention as we drew closer.

"Hey, Rass! What gives?" asked a fair-skinned man slightly shorter than Screaming.

"Come to pay our respect to a lady friend on the twenty-eighth floor. Her daughter died last night," Screaming answered.

There was a broad smile on the man's face when he heard Screaming's squeaky voice. "You got a long walk to heaven. There ain't no elevators working." He sounded suspicious.

"Thanks for the advice." Screaming attempted to go around the man.

"Not so fast." The spokesman wrinkled his nose in disgust. "I just ought to search you motherfuckers, but y'all smell so funky I'm afraid that smell might rub off on me. Anyway, what goes up must come down, so I catch you guys on the rebound."

The men stepped aside and gave us access into the mouth of the building. Paint chips peeled from the walls. The smell of pork lingered above a million stinks wafting in the air. Liquor bottles and broken glass were scattered about the place.

Chico Red led the way towards a burnt-out exit. The stairway smelt of vomit, urine, shit, and all manner of human stink. Roaches climbed sticky fungus walls. The lighting was dim.

"Rass Clatt!" Chico Red exclaimed, momentarily stung. Rare for one so evil. He froze in his tracks between the third and fourth floors. He shook his head and breathed: "Phew."

I came face to face with the object that moved Chico's heart. Hitched up against the wall was a scrawny woman with a needle stuck in her crotch. Her pupils exploded as the drug raced through her blood. She slid down against the wall, her dirty knickers dangling round one of her feet. The garbage beneath her bare buttocks cushioned her meager body.

The men had all feasted their eyes on the grotesque sight and moved ahead of me. This was my first encounter with the perils of heroin. Climbing the stairs to the eighteenth floor was like Bruce Lee entering the dragon. This was the zenith of men creating their own hell and living in squalor. On the eleventh floor there were remains of what looked like chopped-up babies. Three arms and a leg were lined out in front of an exit door as if on parade. A man was taking a shit on the twelfth floor, junkies were jacking up and leaving trails of blood.

We finally reached the eighteenth floor. Customers were going back and forth from apartment 18D. There was a little slot in the door where the money went in. Seconds after, the drug came out like a cash dispenser. The junkies making their cop were blinded by the desire to find somewhere safe to jack up. They just passed us by.

"Brinks," Screaming whispered as a junkie disappeared around the corner at the end of the passage way.

Chico waved us back to the stairs between the eighteenth and nineteenth floors. Jerome was left at the bottom of the stairs to keep a look-out.

"Every hour they send three men down stairs and three come

up. We take them when they change shift." Chico was well informed.

"Seems like you've been planning this for some time," Screaming whispered.

"Not just this base! My Yankee spies have already given me the run-down for at least eight more."

"Then you would have made this move with or without the guns," Screaming said reproachfully.

"Foreign is making you soft. What difference does it make? Anyway, since when have you turned a Christian? Don't tell me you're having guilt complexes from all those women and children you executed in Jamaica."

"Never any kids," Screaming shouted, forgetting where he was.

"Easy," Chico implored, realizing he'd gone too far.

Screaming's face hardened. He was about to attack Chico verbally. "After this . . ."

"Quiet," Jerome whispered. "Someone's coming through the door." He sprinted up the stairs.

Moments after, the exit door on the eighteenth floor was slung open. We made ourselves small on the stairs.

"Hey! Mama you say you got more friends?" The voice was that of a man's, ghetto in tone.

"Sure do and they fuck for drugs too," answered a lilting female voice.

"Bring them right on over," shouted an excited voice.

"Now we out of that shark-infested apartment how's about a quick head," said another male voice.

"Shit, I ain't no bionic lips. Done blow nine of you guys already. I got more spunk in my belly than spilt popcorn in a dark movie house."

"Well, cough on this here one time," the rough ghetto voice demanded.

"Only if you give me another fix," the broad bargained.

"Sure. I'll fix you a free ride from the twenty-fifth floor down without a parachute," the husky voice said.

"Yo! Roach, ain't no need to pop that shit, man. She ain't saying she ain't getting down. She just want some juice to set her loose."

There was a shuffling of feet then slurping sounds traveled up the stairs. "Whoo, wee! Blow, Mama, blow," the pleasure-filled voice pleaded.

The sickly slurping sound was followed by a long grunt of male satisfaction.

"My gear," the choked female voice demanded.

"Right here," said another.

The girl seemed to be blowing another trumpet because the slurping started again. "Shit, honey, you need a crane. This here john's got no life," she taunted.

"Hey! Spanky, move out the way with that there piece of worn-out shit. Let a real man get in." Heavy laughter filled the stairwell.

"Don't choke me with that thing," the girl warned.

"I ain't gonna choke you. Just give me one of them there Linda Lovelace jobs," said a confident voice.

"For them two packages I got two clitoris at the back of my throat," she said excitedly.

The sordid activity lasted for about fifteen nerve-racking minutes before they finally disappeared down the stairs.

"Three more should be coming up shortly," said Chico. "They'll be nice and tired when they get up here."

Twenty long minutes afterwards voices and footsteps traveled up the stairs. "That bitch don't look too bad," said a voice with a nasal twang.

"Spanky got the hots for the little whore," answered another.

Chico jumped into action at the mention of the name Spanky. These were definitely our pigeons. With guns drawn we tiger-pawed our way down the stairs and hovered like death over the unsuspecting trio.

"Don't move," commanded Chico's coarse voice. The three men froze and offered no resistance as they were relieved of their weapons and marched to the apartment door.

"Man, y'all crazy," said the stockiest of the three.

"How much do you value your life?" Chico asked the stocky man.

"I'll do anything." He stared bleakly down the barrels of the two guns in Chico's hands.

"Knock the door nice and easy like everything cool," Chico ordered.

"This is suicide, Homes. They got guns in there trained at the door with orders to shoot anything strange."

"That'll be you three then," said Chico's cold voice.

The three men were paraded in front of the door. The stocky man rapped lightly on the brown door. His two partners huddled close to him, suffering from the shakes.

The cover of the spy hole moved aside. "What took y'all so long?" inquired a rough voice from behind the door.

The stocky man answered nervously: "Spanky and the guys were joshing around with the junkie freak."

Bolts started releasing on the other side. Natty Joe appeared eager. Baby Face Dillinger had a complacent look on his face, intrigued by the action. Screaming positioned himself behind the three men. He was armed with a police assault rifle captured from the Stompers.

The door slowly opened. "What the fuck!" shouted the husky voice as the three men charged inside.

"Don't shoot!" shouted the stocky man as he charged into the apartment.

A barrage of gunshots erupted from inside the apartment. The front door was blown off. The three men and the one who answered the door were mown down by their comrades inside. Bones, blood, skin, and pieces of human organs flew through the door as if they had been put in a blender. The shots continued to ring out. Bullets sailed through the air, ripping up everything in sight and chipping up the walls. The door to the apartment directly opposite was riddled with bullets.

Screaming cranked up the assault rifle and jumped in front of the missing door. He fired rounds of buckshot down the passageway into the apartment. There was a red bulb that lit the long hallway leading to a back room where the Tomahawks were still firing.

Screaming entered the apartment and moved fast, blazing rounds of buckshot to clear the way. Dillinger stepped beside him down the narrow walkway. Together their rifles blazed. Cordite burnt the air.

The shots from inside grew quieter. We shielded behind the cover of the assault guns. Faint voices sounded over the heavy gunfire. "Take it easy. We surrender." The assault guns continued to spit balls of fire until we reached the back room.

Natty Joe and Passo, a short dapper man in his early twenties, opened fire inside the room with two Bren sub-machine guns. Three of the Tomahawks were cut down by the hail of bullets that chewed up the walls and light pieces of furniture. Three remaining Tomahawks raised their hands and surrendered. Their weapons were thrown down at their feet.

The shots stopped and the smoke from the gunfire eased. There was a man on the floor stark naked with a bottle of petroleum jelly beside him. He was on all fours and his ass was stuck in the air.

Chico looked revoltingly at one of the Tomahawks with his pants rolled down.

"Rass, it ain't what you think," the man said.

"Search the other rooms," Chico commanded.

Jerome and myself moved briskly through the apartment. There were three bedrooms, each empty. I kicked off the bathroom door and entered. Jerome pulled up beside me. The sight that greeted us filled us with disgust. There was a man hanging by his Achilles' tendons over a bathtub. He was naked and his throat was cut. Blood drained down into the bath in thick blobs. I closed the door and we returned to the living room.

Passo and Natty Joe had covered the rest of the apartment. Chico Red was interrogating the captives.

One of the captives pleaded: "Rass, please spare our lives. There's heroin, cocaine and a hundred pounds of Colombian Red under the floorboards."

Chico's eyes sparkled. "Where's all the cash?"

"There's plenty of cash. Take it all, and we know a way out of here where no one will get in your way. Ain't that right, Felton?" He nudged his partner nervously.

"Mighty nice of you, but we found our way in here and we'll find our way out. Take me to the stash," Chico barked.

"Right under your foot. Just raise the carpet," the man said quickly.

The worn piece of carpeting was quickly rolled back and the floorboards raised. The Rastamen looked down greedily at the sight below their eyes. Chico Red dropped on his knees and ordered, "Passo, Joe, stay near the door, anyone try to come in shoot to kill."

Natty Joe showed some reluctance to part from the stash, then as an afterthought he smiled and walked off.

"Leave the hard drugs," Screaming said.

"Man, you're crazy," protested Chico.

"The poison stays here," Screaming said.

"The only way I leave anything is over my dead body."

Screaming cranked the riot gun in haste.

Chico Red smiled: "It's a shame those guns can't load themselves."

Screaming in his anger didn't realize the gun was empty.

I moved closer to my mentor. Jerome was by my side.

Dillinger, a man short on words, said: "We're taking all the drugs. When we get back to the base we can decide what to do with it then."

Chico Red traded vicious stares with Screaming, suggesting they had a score to settle.

Chapter 15

Chico Red finished throwing the last of the drugs and money into the duffel bag. He raised himself from the ground and walked across the room. The captives cowered in fright; sweat washed their faces.

Chico passed the captives and stopped a short distance from the panoramic window which was draped with a torn sheet. He pulled away the sheet. Lights from a thousand cars flickered along the boulevard below. He turned his guns on the window, shattering the glass in a million pieces.

Natty Joe rushed back into the room, his eyes wild, the sound of gunfire triggering his desire for blood. Sensing there was no cause for alarm he turned around and headed for his post.

The duffel bag was taken to the window and thrown out. Two men guarding the bicycles awaited the drop under a hedgerow. The mission was complete.

Chico turned to the cowering captors and gazed ruefully at the man with his pants down.

"Rass," he pleaded, sighting the fierceness and revulsion in Chico's eyes.

"Hey! Sodomite," Chico said crossly. "Don't you know that Rastaman don't deal with faggots?"

"I ain't no faggot, Dread." He covered his genitals with both hands. Sweat ran down his face.

The naked man on the ground raised his head. "They were about to bust me out before you guys came along. Look in the bathroom, they done cut my brother's throat."

Menzy, the oldest of the Rastafarian warriors, was overcome with utter disgust. He was a hefty man and wore his waist-length dreadlocks uncovered. There was a streak of grey above his forehead where his hair had started to recede. He walked briskly across the room and stood in front of the captors. "On your knees," he commanded the sodomite.

The man dropped quickly to the ground, his eyes pleading for mercy but finding none.

"Before you die, I want you to confess that Selassie is God." His voice was deep and penetrating.

The frightened man repeated the words, somehow believing he could delay the messenger of death. "Please, please," he cried, realizing there was no hope.

"Die like a man." Menzy's big hands raised the German Luger. "Bad men make the most noise when they're dying," he mused. His eyes narrowed.

The man's screams filled the room, seconds after the bullet shattered his brain. His head exploded like a squashed watermelon.

Instant revulsion overpowered me. Every time someone died in my presence it was like a part of me died. What manner of men had I teamed up with? Death was written in their hearts. They were intrigued by watching men suffer. I had witnessed enough of their merciless slaying for one day.

"Danny! This head's yours." Chico pointed to the naked man on the floor. "Let this faggot be the first man you kill."

The hard faces around me were encouraging me to taste the forbidden fruit of death. They wanted to see me put a notch on my heart, suffer some sleepless nights, go for a few days without eating, battle with my conscience, then emerge a murderer. I pointed the gun at the target and jacked a shot into the breach of the gun.

The man at my mercy pleaded with brown, watery eyes. His complexion was dark. "Look into my eyes when you kill me," he said softly. "I want you to remember this face as long as you live."

"Shoot the faggot and don't listen to anything he has to say," Chico barked impatiently.

The man whispered the Lord's prayer. He stared into my eyes and somehow hypnotized me because I found myself repeating the prayer with him. His handsome face smiled, realizing that I couldn't carry out his execution. The gun dropped to my side.

"Kill him before I do it," Chico said.

"I'm not doing it," I protested. The .45 in my hand seemed to rise of its own accord. I looked down the barrel of Chico's gun. We stared wildly into each other's eyes. A short distance separated us. "Man, you're a vampire not a Rastaman. Haven't you shed enough blood for one day?" I was disgusted.

"If you weren't one of us I would blow you to the other side of the world."

"I won't be alone," I said, full of bravado. My fingers grew sticky on the trigger. No one dared intervene. There was silence apart from heavy breathing. All my mental energy was spent gazing into the cold, calculating eyes of the man who wanted my life. Nothing else seemed to matter at that moment. I was beginning to wonder how long before one of us ceased to exist. Screaming had prepared me for such emergencies. "The answer is in their eyes," he had said when training me. I looked deep into his eyes and for a moment I saw it. Faint and brief but it was there. He was afraid.

He sniggered as though he was doing me a favour. "I admire your courage," he said. "Only the next time you pull a gun on me you're a dead man." He lowered his gun.

Screaming's voice broke the tension. "Twelve men came on this mission and twelve will return."

"Keep him under your wing," Chico hissed venomously.

Menzy intervened once more. He was crafty and knew the air of hostility between the men. He seemed to be biding his time. Without saying a word he turned his gun on the captives and cut them down, sparing the life of the naked man on the floor. "Any man who shows bravery in the face of death deserves to live. Such a man might prove helpful in time to come. Take care of him, Danny," he smiled. There was something in his smile that suggested he would also require my services at a later date.

The naked man recovered his clothes and hurriedly put them on. He was tall and graceful in manner. He took my hat and stuffed it with newspaper to camouflage his flight to freedom. The men were making their way out of the apartment. Instinctively, I stayed behind, not wanting Chico Red to have the chance of wasting me in the back.

Chico dropped further behind while the rest of the men exited through the door. He slipped back into the apartment among the dead men.

From a closet space in the wall of the passageway I could see directly into the room.

Chico holstered his gun and smoothed down the wall near the window. A broad smile covered his face when he uncovered a secret stash hidden in the wall. Quickly he removed stacks of greenbacks.

He was prepared because he took a pillowcase from under his hat and filled it with the money. He then tied a knot in the pillowcase and dropped it through the window. He headed out of the room and past the closet where I was hiding.

I was just about to exit from the closet when two shots rang out from inside the apartment. Chico Red was hit. The gun exploded once more. Chico had no way of recovering.

I jumped out of the closet with the .45 spitting fire. Five shots riddled the body of the assassin.

Chico Red groaned in agony when I approached him. "You saved my life and also took a life," he said, awed.

"Can you walk?"

He smiled painfully. "The bullet hit me in the leg. It seems like it went in and out."

Screaming and Jerome rushed back into the apartment. There was a look of satisfaction on Screaming's face when he saw that it was Chico injured and not me.

We joined the other men on the stairwell and helped Chico down the stairs. He fought the pain, concerned only about the bag of money he'd thrown through the window. Greed was a powerful agent, I discovered.

The guards ambushed us once more inside the stink lobby on the first floor. "That was a short visit," one guard said.

"Not much you can do about the dead," Screaming retorted.

The guard's eyes narrowed. He walked over to the cluster of men who were shielding Chico Red. "Some Rastas shot up a load of Jolly Stompers this evening. Wasn't you guys, was it?'

"We're righteous men. A life is sacred to us," Screaming said.

"Cut the bull," the guard said sharply. He raised his gun to Screaming's head. "Pay some dues for walking on our turf."

"Sorry about the intrusion, but we're poor men. Look," Screaming lifted his foot and showed the hole, about the size of a silver dollar, in the bottom of his shoes.

"Damn, you niggers sure down and out." The guard laughed heartily. The other members of the gang lowered their guns.

"Pass through, but the next time you guys bugaloo on our turf then you got to pay the piper."

Screaming was curt: "Thank you in the name of Rastafari."

The guards stepped aside and let us out into the cold breath of winter.

The two look-out men had gathered the first bag thrown through the window. The last bag thrown out by Chico Red was still there, waiting to be picked up.

Chico Red continued to put on a brave face although overcome by pain. He was picked up by a gypsy cab a short distance away from the apartment building.

Johnny Toobad, one of Chico's staunch followers, slipped away from the fleeing cavalcade. He headed for the hedgerow to recover the bag.

I changed direction and went over to Euclid Avenue subway station to drop off the man rescued from the apartment. His name was Pappy and he was the leader of a group of robbers in the Bronx known as the Stick Up Kids. I had often seen their graffiti slogans on walls.

The men were back in the basement when I returned. Chico Red was also there. He had a piece of cloth wrapped around his wound. The entire take was thrown on a sheet and spread out in the middle of the floor. Menzy carefully separated the marijuana and money from the hard drugs.

Screaming got down on his knees beside the strong-smelling marijuana. "There's enough here for everyone. We gonna burn the hard drugs right now."

Chico Red let off a sigh of hurt. "The money is on the hard drugs. It can't be burned."

"The weed and the money is plenty," Screaming said.

"The drugs stays," Natty Joe said firmly.

"Burn it," shouted another.

"Chico is right. Sell it this once. Once we get on our feet

then we won't need to deal in it any more," Dillinger said eagerly.

"Put it to the vote," said one.

Jerome's vote and mine swayed the decision in favour of burning the drugs. There was a strong air of disapproval among the men as the drugs were taken to the back room and slung into the furnace.

Gathered in the front of the basement once more, Screaming presided over the men who waited eagerly to see how they would benefit from the take—if they were to benefit at all.

"Ganga is our trade. Hard drugs is trouble. The day we trade in powders will be a sad time for all of us." Screaming paced the floor. "We got to take over that Stompers base to move this huge quantity of marijuana."

"One problem," Menzy said worriedly. "The Suni Gods are on patrol throughout the Nineties."

"No problem," Natty Joe raised his gun in the air. "I alone will go out there and chase those Gods off the corner." His words weren't to be taken lightly.

Chico Red swelled up from his squat overlooking the drugs. "When I called for us to take the base, I came up against politician talk. Now because Screaming gives the word it makes everything right."

"We have no choice," Screaming said critically. "The base will have to be taken over tomorrow. Cards will be printed up and distributed along with samples."

"The heads of the Suni Gods must roll before anyone can stand on any corner," Natty Joe said anxiously.

"This is as good a time as any," said Passo defensively.

"No!" Chico gritted his teeth. "The wiping out of the Gods will be carried out by Rano Dread and his men."

The name brought a bitter response from Screaming: "It seems I've played right into your hands."

"What choice do we have. I want a piece of the action," Natty Joe said zealously. "The sight of that big chest Bishme leading a bunch of pussies grieve my heart. I want the personal satisfaction of pushing my gun down his fucking throat."

"Not this time. The outsiders will take off some of the heat that will be raising around here in a few days." Chico squeezed the hurt on his leg.

"Something have to be done about that wound." Menzy seemed concerned.

Chico drew air between his teeth. "I can't go to any of the hospitals. The police would be on me like a bat out of hell." His eyes rested gluttonously on the drugs and money.

"We're rich," Natty Joe shouted jubilantly. "The Tomahawks don't know who robbed them and the Gods are keeping the Stompers out of the Nineties."

"Don't be too over-confident." Chico's voice grew weaker by the minute.

Johnny Toobad, a dimwit loyal to Chico, spoke up. He was dangerous with a gun and was afraid of only one man in the world, Chico Red. "Brookdale is only a few blocks away from here, boss."

"So what?" Chico growled from way down in the back of his throat.

"Kidnap one of the doctors from the hospital parking lot and bring him here." He quickly realized how foolish his suggestion was.

"Kidnap!" Screaming exclaimed. "That's a Federal charge. God forbid if those Feds ever get on your back. They'll ride you all the way to hell and back."

"I know a nurse, but she would have to be paid for coming down here," I said.

"Money is no object," Chico said.

"I'll need to tell her a price."

"One thousand," Chico said.

"Two," I bargained.

"She better be good for that kind of money, otherwise she might end up tending to her own wounds," Natty Joe warned.

"There is over sixty thousand in cash right here. We can afford to pay for Chico's treatment." Menzy was dutifully supportive.

"How soon can you get the nurse here?" Screaming asked.

"Not until the morning."

Chico's pain-heavy face registered disappointment. Menzy walked over and examined the wound. He mused: "I've never met a luckier man. This is the fifth time you've been shot and survived." There was a trace of relish in his tone.

"They say that when the tiger gets old his teeth start to shake." Natty Joe had a sinister smile on his face.

"Don't write this tiger off yet." There was venom in Chico's tone.

That night I went home $500 richer. That was the most money I ever held at one time. My heart was troubled. I was naked without the gun. Screaming had offered to get rid of it after it was used in the apartment.

Mom was asleep at the kitchen table. The television was humming where the station had signed off. I stepped lightly over to the cupboard beside the drainboard and switched off the television.

Mom stirred. She felt my presence and raised her head. "Danny," she said sleepily. She gripped my arm with an urgency. Her eyes were swollen.

"Mom, you look tired. You should be in bed."

"How can I sleep? Look at you. Every day you resemble something from another world." She released my arm and reached into the sleeve of her jumper to pull out some tissue to dry her weeping eyes.

I stood over her, tears welling up in my own eyes.

"Son, please listen to me. Bad things are happening. Rastamen are killing people in their beds like what they used to do in Jamaica. Before I dozed off a police came on the television and said some Rastamen killed a few kids in Wingate Park."

I tried to look surprised. The ganga was swimming in my brain. My eyes were closing, something I couldn't control while under the influence of marijuana.

"Danny, please forget this Rasta business. They're murderers and blasphemers."

"Selassie is God, Mom. There is no other."

She was shaken by my reply and immediately called to God to have mercy.

"Bring back my son, dear God, please, heavenly divine Father." She was carrying a heavy burden, one that was taking its toll on her physical features. "I have never been one for religion, but of late I have started attending services at the

Washington Temple church; I'm born again Christian. I pray night and day for you and all those unfortunate youngsters caught up in this devil religion."

"Mom," I said sternly. "Christianity is the devil religion. You've been brainwashed."

She raised a hand to her mouth and wept once more. Tears rolled down her face and stained her cheeks. "I had a dream, that I saw you swimming in a pool of muddy water."

"Dreams usually mean the opposite, Mom."

She shook her head doubtfully. "Muddy water is trouble, serious trouble."

"Rastafari will guide me," I said flippantly.

There was a new letter rack on the wall beside the refrigerator. The design was unique. Someone had taken the time to put sticks of matches together and make a synagogue, then varnished the finished product.

"Billy made it," Mom said proudly. "He comes around and see me whenever he gets a chance. He calls me Mom." Billy had taken hold of my mother's innocence like a drowning man clinging to a lifebelt. She had shown him a love that crossed the boundaries of race and she had taken the time to find the good in him. He loved her for being poor yet always ready to give: a forgotten pearl neglected by the world, but she had saved him from being a hippie and encouraged him to train to be a lawyer. Mom got up slowly from the table and took a letter from the rack. "It came today."

Immediately I knew it could only be Dave Green. The postmark, Saigon, confirmed my assumption. Tentatively I slid my fingers under the flaps. The letter was short.

> My main man Danny. I am living from day to day where any moment could be my last. Even as I write I'm stoned out of my wits. It's the only way to survive in this jungle. Brothers are dying all around me—white, black, purple, brown. We all bleed the same blood and die in this jungle of hate. Don't reply to this letter because I may not be around to read it.

Mom was moved by the content of the letter. She sat alone in the kitchen while I took a shower. She stood outside the bathroom door when I had finished showering. I was caught off guard when she asked, "What happened to the gun?"

This was the first time she had mentioned the weapon since the evening I pulled it on my father. She must have been searching my bag. I told her that I had thrown the gun away.

The door to Dad's bedroom was slightly ajar when I passed through the living room. I knew he was in there listening to every word, waiting for my downfall on the streets, just to prove he was right.

I awoke early the next morning. Snow had fallen during the night. Outside was blanketed over. Mom was in the kitchen preparing some breakfast for my father before he left for work. I had a quick wash and slipped downstairs.

Nurse Johnson's apartment door was answered by a tall, well-dressed white man who carried a professional air. He had a friendly face and wore horn-rimmed glasses dropped low on his nose. His complexion was a shade below the snow outside.

"Who is it?" shouted the nurse from the bathroom.

"Danny."

"Right with you," she shouted.

Draped with a white towel around her body and smelling of soap, the nurse came to the door. She was a short, squat woman in her early twenties with a peculiar beauty that seemed to grow the more you looked at her. "Danny," she said, somewhat bewildered.

"I need to speak to you urgently." I cut my eyes at the man who seemed to be plastered with a permanent smile.

He gave a curt nod and walked towards the living room.

The nurse held the door to her body. "The only time I see you is when there's trouble. What's the matter this time?" She looked me up and down, then reached out and pulled the hat from my head. She gave a start when my young dreadlocks jumped out of place like the snakes on Medusa's head. "My God! Is that all hair?"

"Every inch of it," I said proudly. "Nurse, a friend of mine has been shot and he needs some medical treatment."

She raised her finger to her mouth and stepped closer to the door, pushing me a little further into the hallway. "Take him to the hospital or call the emergency services." Her voice was low. As if reading my mind she shook her head. "No. I don't even want to hear any more. Rastamen have been creating some serious problems of late. The hospitals are on alert for any of them turning up, if even for a stomach ache. I was on duty last night when they wheeled in some bodies from Wingate."

"This has nothing to do with Wingate," I said hurriedly. She looked at me suspiciously.

"Please, Nurse, you have to help me. I was playing with a gun when it went off and shot my friend in the leg."

Her deep brown eyes widened. "Is that the same gun you almost killed your father with?" She winked an eye and waved her finger. "The way you're going it won't be long before you kill someone."

"Now do you see why I can't go to the hospital? My friend is willing to pay two thousand dollars if you attend to his wounds."

Her eyes lit up like diamonds in the sun. She was behind in her rent and often refused to answer her door when the debt collectors came around. Her breasts heaved under the towel. "I don't know if I should, Danny." She rested one foot on top of the other and leaned against the door frame. She thought for a moment. "Let me talk to Roger and hear what he has to say." Again she crept into my head and back out. "Roger is the best man for the job. He's a doctor." She excused herself and went back into the apartment.

I walked along the passageway to the front door and looked out through the glass. Nathan's sisters were building a snow-man. The violent wind whistling against the crack in the door had stirred up a snowstorm. The white bliss was hypnotic, a wonderland where everything was temporarily pure and clean. I was trapped in the chamber of adolescence once more.

"Danny," the nurse shouted discreetly. She looked about suspiciously over her shoulders before inviting me into the apartment. She escorted me into the kitchen. The circular fluorescent lighting was stained with brown, dripping grease. So, too, was the stove. The floor was sticky and the garbage pan spilled over. Dirty dishes were piled high in the sink. Roaches ran around in skin-crawling haste. There had been no roaches in the apartment when she first rented it.

I crushed one of the little buggers under foot as it tried to cross my path.

"How far away is your friend?" she asked.

"The Nineties."

"Where in the Nineties? You know those blocks stretch for miles on both sides of Linden Boulevard." She was being highly technical but I put it down to her nervousness.

"Between Rutland Road and Clarkson Avenue."

She molded her hands on the fabric of her white uniform. "You did say two thousand dollars, didn't you?" She wanted to make sure I knew the difference between two thousand and two hundred.

Chapter 16

Nurse Johnson didn't seem to have any problems convincing Roger to accompany her. We drove in his Ford along the back streets into the Nineties. The snow was thick on the ground.

The basement reeked of unwashed flesh, marijuana, and trapped air. Chico had broken down into a cold sweat and was covered with a blanket. A mattress was brought into the front room for his convenience. The men gathered around. Some were still sleeping on the floor, too stoned to move.

Roger examined the wound while Nurse Johnson handed him surgical tools from a doctor's black bag. Fortunately, the bullet had exited as Chico had suspected. Within an hour the wound was cleaned and dressed. Nurse Johnson delightedly accepted the money and offered to come back in the afternoon to give Chico a tetanus shot.

There was no school for me that day. Plans for the new drugs house were discussed in full. The men that carried out the robbery would have first priority. Each man would be given a day to sell their drugs. Any money collected at the door he could keep for himself. That man on his day was also responsible for paying the other men who would guard the place against attack.

Chico looked healthier after Nurse Johnson had given him the injection. Fresh snow started to fall. The bad weather had chased the Gods from the streets temporarily. This in some way upset the plan for Rano Dread and his men to come down and wipe them out.

Slim, the junkie informer, came around in the evening. He looked like a distraught polecat as he dragged a twenty-four-inch color television from out of the cold. "Thirty bucks." He was clucking.

"Give him twenty bucks." Chico was propped up on the mattress with his bare back resting against the wall.

Menzy produced two worn $10 bills.

Slim backed up from Menzy's outstretched hand. "Hey, Mr Red! That there picture piece cost over five big ones."

"Ten dollars," Chico said conclusively.

"I'll take the twenty." He snatched the money fast and shoved it into the side pocket of his long, checkered coat. Normally he would have pocketed the money and split, but not today. He hung around as if expecting something.

"What's the news on the streets?" Chico asked.

Slim spoke quickly, like his tongue had just been released from the bottomless pit. "All kind of shit flying. Some Rastas done shot up the Tomahawks' drugs house in Brownsville. They killed a few Jolly Stompers, too." He smiled, revealing his purple gums, but the sour faces surrounding him weren't smiling.

"Give him another ten bucks," Chico said.

Slim's tongue started rolling when he saw the cash. "The police got that juvenile stooge, the one Super Dice been grooming for the assassin's job. Nathan, something like that. They charging him with murder."

I couldn't imagine Nathan in jail. He was claustrophobic.

"The Tomahawks seemed to think it was some Rastamen who robbed them. Folks say the Bear is spitting fire. He threatened to retaliate by shooting up the West India parties over the Easter period." Slim seemed to take some delight knowing that other people were going to experience the hell and torment he faced every day.

Sensing Slim's fuse was running low, Chico instructed Menzy to give him another ten bucks to keep the gen flowing.

"And dig this," Slim continued. "This here gang war ain't because dudes want to be bad, or niggers want to kill each other." He looked about nervously and whispered: "The Mafia. They the ones got Super Dice to start up the war with the Tomahawks and the Vandals." He suddenly went quiet. His tongue iced up and his thieving eyes rested on Chico.

"One of these days you're going to push my generosity too far." Chico nodded for Menzy to hand over some more money.

The sight of the greenbacks didn't thaw Slim's tongue.

"Where's my gun?" asked Chico. He shuffled down the side of the mattress.

Slim raised his hands. "Now, Rass! Shooting me ain't gonna get you nowhere. Besides, who's gonna keep you informed as to what's going down on the streets. Ain't no one got more scope than a junkie. That's how we survive."

"Finish what you got to say and I'll send someone over to Rodriguez' shop with you so you can score."

Slim's face withered. He wasn't amused. His eyes rested accusingly on the bulge of Menzy's side pocket. "So that's it. After all I done for you guys. Mr Red, you promised me that you'd give me three ounces of horse when you robbed that Tomahawks drugs house."

Menzy quickly sealed Slim's lips with a back hand that dropped the scrawny man to the ground. Chico raised a hand, stopping Menzy from following up with a series of kicks.

Slim rubbed the side of his face and pulled himself to a half-sitting position. "That confirms it. Sure enough does. It was you cats that done that robbery." He was unafraid.

"The drugs was burnt," Chico said.

Slim sniggered, refusing to acknowledge the blasphemous words. "Mr Red, all I want is two ounces. Man, I got a big giant ape riding me like the devil in the last race at Aqueduct."

"I said the drugs went up in flames. Every last bit of it."

The reality, though far-fetched, hit Slim like a bomb. He knew Chico wasn't one to jest. Once Chico said no he meant no.

Slim was bitter: "Now you guys on top there's no use for old Slim again. Huh! Treat me like a dog. I risk my life to get information and this is my reward." He got on his feet, pulled all the money from his pocket, and threw it into Chico's face.

"Why, you slimy, good for nothing tramp," Chico cursed.

"I might be a tramp, but you never be half the man I am."

Chico was so fired up he forgot he was in pain and tried to get up. The hurt surged through his body and made him groan like a woman in labor. "Passo, Johnny, tie up the son of a bitch," he commanded.

Slim wasn't having any of that. He turned around and bolted

for the basement door. Unfortunately for him, Screaming was just coming out of the cold. He grabbed Slim and held him while three men bound his hands and feet.

"He knows too much. He has to be taken out of the area, and shot," Menzy said.

Slim's fate turned over in his brain like the colorful fruits on a one-armed bandit. He screamed like a pig condemned to the butcher's knife.

Dillinger had the television plugged in and turned it up loud to drown out the screams. Slim wiggled on the floor trying to free himself. He stopped moving and looked up at Screaming. "Rass, I know you the main man. Sir, that Mr Red ain't nothing but a thief. I was the one who gave him the run-down on the Tomahawks' crib. Bet he didn't tell you about the money he took from that secret stash, I told him about. There was over forty thousand dollars in that compartment. The toerag gonna keep it all for himself."

"He's lying," Chico shouted, averting Screaming's accusing stare. "When he starts to feel the effect of cold turkey he'll confess he's lying."

"Don't torture him," Screaming said. "A bullet in the brain and be rid of him."

"He's my problem. By the time I'm finished with him we'll know every secret this side of the East River," Chico said.

Slim yelled and screamed into the early hours of the night. His tongue ran nonstop like a taxi with its meter running in the rush hour. He spoke of his brother living up in Harlem who supplied guns to the gangs. Different gang hide-outs. Who killed who. While his tongue traveled faster than a speeding bullet his body went through the different changes. He had chills, fits of hysteria, vomiting, and it got worse as the time passed.

Eventually he was taken to the back room and thrown on the floor.

Screaming's nervous father became concerned about the screams and dared to show his face down the basement. Screaming sent him back upstairs.

News of the robbery was stink on the streets. Rastamen came from as far away as Bronx and Queens to ask for favors. Word had spread like wildfire.

Chico advised the beggars to go out and capture drugs houses from the gangs. He offered to lend them guns in exchange for part of their takings.

Later in the night I followed Screaming to check on Slim. He gave a start when we switched on the light. He'd shit himself and wallowed in a pool of vomit on the soot-stained concrete. The stink was unbearable. The whites of his eyes rolled over like he'd seen a ghost. He got hysterical at one stage and shouted, "They gonna kill the mother of that stooge because of what he done to Super Dice and Mo Dean."

"Not Matilda," I thought out loud.

Slim retched but his belly was empty. He spoke feebly. "The hoe Charmane gonna execute her. Let me go I might be able to stop it."

"How you know so much?" I dropped on one knee and held him by the lapels of his coat.

"One of the Stompers shoot up with me sometimes. Junkies don't keep secrets when they want juice. Someone help me please." He started screaming once more, then demanded to speak to Chico.

He was crab-marched back into the front room. The men shied away from him. "A Rasta's mother is going to die also. One of them young Rastas I saw here in this very same basement."

The men drew closer. Slim exploded in a fit of hysterical laughter. Chico wasn't bothered. All his family had been killed in the violent gang wars sweeping Jamaica. He was only interested in clearing his name. "Confess it was a lie you told on me about that money."

Screaming looked at Chico suspiciously.

"Sure I was lying. I never meant to tell no lie on you, Mr Red. You's about one of the most decentest men I ever did meet. Saved my life when that Puerto-Rican Rodriguez wanted to kill me. The monkey is tearing me apart—let me go or else I'll die."

"Once you've been here for four days then there'll be no more monkeys or apes to distress you," Chico said cooly.

Slim's body shook as though he'd just been taken out of a fridge. "One of your boys' mothers is going to die. Give me a fix and I might be able to stop it."

Chico showed some concern. Slim was a bank of information. For him to repeat himself meant something was up.

Slim, although heavily distressed, knew he had Chico's attention: "I ain't talking no more until I get a fix. Kill me but I ain't talking."

I was ordered to rush out to Rodriguez' shop and cop a dime bag of heroin. Slipping and sliding in the snow, I raced for the little shop on the corner. Black folks moved about in the night with coats pulled up around their ears. Junkies and thieves were restless, unable to find sleep.

Rodriguez' shop was packed with his Spanish henchmen. Salsa music blared from a pair of speakers behind a heavily stacked counter. Rodriguez was in his late twenties, medium built, and had shoulder-length hair. He was darker than most Puerto-Ricans.

Out of breath I handed him the money and made the order.

"Take it on the house. A gift." He spoke with a slow Brooklyn accent. He must have thought he'd just hooked another fish.

I was about to charge out of the shop when his sweaty body blocked the door. Sweat circled the armpits of his green nylon vest, dirty and stinking. "Things gonna start getting better around here, Danny. Business has been booming since those Maricon left the area. People ain't afraid to come out and buy drugs any more."

"Mira, if they come back on the corner they'll be sorry," shouted one of the bodyguards, rubbing down the barrel of a shotgun.

Rodriguez threw a confident fist in the air and rocked like Mr Cool. "Right on. Tell Chico if he want a few guns to help him take out the swine that shot him, he can count on me."

"Sure. I'll let him know." I made another move for the door.

Rodriguez had a sparkle in his brown eyes. "Man, you sure in a hurry to go and jack up." He prodded me in the gut with his fingers. "What you doing? Snorting? Chasing the dragon? Skin popping or in the veins?"

"Neither. This ain't for me."

"That's what they all say, Homes. Anyway, remember you guys are my people and I take care of my people. Don't go buying no gear from no gringos or Yankee boys. My shit is dynamite." He stepped aside and opened the door.

Slim seemed to have recovered when the cold from outside entered the basement and he saw me handing Chico the little brown package. "Give it here," he craved.

"Talk first," Chico said.

"They gunning for a lady called Spence."

Screaming's voice cried with mine as we both shouted out: "Jerome!"

"Lay off me," Slim yelled when Screaming advanced towards him.

Screaming got down and wrapped his big hands around his throat. "How you know?" He released Slim enough for him to groan.

"They paid a junkie to find out where she lived." His head hit the dirt-stained tiles and cracked his skull as Screaming threw him back with a mighty force.

Panic played Russian roulette around the room. Jerome's mother was known to many of the men. She was a Christian and often referred to as Mother. She could always spare the time of day for a man in trouble.

"The bicycles won't make it in all this snow," Screaming said.

"Rodriguez!" Chico shouted. "Get him to drive a few men over to New Lots and check things out fast."

We packed some weapons and headed through the door.

Rodriguez was obliging. His old, battered Chevrolet moved through the black slush and ice with much difficulty. He was hunched up around the steering-wheel and used the back of his hand to wipe the condensation from the window.

The bad weather didn't stop black people from walking the streets. They looked mean and suspicious as car lights shone on their faces. Rodriguez entertained us with a story he must have told a hundred times about how Chico rescued him from three men who tried to rob his shop. "Man, I ain't never seen anyone so fast with a gun. It was like a real-life Western. Those jokers fell quicker than a flash of lightning." He glanced across the seat where Johnny Toobad had put his nine-millimeter.

I was seated in the back with Passo and Screaming on either

side. The snow on the streets got heavier as we drew closer to the New Lots area.

Rodriguez pulled up outside the building on the opposite side of the street. Stepping through the slush we waded towards the building. Hobos and tramps lay about in the hallway escaping the cold.

Jerome's apartment was three floors up in the rundown tenement dwelling. Quickly we shuffled up the stairs. The door was kicked off and a bright sixty-watt bulb blazed from inside the hallway. Guns drawn, we made our way into the apartment. There was movement inside.

Rodriguez took out some worry beads and twirled them around his fingers and followed behind us.

Screaming led the charge and gave a start when a mangy cur scurried out of the kitchen and ran through the apartment. The house was ransacked. Things were thrown about the place. There was no sign of Jerome or his mother.

The smell of fresh blood, raw and chilling, hung heavily in the air and got stronger as we neared the back of the apartment where the two bedrooms were located.

The door to Jerome's mother's bedroom was kicked off. What greeted our eyes was to linger in my brain for the rest of my life. Jerome's mother was bound naked to a four-poster bed. The sheets were drenched in blood. She was cut right down her belly. Her sex organs were cut out. Written in blood across the ceiling was a message: *A present from the Mohican Queen.* Rodriguez made the sign of the cross, muttered a few holy words, then raced out of the apartment.

In silence we headed out of the area, each man in the car forced to dig into the depths of his morality, searching for the answers to such atrocities. What could anyone gain from inflicting so much pain and misery? Banks of snow had piled up near the curb where snowplows had passed through earlier in the day. The streetlights were pale.

Five blocks away three hobos leaned against a corner store. They sipped Devil's Brew from paper bags and sang out loud in merriment. Their eyes fell hungrily on the car as it neared the corner.

Rodriguez pulled up at the intersection to give way to a

brightly lit late-night bus with a few passengers on board. The stench of the hobos seemed to get into the engine of the car and came up through the heater. They were dressed in piles of rags with woolen tams on their heads. It was hard to distinguish whether they were black or white due to the amount of grime that plastered their bodies. No one gave them a second thought because hobos were hobos. Black, white, they all smelt repulsive.

They drifted towards the car looking more sober as they drew closer. Suddenly they chucked away their bottles and drew guns. One stepped out in front of the car. The other two rushed around the sides. One stood beside the driver's window, the other beside the passenger door where Screaming sat.

"Police. Turn off the engine and step out," shouted the hobo in the middle of the street.

Rodriguez looked around the car worriedly. "Shit! With all these guns in the car we're all going to jail." There was still heavy mist on the windows.

"Run over the son of a bitch," Passo said.

The cops, sensing something was wrong, crouched in their firing position. "Police!" they shouted.

Rodriguez was panic-stricken. The purple streetlights beaming down on the car reflected his face, glowing with sweat.

"Na tek no chek," said Johnny Toobad in heavily accented Rastafarian dialect. He slowly eased out his nine-millimeter and took aim at the cop standing in the middle of the street. The bullet shattered the windshield and hit the cop in the chest.

The sound of heavy gunfire broke the stillness of the night. The cop nearest to Rodriguez pumped a shot through the window and blew the Puerto-Rican's head off. Screaming and Passo opened fire, cutting down the two cops on either side of the car.

Blood spouted from the mount that once held Rodriguez' head. His body shook with spasms then stiffened. His right foot shot out and stepped on the gas pedal. The car railed up, shot across the street, crushed the bones of the cop who lay dead in the middle of the road, and crashed into a wall.

The world spun around in a whirlpool of confusion. Dazed, we pulled ourselves from the car.

Passo turned around and ran back across the street to where one of the cops had crawled to the safety of the sidewalk. Screaming had to hold on to Johnny Toobad to stop him joining Passo.

Passo, assuming the cop near the curb was dead, walked up to the next officer on the sidewalk and emptied his gun into his body. The heap of clothing jerked up and down and failed to move anymore.

The street was deserted, blanketed over with snow. Sirens whined in the distance. We made haste along the sidewalk, leaving Passo to catch up. Shots rang out once more. No one looked around. We moved with the wind in our backs.

Within minutes sirens were crying out, whining, crushing down on the eardrums and closing in. There was no sight of Passo. Still we didn't worry because the New Lots area had many derelict buildings and alleyways where someone could hide. We got flat, creeping on our bellies and hiding behind cars wherever necessary. Red-eye cop cars with flashing lights sped along the streets.

Screaming, using his knowledge of the area, led us down a deserted street with rows of two-storey houses clothed in the white bliss. Cars were snowed in and branches fell from trees, heavily laden with ice. We stumbled on a Chrysler that had skidded on black ice and crashed. Inside were two men. The radio was crackling and transmitting bursts of broadcast. They were cops and had been rendered unconscious by the accident.

Johnny Toobad suggested we toss the two cops out of the car and use it for our getaway. For once he said something that made sense.

Bright headlights approached at the far end of the street. We were forced to seek cover behind a snowed-in car a few yards away from the Chrysler. The engine was still running.

The car pulled up about thirty yards away and two men jumped out. We were temporarily blinded by the bright headlights. The two men approached with their guns drawn. The smell of their cheap cops' colognes wafted in the air like fresh shit. The forms of the two men gradually eclipsed the bright light and their features materialized in my brain. It was Polaski and McCarthy. The cold that numbed my fingers and toes no longer affected me. I was hot, my blood was boiling. If this was the night for killing cops then I wanted to be the brightest star. The setting was right. The area was dark and desolate. Black people were huddled in their dank rat- and roach-infested apartments. They hated the world, much more cops. The thought of killing the two men was sweet.

McCarthy forced open the passenger door and a body slumped out. He stepped back and spoke with a delightfully pleasant voice. "Well. If it ain't my friend the nigger supercop, Mr Riley."

"Get me out of here," the faint voice pleaded.

A smile stitched McCarthy's face. He gave a quick glance to Polaski who was busy slapping the other cop's face, trying to revive him.

"He's out cold."

"Good! When I blow this nigger away there won't be any witnesses." There was a trace of uncertainty in his voice.

"Don't be a fool," Riley implored. "Help me. I think my back is broken."

"Nigger, I told you your days were numbered." He pointed his gun at Riley.

"You'll never get away with it," Riley said, finding it hard to believe he was about to be cheated out of life.

"You'll never be around to find out," McCarthy screwed up his face as he let off two shots into Riley's body.

"Jesus H. Christ. You fucking meant it!" Polaski shouted.

"Get any ideas and you'll join him."

"No need to worry about me, but we better get out of here fast."

They turned their backs and moved within my line of fire. Screaming pushed me back into the snow and held me down as I steadied the gun. He couldn't understand why I wanted to waste the two pigs.

"What was that?" McCarthy stopped dead in his tracks and turned around in wonder.

"I don't know, but I'm getting the fuck out of here." Polaski made haste to the car. McCarthy looked around and then shrugged his shoulders and walked off.

Chapter 17

The cops were closing in from all sides. The wind kicked up a snowstorm and carried the sound of the sirens across the roofs of the buildings and down the deserted streets.

My body was numb, frozen to the bone. The will to survive was no longer there. "I can't go on." There was no end to the ducking and diving. Whiteness ruled. We were lost in the north pole of hate. Left to die at the mercy of the hungry wolves combing the area for blood. On such nights they took no prisoners.

Screaming picked me up as I fell for the umpteenth time. "Don't give up. Only a few more blocks. The roof to Herzl Park school is in sight." He pointed towards the east.

Cop cars sped down the block, red and blue lights flashing across the face of the snow. The area was hot. The snow on the pavement had turned to deep puddles of heavy slush. There was no life in my legs. I moved along only at the insistence of Screaming.

We finally made it to the tenement building across the street from Herzl Park. This was there I had first attended the day party with Jerome. I had been there several times with Screaming as it was the home of his girlfriend, Ingrid.

All the stragglers had been chased from the streets by the whining sirens. The pigs were out for blood. The way in which the sirens hollered was proof of that.

Climbing the stairs was hard. The life had left my legs. The bulbs were stolen from the hallway and the place was in darkness. Screaming had to draw his gun in case hungry bums or thieves tried to ambush us. To ward them off he spoke in heavy Rastafarian dialect.

Finally we reached the top of the stairs. Screaming rapped on the door. The only light on the landing was that coming from underneath apartment doors and tiny spy holes.

Ingrid released a series of bolts and opened the door. Her brown, frightened eyes asked all the questions as we barged past her and entered the apartment.

Screaming led the way to the kitchen. The streetlights cast shadows of the windowframes across the ceiling. In darkness he stepped over to the cooker near the window and switched on the four burners.

We stood over the blue flame, warming our hands while Ingrid fastened the bolts on the door. She crept to the threshold of the kitchen and leaned against the door frame. The light behind her in the passageway reflected her beauty. She had long, waist-length dreadlocks. Her bare feet embraced the cold floor, her loose-fitting nightie fell below her knees.

Outside the sirens barked like a million dogs locked in a pound. Slowly, the heat surged through my body, unlocking the cold demons that held my senses to ransom.

"Screaming," Ingrid said innocently. Her cushioned lips parted. "I've been having bad dreams of late. The Father is trying to tell me something." She sighed heavily, wanting to reach out to her man as he stood over the open flame, his rags dripping water over the floor.

Screaming's mind was far away, beyond the point where eagles flew. His lips moved and he chanted a psalm of distress. The heat thawed his hands, but the bitter memories of the night were to remain frozen in the corridors of hate.

"If you need me I'll be in the living room." Ingrid glanced at Screaming with her alluring eyes then strolled off, aware that it was unnatural for a Rastafarian queen to question her king. She'd learnt the way of the religion, ever since giving herself to Screaming a year ago when she was in the tenth grade at South Shore. She looked back over her shoulder. A silent chill shook her body. Something was wrong, drastically wrong.

"We're gonna have more problems than we ever bargained for. No one shoots a cop and get away with it," Screaming whispered.

"Passo had the right idea. Kill the fuckers dead before they spread." Johnny Toobad was concerned only about the name he would get for playing his part in the cop shoot-out. He would be feared.

"What d'you think this is? A Western where the quickest gun rule and the star don't die until the last reel?" Screaming couldn't suppress his anger.

"What should we have done—just sit back and let those pigs wheel us off to jail?" Johnny asked, edgy.

"We got to show some diplomacy." The flames reflected the hardness on his face. "Danny, you surprise me. Seems like you want a bad man title for yourself. What's it going to be? Wyatt Earp, Doc Holiday, Billy the Kid, or what?

Johnny was rueful. It was a known fact that Screaming considered him and Passo a set of hoodlums rather than true Rastamen.

Screaming caught the dagger in Johnny's eyes and continued: "Bad men don't last long. Only the love of Jah Rastafari live forever."

"Those two cops whipped me within an inch of my life a few months ago," I said.

"So you risk all of us getting twenty-five to life on that account. It's bad enough the shooting of the black cop will be blamed on us."

"No one saw our faces. What's there to worry about?"

"Danny, you're still wet behind the ears. Listen to that noise outside. It's getting louder every tick of the clock." He stepped away from the kitchen window as the red and blue lights from the police vehicles flashed through the kitchen. He paced the floor restless. "If they catch Passo it won't be long before they find us." He was worried.

"Passo is a strong soldier. Even if they catch him he will never talk," Johnny said confidently.

"Let's hope for all our sakes he got away," Screaming said.

A part of my mind was still in a daze. Time had stood still back there in the filthy tenement where Jerome's mother lay mutilated.

"Settle down, relax. The gullies of Babylon must run red before this Armageddon is over. There's no place in this war for cowards," Johnny said accusingly.

Johnny Toobad, along with many of the young Jamaicans,

was obsessed by Westerns and gangster movies. They lived like their heroes, fast and dangerous. In their world only the gun mattered. They came out of poverty and feared no one. For me it was different. Slowly, I was being hardened by the evil that men inflicted on each other. This was reality.

"Screaming, you taught me the ways of the Rastafarian religion, for which I am grateful. But from this hour I must think as a wicked man. Jerome's mother must be avenged."

He breathed heavily into the glowing flame. "We're all in this together. The Yankees want war, then they'll get war. Tonight's incident has confirmed the need for more men to be brought in from Jamaica. I want men who don't know the meaning of fear. Men whose only interest in life is to fire a gun and kill."

Johnny nodded in agreement. "The youths in the Kingston ghettos would give their right arm to come to this great land of opportunity."

"When all this blow over I'll fly down and select some men personally. This country is going to witness men more danger-ous than the demons released from heaven with the devil." Screaming, too, was moved by the death of Jerome's mother.

The dawn of the new day brought to light the stink of the horrors that raped the night. The morning news focused on the police shootings. Rastamen were being dubbed cop killers. Never before in American history had any mob blatantly turned their guns on cops. The governor of the state was concerned. He sought to know more about the Rastafarians. What made them function? How were they able to survive the wrath of the three hundred strong gangs, the lords of the street?

George Rickets, alias Passo, was charged with killing the two white cops and also Riley. Police combed the area, convinced that the residents were hiding three members of the Militant Rastafarian sect.

Ingrid was sent out to inform the men of our safety. She was gone for some time and returned later in the evening with money, clothes, and a quantity of marijuana.

"The police are running around out there like cross dogs." She spoke of the way Rastamen were stopped on sight and whisked off to police stations. She herself had to make a few detours before getting back.

Jerome came around under the cover of night. The weight of the world was on his shoulders. The moment I saw him I knew he was a changed man. He wanted money to return to Jamaica.

Screaming sent orders to Chico that Jerome should be given $5,000. After four days in hiding word reached our ears that Jerome had flown out. He didn't stay for his mother's funeral. Rastafarian law was that no Nazarene should attend funerals. The dead should bury the dead.

The police vigilance lifted after eight days. One by one we left our hiding place.

There was more sorrow and grief on the block when I got out of the cab on Linden Boulevard. Black folks were gathered around Nathan's house. Wreaths were laid out on the front lawn. The Stompers had struck again. This time it was Nathan's mother. She was ambushed on Church Avenue and strangled with electric wire. The death of Matilda because her son betrayed the Stompers was met with fear and anger by members of the community. They realized that Matilda's death was the start of darker days to come. And they believed that darkness would remain over their community until the hand of God intervened.

There was a three-foot-tall and three-foot-wide bleeding heart wreath leaning up outside the door in front of my parents' apartment. It was decorated with white carnations with bright and dark red roses in the center, giving it the effect of blood dripping from the carnations.

There was a short note attached to the wreath in a pink envelope. I removed the note: it was written by my mother. It read:

> My heart bleeds in pain and sorrow for the days we spent harboring thoughts of hatred against each other. Through our pride and self-conceit we never stopped to say sorry, until this dark hour when I can only cry in silent memory. On behalf of Jessica Palmer and family we would like to offer our condolences.

Mom was sitting in the living room with Billy Weinstein when I entered the apartment. She tried hard to suppress the joy of seeing me walk through the door.

"Nice of you to come home." Billy's hair was neatly trimmed and he wore a black pin-striped suit.

Mom was also dressed up. Seemed like they were getting ready to attend my funeral. Her face swelled up and she burst into tears. "Don't come near me. Blood is on your hands." She jumped up from her seat and stormed out of the room as I was about to put a hand on her shoulder. Her bedroom door slammed shortly after.

"What the fuck you looking at?" I barked at Billy.

"None other than you. Where you been these last few days?"

"Where I been got nothing to do with you. Besides, since when you become my protector?"

"No need to be like that. I'm your friend, possibly the only one you got."

"I need no fucking friends. Think you're some big shot because you're wearing a monkey suit? You're nothing but a junkie."

"Come on, let it out. That's what friends are for."

I broke down and slumped at the center table. Tears that had eluded me all these years were pouring down. Billy got up and patted my back.

"The whole world's turning upside-down," I sobbed.

"I can just imagine," he said thoughtfully. "There's rumors floating around the school that you were involved in the shooting at Wingate."

I needed to confide in someone. Living amongst the Rastafarians was a lonely world of doom. Death was the prologue and epilogue to each day. I was forced to be something that I wasn't. Hatred breathed down my back with every minute I spent in their presence.

Billy was my true friend. I didn't have to prove myself to him. He sat down tentatively and listened to what I had to say. It was strange. The man I protected was the one to give me moral support in my hour of distress.

He sat back in the chair and crossed his arms. "My brother is a lawyer, one of the best. Any problems, I'll get him working for you. He's got good connections in Brooklyn Supreme Court."

"Maybe you could get him to help Passo."

"Get me some details about the guy and four thousand dollars."

I wasn't particularly interested in Passo, but his ability to handle a gun would be needed for the war that was about to start.

Billy snapped his fingers and summoned me from my stupor. "I know this is a bad time, but what you gonna do about the car outside?"

"I don't know how to drive. It was a present from a friend."

"Tell you what. Let me use it for a few weeks and I'll teach you how to drive."

"Got yourself a deal." We shook hands.

He held on to my hands with a strength I didn't know he possessed. "Be careful, there're many hungry wolves out there in the city. I'm glad your mother helped me to find my way before it's too late. Everyone is looking for someone to use. There I was defending this hippie movement when all the time someone was pulling my strings like a puppet. I was another advert for selling drugs."

"The Rastafarian religion ain't like that."

"No, what are they like?" He released my hands. "I won't be needing your protection anymore. I'm dropping out of school. There's a new test called the High School Equivalency. It enables dropouts to get a diploma. I'm like a dog barking at a flying bird trying to chase those high school credits." His eyes sparkled. "This city is a giant oyster dripping with pearls and I want every last one."

The door to Mom's bedroom opened and she stepped out wearing her special occasion waist-length fur coat.

Her hair was neatly groomed, but her eyes were swollen from too much crying.

"I'm taking Mom to meet my family," Billy said jubilantly. "They're so proud of my turn around that they want to meet the new woman in my life."

"All that flattery will get you everywhere," Mom said, finding a smile.

Billy dangled a set of car keys. "Dad's even given me the loan of his Mercedes so I can bring her over."

Fresh tears formed in the corner of Mom's eyes. "Will you be here when I get back?" There was pleading in her voice.

"Sure, Mom, I'll be right here." We both knew I would be back on the streets as soon as I had cleaned myself up.

Mom turned around and headed for the door followed by Billy.

I watched them through the bedroom window as they entered the car. Mom was slightly awkward in getting inside, afraid of spoiling the plush upholstery. She'd never been in such a car in her life. The engine purred and the car pulled off, leaving its tracks in the snow.

The car disappeared down the block leaving me gaping into emptiness. Darkness now shadowed my days. Gone was the warmth in my heart. Gone were the days when everything looked bright. I awarded my body the long overdue rest it needed. Rest from the influence of marijuana and death. Sleep, though short, was not enjoyed. I awoke with the end of a bad dream throbbing in my brain. The streets were calling me once more. I took a shower and headed out.

The evening was dark. Brake lights snaked from the cars stuck in heavy traffic along Linden Boulevard. The cold air was refreshing. The snow had started to thaw aided by a light rain. I crossed the troubled Kings Highway and into the Nineties. The aura of poverty and misery increased as I moved into the heart of the Nineties.

There were strange faces amongst the men as I entered the basement. Men wearing $1,000 suits and sparkling jewelry stood out like lights on a landing strip. Curious eyes fell on me like bullets from a machine gun.

"This is Danny Dread, one of our prominent soldiers," Chico said.

Dark, hateful eyes devoured me from across the room. The owner rubbed a scar that ran down the left side of his face. His waist-length dreadlocks seemed to be spun from mud. Ice sparkled on his fingers and gold heavied his neck.

"This is Rano Dread," Chico said.

Rano was accompanied by eight men, each flourishing in splendor. The men resembled clones from the days of Al Capone. These were the generation of men who only smiled when they had a gun in their hand and were taking a life.

"It's nice to be back in Brooklyn," Rano said in a coarse voice as if inviting a confrontation with Screaming. He pulled greedily on the mouthpiece of a chalice that was lit and handed to him by Baby Face Dillinger. The lighting in the basement suddenly went dim as he blazed the pipe.

Screaming kept his eye on Rano Dread like a bull obsessed with the smell of blood on a matador.

Rano handed the pipe to one of his soldiers, a short man with a light complexion and slanted Chinese eyes. He was no older than sixteen, with shoulder-length locks.

"Take it easy, Chang," Rano said proudly as his soldier sucked on the pipe like an old sage.

Smoke, heavy and thick, crept from Chang's nose and mouth. His body shook, he stifled a cough, and he walked slowly over to Chico who was still bed-ridden. He handed him the chalice. "Behold how good and how pleasant it is for breathren to dwell together in unity." Chico raised the pipe to his mouth.

Vicious stares were traded between the men loyal to Screaming and Rano Dread's soldiers. The roots of hatred among the men were so strong that the walls seemed to be closing in, heavy with tension.

Rano Dread stepped lightly over to the door where a black box leaned against the wall. He picked up the box and carried it to the center of the room. "This is a present from me and the boys." He opened the case and removed a rifle. "Picked up thirty of them cheap in Miami, M16s with rapid fire."

Screaming gloated at the weapons like a hawk preparing to pluck the eyes from young lambs.

Rano offered the first of five guns to Menzy, who hesitated before taking the weapon. The other four were handed over to Natty Joe, Johnny, Chico, and Dillinger.

Natty Joe took the weapon and anxiously cranked it up, filling the room with the sound of an active automatic gun. He went through the rudiments like a gun technician.

"Easy, Joe, such a gun could get a man in trouble," Rano warned.

"It's a shame that I'm out of action or I would christen the gun right now." Chico offered Screaming the gun, hoping to cushion the air of hostility between him and Rano Dread.

"What's this? Charity? Gun don't make a man." He slapped his chest firmly. "What I carry inside here is stronger than any weapon." He gazed angrily at Rano Dread.

Rano smiled sardonically. "Chico, I didn't come all the way down here to be ridiculed. Show me the toy soldiers that is causing all the trouble around here, let me do what I have to do, and get the fuck out of this place." With every word that he spoke he kindled the flames of unrest.

"There'll be plenty of time to take care of the Gods. The heavy snow has chased them out of the area. For now just enjoy your return," Chico said.

"I aim to. This time I intend to stay longer, a lot longer." His eyes made four with Screaming's. "Got my sights set on a little boarded-up shop on the corner. Spotted it on the way in."

Chico was startled. "Take your eyes off that shop," he said cautiously.

"It's owned by some Puerto-Ricans. The owner got killed a few nights back. The fuzz raided the joint and found some tackle and guns. They got five men up on charges."

Rano's eyes lit up at the mention of tackle. "Sounds like them Spics gonna be gone for a long time, and if that's the case I'll just move in and keep the place warm."

Chico was a snake. He struck when least expected. He put up no further resistance. Rano Dread had already made known his intention. Chico lay back, comfortable, already his mind sprinting to find a solution for protecting the shop.

Menzy chucked his rifle on the ground. "Thieves have honors, animals have a code of conduct. You have neither. How could you just march in and demand that shop? What about the poor destitute men in this room? Don't you think they are entitled to something, too?"

Rano argued heatedly: "I didn't march in, I was called in." His voice was coarse and full of hatred. "Remember the stone that the builder refused. That's me." He thumped his chest. "Problems in Brooklyn and it's Rano Dread to solve it because no one down here have any of this." He grabbed his balls. "I can remember two years back when it was you, Menzy, a man I had grown up to respect. Yes, it was on your word that I was booted out of town."

"Give thanks and praise that you're not at the bottom of the sea feeding the fishes." Screaming shadowed his gun resting under a long khaki shirt.

"Pity you didn't have the heart to put me there. Now it's too late. Any attempt to hoist me and this town will be split down the middle in a war that will go on for years to come."

"This is our personal war, why involve anyone else? We could settle it right now."

Rano Dread sniggered. "When or where we settle our dispute is no longer your decision because you're washed up, finished, history."

Screaming dipped for his gun but Rano Dread's young soldier, Chang, was quicker. Screaming froze halfway through the motion of reaching for his gun. Chang weighed him up with eager man-eating eyes.

Rano Dread exploded in a deep gut laugh. "Fool! Spare him, Chang. He's hardly worth the bullet."

The men shuffled about the room in a stand-off. Each man was poised to pull a gun. The Rastafarian movement had only delayed the inevitable war that loomed. It was in the air and would only take one hot-blooded person to start it in full.

Chico Red roared and cursed bitterly. "So this is the end. War amongst ourselves. Spanglers versus Vikings, Trench Town against the Rockfort gang. That's what is taking place in Jamaica now and it's not pretty. Our war is with the gangs, not with ourselves."

"I would sooner get on with the business we came here for and move out." Rano Dread looked, puzzled, at Screaming who had a smile on his face although held at gun point by Chang.

"Tell him to ease up before Chang hang up his gun," Rano said with a degree of uncertainty.

Menzy stepped between Chang and Screaming. "Give me your gun." His voice was warm.

Screaming hesitated. His eyes were on the men he'd sheltered for over two years. He handed Menzy his gun with a look of dissatisfaction on his face. He was my mentor, I knew him well. This was all a show to test the men's loyalty. They failed.

"Hang it up, Chang," Rano said in a defeated tone.

Natty Joe held the M16 firmly under his arm. "Many of you know me from Jamaica, but for any one of you who don't I would like to say one thing. If there's any division among us, then I go by myself. I'm not hopping on anyone's wagon. There is money to be made in this city, we can't afford to fight against ourselves. Once we have taken care of the gangs then any one who want to kill each other is welcome to do so."

Menzy protested: "In the name of Jah Almighty what are you suggesting? To be a Rastaman mean we don't study war. To vow the vow of Nazarene is to cut your locks when a brother die in our presence. We are the vanguards of Rastafari in this country. Generations to come will remember us as the first set of men to pave the way, to discipline Yankees and let them respect us."

The door at the far end of the basement flew open. Long arms of dreadlocks swayed as heads turned.

A clean-shaven man stood at the doorway with his head hung low. He looked like a reject from the five and ten store.

Beside the frightened man was Tony, the stoop-shoulder barber from the main road. Tony had a round face and thick lips that were made for laughing and he was doing just that. He spoke with a deep northern twist. "I never would have believed it if anyone told me that dirt bomb Slim could be cleaned up but here he is." He took Slim by the arm and drew him closer.

"Nice work. The jacket could have been a little smaller but who's complaining?" Chico held out a $20 bill.

Tony shuffled over to Chico, dragging one of his feet, which was longer than the other. He was short and his hair glistened at the temples. He wiped his hands clean on a stained white apron draped around his waist before taking the money.

Natty Joe let Tony out of the basement and served a customer who came to cop a nickel bag of grass.

The tension in the room was temporarily lifted at the sight of Slim, who stood alone in a blue jacket, checkered trousers, and a pair of black shoes.

"What's it gonna be?" Chico said.

"I don't know, Mr Red," Slim stuttered. "I really don't know. I feel as though the weight of the world has been lifted from my head."

Natty Joe offered Slim two little brown packages. "I found these at the back of Rodriguez' shop. It's uncut.'

Slim's pupils went as wide as a grape. He took a few steps backwards, like Dracula recoiling from the cross.

"What's the matter?" Joe taunted.

Slim covered his eyes, warding off temptation.

"Knock it off, Joe. I think he's cured. The old Slim wouldn't need a second offer," Chico said.

Slim slowly opened his eyes. "Mr Red, ain't no need to test me. I'm free. No more drugs." His eyes sparkled and his face took on a saintly appearance. "Jesus came to me when I was kicking. He said, 'Slim, don't worry none. I'm gonna help you get off that there white stallion.' And I saw the Lawd as sure as I'm looking at you right now. He stayed right by my side while that evil stallion rode me down the stretch."

Chico cut him off because it seemed like Slim was going to talk for ever.

"Here's two hundred dollars. Buy a few things to help get yourself on the road."

"I sure appreciate your concern, but I have to turn down your offer. I'm giving myself to Jesus. I don't need no money to enter my Master's kingdom."

"Pity Jesus didn't talk to you before you accepted the offer from the Stompers to trail Jerome to his house." I pulled a Colt .38 from my waist. My fingers curled around the trigger.

Sweat sprang from his face like a mineral pool. His legs jellied. No words escaped his mouth as he looked to Chico for support.

Chico was more surprised than Slim. "This man is under my protection. Back off," he ordered.

"Not even God can save him," I replied, sensing Rano Dread's disapproval at the way I blatantly ignored Chico.

"Please, Danny. They paid me. I didn't know they was going to kill anyone until it was too late." He fell on his knees and raised his hands in prayer. "O God, sweet Jesus, I've changed."

The gun exploded and hit Slim in the heart. Two more shots and he went to meet his ancestors in the land of the unknown.

My body shook as I stood over Slim's lifeless body. I was suddenly alone. The hostility in the room was now on my shoulders. The weight grew heavier as I realized that through my actions I had elevated myself from being just a soldier to being the right-hand man of Screaming, my mentor. Although Chico was enraged he was powerless to execute his authority, because I held his secret. In the eyes of the men about me I had blatantly usurped Chico's power on two occasions, and in the eyes of these men there was resentment for me, knowing that they would always be soldiers whilst I was destined to be a leader. Screaming was full of pride because my actions had elevated him in the eyes of those who would oppose him. He had transformed a boy into a man and had passed onto him the gift of survival. Like death giving way to life, a part of him would live on even when the powers of darkness shattered his world.

Chapter 18

Four Rastamen from the Vanderbilt area in Flatbush came around that night. They wanted revenge for Jerome's mother, and came prepared with guns and two vans. A plan was hatched quickly. First we had to dispose of Slim's body and wash down the basement.

Rigor mortis had set in and locked Slim's body by the time we were ready to move him. His joints had to be broken so that he could be stuffed into a garbage bag. The body was taken into the heart of East New York and dumped on a garbage heap. The smell in the back of the van was unbearable.

Friday night and the action was kicking in Brooklyn. Neons were flashing along Utica Avenue. Traffic was tight in the run-up to Easter.

Screaming sat in silence as we drove along. He was in deep thought. Although he was committed to the gun, he nevertheless loved the Rastafarian religion. He loved it so much that he allowed himself to be humiliated by Chang just to prove how loyal the men were to him. The New York City air had poisoned the hearts of the men he loved. Not even the great powers of Rastafari could save the war. That was inevitable. The Italians, Jews, Irish and Hispanics had all fallen victim to that war.

The vans were parked on Lenox Avenue. Twenty men marched down Utica towards the Rugby Theater. Designer Cadillacs, Oldsmobiles, and all types of expensive cars were parked on both sides of the six-lane avenue. Some cars were double-parked in the street with hazard lights flashing. Crowds of people milled up and down the sidewalk. Sirens were whining like the background music in a suspense movie. The sirens were the ever-present metronome ticking away and speeding up the brain, hollering that all wasn't well, beware.

Our target was the old ten-pin bowling alley that had been converted into an after-hours gambling den. This was under the control of the Stompers. On Friday nights whores, pimps, street hustlers, and those being extorted came to pay their dues to the gang in order to operate on their turf.

A super fly pimp jumped out of a gold limousine that had white-wall tires and TV antennas in the back. Three hot bitches trailed behind him as he bopped across the street. He was draped in a red cape, yellow flared suit, and a broad-brim beaver hat which swayed. They descended the stairs into the gambling house leaving behind a trail of mixed smells, sex, and expensive perfume.

Dillinger led the way following the path of the whores. We crept down a narrow stairwell. Posters were draped on both sides of the walls. The iron security door at the bottom was open.

We charged in behind the freaks and cranked up our guns. The area was bigger than I remembered. The bowling lanes had all gone and were replaced by a dining room, pool tables, dance floor, bar, and a shoe-shining stand where old men bowed to $1,000 shoes.

The whole place smelt of soul food, alcohol, perfumes, and niggers burning all the lethal drugs that were bad for your health.

One pimp had some coke on a Franklin and was about to blow his mind, but he took one look at the guns and froze. The bartender stood still like he was posing for a picture. The Miller High Life sign screwed to the bar shone on his face. Pool sticks were suspended in motion. Some nasty-looking black faces stared at the guns like they could melt the blue steel.

"All you motherfuckers on the floor," shouted Dillinger.

"Fuck this motherfucking on the floor jive. I got too much money for this shit," protested the pimp with the coke still on the Franklin. He kicked at the shoe-shine boy at his feet who was busy stuffing rags and polish into his little black box. He stood up full of bravado. "I wouldn't even let my bitches get on no floor, and this jive-ass nappy-hair bush boy want me to get down there." He fondled his nuts and his towering body leaned over the stand. He had a little goatee beard and a thick Afro under a broad-brim hat.

"Know something? You got a loud mouth, pimp," Dillinger said.

"Nigger, I ain't no pimp. Know a Mack when you see one, sucker. Shit! What the fuck am I rapping with you for?" He clicked his fingers. "Bitches, let's get the fuck out of this place."

Five scantily dressed women sitting around a dining table stood up, rattling the dishes in their haste. One greedy high-color gal hurriedly drained a glass and stuffed the remains of some pig's trotters in her mouth.

Dillinger raised the M16 and put a shot into the ceiling. "I said everyone on the floor and that's my final command." Bodies started hitting the dust. Frightened black eyes pleaded for mercy.

The whores were still on their feet, but looked like frightened foxes caught by hounds.

"Sucker, there's too many witnesses in here. You ain't shooting no one. This is the United States of A., civilization. You dig." The pimp was confident while he floated on a cloud of white dust.

Dillinger raised the gun.

"Motherfucker." The pimp jumped up and down like a spoilt child. "Motherfucker, you can't shoot me." His voice sounded like he was crying.

Several bullets from the M16 hit him while he was still cursing. He didn't drop, just stood there taking shots into his body. Finally he went down.

The whore that was chewing on the hog's foot spilt her guts. All manner of unearthly evil came out of her mouth and splattered over the floor.

The lights suddenly went out except for the one displaying the Budweiser sign. Gunshots exploded around our heads like we'd stepped on mines. Darkness ruled. The people were screaming and shouting as bullets flew about the room.

Our guns rang out. Bullets flew through the darkness with no set destination. The enemy was unseen. The Stompers were prepared for such attacks and were hitting back hard. We were in a hornets' nest and they were stinging.

One of the men from Vanderbilt cried out as he went down. There was only one way out for us—the way we'd come in. Light shone through the glass at the top of the exit door.

I reloaded my gun twice in the dark—an art I had grown to master. Menzy's deep voice bellowed in deep Rastafarian dialect. "Everybody out." Slowly the men started heading for the door. The shooting got fiercer. I was the last man to make the door. The light rolling down the stairs rested on yet another one of my brothers cut down, trying to escape.

Chico Red was outraged when we returned to the base. He couldn't understand how we managed to lose four men in what was supposed to be a touch and go operation. The blame finally rested on Dillinger.

"Next time go in blazing," Chico yelled.

The Easter weekend was marred by further violence when Sugar Bear led a charge on the innocent West Indian parties in Brooklyn and the Bronx. The heartless shooting was dubbed the Easter Massacre.

Three days after the massacre we moved into the drugs house that was abandoned by the Stompers. I stood on the corner of Rutland and East 95th Street with two other men. We distributed free joints and cards with the address for the drugs pad printed on one side.

After one week the drug house was bringing in $5,000 a day. Plans were made to rob more drugs from the gangs.

Keeping guard on the base turned out to be quite exciting. For a joint or a $5 bag of grass, women and girls would cater to our sexual delights. I had sworn against women when infected by Bertha, but staying on the pad had opened my appetite.

The Gods returned to the area on the first day of summer. They painted the floor directly outside the apartment green. The customers were frightened off. Anyone stepping in the green paint and walking on the sidewalk would find themselves in trouble. Armed with swords the Gods stood outside the apartment building. A spokesman for the Gods known as Bishme Allah preached about how they were going to clean up the city and make it habitable for black folks.

Natty Joe stood by the window six floors up looking down at

the army of Gods dressed in their Muslim hats. This was his day and he was breathing fire. "I personally will go down there and blow them away. These scums are stopping me from making fifteen thousand dollars. I put down five thousand on a BMW. The salesman is expecting me tomorrow to make the final payment."

"Rano Dread will be here by nightfall. All we have to do is leave the area round about eight o'clock. By morning there will be no more Gods." Chico got up from his sunbed and walked around in his shorts. Under his arm was a double-barreled shotgun he had bought from a junkie.

A crowd gathered across the street and listened rapturously as Bishme preached about the devil white man and the way he made drugs for black men to kill themselves.

Two Thunderbirds with tinted windows passed and circled the block. The cars went around the block a second time. Guns were on the windows as they came around the third time. Bishme dived for cover when he saw the dark holes of death drawing closer to his life.

Gunshot barked abruptly from the windows of the cars. Machine guns and buckshot were pouring rounds of bullets on the Gods. Innocent bystanders were cut down in the hail of gunfire. Blood washed the sidewalk. Tires screeched and the cars sped off down the block.

Police and ambulancemen were quickly on the scene. The dead were thrown into meat wagons and carted off. The cops didn't waste too much time hanging around. They took a few statements as a matter of formality then left the area.

There was no need for Rano Dread and his men. The Gods were cut down by the Stompers. Business was back to normal by nightfall. The following day Natty Joe bought a silver BMW.

Trading throughout the summer was good. Chico was now in control of Rodriguez' shop. Several drugs houses were captured and many of the men were running their own businesses.

Screaming, along with Natty Joe, took control of the first drugs house to be established. I worked for them in between going to school. Truancy notes were piling in my house like the

Post Office shelves at Christmas. Several times the Dean had summoned my mother to the school. Even on those days, I was absent.

Jerome returned from Jamaica a changed man, one who hated the world. He brought with him four men who were to help him in his war against the world. He recruited Patrick, who was to lead a short life as a gangster.

One Saturday night Jerome stuck up Nine Fingers and his men at a dance in Bedford Stuyvesant. Patrick was actively involved.

Nine Fingers put out a contract on Patrick which was quickly acted on. Patrick died in front of Tilden High School. His death was witnessed by many frightened students.

Screaming, unlike Natty Joe, didn't become a victim of wealth. He was committed to the unification of Rastafarians. This was to prove fatal and led to his downfall. He made many visits to Jamaica, each time returning with men who were committed to the gun. The gangs were terrified of his name and he reaped vengeance around the city.

Near the end of the summer Screaming disappeared. He wasn't to be found in any of his usual hangouts. Five days later no news had been heard of his existence.

On the first Sunday morning of his disappearance there was screaming and shouting at the front door when one of the regular customers stumbled on a carrier bag outside the door.

The noise triggered panic inside the apartment where armed men were on twenty-four-hour guard. There was a foul stench as we neared the door. Natty Joe removed the security from behind the door and slung it open.

The woman was still crying out, horror-stuck. There in front of her was a Big Apple shopping bag with blood soaking through the bottom. Inside the bag was Screaming's head.

Chapter 19

Spring was in the air. There was still a cold chill left behind from the winter. The sky was gray and thunder threatened rain.

Dressed in a blue overall I sat on the edge of the curb and tightened the lug on the rear wheel of the Mustang. I now had waist-length dreadlocks that I tied in a ponytail. The Dean of Tilden High School had finally expelled me in the fall of 1972. He had made the decision after I drew my gun on one of the security guards in the school.

Mom continued to preach to me with tears in her eyes, but this did not stop me from joining up with the brotherhood of bandits from the Bronx known as the Stick Up Kids. The brotherhood, numbering twenty-five, was formed in the Spodeford Juvenile Center in the Bronx. This was a maximum-security prison that housed juveniles under the age of sixteen.

I was drawn into the brotherhood by Pappy, the man I had rescued from the Tomahawks' drugs house. Pappy was one of the three leaders of the Stick Up Kids; it was a heartless, ruthless gang with a passion only for money and their allegiance was to each other above even that of a family.

They specialized in robbing number joints, gambling houses, after-hours clubs, and places where the people couldn't call the cops. Our rule when carrying out a job: "anything move, shoot it."

It was drizzling now. I looked in the direction of Linden Boulevard. Dave Green stood in the middle of the street, heaving and panting and daring the cars to run him down. Finally he got back to the sidewalk and headed down the block for the umpteenth time.

I stood up, hoping this time he would recognize me. "Dave, it's me, Danny."

His cold, muscular face hardened and he jumped back in a karate stance. The dog tags on his neck rattled as his bare chest bulged. "Come on, make a move. I'll tear your fucking Commie head off." His eyes were wild like an untamed animal's.

"Hey! I'm your fri—"

He threw me on my back and pinned my hands to the pavement with his heavy combat boots. Stunned, I looked into the mad face of death. The stench of his body was suffocating. I was unable to reach for my gun.

"The war is over for me. Keep out of my life." His voice was harsh. Gone was the warmth in his brown eyes that had led me to accept him as a brother. He was a madman. He released me as though something behind all that madness was telling him not to do me any harm.

The pavement shook as he marched down the block towards some young kids who were hiding behind cars, ready to taunt him. The mood was right for their entertainment.

"Here comes the boogie man," shouted one kid.

"Murderer, killer," shouted another.

"Wanna kill kids? Then catch us if you can," shouted a little girl. They were delighted that they could get the soldier bubbling like soup in a pot.

Dave slapped his chest like King Kong. "Fucking Commies, I killed you once. I'll kill you again." He gave chase. The crafty kids scattered in all directions.

Dave stood in the street looking about in a state of confusion. The kids bombarded him with missiles of rotten fruit and eggs.

The corruption of the city had put my emotions on ice. But as I stood there, eyes witnessing the destruction of a once promising black man, I wondered: Where did it all go wrong?

I shook back the feeling of hurt because in this city, void of pity, emotions were best left on ice. My eyes rested on Nathan's house, a dark and desolate dwelling, a ghost encampment occupied by a drunk. The Stompers had claimed Alphonso's life in a shoot-out at a disco six months back. Nathan had hung himself after being repeatedly sodomized on Rikers Island. Only after his death did the authorities admit that they were in error putting him on the island because he was too young.

I was suddenly shaken from the gloom by the sound of a car,

its tires screeching as it bent the corner from Linden Boulevard. I was flat on my belly with my gun drawn.

The car went out of control and crashed into a tree near Nathan's house. Two stunned Puerto-Ricans jumped out, frightened by the bark of a police siren. They strolled down the block cool and calm like they lived there.

The cops' car swung around the corner and stopped beside the wreckage. They took a quick glance inside the car and sped off down the block, blind to the two jitterbugging Puerto-Ricans.

I walked off towards the house, my mind drowning in a state of gloom. What was this wicked life all about, I asked myself. Ghosts surrounded me. Everything about me seemed to be dying. My gun never left my side. Somewhere out there in this city without pity, there was a bullet with my name on it. I wanted to go out blazing whenever that dark destroyer struck.

The neighborhood had changed rapidly. Garbage pans were piled high and stinking. Rats and roaches had crept in and taken over the houses. Gone were the white faces that somehow said total anarchy didn't rule.

Max, the last of the sitting tenants, had gassed himself in his apartment. He had taken it to heart when Sophia, the old Jewish spinster on the first floor, was found dead in Buffalo Park. She was badly mutilated. The attackers had plucked out both her eyes, cut her throat, and raped her several times.

Muggers and petty hustlers had started hanging out on Church Avenue. The Jews had sold their businesses and left the area for safer havens.

I shook off the heavy burden of despair and went upstairs to take a cold shower. Chico Red was having a dance and I was taking along my girlfriend, Destie. She was the sweetest thing in my life.

Destie looked stunning as I picked her up that evening. She was petite, with Indian ancestry. Her complexion was coffee-smooth. She was unusually quiet as we left her father's house in the Bronx. Her brown eyes were fixed on the city's dazzling lights that spun around the car. Nervously, she molded her tiny hands into the fabric of her short, backless dress that had risen up above her knees, giving me a glimpse of promise.

Excited, I reached over and rubbed her leg with intention of taking her before the party. It had been three days since I last made love to her.

She shied away from my touch. "I'm in trouble," she said critically. "I think I'm pregnant." She spoke as though she'd rehearsed the lines.

The world seemed to stand still for me at that moment. Her words hit me like 115 volts. Destie was only fourteen years old. I had taken her maidenhood on a cold winter's night when she sought the warmth and comfort of my arms. Now she was sucked into the arms of womanhood. She dabbed at the flowing stream that blurred her vision.

There was a stirring in my loins accompanied by the shock that I could father a child, a task I had always credited to the skill of other men. "What makes you so sure you're that way?" My nostrils were filled with the pleasant odor of her perfume.

"Why do you always take me for a fool?" she said affectedly. "There're certain things that a girl knows." She covered her face and sobbed. "I'm not keeping it."

"Abortion!" I was outraged. This was strictly against my religion.

She spoke from behind her hands. "Think of something, Danny. You always seem to have the answer for things."

"Leave it to me," I said quietly, suddenly faced by one of the biggest decisions I ever had to make in my life.

"I'm not going back home neither. My father is getting suspicious. He heard me being sick in the bathroom the last few mornings." Her voice was broken.

Destie had all the intentions of shacking up with me but I wasn't ready to take on such responsibilities. She touched my hand that rested on the gearshift. Her young brown eyes were slowly finding the angle of seduction.

Angry lights of red and blue froze the tense atmosphere in the car. A single bark from a police siren triggered panic. The city pigs were down on me like death in the night. They indicated for me to pull over.

My mind began to race, calculating the many armed robberies I had committed since meeting up with the Stick Up Kids.

Destie's brother was doing seven years for a job we pulled off on Lexington Avenue where a cop was shot.

Traffic was light in all four lanes along Fifth Avenue. I considered making a run. The pigs' siren barked once more. Quickly, I slipped the .45 Magnum from my waist and handed it to Destie. She drew her raincoat from the back seat and pulled it over her shoulders, then hid the gun under her dress.

I pulled up beside the curb. Eyes looked up from a mobile hot dog cart. Pedestrians on the sidewalk jacked up to witness the shakedown.

Two white uniformed cops moved cautiously towards the car. Their guns swung low on their hips. I turned down my window and stared into the blue eyes and red face of authority. He spat out my offence without delay. "Ran a red light on the corner of Forty-Eighth and Fifth. Get out of the car." He stepped back, fingers brushed the butt of his gun.

I got out of the car with my hands slightly raised. The cops' depraved eyes undressed me, starting with the thick gold chain and pendant hanging from my neck.

The pendant seemed to have the cop hypnotized. "Remove your hat," he commanded.

Ropes of dreadlocks dropped down below my shoulder. The judge and jury eyes of the spectators were stunned as I stood there holding my leather hat in my hand.

"What you waiting for? You don't seem like no novice to me." The cop's tone was full of sarcasm.

I spreadeagled and put my hands on top of the car. His hands moved over my body and between my legs. Completing his search he got back to his position and barked: "Driver's license."

I lowered my hand to take the license from my back pocket.

"Don't try it, buddy," he warned. "Just keep your hands where I can see them. I ain't about to let no Rastaman put no bullet in my brain, as seems to be the fashion with you people." He was referring to the two cops gunned down in Queens three months back.

The faces on the sidewalk drew closer. They'd returned a verdict of guilty. A black face in the heart of the city could only mean one thing—trouble.

The cop was on a stage and I was at his mercy. "Proceed and remove your driver's license." He seemed to be coaching the public on the proper way of conducting a stop and search.

He snatched away the license and walked back to the police cruiser. After feeding the details through his two-way radio he returned looking like some great miscarriage of justice had been committed. He stared me out, waiting for me to crack. I had been through this kind of shakedown several times and the procedure never changed.

"What's in the trunk?"

"It's locked. The keys are in the ignition." I kept my eyes on his itchy fingers as they brushed the butt of his gun. The police were secretly conducting a shoot-to-kill policy on Rastamen. The city was filled with young cops seeking revenge for their colleagues gunned down since the beginning of the seventies.

The other cop who was covering the passenger window where Destie sat looked at me and smiled. This was typical of police. One would be mean as shit and the other would be the nice guy. They changed roles depending on the situation.

The cop who had taken my details opened the door and raised his hat politely to Destie. He got down on his knees and started looking around the car. He twitched his nose like a sniffer dog and crawled over on the back seat.

My heart started to race faster than Jesse Owens'. I wanted to tear away and lose myself in the thick jungle of businessmen, tourists, and working-class stiffs that gathered on the sidewalk. Behind the driver's seat was a bag of food stamps taken from a supermarket up on Hundred and Tenth Street four nights back.

The pig did a thorough search then climbed back to the front and took a seat beside Destie. "Looks like you're due any time now, miss. Is Palmer the father?"

She nodded and accommodated a smile. Her fingers drummed lightly on the bulge of her stomach where she'd hidden the bag of food stamps.

The cop tilted his hat once more and slithered out of the car. He handed me my driver's license. "Be careful next time. There could have been a major pile-up back there."

Destie was far from happy when I returned to the car. She kept her cool until the cops gave us some slack after tailgating for four blocks. She pulled the bag of food stamps from under her coat and chucked them down by her foot. "Why do you keep lying to me? Aren't you satisfied my brother Tony is doing time? Do you want to go and join him?" The dimples in her jaw sank as she swelled with rage. "You promised me that you were going to stop robbing," she said bitterly.

"Those," I smiled innocently. "I found them amongst some old clothes when I was cleaning in the basement this morning. I'm gonna drop them off for Sheron and the baby. Jerome has been neglecting them of late, and I am the godfather."

"I don't believe you. Any time you're telling lies your eyes get wider." She stared through the front screen. "Pappy is going to get you killed. Just because you saved his life, that don't mean you got to be his lap dog."

"He's cool and he ain't doing no more stickups, he's a Muslim now."

"Like the devil turned Christian. There ain't a righteous bone in his body. I knew him long before you. In case you forget, it was him an' my brother that started the Stick Up Kids." She gave me a sidelong glance. "Either you give them a walk or our relationship is over."

How could I explain to the girl I loved that I was obsessed with armed robberies and enjoyed the thrill and excitement of holding someone at gun point while relieving them of their valuables? "Look at the good side. Had it not been for Pappy we might never have met."

She raised her eyebrows. "I'm not sure that was a good idea at all. Everyone that comes in contact with you seem to have a tragic end. You're like acid." She paused. "I don't like those Rastamen you associate with, either. They give me the creeps."

It was after eight when I reached Brooklyn. Crowds of people were gathered outside Chin Randy's record shop on Schenectady Avenue. Reggae music had hit New York like a storm. Randy's was the main distributor at the time. They carried the latest hits up from Jamaica.

I pulled up on St John's Place where rows of rundown tenements formed a concrete chain along both sides of the road. Black folks milled around the sidewalk. Winos and red-eye hobos staggered to nowhere. Junkies were chased up and down with monkeys on their backs. People were on the roofs and fire escapes. A stink escaped from the garbage that lined the street and sidewalk.

Jerome had captured one of the dirty apartments for Sheron and the baby. She was overjoyed when I handed her the bag of food stamps amounting to $5.000.

My next stop was in New Lots to see Ingrid. She still had not come to terms with Screaming's death.

Natty Joe's car was parked outside one of his drugs houses on Rockaway Boulevard. He'd taken control of that pad when he kicked off the door and killed four members of the X-Vandals gang. He was running a gold mine, but still his name was called on several shootings and murders in the area.

Destie remained in the car while I ran up to Ingrid's apartment. Passo and Johnny Toobad had a drugs pad two flights up on the fifth floor. Six of their fierce warriors stood outside the apartment building. Traffic was heavy in the building where the smell of marijuana wafted amongst the stench of poverty. Two girls no more than fifteen years old passed me as I climbed the stairs.

"They selling some good shit," one of the two girls said delightedly.

"Paying for it with ass, so what you complaining about," said the other.

Ingrid opened the door and led the way into the living room. She'd decorated the living room with all of Screaming's belongings. His bicycle was resting on a silver stand near the old cabinet television. "He's gone to prepare a home for both of us." She was on her knees wiping the spokes of the bicycle. Her beauty was still captivating, but her mind was as cloudy as a winter's day. "No, he's not dead." Her eyes sparkled, then she sat on the floor in a daze and stroked her silky locks.

I handed her a crisp $100 bill. She took the money and put it carelessly on the little center table. The face of Ben Franklin swayed in the incense-filled air as it fluttered to the ground and landed on a white fur rug.

I returned the money to the coffee table, silently admiring the beauty that she was storing in a freezer for a dead man. "Chico's keeping a party tonight. Would you like to come along?"

She looked up angrily. "I don't want anything to do with Chico or any of those men my king had brought together." Her tone was sharp and full of venom. "They killed him, Danny. I'm not sure, but one of them or all of them killed him. My king wanted peace for everyone. They didn't want that. They wanted riches here on earth. That's why the . . ." Her voice trailed off and she dissolved into tears as the embers of grief were kindled.

"Don't blame any of the Rastamen for Screaming's death. The Stompers done it. They were the only ones that had any reasons for doing it."

She thumped her chest and gritted her teeth. "Something in here tells me different. I see my king in visions and I'm convinced it was one of his brethren that killed him." She drifted into the dead world once more. Her hands recovered one of Screaming's old shoes from under the coffee table. She stared longingly at the shoe then started to dust it, adding to the sparkling shine that was already there.

I let myself out of the apartment, doubting if she would notice my absence.

One o'clock and the dance was swinging. The residents of Crown and neighboring streets got no rest that night. The dance was held in the tenement building where Rano Dread had a drugs pad. Chico had given him a handsome start, mainly to divert his interest from Rodriguez' shop.

Music was supplied by Skattelite disco, a sound system owned and operated by Jah Stagga, a brother of one of Jamaica's leading sound system engineers.

Reggae music to Rastamen was like rock to the hippies. Reggae carried the teachings of oppression. It originated in the slums of Kingston, Jamaica. Reggae was hypnotic and raw. It could make you cry, make you happy, or just make you want to take out your gun and fire shots.

Rastamen were out in their numbers. Hair was swinging and swaying in a ganga and sweat stink atmosphere. Four rooms in the apartment were jam-packed. People had spilled out on the landing where the air was cool and less stuffy. Rows of Rastamen and -women leaned against walls burning big spliffs the size of ice-cream cones.

New dances came up from Jamaica with the rising number of

immigrants. There was the Bicycle Skank, Yamaha, Ace Ninety, Cool, and Deadly. These dances were called skanks which simply meant any dance that you could fit to the heavy bassline of reggae music.

The rugged bassline shook the walls and dimmed the lights in the hallway. Faces screwed up and men surrounded me. Those were the days when a smile cost a million bucks. The young generation of Rastamen had nothing to smile about. They would sooner kill you. To smile meant they were weak and soft and no one wanted that title. Step on a man's toes inside a dance and you had to draw your gun to say sorry. Such was the air of hostility that existed. The unity that Screaming sought was now a myth.

Music and dance were the introduction to fiercer things coming out of Jamaica. Terrorists and murderers were arriving by the planeload. They had one intention—to get rich at any cost.

The gangs and the police were the first to witness the wrath that the wave of Jamaicans could inflict in the name of the Rastafarian religion.

Rastafarians were slowly getting a name as the marijuana dons. The law agencies were classifying them on the same scale as the dreaded Mafia, a category the gangs had failed to reach.

The Rastafarian name on the streets was revered. This inspired glory-seeking individuals to capitalize on the name. People from the other West Indian islands started adopting the religion. They, unlike the Jamaicans, didn't have a history of tribal wars. Neither were they the forerunners in the fight for West Indian liberty on the streets. Finding a bed of roses and a road already paved, they took hold of the religion sounding and looking like the Jamaican Rastas.

There was a great deal of mistrust between the Jamaican Rastas and the new recruits from the other West Indian islands. For this reason the name Yard Men came into use. The Jamaican Rastas considered themselves a superior force in the Rastafarian religion. They refused to accept anyone that wasn't from "Yard," which was the name they gave to Jamaica meaning home.

The big chests and hard faces that surrounded me on the

landing suddenly took on a humble look as an army of Rastawomen appeared at the end of the hallway near the stairs. The women were dressed in African head wraps, long skirts, and double-breasted cashmere coats. On their feet were low desert boots.

Jerome led a posse of men up the stairs behind the women. They stopped in front of the Militant women who handed each man a gun from under their coats. Jerome had grown much taller, his hat leaned to one side like the Tower of Pisa. His body bounced to the rhythm of the music as he drew closer, leading his band of ruthless murderers towards the frightened crowd.

The deaths of Screaming and Patrick were the final nails in the coffin for Jerome. He had returned from Jamaica with four members of his old childhood gang. After a year he sent for sixteen more members and now had his own posse known as the Fields, short for the Field Marshall Generals. They were the first Jamaican posse to be formed in the States.

The Fields were well armed. Jerome had led them up to Hundred and Twenty-Fifth Street where they robbed and killed Slim's brother, the one who supplied the gangs with weapons. They were notorious for shooting up dance halls and robbing weed houses. Jerome's name was on everyone's tongue—even Rano Dread, who lost two drugs houses to the Fields and was unable to do anything about it.

Jerome's Militant frame walked over to me. His posse stood behind him. Their faces were sour and screwed up. Some wore dark welding glasses to hide the fire of death that burnt in their eyes. "Long time my brother." He rested a hand on my shoulder. His eyes were red and filled with hate.

"I came here specially to see you. It's been six months. I passed your base several times, but not seeing your car I didn't bother to stop."

"Danny Dread. You still the biggest liar I ever met. Hear you been burning tires in the Bronx. How about driving for me sometime?" He eyeballed me from head to toe. "Looking good. That was a wise decision you made the night you saved Pappy's life." He leaned closer and whispered, "There's always a place in the Fields for a man like you."

I politely declined the offer that many of the fiercest men of the day would have gladly accepted.

There was a bitter look on his face. He didn't like being turned down. Warning signals started going off in my head. There was a gap between me and Jerome, one that would explode in time to come. Jerome wasn't happy about the way I was friendly with Nine Fingers and members of his gang after Patrick's death.

His eyes were restless. "Where are all the rats?" he shouted over the heavy beat of the music.

I tossed my head towards the apartment where the music blared. He drew closer and whispered, "The lawyer you got to represent Passo. I need him for one of my men. The same one who turned over Nine Fingers' brother. He's coming up in front of the grand jury in two weeks."

"No problem. His name's Jack Weinstein, brother of the hippie kid we used to bodyguard in high school. I'll drop his details by your camp tomorrow."

He made as if to move off. "I don't know why I even bother coming to this party. They treated me and you like dirt after Screaming's death." He groomed the twines of locks below his chin. "They are all rich men now with many drug houses around the city." He paused and moved up a gear in his bitter trail. "All what they done didn't hurt me like how they allowed that Chang to pull his gun on Screaming and get away. Screaming could have out-drawn that little scum but he didn't. He allowed everyone to think different, but me and you know what he was all about." His voice then went cold like the look in his eyes. "Screaming sacrificed himself for his brothers. Not me. Men are going to weep and gunshot is going to gnash before my war's over." He was harboring the ghosts of the past and allowing them to poison his brain.

"They can't use us anymore. We're free, grown men running our own operations."

"Woe to anyone—man, woman, or child—who cross my path." He plucked a few ropes of locks from under his crown and let them hang down the right side of his face. He looked over his shoulder as he walked off. "Stick around. We have to smoke a chalice together before the night is out."

The crowd on the landing showed me their teeth. I was no longer just another Rastaman leaning against a wall with a pretty girl. I was a friend of one of the most feared men in Brooklyn.

Chapter 20

Five o'clock in the morning and the dance was in full swing. Rastamen were arriving from all over the States, some from as far away as Texas and Kansas City.

Jah Stagga was around the amplifier, with multi-colored lights flashing in his face as he operated the mixing board and drew selections that brought back memories of Jamaica, when sound systems played under the stars on a cool Saturday night. There was enough marijuana smoke in and out of the apartment to stone the whole of New York City.

I left Destie with a few of Jerome's debs in one of the back rooms and joined him in blessing a pipe. The chalice was blazing in my mouth when the needle scratched across the music.

Chico Red's voice amplified through the dance. "Praises to Jah Almighty," he roared. "The Jolly Stompers have sent two of their emissaries to negotiate peace."

There was silence, then a soulful voice declared the messages of peace: "My brother, for nearly three years the gangs around the city and the Rastafarians have been waging war against each other. I can't speak for the other gangs, but I can speak for the Stompers. My boss Super Dice want no more blood shed between the Rastafarian brothers and the Stompers. He's willing to overlook all the bad water that has passed between us. Also, there will be no action taken against the Dreads that captured some of our establishments. Super Dice want all of us to join together and defend this turf so we can all enjoy the royalties. Furthermore, the boss want it to be known that the Stompers were not responsible for the death of Rastaman Screaming. Here is a treaty of peace that I would like Chico Red to sign, putting an end to the war."

Silence reigned, then the microphone crackled and Chico's voice thumped through the giant speakers. "I have signed the treaty. Let peace reign."

Jerome slapped the chalice from my hand. "This is my war. It has nothing to do with Chico. I was the one who lost a mother." He stormed out of the room, followed by his men.

The music started blasting once more. The crowd was thrown aside as Jerome and the Fields hurried out of the apartment.

The sound of gunfire erupted from outside in the hallway. The crowd stampeded. Men with guns drawn held onto their partners and made for the safety of the back rooms and the fire escape.

I sought Destie in the midst of the confusion. She was still in the back room trapped in the mass of hysterical bodies that crammed into the room.

I drew my gun and fired a few rounds into the ceiling to clear the mass of bodies. A woman responding to the sound of the gunshot jumped straight through the glass window and landed on the fire escape. The rest of the crowd dropped on the floor.

Destie rushed into my arms and together we turned around and headed for the front door. The sound of gunfire echoed out in the hallway. The crowd were huddled together in fright as we moved through the apartment.

Outside the apartment door the two Stomper emissaries lay dead with gunshot wounds in their heads. The crowd were on their bellies screaming. Rapid gunfire erupted in the hallway as Chico Red and Dillinger traded shots with the Fields.

I pushed Destie back through the front door as bullets tore down the landing, chopping up the wall and ricocheting off the ceiling. The Fields women were on their knees and firing their guns like trained vanguards in a revolutionary army.

The gun fight lasted for nearly twenty minutes. The Rastamen from out of town were forced to get involved when the Fields threatened to storm down the hallway and kill every moving thing. Eventually the Fields were chased from the building, leaving behind a flowing river of discontent.

Rastamen and their partners rushed down the hallway in an attempt to escape the wailing police sirens. The cops were responding to the call of distress.

I was able to make my way down the stairs amongst the hysterical crowd. Many were wanted men who had run away from the state to escape capture by the local cops.

The lights on the police vehicles were flashing in the street outside the tenement building. Cops with their guns drawn took up positions behind parked cars along Crown Street.

Rastamen, fearing for their safety and stoned on marijuana, opened fire on the cops. The morning was woken by gunfire on the streets. The area was swarming with cops from at least six different stations. Red and blue lights were flashing. Rastamen were running in all directions with their guns barking. I was on my hands and knees trying to keep a hysterical Destie from cracking up. Slowly I made it to the bottom of Crown Street where the Mustang was parked.

Destie had a few cuts and bruises when we reached home. Her nerves were completely shattered.

The seven o'clock news highlighted the shootings in the Crown Heights area. Police were advised to step up their vigilance against the Militant Rastafarian sect. One member of the glory-seeking Rastafarian sect was interviewed on the radio. No Jamaican Rastaman would ever have agreed to such an interview. The man spoke with a Trinidadian accent. "The Rastafarian movement is non-violent," he stressed. "Criminals take on the Rastafarian cloak to shield their identities. The men from Yard are mainly responsible for the shootings and murders."

The law agencies at the time could not spot the difference between the Yard men and the so-called true Rastas. As far as they were concerned all Rastas were the same.

I received a call from Billy Weinstein around lunch time. He was excited: "Jack has just been appointed District Attorney."

"What! Heavens, Billy. I don't know why you're so happy. This could mean serious problems."

"Man, this is the best thing since Jesus Christ."

"Jack has gotten the reputation as the Rastaman lawyer. Now he'll be spitting swords against us."

"Not you, Danny. Jack will never raise a finger against you. He appreciates the good job your mother is doing taking care of my father." There was a sadness in his tone. "The cancer is getting worse, kid. I don't think he's going to last the year."

"Sorry to hear." My voice lacked sincerity.

"For Christ's sake, relax. With Jack in the DA's seat I'll be winning cases left, right, and center."

"That won't be for some time yet, schmuck."

"Hey! Watch that schmuck talk. Anything can happen in this city. Shortcuts can always be arranged." He rang off in a jubilant mood.

Destie stirred under the covers. Her radiant features reflected under the glow of the bedside lamp. I had fixed up a room in the basement and installed my own phone. The street-level windows were blocked out so no light from outside could get in. I lowered the bedside lamp and crept under the sheets. Destie was naked and my hands found the mound of hair that warmed her crotch. She moaned with a sense of delight as I probed her darkness with my fingers, scenting the air with her sex. Sleepily she rolled over and parted her legs for me to enter. We made love for nearly one hour.

While she slept that Sunday afternoon I was faced with the problem of her abortion. Finally I decided that she was right. She still had three years to go in high school.

The following day I took her down to Kings County Hospital. We sat in the crowded lobby nursing ticket number 52. Five o'clock in the evening and we were no closer to being seen by the doctor. Eventually we gave up and returned home.

We sat in the basement watching the television and eating a take away from the West Indian restaurant on the corner of Fifty-Third and Church.

Later in the night, when Destie went upstairs to take a shower, I slipped out of the house. Night had set over the city. Time was approaching when I should meet up with the Stick Up Kids on the corner of Rochester and East New York Avenue. They were coming from the Bronx, but they also had to pick up a stolen car in Bedford Stuyvesant.

Whores in skimpy garments paraded up and down both sides of the avenue. Pimpmobiles cruised by, keeping an eye on the whores. They were hot, some even smelled like sex.

Buffalo Park ran the length of the avenue. That's where the whores entertained their tricks. Niggers were grunting in the park like hogs which had been put out to mate.

I felt like a target for the police cars that cruised by as I stood there on the corner with a gun down my back. This was Batman and Robin's territory. They could spot me from a mile off. I walked up and down, hoping one of the many cars pulling up to the curb was my boys. They were late. At one stage I had to restrain myself from shooting a Puerto-Rican who thought I was game. I stood on the curb waiting to cross the street when one of the whores crept up behind me.

"Natty Dread! For the right price you could have the best pussy this side of Brooklyn." The voice was sweet and had a Diana Ross lilt.

This was the same voice that provoked my passion when I was much younger. "Nadine," I said, keeping my eyes on the approaching cars. The shadow of the woman in a short mini-skirt took a few steps backwards. "Nadine." I turned around quickly.

She recognized me right away. There was a startled look on her face as if she wished the ground would open and swallow her up. Her professional instincts took over and she rocked arrogantly on her stiletto heels. Her beauty was fading but still her legs were shapely and long and she had a head of Afro glowing under the streetlights.

"Now you know right. Spread it all over the neighborhood. I don't give one fuck. Nathan, Mom, Alphonso—they're all dead. Dad's hitting the bottle. Paula and the twins, they humping ass with me. The rest of my brothers and sisters are in care." She was bitter and looked at me as though I was to be blamed.

"This isn't the way." I was choked.

She sniggered and threw back her head. "There ain't no other way but selling pussy," she said dryly.

I pulled her to me. "Go get the twins and meet me here in one hour. I'm making some good money. I can help until you can sort yourselves out."

Her hand found the gun resting down the back of my pants. Hastily she took my arm and led me towards the entrance of the park. We walked into the darkness in silence. Her heels clicked along the stone pathway that ran through the center of the park.

We both knew the area well. This very park had served for our entertainment only a few years back. Now Nadine was a victim of the same environment, using the canopy of the trees, bushes, and hedgerows to solicit her trade.

She stopped by a bench near the concrete steps that led to the basketball courts. "The pigs were coming. I could spot them from a mile away. I know you packing so just chill here for a while," she whispered softly over the sound of sexual pleasures crooning in the background.

I took a seat beside her, somewhat rebuffed by her stale whore's perfume and lingering stink of sex.

Nadine's hand lighted on my leg and her fingers trailed towards my prick. "Still got the hots for me?" She squeezed my penis, which was showing some sign of life.

I removed her hand. "Listen, you gonna let me help you or what?"

"It ain't that easy. I'm strung out along with my sisters. Not only that but we got a bad ass pimp on our backs that don't fuck around." She parked her tongue for a spell and tried to move my passion once more. "Here's your chance to get that fuck you always wanted. I know you been wanting me from the first day you moved on the block."

"That was in the past. I got a permanent girl now and she's expecting my baby."

"So you gonna be a daddy?" she teased. There was a vestige of innocence in her voice.

"I would love to be a daddy but she wants to get rid of it."

"Ain't no big thing, honey. I've flushed a few myself. No one in their right mind should bring up a kid in a world like this. Paula got some doctor up there in Manhattan, chopped a six-month baby out of her belly last week." She shuffled in her pocket book. "I got that doctor's card right here and he real cheap too." The inside of her pocket book smelt like a rubber factory. She struck a match. The yellow flame brought to life the sordid picture of vice surrounding me.

"Out that goddamn light," shouted a husky male voice.

"Since when you need a light to fuck a hoe," shouted a wisecracker.

"Hey, bro, make sure she ain't got no dick," shouted another.

"Here it is." She blew out the match.

The card was like a ticket to the electric chair for my unborn child. It felt heavy as I pushed it in my pocket. My eyes had adjusted to the darkness. The shadow of a young girl drew closer. She stopped where we were sitting and wiped her mouth with the back of her hand. Her long hair fell about her shoulders.

"Come back here gal, youse ain't finished yet," shouted a dirty voice from three benches down.

"Fuck you, scumbag," the girl shouted in a childish treble.

"Here! Mama, I'll lay another twenty on you if you come back," said the husky voice.

"Not on your life. The only thing gonna get laid on you is my knife through your ribs."

"OK, but you don't know what you missing. They don't call me Big John for nothing."

"Shut the fuck up," someone shouted. "How's a man supposed to concentrate with all that rapping?"

Nadine snapped in a hushed voice: "Paula, you turning down good money. You know business tight on a Monday night."

I couldn't believe that this beautiful girl was Paula.

The pot-bellied foul-smelling man she was entertaining earlier crept up behind her and squeezed her ass. She turned around and gave him a slap across the face. The man cackled like an old fowl as he walked away, disappearing in the darkness.

We moved from the park back to the sidewalk. Paula didn't seem to recognize me and Nadine made no introductions. She was beautiful and the pressures of her trade were maturing her body at a fast rate.

Terror washed Nadine's face as a pink Cadillac with white-wall tires and TV antennas pulled up a short distance from where we were standing. Hazard lights started flashing on all sides of the car. Traffic came to a standstill waiting to get around the Cadillac.

The whores crept from all corners and flocked around the

cars. There was a crash and the sound of metal crunching. A tall, hefty black man jumped out of an old battered Chevrolet. He had a big hunting knife glistening in his hand. He was out to claim some insurance. "Nigger, you done hit my car," he yelled, making his way towards a Mercury Monarch where a frightened-looking man sat with his family.

"Sorry." The man turned down his window and apologized.

The man with the knife was having none of that. "What you mean, sucker!" He shoved the knife through the window and tried to stab the man.

Frightened, the man drove off, taking the screaming attacker with him.

With so much activity taking place around me I forgot I was on a mission.

The pimp, covered with a mass of fur and wearing a broad hat, stepped out of the car. He looked about like he was on top of the world. Diamonds glistening on his finger and platform shoes trucking on the sidewalk, he drew closer, leaning his body and bopping. "Bitch, where y'all been hiding?" He sounded like James Brown.

Nadine moved towards the half-pint pimp. "The pigs was on us, Daddy, so we hit the park for a little shade."

The pimp squeezed his nuts and looked at me bitterly. "This the jive motherfucker stopping you from making my money."

"He an old friend, we grew up on the same block."

Paula's eyes lit up as she placed the face in her memory.

"Bitch, I don't give a fuck who he is. Time is money." He was on a stage. The cars were piled up and hooting impatiently. Whores were looking on shivering in their boots, glad they weren't the ones at the mercy of the pimp's wrath.

A tired-looking whore staggered out of the park and yelled, "That's Silver Knight, he one mean motherfucker."

The pimp must have heard because he sprang into action and slapped Nadine to the ground.

"Back off." I eased out the gun and cocked it in the same motion. Normally I wouldn't have given any warning but there were too many witnesses.

The pimp stared at the weapon like his whole world had been put on brakes. His legs did the Charleston and his Mexican moustache twitched nervously. "Brother man, you ain't got to use that there speaker on me. It was all a misunderstanding."

Nadine got up off the ground. "Danny, it's all right. Daddy don't mean no harm."

"That can't be the bad Silver Knight pleading like one of his prized hoes," shouted a shapely transvestite.

There was a look of sheer pleasure in Paula's eyes.

"This here's my man," Nadine pleaded. "Without him me and my sisters would be sleeping in the gutters."

The pimp smiled as Nadine held onto his arm. "She's right, brother. I take care of all my girls." He reluctantly put his arm about Nadine's body.

The traffic started moving and Pappy pulled up in the stolen car. "Got problems?" He leaned through the window.

"Nothing I can't handle."

"Let's chip, Homes. We running late."

"Danny, take me with you," Paula said in a frightened tone.

The pimp let out a groan as though he'd been hit in the belly.

"She ain't serious," Nadine said. "Go on, we cool now."

"I'm too serious. I'm tired of turning tricks." Paula took a few steps backwards as Nadine approached her.

"Daddy's gonna make it real nice for us, babes. Don't leave, I need you." She sounded desperate.

Paula's eyes made four with the pimp's.

"Honey, I'm gonna take real good care of you like I do all my little babies when they good."

"Hey! Homes, you coming or what?" Pappy shouted.

Paula bit her lips and clasped her hands together as the pimp took out a little brown bag and held it out like bait. "Daddy, I hope you ain't fixing to welsh on me." Her eyes sparkled.

"It's all yours, baby, and you get to spend the night in Daddy's waterbed too." He stretched out his hands as Paula drew closer, bewitched by the bag of dope.

I put the gun away and stepped towards the car. There was no saving Nadine and her sisters. They were slaves to King Heroin. As I stepped into the car I was overpowered by a sense of foreboding, something telling me that I would never see them again.

Here was the coquette of doom, a seductress who lured her

victims with a promise of the stars, supplied in a small cellophane bag. But she delivered only death: a slow and lingering death where she bled away rational thought and rewarded her mindless slaves with the festering sores of hopelessness. This seductress became a goddess but a merciless macabre deity, whose angel pimps were made masters in a world where they would otherwise have been nothing.

"Well, don't you want to know why we're late?" Pappy drummed his fingers on the steering-wheel.

"It doesn't matter." My voice was stern.

"That's the right attitude to have when going on a robbery. Kind of make everything that much more serious. Anyone make a wrong move get whacked."

Die Hard and Jelly Bean were in the back staring out of the window. They resembled college students but they were master robbers. These were two of the original members of the Stick Up Kids, who formed the gang from the age of twelve. They had graduated from street muggings and petty thefts. In the Spodeford Center they were motivated by the Homicide Twins, who at the age of twelve were carrying out contract killings.

We drove through Brownsville and further in East New York. Pappy was laying down the rules for the next robbery.

"Then after two more jobs I'll just slip on down to Hawaii and get me some of them Hulli-Hulli girls." He glanced over at me. "And what's the matter with you? Don't tell me you got the hots for some hoes."

"Lay off my back." I needed to release my frustration on someone.

He mused: "Some guys just can't be satisfied. I done gave you one of the sweetest little girls to come out of Jamaica and you want to go blowing your money on some two-bit junkie whores."

The two men in the back fell about with laughter.

"Hey! You a pussy sucker," I cursed.

He licked his lips: "Love it, too. Dread, you should try it sometimes. That juice just dribbling down your face—and the girls love it."

I gave him a quick backhand across the chest. "If it wasn't for me them Tomahawks would have eaten your pussy the night we saved your naked butt from being raped."

"Man, you always got to bring up that scene from the past. I didn't need your help. They would have to kill me like they done my brother before they would get my ass."

"Ease up, y'all," Jelly Bean said in his soft tone. "The Dread didn't just save your life. He's your guardian angel."

"Some guardian angel," Pappy hissed. "He's worse than a hole in the head."

Die Hard grunted: "Had it not been for Danny's connection with Sugar Bear and Shorty Gold Tooth we would all be dead, so fuck the rap." He had a voice like Michael Jackson's and gray sleepy eyes that thrilled the girls. He was tall and had a light complexion.

"I ain't afraid of no Tomahawks. They tried to kill me once and failed. I'm invincible." He accelerated around a slow-moving car.

Jelly Bean sniggered: "The night they held us at gunpoint in the Iron Rail club you looked scared enough to me." He was the joker of the pack and wasn't much of a looker, didn't care too much about clothes and sometimes carried a heavy perspiration odor. He had a big nose that looked like someone chewed it up and spat it out.

Pappy was fired up. "Shit, you rapping about being scared. What was I suppose to do? Confess to robbing their numbers joint? I was at home with my girl that night."

"I know different," Die Hard said.

"Best let all that shit be forgotten. Shorty the General says Danny saved his life, so he gonna give you some slack." Jelly Bean looked up accusingly and met Pappy's guilt-stricken eyes in the rear-view mirror.

Clicks of automatic weapons sounded in the car as we pulled up on the dark street in East New York. We went around the block and scrutinized the gambling house that was soon to fall victim to our assault. The residents of the area were out in their numbers. Winos stood in front of liquor shops licking their tongues. A group of sour-looking women were cursing each other. Kids were running up and down. Black folks were sitting on the step-ups of four-storey semi-detached houses.

The gambling house was situated in the center of the block beside a burnt-out derelict building. The stairs leading to the front door were painted bright red and the railings were painted enamel black. The basement trailed off to the left underneath the stairs.

Hustlers made their way along the broken concrete slabs and passed the piled-high garbage pans stinking of soul food. Paper plates and cups were scattered on the ground beside man-gnawed chicken, pig, and cow bones. The gamblers descended a few stairs and disappeared through a brown security door.

The bum that occupied the derelict house staggered over to the car as we lay in wait. "Fuck off," Jelly Bean shouted as the rising stench from the bum drowned the pleasant smell in the car.

The bum's face lit up with a wry smile. He dragged his tired load across the road and painstakingly climbed the stairs and disappeared into the blackness of the derelict house.

Headlights shone at the end of the block and shortly after-wards a car pulled up. A young white man in his late twenties got out of the car and walked up the stairs into the house.

The three Stick Up Kids left the car. Pappy's lean body led the way followed by the short, stocky Jelly Bean. Die Hard was the cool diplomat. He walked like an ostrich in full stride. His long legs carried him across the road in quick time. The three men merged with the other hustlers entering the gambling house.

I remained in the car until they were safely inside. Rastamen had a bad reputation for robbing people. The sight of one would only set off an alarm. I gave the Stick Up Kids enough time to ambush the fat, six-foot giant at the gate who was the only opposition. The fat man, known as Big Fats, had a feared reputation in the East New York area. He had often boasted of his Mafia connections. Some of his enemies had been known to be found at the bottom of the Hudson with cement blocks on their feet. He was a confident man, one who drew pleasure from terrifying black folks. Just to be nasty he would grab anyone giving him trouble and bite them up like a Rottweiler.

Chapter 21

The three Stick Up Kids had the people on the floor when I entered the dingy gambling house. The place was brightly lit and drowning in smoke and stale odors. Money and dice were still on the floor where crap games were interrupted. Poker tables were abandoned. Fierce black faces looked up from the floor.

The fat man was the only one standing, his deep shade of black burnt with rage. Jelly Bean's Magnum was shoved under his ribcage.

"Where the white man?" Jelly Bean asked.

The fat man smiled on one side of his face. "Come on, you know there ain't no white folks within fifty miles of this here stench." He was dressed in green army fatigues and smelt like a bison. He raised one of his big heavy hands.

Jelly Bean shoved the gun into his gut, causing him to groan. "Don't try it, you Friar Tuck-looking motherfucker."

Fats' heavy paw remained still in the air when he heard the cock of the mighty cannon. His hands slowly dropped to his side, trying to hide the big sparkling diamond on his finger. He huffed like an old steam engine as I walked over to him, my knife glistening under the bright unshaded bulbs.

"I want that ring," I said.

He grunted and stiffened his body. Bubbles of sweat sprang from his crocodile-hard skin. "Motherfucker," he screamed as I gave him a telephone cut from the tip of his ear to the point of his chin. Blood trickled on the blue and white tiles below.

The knife went up again. "No more! Take the ring," he yelled and slid the ring, sticky with blood, from his finger. It was warm.

The sight of rich blood spattering on the floor had done

something to the frightened black folks. The women screamed while the men closed their eyes and prayed to the God they'd forgotten until that point in their lives.

Jelly Bean pointed the gun at Fats' head. "This is the last time I'm gonna ask for the white man. Any answer other than the one I want, then kiss the world goodbye."

"He upstairs. But, mister, them there is Mafia. They'll hunt you down to the end of the earth."

"We'll worry about that—get him down here."

The whites of frightened black eyes rolled over and they looked up like hippos rising from a mud bath.

"Life is hard enough for us black folks. Ain't no one gonna get hurt. We just going to settle a score with the honky and get out of here," Pappy shouted reassuringly.

The mention of white folks going to be ripped off brought some light to the frightened black faces on the dirty floor.

Jelly Bean and Pappy marched Fats across the room to where some wooden stairs led to a solid metal door. There was a lighted bell on one side of the door frame. The broad light above the pool table cast the fat man's shadow across the floor as he climbed the stairs leaving a trail of blood.

Fats stood on the top stairs and looked over his shoulder before pressing the bell. There was silence in the room. Shortly afterwards a white voice sounded on the other side of the door.

"What took you so long? I was beginning to think you ran away."

"No, sir, Mr Castello," Fats said in his best nigger voice. "I was just getting things together. Things kind of slow tonight." He turned round and looked at Pappy who indicated for him to come back down. The wooden stairs creaked as he made his way down. He reached the bottom and got on his knees. His jaw was split wide open but he was too afraid to notice the pain. He stared into the nose of my gun.

Pappy rushed to the top of the stairs and waited eagerly while the bolts were released on the door. The door opened and he shoved his gun through a set of bars.

Castello shrank back. He was the same white man we'd seen climbing the stairs. Dandruff fell from his sandy colored hair and rested on the shoulder of his brown two-piece suit.

"Open up," Pappy demanded.

Castello quickly turned a set of keys in the lock of the iron door that separated him from the mean-looking black eyes. Downstairs on the floor he could see his black body-guard on his knees looking into the muzzle of a gun.

Pappy pushed the gun under Castello's chin as soon as the iron gate was opened. He motioned for us to follow.

Jelly Bean was left downstairs to keep guard. He had a Bren sub-machine gun with a loaded clip.

Castello led the way up some winding stairs and exited in the hallway on the first floor. He stopped outside a door where classical music was coming from inside. "We don't have much money," he said.

"We!" Pappy gave him a mighty push into the room.

An old man, startled and confused and wearing horn-rimmed glasses, looked up from behind a desk. He dropped a piece of gold into an open drawer and sat up straight on a Chesterfield sofa. On the desk in front of him were a few pieces of jewelry and a magnifying glass. The Anglepoise lamp fixed to the desk was turned up bright.

Pappy gave Castello a shove. "The safe."

The old man's eyes popped out, his jaw dropped and his face hung down. He toyed nervously with a chain hanging from the button of his waistcoat and resting in his pocket.

"Please Dad, don't give them any trouble. Do as they say," Castello pleaded. The color had left his body.

"So that's the old Castello!" Pappy exclaimed.

The old man sucked in his breath stubbornly. He looked mean and cocky like the picture of a younger man with a handlebar moustache which was hanging on the wall to the right of his desk. "There is no safe," he muttered.

He raised his hands in a feeble attempt at stopping the butt of Pappy's gun as it hit him across the forehead.

The young Castello rushed across the lightly furnished room and held a handkerchief to his father's wound. Blood poured down the old man's face and nastied the collar of his white shirt.

"Give them what they want, Dad. We're quite comfortable.

Things are not the way they used to be. Give it up and let's walk out of this alive."

The slug only served to harden the old man's resistance.

Pappy cast a violent stare at the two men. "Give him the ear treatment, Homeboy."

The younger Castello wrapped his arms around his father's neck. "He's only an old man with a bad heart. He won't be able to stand too much of this."

"Whatever happens to him is his own doing," Pappy said mercilessly.

The younger Castello backed up towards the window as I drew closer, holding a knife in one hand and the gun in the other. He screamed as I put the knife on his father's ear and removed it with a single swipe. The ear fell on the desk and wiggled around like a worm.

Castello took one look at his father's severed ear and fainted. The old man shivered like he had the fits. He was dripping with blood, but all that escaped his mouth was a groan.

Pappy took a butane lighter from his pocket and turned up the flame. He got down on one knee and put the flame to Castello's face. The burnt flesh smelt like sizzling pork.

Screams healthy and afraid filled the room. Castello was forced back into consciousness. He jumped up and looked around as if he'd been jerked out of a bad dream. He crept to his father's side and held on to his baggy trousers. "Please, Dad," he whispered desperately.

The father stiffened and jerked his foot away from his son. "There's nothing to know." He was stubborn.

Castello slithered across the floor, his blue eyes crazed like a madman. "I know it's in the wall, Dad." He got up and rushed to a silver candle holder screwed to the wall opposite the painting. With little effort he turned the candle holder. The wall crackled and slowly moved aside, revealing a tiny room no bigger than a closet. There was a safe on one side of the wall and a mysterious door. The room carried the noxious odor accredited to bums and winos.

The old Castello breathed heavily and gave his son a rigid look of betrayal.

"Only Dad knows the combination." He rested his fingers on the safe's numbering knob.

Pappy stepped around the desk and flicked the lighter in front of the old man's face.

The old man was on his last legs. Greed kept him kicking even though pain was slowly drawing on his last remaining strength.

"Give me a chance. I can but try." The young Castello stared into the muzzle of my gun and busied his fingers on the safe's dial.

"No," the father protested faintly.

The son's fingers were busy on the knob. His ears rested on the body of the safe, listening for the right click.

Fifteen minutes later Castello was no nearer to finding the right combination. There was a slight smile of contentment on his father's face. The smile quickly turned to a frown as the safe clicked and the young Castello stared at us like a lunatic.

The safe flew open. Valuables came bursting out and dropped on the floor.

Before we could move towards the safe we were held still in our tracks by the sound of gunfire coming from downstairs. The Bren was coughing out bullets.

With a sigh of relief Castello stepped back, knowing how close he'd come to death. He rushed over to his father who was stiff in his chair with his hands over his heart and his eyes looking up at the chandelier. "Dad," he shouted.

The gold and greenbacks continued to fall from the safe like a volcano erupting. We were happy to stand there and watch our dreams materialize. There was more money and jewelry in that safe than our poor eyes could ever imagine. The diamonds sparkled and sent off shooting stars as if proclaiming their worth.

The woman who set us up on the job, Ruby Chambers, had specifically requested the jewelry. "Keep all the money. Just let me have the gold," she said with sparkling eyes.

Two hefty kicks and Pappy had the mysterious door open. A funky smell like a stink bomb crept through the open door. Pappy staggered as the stench almost caused him to spill his guts. Holding a hand over our noses we stepped over the valuables and walked through the door into a brightly lit passageway. The bum's clothing was thrown down in a heap beside a wash pan full of shit and alcohol.

We followed the hallway and found a door that led to the burnt-out derelict house next door.

Ruby Chambers was a woman with a greedy outlook on life. She'd watched the gambling house for two months before calling us on the job. "Every Monday night that Castello go into that house as sure as my skin is black, and I ain't never seen him leave that house with anything resembling what money is kept in."

As we raced out of the hallway back into the room the whole mystery started to fit into place. The bum that we'd seen coming out of the burnt-out house was old Castello smuggling out all the money in shopping bags. Who would ever think of robbing a bum?

The old Castello had suffered a heart attack. His son stood over him in a state of shock. He put up no resistance as we tossed his father out of the chair.

I tied the young Castello to the Chesterfield while Pappy and Die Hard filled the two duffel bags with the money and the jewelry from the safe.

We headed out of the room and made our way downstairs. The fat man had holes in his body like a sieve and the frightened black folks on the floor thought we were going to mow them down before leaving. They were ordered to get up off the floor and hand over all their valuables before we left.

Ruby's soft bedroom eyes glistened as we entered her high-rise apartment on Ocean Avenue. She was all done up, awaiting our return. Her ball-bearing hips rolled as we moved across the shag-pile carpeting to the living room.

Ruby's eyes sparkled when Pappy emptied the bag of jewels on the plush red carpet next to the center table. She was a beautiful woman, tall and shapely. Her house coat fell away from her body revealing her dark nipple teats. Overwhelmed, she dropped on the floor and scooped up the jewels. "Wow!" She moved from one piece of jewelry to another. "Is y'all sure this is everything?" She was high on greed. Her huge breasts quivered with avaricious appreciation. She caught our eyes feasting on her loveliness and smiled like a naughty school girl. "I would've liked to see the look on that nasty fat two-timing bitch when you guys held him at gunpoint." She gently laid down a necklace and raised her fingers like they were a gun. "Did he squirm?" She picked up the necklace once more and held it to her throat.

Pappy coughed, reminding her we were there. "Well, that settles it. Ever need our services, contact us through our man on the street."

"What?" She lowered the necklace. "Ain't no separating us now, honey. I been planning something like this for at least two years." She winked her long made-up eyelashes and pouted her lips. "My Fats tell me everything when he want some loving. It just drives him wild when he sees me making it with another woman." She pulled a face and whispered, "We all gonna be rich." She rolled on the floor and laughed out loud but we didn't share her joy. "What's wrong? Everything went smooth, didn't it?" Her eyes widened.

"Couldn't have been any smoother." Pappy stared into her eyes.

She stood up and pulled away her silk house coat and started a provocative dance to whet our appetites. Her hand circled the bulge of her crotch through a pair of yellow bikini panties. She wiggled over to me. "Ever had your dick sucked by a woman with ice cubes in her mouth?" She wound her crotch into my body, then stepped back and widened her legs. She groaned passionately as two of her fingers disappeared into her cunt. Slowly she drew them out dripping with honey and slipped them into her mouth.

The phone rang. "Who can that be?" she sighed with annoyance. She strolled across to the black leather settee and slumped down heavily then picked up the phone from a glass coffee table. "Yeah, that's me." She curled her fingers around the telephone cord. The smile suddenly disappeared from her face. She clutched her house coat about her body as if suddenly realizing she was naked. The phone fell from her hands and she turned into the exorcist. "Fools, you killed him. I didn't want my Fats dead." She combed her fingers through her hair hysterically.

"He pulled a gun on me," Jelly Bean said.

"I'm gonna make each and every one of you pay," she hissed venomously.

"We go down, then you go with us," Pappy said bluntly.

Jelly Bean pulled out his gun. "Fuck the rap. We bump this lame bitch off right now," he said belligerently.

"You lost control of your senses or what?" Pappy said angrily.

Ruby stared at the gun and made a rush for the front door, screaming. She yelled even harder as Pappy blocked her path and held her in a yoke.

"Listen up." Pappy tightened the grip around her neck until only a slight whimper escaped from her mouth. "It was an accident. No one meant to hurt your old man. You got the jewels. Why don't you just chill out?" He released her and she fell to the ground. "Rack up the peace, Homes. She just a little nervous, that's all."

Jelly Bean gave one of his innocent smiles then leveled the gun at Ruby and fired once.

The frightened woman didn't have time to scream. She just rolled over on her back and breathed heavily. Blood spouted from a hole in her belly.

"We better get out of here." I picked up the necklace from the pile of jewels and headed for the front door.

"Sucker! Weren't no need to shoot the freak," Pappy protested.

"Don't tell me you turned a Christian," Jelly Bean retorted.

"You done killed her old man. What do you expect her to do?"

"She still alive!" He raised the gun once more, but I blocked his shooting path. Die Hard and Pappy rushed across the room and restrained him.

"Man, if we don't silence her we all going to be doing some serious time upstate."

"I ain't about killing no woman," Pappy said.

Jelly Bean was disarmed and pushed out of the apartment while Pappy and myself gathered the jewelry.

Ruby was groaning on the floor as we went through the front door.

Destie was awake and watching the late movie when I got in.

She had the sheets pulled up around her body. "Where have you been?" she asked furiously.

'Twelve Tribes' meeting in the Bronx." I took a seat on the edge of the bed.

"How could you just slip away without letting me know? It gets pretty scary down here." She got up from the bed and swept across the room to the light switch.

"Turn out the light." I raised a hand to shield my eyes from the beam.

"No, I want to look into your eyes." She walked back across the room and stood over me. "There's blood on your shirt!" she exclaimed.

I jumped up quickly and strutted over to the wall-length mirror.

"You've been out robbing." She beat against my back with her tiny fists. "Don't lie to me," she yelled, tears rolled down her cheeks.

I turned around quickly and caught her wrist as she was about to pound me once more. "The last one. I only done it so we would have money for the abortion and to find somewhere to rent."

"The blood!" she screamed. "Who have you killed? I don't want no part of any blood money."

"Die Hard cut himself. I was sitting beside him in the car. It must have rubbed off on me."

She broke free and ran to the bed. "Don't come near me until you've had a shower," she shrieked.

A shower was out of the question because that meant I had to go upstairs and risk bumping into Mom who was as sensitive as a mine in those wee hours of the morning. And there was the possibility of bumping into my father on one of his random trips in the dark to take a piss. It seemed like Mom never slept anymore. It took only the sound of a car engine or the slam of a front door and she would jump out of bed and rush to the window, fearing it was me driving off to the bloodbath that dominated her nightmares. Every time she heard a siren her heart would leap and her belly would drop to her knees. My father never spoke. He had always expressed himself with the belt, but those days were gone. All that was left for him was to join Mom in prayer, but his prayers were different, he prayed to God to bring me a swift ending and deliver his wife from eternal torment.

I stripped and examined every piece of clothing for traces of blood. The closest thing to having a shower was a quick wash at the sluice at the far end of the basement.

Destie made herself small as I entered the bed. That night we slept apart, each drowning in our own sorrows.

Early the next morning I took Destie to her house to collect her clothes. Her father Ivan, the television zombie and race horse fanatic, was there to greet us. He was a short man with parasitic eyes and a sarcastic nature. He was harmless.

I took a seat in one of the matching armchairs opposite the settee where Ivan was sitting. He stared into a steaming mug of coffee that Destie had made for him the minute she entered through the front door. The yellow of the morning sun crept through the window and shone on his bald head.

He mumbled: "Now you've turned her into a woman I hope you intend to look after her because I don't want her back in this house."

"We're going to rent an apartment and live together."

"Destie don't know how to wash her own panties, much more to look after a man." He picked up the newspaper from the floor which was already turned to the races.

I removed a wad of money from my pocket, a bait to soften his heart. His eyes sparkled. The grey kinks above his temples seemed to quiver with delight.

"Buy yourself a drink."

He dropped the paper and leapt across the room. "Boy, you better save something for a rainy day." He snatched the $300 from my hand and shoved it in his side pocket. He took a pen from the top pocket of his blue bush jacket then returned to his seat and picked up the paper with renewed interest. He stole a quick glance at the wad of money in my hand before I put it away.

He whispered: "Between me and you I'm glad to see the back of Destie. She is such a pain in the ass."

Destie crept into the room in silence. "I heard that, Dad," she said angrily.

"So what?" Ivan barked stubbornly, his eyes fixed on the paper.

"This summer when I get a job with the Manpower you won't be seeing one red cent," she said spitefully.

Ivan put down the paper. "I raised you to the point where you start taking cock and this is the thanks I get." He put out a hand to shield himself as Destie started beating him across the head with a cushion. There wasn't too many things that bothered Ivan. He was in his late fifties, a playboy who hung around with the widowed and divorced West Indian women in his age group. Destie was in every way like her father, having adopted many of his sarcastic ways. She crossed her legs and dropped into the settee beside him.

Ivan stared curiously into the paper. "Danny," he said pleasantly and formally, "who do you fancy in the two thirty at Aqueduct?"

"I know nothing about the horses."

"Don't blame you. The dogs are more reliable. At least they don't have any crooked jockeys on their backs pulling them up when it suits them." He folded the paper. "One of these days I will have to take you down to Belmont. I will show you how to back winners." He was excited. "It's better when you're there watching them run in the flesh. Somehow the horses can feel your presence and win just to make you happy."

"Dad, keep quiet before you have Danny believing all that rubbish."

There was a trace of guilt on Ivan's face. "Destie, you're so stupid you wouldn't know the back of the horse from the front. Why you feel so many people go to the races when they can switch it on television or listen to it on the radio?"

What Ivan didn't know was that on many Friday nights I had attended the races, keeping a watchful eye on the winners, then trailing them and relieving them of their winnings.

"Dad, I'm going to live with Danny." She toyed nervously with the ends of a square cushion.

Ivan looked up from the paper. "I thought you lived with him already, without my permission. Go and do what you want to do. You're a big woman. Don't come crying when anything goes wrong. When you write your mother in Jamaica let her know that it was you who chose to leave this house."

Destie jumped up in a huff and threw $50 on the table.

Ivan smiled: "I've yet to have a child as considerate as you," he patronized her.

"Only when I give you money."

Ivan's smooth tongue was in motion. "Listen, you and Danny are two young people. Go and make life. I wish you the best of luck." His words carried mixed blessings. He added: "Leave the door keys on the way out."

"No." She stormed out of the room and returned shortly afterwards with two small suitcases.

Ivan stood at the window with a condemning look on his face as I pulled away from the curb.

Chapter 22

It was late afternoon when we left the doctor's surgery in Upper Manhattan. For the fee of $500 we took the life of our unborn child. Somehow that guilt was made to rest heavier on my shoulders.

The trains back to Brooklyn were packed. The stench of burnt oil and corrosion in the tunnels hung heavily in the air. Bodies rocked from side to side as the train moved from station to station. The white faces had all disappeared by the time we reached Atlantic Avenue.

The car was parked outside the subway station on Eastern Parkway. There was silence as we drove home.

The following day I rented a room in a basement on Montgomery Street in Bedford Stuyvesant. The block was made up of neat rows of semi-detached houses.

"Not pets or drugs," the balding landlord warned.

Within the next few days we were settled. Destie had slipped further into a state of depression. She refused to eat and would sit in front of the television all day in a daze. The room was small and could only hold a bed and a little dresser. There was a makeshift closet beside the ground-level window that looked out into the garden where the landlord parked his car. There were several other rooms in the basement. Everyone shared the same bathroom and kitchen.

Pappy and Die Hard came around to see me three days after I moved in. Destie rushed out of the room when Pappy entered. He shrugged and sat on the bed. Die Hard leaned against the wood-paneled wall. The sun outside was shining but there was always a darkness in the basement—even with the light turned on.

"We got problems," Pappy whispered heavily. "The heat scorched Jelly Bean."

The floor started to give way beneath my feet. "Quit jiving."

"No jive. He on the rocks." Pappy looked like he hadn't slept for days. "They got him on half a million dollar bail."

"That ain't no bail. It's a ransom," I declared.

Pappy scratched his head. "We got to get him out, Homes." There was a sense of urgency in his tone.

"Between us we must raise fifty grand, for the bond. If not we hit the streets."

Pappy shook his head hopelessly. "There's no hitting any streets, we're all under fire. The freak Ruby Chambers is still alive and she mouthing off to the never end."

"What about our man on the streets?"

"He on his toes."

"I figure the cops got him, too!" Die Hard exploded. "They raided the warehouse this morning. The only way they could know where we hang out is by that dime-dropping son of a bitch."

"Don't jump to no conclusions," Pappy said hastily. "We've been through tougher shit and he's come through for us."

"Twenty-five to life would turn any motherfucker into a rat." Die Hard avoided my eyes as I looked at him suspiciously.

"Between the three of us we can come up with at least thirty grand. Any bonds man in this city would be glad to take that," I said.

"Only me and you willing to put up any money," Pappy said.

"Man, I got a family to support." Die Hard seemed agitated.

"Sure that's all you supporting?" Pappy gazed at him accusingly as he sniveled and rubbed the bridge of his nose.

"What's that suppose to mean?" he asked.

"Nothing." Pappy punched the palm of his hand. "There's only one way out of this." He looked over his shoulder, startled by the boisterous laugh of the faggot who rented the room at the end of the basement.

As if reading Pappy's mind Die Hard shook his head. "Count me out."

"Ain't no one getting let off," Pappy said. "We're all in this together."

"The sooner we get it over with the safer it will be for all of us." I was committed.

"Shit! What's come over you guys?" Die Hard stared at us as if we had gone mad. "I don't want any part of wasting no dame."

Pappy ripped a page of A4 paper from the pad sitting on the dresser. He tore the paper into three unequal pieces, then left the room. He returned shortly after. "Choose."

Die Hard hesitated and made the first draw. I was next.

"I can't do it," Die Hard shouted. He checked the other two pieces of paper to make sure he hadn't been duped.

"Either you carry out this execution or face the consequences." Pappy's voice was ice.

Die Hard sighed heavily. He knew the punishment for welshers and dime-droppers. He was the one who made the rule. The fate of Ruby Chambers now rested in the hands of the reluctant Die Hard. His mission was to go to the St Lukes-Roosevelt Hospital in Manhattan and blow Ruby away. The smooth purr of the Seville's engine signaled their departure out of the driveway.

Destie came rushing back into the room with the faggot on her heels. She knew how much I detested the pansy, but still she allowed him to sit on the bed. He was dressed in a flimsy kimono and was the ugliest human being I had ever set eyes on. His lips were ten times fatter than any nigger's I ever did see. And he had the nerve to wear bright red lipstick.

The pansy could tell by the look on my face that I was in no mood for jokes. "Destie," he said in a put-on effeminate voice. "When you have some time come down to my room. I have some pictures of my boyfriend you might like to see." He left the room.

I slammed the door. "What you go and do that for?" Destie yelled.

"I don't want him back in this room," I protested.

"Why? You have your friends," she said angrily.

"Not like that."

"I'm like a prisoner stuck in this old, stuffy basement. She's the only one I have to talk to."

"Keep him out of this room before I . . ."

"What, Danny? Before you kill him? Haven't you had enough . . .!"

In a fit of anger I slapped her across the face. She screamed.

"Don't you ever accuse me of killing anyone." I stood over her with clenched fists. She cowered in fright as I stepped over her curled-up body on the floor and left the room.

The pansy stood over the cooker frying some pork. He gave me a dirty look as I stormed through the kitchen and up a flight of stairs that led to the door. I thought of going back for my gun but resisted the temptation. I needed a walk to cool my brain.

The night was fresh. People were up and about. A group of kids with roller-skates hung round their necks made their way down Bedford Avenue towards the Empire roller-skating rink.

I knew the area well and walked out to Washington and Montgomery where some Rastamen were selling grass in front of the park. Bicycles were still a major source of transportation for many Rastamen.

The park was a hive of activity. Reggae music blared from one of the high-rise apartment buildings that surrounded the park. Rastamen were seated on tables near the curb. They sold marijuana while Yankees and Puerto-Ricans pushed hard drugs. Customers and loafers were plentiful.

Two of Jerome's Fields were sitting on bicycles beside a group of Rastamen who were smoking a chalice. They called me over and repeated Jerome's desire to have me join the Fields. My answer to them was the same as I gave Jerome.

As I stood there the men started moving about agitatedly. An unmarked police car with three white men slowed down as it passed the park. The car stopped in the middle of the street.

"What the fuck you looking at?" one Rastaman asked. He unbuttoned his army jacket to show his weapon.

"Blood Clatt pigs," shouted another man in heavy Rastafarian dialect.

"Blood Clatt," repeated one of the white cops. He smiled and waved. "Have a nice day." They drove off laughing.

The men mused at their victory, sending fear through the

hearts of Babylon. They loaded a chalice and burned the weed right there on the sidewalk. The cops' car drove by once more. This time they didn't bother to stop.

Remembering what Pappy said about the heat, I suddenly felt that the cops' eyes were on me. I reasoned with myself and thought it couldn't be me.

I walked away from the men and headed for Franklin Avenue to find a phone box. A woman with weeping eyes stormed out of one on the corner of Eastern Parkway and Franklin.

The phone was buzzing as I picked it up. Through the glass window in the booth I could see men moving around outside in a suspicious way. My eyes darted all around. The door to the booth suddenly flew open.

"Don't move, you fucking cocksucker," shouted a hefty black man dressed in army fatigues. He was joined by two other white cops.

"Hey! Blood Clatt?" said one of the white cops.

"On your fucking knees and put your hands behind your back," the black cop ordered. He read out my rights and dragged me off to one of their unmarked cars.

The sirens sounded and intermittent broadcasts crackled from their two-way radio as they drove down the hill towards Empire Boulevard, destination 71st Precinct.

I was booked in and marched up the stairs to the interrogation room. There were pictures of Rastamen posted all over the walls. I even saw one of me sitting on one of the tables in Ninety-Fourth Park. I had a shotgun in my hand. Batman and Robin awaited my arrival.

"We meet again," McCarthy said wryly. He sat comfortably behind his desk. "I always knew you would make the big times, kid." He flicked a cigarette from a full pack of Kools and offered me one.

I turned down the offer. The room was stuffy with the smell of pigs and their cheap cologne.

McCarthy took a long drag on his cigarette. "I thought the gangs would have taken care of you a long time ago. Of course I could have pulled you in on several occasions. Cutting off Nathan's ear was a bit naughty. But then you seem to have a habit of cutting people, like old man Castello." He was calm and treated the whole matter flippantly. "Old man Castello got what was coming to him, but nevertheless you fucked up. White people are special stock. When you start fucking with them then the law comes down on you hard. Ain't no one gonna cry when you hit a few niggers in the park or waste a few Puerto-Ricans."

McCarthy charged me with robbery, two counts of murder, and one attempted murder. He knew from past experience that beatings were a waste of time.

"This is the end of the Stick Up Kids, Pappy, Jelly Bean, Die Hard, Tony Scarlet, you. It's lights and I am proud to be the one that's going to put them out." He turned to the cops who arrested me. "Get him out of here. I want him in court tomorrow morning."

I was whisked away down town to Schimmerhorn Street for processing. There I was mug-shot and fingerprinted. The booking area was like a circus. Men were thrown into big, stuffy cells stinking of cigarette smoke and unwashed bodies. Prisoners from all over the city were there.

I was allowed a phone call then thrown into one of the crowded cells. The ruthless and the bad had taken all the seating on the long bench that ran the length of the back wall. There wasn't much room to move, not that I wanted to. I stood near the bars at the front of the cell, pushed aside every time they put in another prisoner.

There were striplights in the ceiling stained by burnt cigarettes.

"Here comes the dudes from night court," shouted a Puerto-Rican. There was a surge of bodies charging the bars, straining their eyes to see if they knew anyone.

"Hey, Homeboy!" shouted a black man reaching through the bars.

"Shut the fuck up," yelled an old black jailer with a limp.

"Come in here and pop that shit," shouted one prisoner.

The men from night court were thrown into the cell. Their faces were sour, resentful of the fact that they couldn't make bail in court. Some had fifty cent and one-dollar bails but still couldn't pay it.

One of the new men in the cell tore his way through the mass of bodies and made his way over to the bench. "Hey, mighty whitey. On the floor, sucker," he grunted in a rough voice.

There were three white prisoners in the cell. Two were already on the floor. The other was on the end of the bench, his body shaking. He was a dope addict and was clucking. He didn't have a chance to move.

The sorry-looking nigger pounced on him and started bashing him about the head. "Man, you deaf or what?"

"All right." The white man slid to the foor and landed in a mass of vomit.

There was more action in the cell when a Puerto-Rican walked over to one of the other white men on the floor. "What you in for, Homes?" The Puerto-Rican feasted his eyes on the white man who was well dressed and seemed out of place in the jungle of crooks.

"It was all a mistake," the man answered nervously.

The prisoners laughed.

"I want that there jacket you wearing," the Puerto-Rican demanded.

"I want his shoes," shouted a bum.

Terrified, the white man held on to his jacket as the Puerto-Rican ripped it from his body. The other prisoners bared down on him like hungry lions tearing at dead meat. When they'd finished the man was down to his underwear.

"What y'all say this honky suck some dick?" the Puerto-Rican said while he slipped into the jacket.

"He got the lips," said one.

The white man screamed as they took turns abusing him. The guards heard all the shouting and cries for help but they just kept on about their business.

The sordid activities continued through the night. Robbers were robbing robbers. Pickpockets stealing from pickpockets.

That was the longest night I ever spent in my life. In the morning we were shackled and taken to the basement of the Brooklyn tombs. Down there was dark and damp. Again we were thrown into huge cells known as bull pens. Cops roamed about outside dressed in suits. They were preparing to take their prisoners into court. The courtroom was located upstairs.

Prisoners from Rikers Island and Sing Sing were brought in. The men smelling of prison stench came into the bull pens prepared for action.

Many of the older prisoners from Sing Sing just took a seat and waited. Some spoke with lawyers and cops at the gate.

The Rikers Island men were only interested in robbing the new prisoners. Within minutes they had robbed the men who had robbed other men down at the processing center.

The jailer brought around some coffee and sandwiches and passed them through the bars.

McCarthy appeared shortly afterwards with a black briefcase in his hand. "Palmer!" he shouted.

"Shit!" exclaimed one of the men from Sing Sing. He spat out a mouthful of hot coffee. "Man, whoever got that motherfucker on their back is in for a lot of trouble."

"Palmer," McCarthy shouted once more. "You're in court in one hour. Have you got a lawyer?"

I refused to answer and gave him a hard stare.

"A lawyer will be provided if you don't have one." He smiled deviously and walked off.

"Don't fall for that shit with them legal aid lawyers," shouted an old man with a pile of minutes on his lap. "Any lawyers they give you is a fraud. They worse than the pigs."

Half an hour later I was taken upstairs and thrown in another bullpen closer to the court. I had completely resigned my freedom to the dark chambers of jail when the warden called me to the bars.

"Lawyer to see you," he said.

Billy Weinstein and an aging lawyer in his late fifties were seated around a Formica-top table in an area set apart from the cells. The warders marched me into the area and stood off a short distance and cast their eyes over the activity in the room.

Billy shook my hand. "Don't worry, we'll get you out of this."

"Would you like a cigarette?" the lawyer asked. His eyes darted around and rested on the guards. "This isn't the place to talk. Walls have ears and such a case as yours will need careful planning." He looked carefully into my eyes. "First, I must ask did you make any statements at your arrest?"

"No, sir."

"Good! Many people are sent to prison on their own statements. Undoing what is said in statements can be a very lengthy and unsuccessful venture." He cast his eyes at the two wardens standing a short way off and mumbled, "The DA is a friend. I am asking him for low bail as this is your first offense." He stared at my locks. "Being a Rastafarian could complicate matters. Is there any chance—"

I cut him short. "I will never put a razor to my head if it even mean that I have to go to jail, sir."

"Call me Weatherman." He shook my hand and closed his briefcase.

Billy smiled. "We'll talk once you're given bail. Mom is in court. She is willing to put up her house if necessary."

"Is she all right?"

"She's a strong woman, shaken but all right. Your father is against her offering any help whatsoever."

I was bitter that anyone could actually want to deny me the right of freedom in such circumstances.

"It's to be expected," Billy said.

The lawyer checked his watch. "Time is drawing near," he said in a businesslike tone.

We shook hands and the guards escorted me back to the bull pens. Twenty minutes later I was taken into court. Polaski and McCarthy sat in the front row behind the DA. Mom sat in the center row with a handkerchief, rubbing her eyes as the charges were read out. Behind Mom were three white men. They seemed somewhat out of place sitting there amongst all those sorry-looking black people.

I was charged jointly with Jelly Bean, Die Hard, and Pappy, who was in Bronx hospital on the critical list after being shot by Officer Polaski.

Bail was set at $5,000 on account of my age and lack of past criminal record.

McCarthy and Polaski stormed out of the courtroom and stared at me bitterly as I stood in the crowded lobby. Billy, Mom, and the lawyer saw the dirty look they gave me as they barged their way through the crowd and left the court building.

"That's one hurdle out of the way," Weatherman said. He

offered me his card and made an appointment for me to visit his office the following day. He shared a few words in confidence with Billy before walking off.

Billy was at the wheel driving his father's Mercedes. He reached over and squeezed Mom's hand as she sat quietly on the seat beside him. "It looks bad," he said critically. "Die Hard claims that you and Pappy intimidated him to go to the hospital and kill the woman."

Mom turned around and looked over her shoulder. The horror of my ways was slowly taking root in her head. She cried.

"How about your brother?" I asked apprehensively.

"No such luck. He's been appointed to investigate the Rastafarians and their involvement in organized crime."

"But you know that's a farce."

"I don't know any more. Rastamen are getting heavily involved in drugs, racketeering, and extortion. They are becoming a threat to the system. And with the recent police shooting they've really brought the heat down on themselves."

The trains were clattering above Broadway. The city, wallowing in filth, passed by the window. The heat of the day had set in and people moved about like zombies along the sidewalks. The buildings were dark and gloomy. Beyond the gloom was the bubbling inferno of those who made the city a living hell. They were like maggots feeding on stench and decay. Faces on the pavement stared at the car, their brains ticking like potential time bombs. Hungry hustlers had taken to the streets, dancing to the rhythm of the city, the permanent noise of airplanes, cars, sirens, helicopters, guns. The orchestra made up of the poor, junkies, robbers, murderers, whores. They were all part of the world I had grown up to know and love.

My brief spell in jail had opened up my appetite for better things. Things I knew I would only achieve by using the gun.

Billy pulled up outside the house. The neighbors were out shuffling around for some reason or other.

Mom thanked Billy and left the car. She chatted with a few of the neighbors before climbing the stairs. She looked much older. The strain had stooped her shoulders and slowed her down physically.

"Be careful how you move about," Billy warned. "The heat's on your ass and it ain't just from cops."

"What do you know that I don't know?"

"Old Castello might have been a fool, but his daughter is married to a leading member of the Bonatto faimly. That spells Mafia and they are one hell when it comes to vendettas."

"I learnt something in those bull pens. This is a dog eat dog world, where the bigger dog eat the smaller dog. This is one small dog that ain't going to be eaten by anyone. I'm going out there to rape this city."

"Before you do any raping make sure you get yourself a part-time job or something. It will help when the trial starts."

"Drop me somewhere." I suddenly remembered Destie.

"What about Mom? She needs to be alone with you for a while."

"Fuck you, jerk. I'll take a cab." I jumped out of the car and came face to face with Dave Green. His eyes were red and his hair was uncombed. He was deteriorating rapidly. I stopped and stared at him for a while. I wanted to reach out and be a part of him, but it was no use. Once again I had to put my emotions on ice. Things were changing rapidly, the streets had become a battleground more ferocious than the jungles of Vietnam.

Billy drove beside me at a slow pace as I headed for the Winthrop Cars cab station on Clarkson Avenue. He wound down the window: "Get in."

"No lectures."

"Have it your way."

I got into the car and we rode along in silence. When I reached Montgomery Street my car was completely vandalized. Everything, from the windshield onwards, was gone. There was further shock as my eyes adjusted to the dimness in the basement.

The faggot was standing in the kitchen with a smile on his face as I rushed past him. The door to the room was open. Inside was ransacked and there was no sign of Destie. All my valuables, including my gun, were gone.

The faggot burst out in a loud, boisterous laugh of contentment. "She's gone, honey," he jeered.

"What happened to the things in the room?"

His face hardened. "How the fuck should I know. I ain't your goddamn watch dog." He rested his hands on his hips and rocked. "What you doing with a young girl anyway?" He batted his false eyelids. He was tall and almost touched the ceiling.

"Get yourself a real woman, one that can take care of you and give you nice things," he said suggestively. He started making funny eyes at me and slowly releasing his kimono. His lips pouted like clappers and his silicon breasts stared at me, pointed and wrong.

"Like what you see?" he asked, mistaking my shock for lust.

My eyes rested on the drainboard beside him where a long kitchen knife was sticking up in the air.

The faggot was quick. He picked up the knife and slapped it against his palm menacingly. "Honey, if you fuck with me I'll carve you up like mincemeat," he said in a rough man's voice. He came at me, poking the knife in jest and laughing at my response. He wore a funny pair of slippers on his large feet, exposing his big toe that was dressed with a blood-drenched gauze.

I remembered Destie telling me the day before that the faggot had the nail of his big toe removed so the doctor could shape it to grow like a woman's. Taking advantage of his handicap, I mashed his toe as he shuffled about me.

He screamed out so loud one of the tiles fell from the ceiling. The neighbors rushed out of their rooms and looked on curiously as I stood over him with the knife firmly in my hands. I wanted to slice him from his throat down to his belly. I threw the knife in the sink and left the house in a huff. The faggot was lucky I was on bail and couldn't take another charge. His screams followed me through the driveway.

Broke, I walked up to Eastern Parkway and Franklin and entered the subway for uptown. Police were on guard, but I jumped over the turnstile and ran down the stairs.

One cop chased me, but I was fortunate a train was coming and I jumped on. The train was the number five express for the Bronx. It skipped past the stations like a mad mule in haste to nowhere.

When I reached Destie's house only the dirt shadow of where

her dad parked his car remained. There was no answer at the door.

I jumped another train back to Brooklyn and returned home.

I phoned Destie's house every half-hour with no luck. It was after midnight when her father answered the phone.

"She's not here," he barked.

"Please, sir, could you tell me where she is?"

"Where you can't get your filthy hands on her—that's for sure. I allow you to take her from my house and you beat her near death." He hung up the phone, leaving me gaping into the receiver. To make matters worse he took the phone off the hook for the rest of the night. My world crumbled about me. That night I could find no rest.

Mom and Billy came along with me to the lawyer's office the next day. He was situated twenty-four floors up in one of the modern skyscrapers across the street from Brooklyn Supreme Court.

A beautiful secretary led us through the brightly lit area into a room where a bespectacled Weatherman sat behind a mahogany desk. The office was spacious, with picture windows looking out over the towering skyscrapers of the city.

Three padded seats were already set out before Weatherman's desk. Mom sat in the middle seat. Weatherman got down to business as soon as we were seated. "First let me tell you the major obstacles." He counted off his fingers: "Ruby Chambers, Donovan Thompson, and Allan Sullivan, alias Die Hard. Thompson has admitted no part in any of the charges other than he commissioned jobs for the Stick Up Kids on the street. In other words, he was a messenger. Ruby Chambers is cooperating fully with the DA and Sullivan has made statements involving you. I need complete honesty if we're to gain a strong foothold in the case. I will have to know the full details."

I turned to Billy for some sort of confirmation that I could actually trust this man. He had been, after all, a friend of the Weinstein family for years.

"Couldn't we tell them that it was the marijuana that made him behave other than himself?" Mom said innocently. Weatherman smiled at the likely prospect of a judge accepting such a feeble excuse.

He listened intently to my side of the story with a poker-faced look. "Would you agree to a line-up? The chances are if this woman saw you twice briefly then she might not remember you. Second, if you could get a few friends on Rikers Island to sort out those other two then we stand a very good chance."

"How long is he looking at if all goes wrong?" Mom asked worriedly.

"Mrs Palmer," he said confidently, "wrong is a word that I hate to use. I am confident of success in this case. The Weinsteins are my close friends. They would not have recommended me had they not thought I was competent. There is another positive aspect in this case. Castello's son has disappeared and won't be pressing any charges."

I breathed a long sigh of relief.

The meeting concluded, no sooner did we reach the street than I rushed for a telephone box. A middle-aged man was in the box rapping for ages. Full of vexation, I grabbed him and dragged his screaming body outside.

"Police!" he shouted.

There was still no answer at Destie's house. Thinking I must have gotten the wrong number I dialed three times. Still no answer. I asked the operator for assistance. Frustrated, I ripped the phone from the box and threw it on the pavement in front of the man who was still shouting for the police.

"Forget about that girl. She's the one responsible for you doing all those crazy things," Mom said, breaking the silence in the car.

That afternoon I went for a stroll outside of my old high school. The handball courts were still stained with our names. Students were cutting out of classes, the pretzel man was there. So, too, was the beat cop, Ralph. The red 'X' was still painted on the pavement where Patrick had lost his life.

The younger kids attending Mayer Leven Junior High were out in the school yard as I circled the block and walked along Ralph Avenue. Spotting a phone box near the Italian delicatessen, I called Destie's house once more. On the second ring the phone was picked up by her little brother. "Dad put her on a plane back to Jamaica," his childish voice declared.

She might as well have been sent to the moon because there was no way of me getting to ʰer.

Weatherman got me a part-time job in the Brooklyn public library on Grand Army Plaza. I worked below the many decks, running calls for reference books. The work was hard and tedious. I was in charge of the science department. There were always trolley loads of books to be reshelved. To make matters worse the supervisor would put books out of place on the shelves, then come down on me for not keeping my area in order and reading the books.

The grand jury indicted me and the case was sent up to the Supreme Court for trial. Polaski and McCarthy were pushing for a conviction. Weatherman changed his tune and started introducing me to the idea of copping out and getting a lenient sentence.

Chapter 23

The gangs were fighting to the death, fired up by the heat and the desire to settle old grievances. The cold and miserable winter had sent many of the gangs underground. The heat brought them out. The only way they could breathe the summer air was to defend their turf. The ghettos went up in smoke.

The Suni Gods took to the streets armed with sub-machine guns. They were intent on crippling vice, one of the most lucrative arms of the gangs. They once again turned their guns on the prostitutes walking the strip and defenseless junkies copping dope.

The presence of a power mightier than the gangs could be felt in the death-gripping atmosphere that set over the city. The Mafia were moving in once more. They thrived on the gangs' all-out war against each other. This allowed them to get back into the ghettos of Brownsville, New Lots, and Saratoga Avenue. These areas were once owned by the mob who boasted that Murder Incorporated started out on Saratoga Avenue where Al Capone grew up.

The Rastafarians were carrying out a vendetta against the Tomahawks who shot up the innocent West Indian parties. The Easter Massacre had claimed many lives and left permanent injuries. Rastamen were purchasing sophisticated arms with the money earned from their thriving marijuana empires.

The gangs were easy targets. They hung out on street corners or in parks or groups. The Rastamen would just drive past and mow them down regardless of the consequences.

The gangs had never witnessed such acts of barbarism as practised by the Rastafarians. More and more every day they sought to bridge the gap and make peace with the Rastafarians. The gangs considered them a set of psychos better left alone.

The Stompers were losing ground. Jerome and his Fields reaped vengeance on them.

As the hot days and lonely nights took their toll I returned to the Nineties to work as one of Chico Red's guns. He was always on location at the store once owned by Rodriguez.

Chico took me into a back room and handed me a spliff. "You deserted me for some Yankees, now they've turned their backs on you."

"I had no choice."

"The patient man gets to ride the donkey. Look at me, I am a businessman." Although he was successful he still dressed in Militant clothes and carried his gun on his hip.

"I need help. A start to get me on my way."

"Start. It takes a lot of gun power to run a drugs house. The Fields are kicking off doors and killing people all over the city. Junkies having a bad day might just come to the door and blow your head off, just for something to do."

"Maybe I should have gone to the Fields."

"Jerome will not last out the summer." He walked around the room puffing on his spliff like it was a cigar. Somehow his conscience must have alerted him to the fact that he owed me a favor for not ratting on him about the money he took from the Tomahawks raid. "The gangs see me as some kind of leader for the Rastafarians. They come to me seeking peace. They think because we all have this hair then we are one. But they would be surprised to know we are as much at war against ourselves as the gangs are. I will give you a start but you must work for me for six months."

"Then what?" I asked suspiciously.

"I will finance your drugs and give you a few men."

The body count piled up as the gangs went at each other's throats. Drive-by shootings claimed many lives. Business for the gangs was at an all-time low. This increased the sale of marijuana.

Near the end of the summer Sugar Bear called for an all-around truce after a band of hooded men stormed into one of his whorehouses and massacred every living thing. A meeting was scheduled within days. Members of the three hundred different gangs around the city were invited to meet under one roof. The venue was the armory in the Bronx. This was the first time in the history of gang warfare that so many gangs had agreed to meet under one roof.

The meeting was chaired by leaders of New York City's larger gangs. These leaders conveyed the message of the city's councilors who had worked alongside the heads of the gangs in bringing a solution to end the gang warfare. The government was prepared to offer the gangs a building for their recreation. This building would be furnished with workshops for theater and dance. GED classes would be available, so the youths could continue their education and art training programmes to coax the graffiti artists in off the streets to put their work on canvas. The building would have a recording studio; members of the gangs would be assured jobs with the government urban programs.

This was all geared to nurturing street culture palatable and marketable. It was put to the vote and the majority of the gangs voted in favor of forming the family. As a family no gang could attack a rival gang without the consent of the family. Ling Wo of the Chinese War Lords and Dominico Vercotti of the Italian Destefano gang refused to be part of the family of blacks, who they saw as cowards and traitors.

The family was to elect an official title: "I Cry" or "Inner Circle Round Table of Youths." I Cry was agreed but the Suni Gods wanted no part of it: they felt government money meant government control, in other words white people telling *them* what to do. At the conclusion of the meeting Sugar Bear called on the family for the heads of Super Dice and Charmane. Super Dice was responsible for accepting money from the Mafia to start up the bloody war between the X-Vandals and the Tomahawks. The Mafia thrived on gang warfare because death gave rise to the oppression which in turn opened the doors to hard drugs, and as long as the gangs were at war they would have no time to engage in the lucrative drugs-running business. The family returned a verdict of guilty and Super Dice was gunned down by Sugar Bear. The same weapon was passed to Jerome who promptly executed Charmane. She died with a fire of abuse erupting from her mouth at Jerome.

The gang wars in the city ended, but another war was to start, one even more ruthless and bloody than the first.

Chapter 24

Weatherman had secret talks with the DA, who promised a shorter sentence if I copped a plea. Seven years seemed like a lifetime to me. I turned down the offer and told Weatherman to prepare for trial.

"Trial could result in you getting twenty-five to life," Weatherman warned.

"I'm innocent," I declared boldly.

"The evidence against you is very strong. When I first took this case it looked simple enough, but those two officers, McCarthy and Polaski, have gone out of their way to make a fight of this. You being a Rastafarian doesn't help matters either. Rastafarians have a permanent stamp on them as cop killers."

The two cops were going all out against me. It was then I contemplated a way out. I had discussed it with Billy before the meeting with Weatherman and he suggested that if all else failed then that would be the only way out.

Weatherman listened intently then scratched his forehead. "You do realize what you're saying? To accuse these officers would be to admit that you were at the scene of the crime. Worse yet, McCarthy could turn around and charge you for shooting this officer Riley."

Billy stirred in his seat. "Who needs to know that Danny was present? All you have to do is drop a line in McCarthy's ear. That should make him stop and think."

Weatherman smiled devilishly. "Mr Weinstein, are you suggesting I bribe an officer of the state?" he bantered.

Billy's face lit up. "It won't be the first time," he said knowingly.

"You're going to make one hell of a lawyer, Mr Weinstein," Weatherman said.

Court was in session the following day. That was one of many hearings leading up to the trial. The correctional facility on Rikers Island had failed to produce my co-defendants. The case was adjourned for the following week.

The scene outside the court was one resembling the gallery in the stock exchange. Criminals in $2,000 suits were milling up and down amongst the cops in cheap gaberdine two-piece suits and lavishly paid lawyers sporting pin-striped suits and carrying briefcases.

Weatherman waded through the forest of fast-moving bodies and made his way over to the two cops as they left the courtroom.

From a safe position near a water fountain, I stood beside Billy Weinstein as Weatherman and McCarthy were locked in a heated discussion. With every word that Weatherman spoke the cop jerked like he was being hit by poisoned darts.

McCarthy, unable to take anymore, grabbed Weatherman by the lapels of his expensive suit and nearly lifted him from the ground. The fast-moving bodies in the hallway turned around and fixed their eyes on the scene. McCarthy released Weatherman who fought feebly to steady himself as he hit the ground.

McCarthy stood with both hands on ample hips and looked up into the eyes of God. He huffed, suddenly plagued with a thousand decisions and visions of occupying a jail cell himself.

"Weatherman," he growled as the lawyer shied away from his monstrous presence. "You owe me one." He pushed his way through the onlookers and left the building with Polaski trailing behind him.

Four weeks later the case was dropped. Ruby Chambers had mysteriously disappeared. Jelly Bean and Pappy were indicted on a total of twenty-eight armed robberies. Die Hard was given a deal by the DA in exchange for information.

I quit the job at the library and worked full-time for Chico Red. My only intention was to fly down to Jamaica and find Destie.

Rastafarians had popularized reggae music in much the same

way as the hippies boosted rock and roll. Bob Marley and the Wailers, one of the many popular reggae groups, carried the music across the west.

Mom watched a documentary on Channel 13 one Sunday afternoon. "Who would believe Bob and his little band would reach so far," she mused.

I remembered back in the tenements when Bob and Peter Tosh used to practise with homemade instruments. They made a terrible racket. But for us kids it was exciting. Mom had once thrown a pot out the window and yelled at Bob to keep quiet.

Eight weeks after the meeting at the armory, Ling Wo was assassinated by members of the Destefano gang. China Town and Little Italy were at war.

The Fields grew increasingly unpopular amongst the Jamaican community and the West Indians alike. They created a threat far greater than the gangs. Jerome was an executioner and he knew who to execute. The Rastafarians from the other islands were his main targets. His philosophy was that if you weren't a Jamaican then you had no claim to the religion.

The terms Yard Men to describe the Jamaicans and Smallies to describe those Rastamen from the other islands became popular.

The law-enforcement agencies slowly became aware of the difference between the Smallies and the Yard Men. The Smallies declared openly to law officials that the Yard Men were criminals—wolves hiding in sheep's clothing.

In August of that year the carnival came to Brooklyn, a joint enterprise sponsored by the West Indian community. Afro-Americans came out to enjoy the parade that stretched from one end of Eastern Parkway down to Grand Army Plaza. Five miles of floats, steel bands, sound systems, and jumping up. People took to the streets in merriment. This was the bank holiday.

The event was marred when members of the Fields opened fire on a group of Smallies selling marijuana on the corner of Utica and Eastern Parkway. Innocent people got caught up in the shooting which left six dead and countless injured. The dead included a nine-year-old girl.

The Fields didn't just restrict their war to the Smallies and the gangs. They robbed Yard Men who could not stand up to their might. On weekends they would gate-crash parties held by the older Jamaicans who were terrified by the presence of Rastamen. At these parties they would subject the people to all manner of degradation before robbing them.

Three weeks before Christmas Jerome and his posse of Fields kicked off Rano Dread's door and killed eight men inside. Rano Dread's life was spared so Jerome could use his influence to organize a grand Christmas dance. Rastamen turned up from all over the city. Chico Red, Menzy, Natty Joe, and many of the original men from the days of Screaming were there. Jerome and his posse turned up at the dance in the early hours of the morning. What followed next was later dubbed the Christmas Massacre. Natty Joe was shot in the belly and three of his men died. The war that Screaming predicted had finally started.

I was now involved in a war that was to see no end. The Rastafarian religion was to take a nose dive inflicted by many scars. Scars that would never heal.

Three months later the war had intensified. There were at least twelve feuds waging amongst the Yard Men. Natty Joe led the major war against the Fields. He was a one-man army, taking no prisoners. His main target was Jerome.

Things became desperate on the streets. Innocent Jamaicans were caught up in the bloody war. There was no longer a choice as to whether or not you wanted to be a Rastafarian. You had to join or be mown down by the warring sectors who all considered their war just.

It reached a point where I couldn't take a shit without having my gun at my side. Whenever I pulled up at a traffic light I had to have eyes in the back of my head. Parties and dance halls were no-go areas.

I finally approached Chico Red to let me have enough money to start my own pad.

"This is not the right time," he said. "I need all the manpower I can get, men loyal to me who are not afraid."

"Living from day to day behind an iron door isn't my scene. I need more out of life," I protested.

"There is no life outside these doors." He paced the floor with his gun in his hand. "Every Rastaman out there is a potential time bomb. I've lived through tribal war. In a few months everyone will settle down to one side or the other, then we'll know exactly who we're fighting."

"Either I get a start or I find my own way out."

"We'll talk about it next week," he said dismissively. "I want you to drive me down to Florida. A Colombian is giving me a good deal on a consignment of marijuana."

I got up from the seat overlooking his bed. "Take care."

"You're making a sad mistake," he shouted as I headed for the front door. "If the Fields don't get you then Natty Joe will."

"I'm not afraid," I yelled without looking back. Sprango let me out of the apartment.

From that hour Chico Red was one of my archenemies. There was regret in some of the men's faces when I walked through the door. Instincts told me they would be there for me should I ever need them.

I went home and called Billy Weinstein. We agreed to meet at eight o'clock that night. He picked me up driving a Cadillac Seville. He seemed to have stumbled into a gold mine. My eyes rested on his diamond-studded Rolex as he curved his hand around the steering-wheel.

We pulled up on the corner of Church and Utica where groups of young men stood on the corners. The lights were on red. Two cars in front a woman sat huddled around a steering-wheel. One of the restless youths smashed the window on the passenger side of her car and made off with her pocket book. The area had gone completely downhill.

Billy had added a few pounds around the belly since his high school days. The sound of Otis Redding crooned softly through the stereo system. He pulled away from the lights.

"I need your help badly," I said.

"We got plenty of time to talk. First we got to find somewhere safe. Walls got ears." He stubbed his cigarette into the ashtray and changed the subject. "I got a woman in my life," he said proudly.

"About time. I was thinking you would end up the other way."

"I had my share of women—just keep it quiet, that's all." He paused and his eyes sparkled. "She's beautiful, Danny, I want you to meet her sometime. Told her all about you. I met her at Dad's funeral. I want to tie the knot in our relationship before anything goes wrong."

"What could go wrong for you? You're already on your way to becoming a lawyer, and with Jack's help nothing can stop you from reaching the top."

There was a smirk on his face. He fell quiet. I just seemed to be punching the wrong keys. Every word offended him.

The lights of the city spun around the car as we headed for Brooklyn Bridge. He drove down by the Hudson where bright lights silhouetting on the bridge stretched over the dark face of the river. On the other side Manhattan in its full glory twinkled under the starless sky.

There was a nip in the air. Billy parked up the car and we walked over to the railings that ran the length of the river bank.

"Beautiful," he said, feasting his eyes on the lighted towers of dreams. "The greatest city in the world. It can all be yours, Danny. This is the only city in the world that a man can own even though it's owned by others. I love it."

The bright lights along the river radiated the pleasure on his face. Beyond his delight I could tell something was eating him up.

"Why you been cutting me off all evening?"

He took a deep breath and held onto the railings with a sense of urgency.

"What is it?" I grabbed him forcefully by the arm of his leather jacket.

"I've got myself involved. How do you think I could buy the car and the house on Long Island and still have money?"

"Hey, slow down. I'm missing the periods."

"Shucks! You always had a way with words." He smiled briefly. "The Mafia propositioned me."

"And you accepted their proposal like a fool," I said harshly.

"Quiet." He looked around nervously.

"They'll be on your back until you're dead once you've accepted their money."

"For Christ's sake, when Dad died he left nothing but bills.

There was just enough money in his account to keep a roof over Mother's head. I had no choice. All your court proceedings they were there. They wanted you to pay for old man Castello."

Memories of the tight white faces that were always present in the courts flashed back in my brain. I remembered thinking at the time they just didn't fit in with the other people in the court. "To save my life you got involved?"

"I love you, kid." He embraced me warmly.

Something moved inside of me. His aftershave lotion rested at the back of my nostrils.

He held me at arm's length. "It's not so bad. They're paying for my college tuition and want me to work for them once I've graduated."

"What about Jack?"

"Jack." He threw his hands in the air. "I've been avoiding him. He's got his hands tied investigating the Rastafarians both here and in Jamaica. They could be a strong nation if they came together and stopped the fighting. Even the Mafia fear them."

"The war is the end of such hopes. With every day the grievances are multiplying. More and more men are arriving from Jamaica and taking sides. I don't want to spend the rest of my days creating enemies and defending someone else's drugs establishment. I want to lead my own posse and sell my own drugs, and if war come my way then the streets of this city will run red with blood."

"Best of luck, you've just turned a man. We're in this together. Before I die I'm gonna live some life, get married, have a few kids, and get rich. Fuck it! Go and lead your posse. I will settle to being led. Who knows what way the wind will blow." He removed an envelope from his breast pocket. "Five grand. You need any more, just ask."

"This is plenty." I was extremely grateful.

"Got something else for you." He walked to the back of the car and opened the trunk. Two lights came on from the side panels.

There in front of my eyes was a brand new AK-47 in a plastic bag. There were five more plastic bags containing marijuana, the smell kept down by the tightly sealed packets.

Billy showed his teeth. "Ten kilos of Colombian Red. That

should be enough to get you started. This batch is on the house. Want any more and it will cost you seventy-five dollars a pound."

My mind started clicking like a calculator. Chico Red was paying $200 a pound, and he had to go all the way to Florida and risk driving it up on the hot 95 North. All I needed was a base and after a few weeks I could undersell Menzy and the other dealers in Brooklyn.

"I knew you'd like the arrangements." Billy squeezed my shoulder.

I returned home and locked myself in the basement. I had the goods. All I needed was some men and an apartment to work from.

That night I hit the streets with preconceived ideas of the men I wanted. My first stop was the Salt and Pepper Club on Utica Avenue. Jamaicans had converted an office space into an exotic club where reggae music played all night and women in the nude performed wonders on the stage. In the dancing area hitched up against a wall with a woman was one of Chico Red's men. He became my first recruit.

My next stop was the Rocking Horse club down on Franklin and Pacific where they had a dingy after-hours joint run by some old Jamaican men who boasted of their days in Jamaica when they roamed with the likes of notorious men like Joe Rigin and Wappy King. The bartenders were old whores from Jamaica, women with long, wicked scars on their faces.

In the club I found one of my deadliest soldiers, a man in his late twenties. His name was City Puss. He was a compulsive gambler, tall, and had a reputation for handling a knife.

In the first week I rounded up eight men. They didn't all come up to the standard of the Fields, but I carried the heart for all of them. Our first target was a Dominican drugs house down on Bergen Street. The men surrendered quite easily after we kicked off their door using all the skills I had picked up from the many raids I had been a part of. The Dominicans were Rastafarians, too. I gave them the choice of being my enemies or working for me. They accepted the latter.

The business kicked off in the first two weeks. I was selling only large quantities which cut down the traffic at the door.

In three months I had bought a new BMW and screwed half of New York City. I was even paying the beat cop $700 a week for turning a blind eye.

Billy was surprised at my ability to move marijuana on a big scale. He was the one who suggested I expand the business. He was right, but first I had to go down to Jamaica and find Destie.

Three days before I left for Jamaica, Sprango, one of Chico Red's soldiers, knocked on the door and asked if he could seek asylum from Chico Red. I debated the offer and finally allowed him to join up. To prove his loyalty he gunned down one of Chico's men on Fulton Street in a fierce shoot-out. Still there was something about Sprango's mannerism that I couldn't come to terms with.

The night before I was to fly out I had dinner with Billy and his fiancée, Henrietta Bosco, in one of Manhattan's posh restaurants. Henrietta had warm blue eyes. Her hair was auburn and rested on her shoulders. She was a supporter of women's lib and a sympathizer of the black liberation struggle. She was one of the many women who attended demonstrations to stop troops from being sent to Vietnam.

"Will you be attending the wedding?" She toyed with her dessert.

"Wild horses couldn't keep me away," I said.

"Can you keep a secret?" Billy smiled happily with his wife-to-be.

"No," I answered jovially. Muzak poured through the speakers in a discreet intimacy.

Henrietta's beautiful face lit up. She squeezed Billy's hand, delighting in what he was going to say.

"Well . . ." He looked around at the expensively clad people sitting at other tables with napkins around their necks to protect their threads from gravy stains. "I'm about to be a father," he announced proudly.

"That's a secret I would never be able to keep." I shared my friend's joy.

"Want a next surprise?" Billy was excited.

"Fire away." The vintage champagne lightened my head.

"You're elected the godfather."

"It won't be the end of the world," Henrietta smiled at the

stunned look on my face. "Someone has to lend a hand when she starts crying."

"She!" Billy exclaimed.

"Yes. She." Henrietta answered firmly. She was a dominant woman and had a delicately beautiful smile that somehow said it all.

"How do I take a girl on camping trips or fishing?" Billy stuttered, careful not to rub her violent side too briskly.

"My dear, you will just have to learn," she said wearily. She left a red mark on his face where she squeezed his cheek. "And let's have no more of your chauvinism," she added firmly.

Billy shrugged. "I forgot to tell you. Henrietta is leading the movement on her campus."

Henrietta crossed her hands on the table. "Do you know this country is more bent on suppressing ideas than Russia? Take the Rastafarian religion. The media are trying to convince the public that they're a set of gun-toting marijuana fanatics."

"I hardly think this is the place for politics," Billy said cautiously, regretting he'd started her off.

"Not politics," she objected.

"More like propaganda," I said.

"Exactly," she agreed.

The waiter returned with yet another bottle of champagne. He looked at my locks with a degree of scorn before popping the cork and pouring some into Henrietta's glass.

"Five hundred bucks," Billy whispered, careful not to let Henrietta hear him bragging about wealth.

The waiter placed the bottle in the ice bucket and gave me another astonished look before leaving the table.

Henrietta raised the flute glass to her lipstick-free lips. "One of these days I would like to hear about your religion," she said curiously.

I gave her a brief introduction—one that seemed to woo her affections.

The following day I was on a plane to Jamaica.

Chapter 25

I spent two weeks in Jamaica, a week longer than I intended. As the plane journeyed through the sky I squeezed Destie's hand, silently admiring her beauty while she slept. I was in a new frame of mind. Everything just seemed to fit into place. The Rastafarian war sweeping New York City was only a reflection of the bloody feuds that had their roots in the ghettos of Kingston, Jamaica.

While the plane drew me closer to the city of dreams and discontent, I felt like I had just graduated from a major college. I realized how Marco Polo must have felt on his return from China or Malcolm X after making his pilgrimage to Mecca. On arriving back in the city I left Destie at my parents' house. I was anxious to see what was happening at the drugs pad. It had been a week since I spoke to City Puss. The business was still in order.

The streets of Brooklyn were crowded with young men, victims of the peace between the gangs. Rastamen walked around in groups of threes and fours in the heat of the afternoon. The war had destabilized them. The screech of tires or the honking of a horn could cause them to pull their guns in quick response.

As I drew closer to the drugs house I was overcome by a sense of foreboding. Something was wrong. I could feel it.

There was a familiar stench that hit me at the back of the nostrils as I entered the apartment building. The residents couldn't distinguish the stink from the million other stinks that filled a place in the grip of depression. The stench was reminiscent of dead bodies rotting in the sun after a night of gang warfare in Jamaica. For a moment I thought I was having a flashback.

The smell of death grew stronger as I neared the apartment door. There was no answer from inside as I knocked the door. My fingers trembled as the key turned in the socket. The security catch had been removed from behind the door. Inside the stench was unbearable. Flies that seemed as big as jumbo planes buzzed about in the putrid air of death. I switched on the light in the passageway. My eyes were gripped by the horror. City Puss was lying in the passageway with two shots in his chest.

I rushed into the living room and all seven of my men were dead. Shot in the head.

How could seven ruthless men be caught off guard and executed in such a manner? There was no sign of forced entry. That meant the killer or killers were known to my men. I turned over the bodies and looked into each man's face. Maggots, fluffy and white, climbed out of the bullet holes in their heads and rats had started gnawing at their features.

I had fallen for the oldest trick in the book. Sprango was not among the dead. He was one of Chico Red's soldiers who had joined up a couple of days before I had left for Jamaica.

The long and evil arms of the world had reached out and forced the final nail into the coffin. Bursting with revenge, I left the apartment. According to the Rastafarian doctrine it was lawful for a Rastaman to shear his locks when uncovering the corpse of brethren.

Shaving my locks was out of the question, but putting a razor to my face wasn't. I jumped on a train up to Forty-Second Street and bought a make-up kit. The next stop was Delancey Street to buy some women's clothes. Later in the evening I drove up to Tilden cemetery and dug up a .45 Ingram that I had oiled and planted.

The following day, while Destie was out job hunting, I dressed in front of the wall-length mirror in the basement. The make-up took me some time to perfect. Dressed in a short miniskirt, black fishnet stockings, and matching stiletto heels, I left the house. The Afro wig actually looked real and hid my dreadlocks.

Dad was outside washing his car when I stepped out of the house. It took him some time to recognize me. His eyes followed me down the block with much scepticism.

I parked up a block away from Chico Red's shop. Men whistled and catcalled as I wiggled my ass down the block. The Ingram rested under my arm, shielded by a thin black windbreaker.

Outside the store was a hive of activity. People milled about bouncing to the sound of soul music blaring from a set of speakers outside the record shop on the other side of the street.

Sprango sat on a car outside the store. He was whittling a piece of wood with a penknife. Jewelry glistened on his fingers. His gray, lustful eyes followed me, undressing me with every step that I took.

There was no doubt in my mind: if he was the traitor he'd surely moved up a rank in Chico's army.

"Hey, girl, whatever you need I can supply it." He got up off the car and took my arm. "A nice girl like you don't need to spend money," he whispered. His face suddenly went hard as I batted my eyelashes flirtatiously and gave him an inviting smile. "Do you have a brother?" he asked.

I shook my head and enticed him with yet another suggestive smile, before lightly tugging away my arm and walking into the shop.

Three men sat behind a bullet-proof screen and served the customers. They looked up, fascinated by my beauty and the aroma of my strong perfume that sweetened the air of stale marijuana.

Sprango rushed in from outside. "She's mine," he barked.

One of the men behind the counter turned down a big ghetto-blaster pumping out some hot reggae music. "Hey, what makes you think such a beautiful girl would want a slob like you? Baby, how'd you like to come around here and have a nice smoke?" I wiggled towards the counter and turned innocently towards Sprango.

"Can't you see it's me the girl likes?" Sprango eased up his yellow pin-stripe shirt to show off the gun resting on his hip.

"There's enough woman there for all of us," said another of the three men behind the counter. He got up and walked towards the door.

The door opened and the strong smell of marijuana and

cherry incense crept around the excited Rastaman as he stood in front of me squeezing his privates.

Sprango held onto my arm as I moved towards the open door as if I were a prized slut. "Play your cards right and you could be onto a good thing." He looked over his shoulder before following me into the room. His hands found my body.

I side-stepped him and did a little shuffle positioning myself so I could have all four of the men in my line of fire. Stunned, they stared meekly down the barrel of the gun as I slipped it from under the windbreaker. "Kiss the world goodbye, Sprango."

He opened his mouth but no words came out. The four men dropped to their knees. In their last moment before slipping into death's eternity they were suddenly aware of their executioner.

The gun kicked and bullets spat out of the muzzle with such force that it threw pieces of the men against the wall in thick blobs. Customers came into the shop and ran back out when they heard the rapid sound of gunfire from behind the screen. Quickly I moved through the back of the store. Chico Red was fortunate not to be there.

I took a bag of money from Chico's office before leaving the store. Outside in the humid breath of summer the residents had hidden behind cars. The sidewalk was deserted. Eyes beamed down on me from a thousand windows. To make my final exit I emptied all the bullets in the magazine, spraying rounds of bullets in the wake of my departure.

The money amounted to a little over $10,000. There was just enough for me to buy a new gun and set myself up in business once more.

The following morning I took Destie to a real-estate dealer on Church Avenue. We picked out an apartment on Parkside Avenue in the Flatbush region.

Four days later we moved in. Most of the money was spent buying Destie new clothes and furniture for the apartment.

Destie was able to get a job working in the city as a key-punch operator. I was confined to the house. Rumor was out that Chico Red had put a contract on my life.

I tried to call Billy on a few occasions but got no answer.

The streets of Brooklyn were loaded with human voltage. Rastamen were riding in posses and swinging guns like the days of the wild, wild West.

"I Cry" suffered their first major setback when an argument started on who should lead the coalition. Sugar Bear insisted that he should hold the position because he led the largest gang. This was strongly opposed by the other leaders, but a handful of them eventually sided with Sugar Bear. This led to a division in "I Cry" with Sugar Bear and his rebels splitting away and taking thousands of dollars of the government funds with them. They were quick to branch out into wide distribution of hard drugs.

The former gang members started to lose faith in "I Cry" when the policies determined in meetings took time to become law. They felt cheated; angered and disillusioned they armed themselves with spray paint and attacked the walls and monuments of the city, resulting in a psychedelic nightmare which was later dubbed the graffiti explosion of the seventies.

The government acted swiftly to this angry backlash and injected more money into making "I Cry" work. The scheme finally took off and the chosen building was located in Manhattan on neutral ground. The youths referred to the building as the "Door" as it symbolized the door of opportunity.

The leaders of "I Cry" ensured that it maintained its black and Hispanic identity and the Suni Gods then became integral members. This coalition was to surpass the gangs and their conflicts in importance in the eyes of the youths.

It was another two months before I set eyes on Billy Weinstein. He was in Baltimore with Henrietta and her family; while there they tied the knot.

Survival on the streets became impossible. I didn't know who to trust. Several times in crowded areas I was involved in shootouts with members of the Fields or Chico Red's men. The latest shoot-out was down in the subway station on Utica Avenue. Three of Jerome's men tried to sneak up on me while I was waiting for a train. I had escaped by shooting one and running through the tunnel. Miraculously I made it to the other side of the tunnel on Sutter Avenue.

While I was in Jamaica I had met up with one of my old friends from the ghetto. His name was Django and he was on the police "most wanted" list. I decided to assist him in gaining entry to the United States. It took me five months to arrange his visa. During that time Billy and Henrietta became the proud parents of a bouncing baby boy. His name was Abraham.

On a cold January morning the plane carrying Django landed at Kennedy Airport. He was nine months my senior and celebrated his nineteenth birthday the following week.

Billy Weinstein sold me two more AK-47s. With Django by my side we quickly acquired a reputation that ranked with the likes of Natty Joe's, who was singlehandedly defeating the Fields.

Billy kept me supplied with consignments of marijuana. I was running a store front on Nostrand Avenue. The main road was healthy for business. Customers would park up outside the store without fear of being robbed in high-rise apartments or down side alleys.

Django became increasingly worried by the state of violence on the streets. He suggested that we send for five more men from Jamaica.

Billy helped me arrange the visas for the men. They were known gunmen, some wanted by the authorities in Jamaica. News of the men coming to join me in the States was on the streets of Brooklyn before the men actually arrived.

The roles of oppression had been switched. No longer did I have to sit around and wait for trouble to come and kick off my door. I had six dangerous men by my side. It was time for me to go out and turn aggressor.

The Rastafarian war, as Chico had predicted, had settled down to some extent. The two major fighting forces in the city were Natty Joe and the Fields.

The FBI got involved when the murder rates seemed to take an upward surge. Natty Joe had become obsessed with killing. There were times when he could have killed Jerome and ended the war. He killed three of the Fields in a shoot-out but spared Jerome's life. He ordered Jerome: "Go and get some more men. This war is just getting sweet."

Jerome did exactly that and disappeared to Jamaica once more and returned with men who shouldn't have been let out of a bottomless pit.

The Smallies once again proclaimed themselves as the peaceful Rastafarians. They sat with FBI officials and discussed at length the ruthless men from the Yard and their activities. The FBI built up a file on the Jamaican Rastas, who they codenamed the "Yardies."

Christmas 1974 Mom cooked a big dinner and invited a few of the neighbors. There was plenty of pork, turkey, and fried fish spread out on the kitchen table. Decorations ran throughout and the apartment rang out with the singing of carols. The neighbors had somehow managed to get Dad drunk. Late in the evening I visited the Weinsteins and my godson Abraham.

"He's growing into a fine boy," Billy said as I held the sleeping infant on my lap.

"He looks more like Henrietta every day," I said.

"Someone called my name?" Henrietta danced into the room holding a baby's bottle.

"I was just saying how much Abraham looks like you."

She curled her fingers around her hair that had grown below her shoulder. "He's even got my hair. But that nose is definitely his father's."

"Thank you. I was beginning to think he was conceived by immaculate conception," Billy said.

"Oh, Billy," she sighed ridiculously.

She took the baby gently from my hands. The birth of the child had changed her outlook on life. She'd abandoned the Women's Lib movement and had settled down to be the good old Jewish wife Billy wanted.

"For someone who wanted a girl, she just sits for hours and stares at him," Billy said.

"Billy! How many times during the night do you wake up to make sure he's still in his cot?"

"You've been spying on me," Billy said.

Abraham had brought sunshine to the Weinsteins' life. They seemed to have everything going for them.

The Christmas holiday was marred when Natty Joe turned on some of his own men and gunned them down at a party.

Django and my men from Jamaica had settled down into the city life. They had girlfriends. Django had a Yankee girl, a treat once denied to West Indians. Rastamen had opened Yankee hearts, forcing them to respect West Indians.

The summer of 1975 promised to be quite prosperous. The war was predictable. I could avoid it as much as I could be actively involved in it.

Billy Weinstein greeted me with some bad news on one of my weekly pick-ups. The striplight in the old warehouse beamed down on the brown packages. "This might be the last of this gear," he said.

"No problem. What next? Panamanian or Mexican Blonde?"

"Wish it was. My people are moving away from the marijuana trade."

"What?"

"Too bulky, smells, and the return just isn't worth the bother. Hard drugs, Danny, that's where the money is. The gangs who once posed a problem on the streets are no longer a threat. The Mob is moving into powder distribution."

I looked down disappointedly at the last of my consignment.

"Listen, the Smallies are cashing in on the sale of hard drugs. Why not do the same? In two years you could clean up and get out of this business once and for all."

"I'm not interested in selling poison. The Smallies are hypocrites. They resent us for turning the gun on each other yet they trade in hard drugs, drink alcohol, and eat pussy. I live on the streets. I see what heroin and cocaine do to people."

"The world is a rat race. Morality is no longer an accepted currency for trade. You got to be one of the rats with a strong instinct to survive. The city is still a jungle but not because skyscrapers have replaced the trees."

"I'll remember that, but I will never handle hard drugs. Robbing a few kilos and selling it once in a blue moon is bad enough."

"I have a contact in Miami that could supply you with grass. The price will be more and you will have to transport it to New York yourself. The roads are hot. So, too, are the airports."

"I'll take the chance. How much more per kilo will I be paying?"

"One hundred, maybe hundred and fifty."

The price was ridiculously high. "How soon can you fix me up with these people?"

"Anytime you ready. I can give them a call and arrange things."

"Right away. I don't want the drought to reach me and can't get any ganga to run any of my five shops."

Billy left the warehouse. Shortly after I followed. Dark days were ahead. Some of the other dealers had already experienced the drought and collapsed.

Django opened the door with a sixteen-shooter in his hand. He'd put on some weight since arriving in the States. He was medium built with thick bushy hair combed backwards. His complexion was dark and he wore the best clothes money could buy. There was a gleam in his eyes when he saw the fresh packages of marijuana that I brought through the door.

The rest of my men were seated in the living-room. The sound system we hijacked from a dance in Connecticut was playing and turned down low. The television was on. Each man had an automatic gun in front of them.

The toilet flushed and gave me a start. "I thought I said no more women in the shop. This is business, not a whorehouse," I protested.

At that moment a man of medium height shuffled into the room wiping his hands on a washrag. Having women in the shop was something we overlooked once in a while, but men were never tolerated.

"This is my good friend from Queens. He once saved my life in Jamaica. He's hot and needs somewhere to hide out for a few days," Django said.

There was something in the man's deep-sunken eyes. He was dark, with blemishes on his face. His hands were rough—a clear sign that he was a gun slinger.

"Teeny Bop." He offered me his hand, then smiled with an air of hatred as I walked off into the next room without accepting his handshake.

Django and two of the men accompanied me into the back room to sort out the consignment. It had to be weighed and mixed with an inferior brand that I kept on hand.

"What the hell's going on?"

"Take it easy," Django said. "The brother is safe."

"Something's not right about him."

Django entreated: "Give him a chance. If in one week you still feel the same way about him then we get rid of him."

"He's not to handle any of the guns. If he go through the door without one of the men accompanying him then he stay out there."

"Fair enough." Django wasn't too happy about the arrangements.

Billy was unable to secure a deal for me in Miami. Faced with the prospects of a dry summer I was forced to indulge in acts of piracy. We robbed some of the Smallies to meet our demand.

The drought had officially hit the city. The Mafia had crushed the ganga trade and flooded the streets with powders.

Four of the shops had to be closed as a result of the marijuana drought sweeping the city. My gang had turned to armed robberies. During Labor Day and the carnival festivities we stuck up all the celebration dances and money-raising functions around Brooklyn.

Finding myself with an excess of women's jewelry from the robberies, I drove over to New Lots. Teeny Bop and three more of my men accompanied me.

Ingrid opened the door. She'd shed her heavy mane of dreadlocks and now sported a curly perm. She looked stunning as she escorted us into the living room. Gone were any traces of Screaming or her Rastafarian past.

"It's been five months since I last saw you." She parted the curtain, flooding the room with sunlight.

Teeny Bop stretched out in an armchair as if he belonged. His eyes rested on Ingrid's long, shapely legs and child-bearing hips.

"Excuse the place, I'm working as an accountant now and have no time to clean. Would anyone care for a cold drink?"

"Sure," Teeny Bop answered quickly.

"Orange juice?" she offered.

"That'll be fine," he said.

Ingrid gave him a warm smile before leaving the room. She returned with a carton of orange juice and five glasses stacked with ice resting on a tray.

Teeny Bop held on to her hand as she gave him his drink. "You're a very beautiful girl," he complimented her.

"I've seen better days." She was bashful.

"Well, no more of that, I'll make it my point of duty to make sure you're dined as appropriate for one so elegant," he said.

Ingrid crossed her hands in front of her and went weak at the knees. She was taken by the smooth-talking rat. She sensed my disapproval by the look on my face.

"My new job is very demanding. I doubt if I would have much time to go out," she said.

Teeny Bop smiled wryly. It was as if he deliberately tried to antagonize me.

"I got something for you." I gave her the bag of jewels, two link chains, a woman's Cartier watch, rings, and bracelets.

Her eyes sparkled. She smiled at each of my men as though thanking them individually. Teeny Bop nodded as if it were he who was making her the present.

I could feel the electricity passing between the two. It grieved me to think that such an undesirable would bed one of my best friends.

The picture of Ingrid smiling warmly with the rat lingered on my mind as I dropped off the men and drove over to Long Island to visit the Weinsteins.

Billy was away on business and Henrietta was at home nursing a Scotch. She was troubled. "Abraham is sleeping." She slipped over to the bar.

"How could he be sleeping at this time of the day?"

"Ssh! I had enough trouble putting him to sleep," she whispered.

"I brought him a present."

"Where will I find room to put all these presents?" She breathed heavily. "And I hope it's not that pony you promised him."

"No, it's just a few books." I handed her a shopping bag with a bunch of books I'd picked up in a shop somewhere in the town.

Abraham strolled into the room dressed in his pajamas and rubbing his sleepy eyes. "Uncle," he said happily.

I met him halfway across the room then picked him up and swung him around. "How are you, tiger?"

"Have you come to take me to the park like you did yesterday?" He was excited.

"Last week," Henrietta corrected. She put her glass on the center table and slumped back into the settee.

"Not today. I have a present for you."

"My horsie?" His eyes were wide and full of childish dreams.

"When Dad gets a bigger house with garden space, then I'll get you that horsie."

"Don't you go encouraging Billy about getting anywhere else. This house is so big I'm afraid of getting lost," Henrietta said.

Abraham planted a kiss on my cheek. "You're the best uncle in the whole wide world."

"Only because he spoils you rotten. Now get back to bed or you won't be getting that pony." She got up and took him upstairs. Shortly after she returned and strolled across the lush gray carpet towards the bar. The living room was exquisitely furnished, with a wood-frame picture window looking out over the wealthy Wasp surroundings.

"Scotch?" Her offer carried an urgent tone.

"My religion forbids the taking of alcohol."

Henrietta already had the glass and poured the drinks. It seemed that what she had to say required the astringent taste of alcohol to thaw her tongue.

She returned with the drinks and seated herself opposite me on a long settee. "Billy!" she said after a moment's silence. "He's been acting strange lately."

"He's always been strange. It will take some time to get used to his ways."

"You've been his friend since high school—maybe you can explain a few things to me. He's been associating with some very rough people. They're not what one would call your everyday businessmen."

"I know nothing of Billy's friends."

"I'm aware of that." She was patient. She took another sip of her Scotch and twirled the ice around in the glass with her finger. "All I wanted in life was a little house, a husband, and a few children. Now I have all this and it doesn't seem real. I'm living a lie. I overheard Jack and Billy talking in this room one night. Jack actually thinks that my family is responsible for all this. Billy married me in Baltimore because he didn't want his brother to know how poor my family are. I was so foolish. I believed Billy when he said his father left him a fortune when he died."

"This is family matters. I would hate to be drawn into the middle."

"This is more than family matters." Her voice was bearing a slight edge. "If Billy's not careful we'll both have to bury him very soon."

"He's on his way to becoming a very successful lawyer."

She looked up angrily from her drink. "Somehow, I don't believe you're as naïve as you claim to be. Three months ago one of the Mafia hit men decided to turn State's evidence against the Bonatto family. His name is Louis Mazonette." Her eyes met mine.

The case about Mazonette had made big headlines, climaxing when he was found dead in his cell two days before he was due to give evidence in front of the grand jury.

Henrietta sat up straight, her bare feet sinking into the carpet. Her toes twitched nervously. "I think Billy has something to do with Mazonette's death," she whispered.

"The man was under Federal guard. There was no way for Billy—or anyone else for that matter—to have gotten to him."

"Billy got to him, somehow. The papers stated that Mazonette died with a letter from his wife in his pocket."

"For God's sake, a note hardly places Billy in any position where he could have been a threat to anyone."

"I found a woman's ring in Billy's pocket wrapped in a white handkerchief. At first I thought he was having an affair with a married woman until I looked closer at the ring. The name J. Mazonette was engraved inside."

"It still don't add up. I think you're getting all worked up for nothing. Have a talk with Billy and hear what he has to say."

"Worked up indeed!" she exclaimed. "Billy went along with Jack to one of his interviews with Mazonette the day before he died."

"If Billy made any false moves Jack would have suspected, so that disproves your suspicions."

She stared into her drink, her eyes watery and glazed. "I don't have much to go on, but one thing I'm certain of. Billy used that ring in some way to intimidate Mazonette." She was annoyed that I didn't share her views.

"Suppose what you say is true, then what?"

She threw up her hands and sighed. "I married him for better or worse. We're in this together. I just wish he'd learn to trust me."

"Give him time, let him sort himself out."

"Billy's weak. He puts up a big front, but he's a coward. I can't just sit around and watch his life go down the drain."

"Let me have a word with him, if that will help. Whatever is chewing him up he'd let me know."

"No." Her face hardened. "Let me handle this. Just stay close in case you're needed." She was a tough woman, tougher than I expected. She was actually thinking of gunpower to save her husband if necessary.

Chapter 26

Business at the shop had hit rock bottom. The last of the marijuana had finished that very day. There was money to buy a few kilos but the supply was not available.

The men sat around with their guns in hand, bored and looking for action. The customers trailed in and out, disappointed at not being able to cop some good grass.

Teeny Bop suggested we rob one of the Smallies down on Empire Boulevard. "He just received a shipment from Bermuda."

Django's eyes sparkled. "What are we waiting for, let's go."

"Not that easy," Bop said knowingly. "He won't open the door for no Rastaman, especially Yard Men."

"No problem. We find a few Yankees to front the move," Django said.

"I got a better idea. Tomorrow my younger brother Carl is getting released on bail from Rikers Island. He used to roll with the Gods on Buffalo Park. He's the right man for the job."

The following afternoon Django drove Bop up to Queens to pick up Carl.

Carl was slightly taller than his brother. He was well dressed and had green stains on his teeth which had earned him the name Jungo. There was something about Jungo that I identified with. He was short on words and had an air of confidence about him.

That night we packed our guns and headed out. The building was in good shape. The apartment was located on the ground floor. The air smelled of disinfectant and the walls were painted cream, with mirrors and flowers along the lobby.

Jungo walked up to the door while we kept a safe distance out of sight. "Neville Springer," he answered after being asked a question from inside. The door opened and Jungo disappeared into the apartment. Seconds after, the door opened once more.

Teeny Bop led the way. Jungo had the tall Dreadlocks by his long manes and pushed a gun into his side.

The apartment smelt of incense and was well furnished. Pictures of Haile Selassie, Marcus Garvey, and reggae artists decorated the freshly painted walls.

The Dreadlocks was led into the back room and slung into an armchair. He put up no resistance and willingly showed us to the marijuana and a quantity of money.

Teeny Bop uncovered a briefcase from behind the settee. There was a hungry glow in his eyes when he opened the briefcase and saw stacks of greenbacks.

The robbery was one of the easiest I had ever been on. It was like taking candy from a baby. We walked along the passageway towards the front door. A gun clicked from behind us.

"Don't move." The frightened Dreadlocks held a snub-nose .38 in his hand.

He stuck us up and brought us back into the living room. His massive hands held the gun with uncertainty. He was faced with a decision of what to do with four men.

Jungo pulled out his gun, sensing that the man had not the nerve to kill us as would have been the option to any Yard Men.

The Dread stared at the gun in Jungo's hand. "Drop it!" he shouted, sweat springing from his pores.

"Fuck you," Jungo growled. "Drop yours before I blow you to the moon."

Teeny Bop looked about the room nervously. Visions of occupying a plot in the cemetery and not being able to spend the money in the briefcase flooded his brain.

The big Dreadlocks quivered as Jungo walked up to him and took away the gun. Tears rolled down his face. He farted and his knees buckled.

Jungo slapped him across the face as he got on his knees and started praying. "Let's get out of here."

We left the Dreadlocks tied up and made our getaway. Jungo proved to me at that point that he was not bloodthirsty. He didn't just take a life because it was there to be taken.

Ten kilos of sensemelia and $9,000 were taken from the Smallies' crib. The drugs lasted five days, then the customers had to be turned away.

It was a cool Saturday night. The heat had abated and the night came with a hint of winter building up beyond the Canadian Arctic.

There was a dance on at Buffalo and Rochester. This was a territory beyond the bounds of the Fields. Natty Joe was fairly popular in the area. He wasn't so much liked as feared.

The night was to bring many surprises. Ganga was burning, music was volcanic. The dingy apartment building was packed. People had spilled on the landings and stairwell.

The atmosphere was tense. Men were arriving in posses.

Teeny Bop strolled up the stairs with Ingrid by his side. I couldn't believe my eyes when I saw her holding onto his hand. I had no desire to possess Ingrid physically; she was like a sister I never had.

They came to a stop where my men were standing. Ingrid gave me a kiss on the cheek, somehow knowing I was hurt to see her with Teeny Bop.

I was so hurt and worked up that I didn't see Menzy walk down the hallway with a posse of men dressed in three-piece suits and expensive beaver hats. His hand lighted on my shoulder, the smell of expensive men's cologne rested at the back of my nostrils.

"I want to have a word with you." He gave Teeny Bop a dirty look from the corner of his eye.

My men quickly moved into position ready to pull their guns should the situation call for it.

"We got no war, Danny. We're from the old school." His eyes made four with Teeny Bop and they stared heatedly at each other for a moment.

We walked a short distance down the hallway. Menzy put a hand on my shoulder. "Be careful how you're moving with that rat Teeny Bop. He's an informer."

Instinctively, I looked down the hallway. Teeny Bop was staring at me. He was definitely uneasy.

"My good friend is doing twenty-five to life as a result of him turning State's evidence." He paused. "Time's changing, Danny. It's getting harder for a man to run a business because of the Fields and Natty Joe. I'm looking for a few good men to help rid the city of their filth."

"Leave it to the police, that's their job."

"No, our job. I already have the backing of many Jamaican people both young and old who are willing to back me in forming a posse to wipe out the Fields. Nothing will be able to touch this force once it is erected."

"Menzy, I have always respected you as an elder but it seems like I'm always hearing this kind of talk. I rejected it then and I'm rejecting it now. I stand alone."

"This might be the last chance you will ever get. Big things are at stake. Mass shipments of marijuana from Jamaica on a scale never before seen. I am offering you a chance to be one of my men, one of the Renegade Posse."

"I'll take my chances in the wide ocean like the little fishes."

"When you get tangled up in the net don't come running." He strolled off towards the dance and led his men inside.

Teeny Bop slipped away with Ingrid shortly after Menzy entered the dance.

The following weeks witnessed a massive surge of support in favour of the Renegades. The Jamaican public was behind them. They ensured security where the Fields and Natty Joe had often threatened death and insecurity.

After a while, I was forced to acknowledge the good that the Renegade Posse were performing. Their numbers had quietened down the activities of the Fields.

Natty Joe was finally picked up on two murders and a rape charge. He was in Sing-Sing while cooling his heels and ordering the executions of anyone that would stand up against him in court.

Six months after establishing themselves the Renegades moved into the sale of hard drugs.

Reggae music came to Madison Square Garden at the end of fall 1975.

Django and I went to see Bob Marley, whom we knew personally from living in the same tenement yard.

With little opposition the security guards led us around the back to Bob Marley's changing room. Bob quickly excused the make-up artists and stragglers who were in his changing room.

"Django." Bob embraced him warmly.

"This is Danny Palmer," Django said.

Bob stepped back and rubbed his chin. "He's taller than me. How's Mom? I still have the scar where she hit me with the frying pan for making music in the yard."

"She's fine. She talks about you all the time," I said.

"We don't have much time, I'm on in fifteen minutes. My brothers, we must eat from the cup of peace. In this troubled time such an occasion may never come around again." The chalice was already loaded and sitting on the dresser. Bob's eyes near popped out of his head when we removed our guns from our waist and put them on the table. He looked down at the weapons and his eyes filled with tears.

He shook his head. "It was a terrible day when that instrument was invented. This is the reason why I sing, not for the money or the fame. When music hits you man you feel no pain. I hope to warm the hearts of man and stop them killing each other." He chanted a short psalm and offered me the chalice.

I passed the chalice to Django. He in turn handed it to Bob. The smoke was thick in the room when Bob took the pipe. Hungrily, he filled his lungs. Suddenly the water sprinklers in the ceiling exploded and showered down water on our heads. The smoke had set off the alarm. "Jah!" Bob shouted and burst out laughing. We all laughed.

Bob went on stage dripping wet. He preached his message of peace to the thousands of people who turned out to see him.

The marijuana drought lifted in the winter of that year. The market witnessed the beginning of Jamaican ganga. Through one of Jungo's contacts I was getting a steady stream of supply from the Bronx. Business was slow until the Yankee customers were weaned off the chemicalized marijuana they'd been smoking through the drought.

On a cold day in February 1976 tragedy hit a group of people standing at a bus stop in Queens. Dave Green walked down the block and mowed down fourteen people. Nine died and the others were critically injured and taken to hospital. The police finally shot him when he barricaded himself in a house. It was not until Dave Green died that I realized how much he meant to me. What a waste of a great man's life . . . He was more than a hero to me, he was a source of inspiration to me; he made me proud I was a Jamaican. The void left by his death caused an ache of despair in all who had known him, and his sacrifice was so futile, he was a pawn in a war that all decent men opposed.

Dave was not just an inspiration to me, he symbolized black achievement to all those underprivileged youths who, without such inspiration, could see no way out of their ghetto lives but for crime. Dave had been respected by the most ruthless in the gangs and the weakest of the victims alike, but the white man's world had taken him, wasted him in macabre theater. They left him a phantom to moan on the winds of desolation. This wounded me, but the hurt was replaced by a bitterness that I could only appease through crime, which I now embraced with new fervor.

Billy Weinstein was committed to the Mob—hook, line, and sinker. Dinner had just finished and we retired to his private study. He walked behind his desk and pulled a brown package from out of a drawer. Eagerly he poured four grams on the glass surface of the desk. His nostrils opened and closed as the white dust disappeared from the table. He sat back, lost momentarily, while the drug raced to his brain.

I could only watch in amazement as he got up and walked to the bar and poured two large glasses of Scotch. "What's the deal? You know my religion forbid the drinking of alcohol."

"Cut the shit. Your religion forbid many things but do you go by all the rules?" His voice was edgy. He walked over and forced the drink in my hand. "Henrietta told me you shared cozy drinks with her while discussing me."

"Wasn't exactly cozy." I took the drink.

He stood over me. "And what do you think?"

"It's not my business to think."

He drained the drink quickly and stared bitterly at the empty glass. "You believe I had something to do with having the scum knocked off." He squeezed the glass tightly and slung it against the wall, tearing a picture of his father above a fireplace. "I'm glad I helped to get rid of the slime. He was about to blow the cover on every racket this side of the river." He shoved his hands in his tailor-made slacks and walked about the room. "Organized crime runs this city, not the Mayor or the President or any goddamn commissioners. Criminals, for Christ's sake. Men who can hardly read and write, men who can't write a million yet own billions. I'm part of that syndicate and sooner or later you'll be too."

"That's where you're wrong. I'm part of me, no one else. My days of being used are over. No Chico Red or Renegades or anyone for that matter's going to control me. I'm a free man."

"What d'you really know about the Renegades?" he asked.

"They're just another set of exterminators set loose on the city."

"That's part of it. They were put together by none other than Mr Mazonetti, who also propositioned Super Dice to start the gang wars."

"I think you got it wrong. Menzy don't have such contacts."

"Do I? This Menzy was hand-picked by Mazonetti to execute your friend Screaming because he was thought to be dangerous."

"What did Screaming have to do with all this? He was no threat to anyone." I was completely bewildered.

"That's where you're wrong again. Screaming was the only man that could keep the Rastafarians together. Notice that soon after Screaming's death the war started. Mazonetti was afraid that if the Rastafarians united they would control the sale of hard drugs on the street."

"The Renegades," I mused bitterly. They'd won the confidence of the Jamaican people then turned their guns on them when they reached where they wanted to go.

"Mazonetti gave them the name as a joke. Named them after the Apache Indians who became renegades. The marijuana flooding the streets from Jamaica is no fluke. The syndicate is using the island as a ship-out point for cocaine. Four years ago the syndicate became involved in the island. The government allowed them a free ticket to export marijuana in return for their foreign exchange. Hidden in those shipments of marijuana is the cocaine." He walked over to the bar and removed another glass, then poured himself a drink. "What I've told you should be kept in strict confidence. Jack allowed me to listen to a few tapes made by Mazonetti. He thought the experience would come in handy to me one day."

"It's my duty to waste the fraud, Menzy." I was bitter, remembering how he tried to get me to join his posse.

"Take it easy, Danny. Menzy is already on the cards. He's running too hot, the Feds have a dossier on him a mile long."

"I want him to die the same painful death that Screaming suffered."

"I will personally see to that." Billy was serious. He'd got the truth of his information from his brother so there was no doubting what he was saying.

The Renegades were the second Jamaican posse to be formed in the States. They controlled large consignments of marijuana and made it available to those loyal to them. They ruled the Brooklyn area with an iron hand. Their numbers far outnumbered the Fields, who were diminishing daily. Some of the Fields deserted and joined up with the Renegades.

The Mafia were once again in the driving seat. There were no gangs to interfere with their business ventures. They had one of the strongest posses in their pockets and also some former gang members who had survived the Family.

As the drugs problem increased Jack Weinstein was elected Assistant Attorney General. He was now the nation's number three man in law enforcement. He expanded the dominion of the FBI and set up a special task force to fight organized crime.

Teeny Bop had secured a firm relationship with Ingrid, who was expecting his baby. They rented an apartment in Staten Island. Bop journeyed to Brooklyn every day. He brought with him fresh ideas of places and people to be robbed. I went along with his ventures. They were after all a source of income.

Slowly Bop introduced a few of Natty Joe's men who were experiencing difficulty as a result of their boss being in jail.

The men, though extremely dangerous, proved to be quite awkward on jobs. They were like babies tripping over their shoe strings.

Teeny Bop started to regret bringing in Natty Joe's men who

were now left out on many jobs yet shared the profits. Grievance brewed within the four walls of my drought-stricken drugs house.

The weapons were set out one Saturday night shortly after Natty Joe's men had left the apartment to go to a dance in Queens. There was a news flash on the television that interrupted the Groucho Marx show. The female newscaster announced: "Two police officers from the 71st Precinct were seriously wounded when members of the Rastafarian sect opened fire on them. Two men are now in custody, one critical in hospital. The two officers are Detective Sergeant McCarthy and his partner, Officer Polaski."

There was complete silence in the room as the newscaster announced the names of the men involved in the shooting.

One was Lenny Chang, the same man who pulled a gun on Screaming on the instructions of Rano Dread. Chang had set up dealing drugs in the Brownsville area. They were said to be in constant conflict with the Yankees in the area.

That night Ingrid's aunt held a party down on Avenue A. Teeny Bop only went to functions where he felt safe. The party turned out to be quite nice.

On the way home we dropped off Django at his girl's house in Bushwick. Teeny Bop was at the wheel. A reggae eight-track was pumping music through the heavy back speakers. He pulled up at the lights on Empire and Utica. The lights from the White Castle hamburger joint and the Kentucky on opposite corners shone into the car.

"That's my watch," I shouted.

Teeny Bob quickly one-handed the steering-wheel and shook down his shirt over the piece of jewelry. "I bought it in a pawn shop." He was agitated.

The watch was mine without a doubt. I had fallen asleep one afternoon when some whores were in the back of the store. When I woke up the freaks were gone; so, too, was the watch. The watch was solid gold and came from a gambling house robbery. The previous owners had offered $5,000 for its return. "To eat from one's vineyard is sweet to the soul but to steal from thy brethren is bitter to the belly."

Teeny Bop's face hardened. "You threatening me?"

"Take it any way you want."

"So what if it is yours anyway? It was me who set up the robbery that it was taken from."

His impertinent outburst caused me to reach across and grab him. The car jerked to a stop in the middle of the road. Quickly, I slipped out my gun.

Jungo reached over from the back seat and held onto the weapon. "He's my brother, Danny. Chill out, please."

"I had a friend who once told me that when you draw your gun always make sure to use it."

Teeny Bop shrugged and pulled off.

"Let this one ride, Danny. Me and you are too close to let a little thing like a watch come between us. I personally will stick up a jewelry shop and get you a watch. Monday morning go to any jewelers and choose a piece. I'll walk right in there and get it for you."

I replaced my gun knowing that one day I would have to take this man's life.

Teeny Bop knew that once he crossed me his days would be numbered. He was also uneasy about Menzy and feared the Renegades would try to gun him down. He eventually moved to Staten Island where he linked up with a big drugs dealer. Shortly after, he returned to Brooklyn and set up the dealer's house to be robbed.

Chapter 27

It was a cold December night in 1976 when me and three of my gang crossed over into Staten Island. The drug dealer on the ground floor of Teeny Bop's building was expecting a shipment of marijuana.

I was uneasy because this dealer had a Great Dane as big as a horse. Men of any size I could stand, but not dogs.

"Don't worry about the dog. I'll rip him apart with my bare hands." Django was confident.

No matter what anyone said my mind wasn't on the robbery. I was relieved when we drove up to the parking lot in front of the building and the dealer's car was out.

We got out of the car and marched up to the building. I knocked on the door and waited. There was no answer, not even the sound of the dog barking could be heard. We returned to the car and waited in the cold. Two hours later the dealer still hadn't arrived. I decided to put off the robbery until the next day.

Django spurred the car into action and we rolled off through the quiet streets of Richmond.

"Jack up. I need some cigarettes," one of the gang said.

The shop was on the main road behind a bus stop where people with their heads pulled down below their coat collars stood shivering, at the mercy of the cold.

A bell over the top of the door rang as we entered the shop. Behind a counter stood a frightened-looking man in his late twenties and as white as the snow at the top of the North Pole. He shifted about nervously as we walked about the shop. There were a few white customers inside the shop. They left the premises as soon as we entered. One woman was cashing out and left everything on the counter.

I picked up a handful of candy bars for Destie, and Django ordered some cigarettes. One of my men, Smiley, stood near the door. He'd never gotten used to the cold and he was shivering like he was on dope.

Django stood by the counter and was reaching inside his pocket for his wallet. "Why you looking so nervous?" he asked the store assistant.

"Nothing." The assistant's eyes rested on me, then Smiley.

"The son of a bitch done pressed a silent alarm." Django reached over the counter and grabbed the man in his chest, pulling him over the counter. He held the man with one hand and pulled his gun. "Get out of here," he commanded.

"What about you?"

"I can take care of myself."

As I stepped out of the store a cop jumped out of a car parked in the middle of the street.

"Don't move!" He crouched in shooting position and leveled his gun at me.

Visions of prison and seedy jail cells plagued my mind. The only solution was to run. The cop was about ten yards away. His eyes made four with mine seconds before I did a ninety-degree turn and ran.

The cowering people at the bus stop stopped him from shooting me in the back. I didn't know that at the time. My feet took to the wind and I ran faster than I'd ever run in my life. The stillness of the night was broken by the sound of gunfire. A bullet whistled past my ear as I ran down the long block. Two more shots. I was actually laughing even though the next bullet could terminate my lease on Earth.

The world was spinning fast. Sirens howled in the night. The rhythm of the bullets suddenly changed. They were bad boys' bullets; not cop-trained bullets, but wild, untamed bullets—reckless and lethal. Hell was breaking out behind me, but still my feet made haste. Tired, I jumped over a fence and landed in a forest in someone's backyard. Lights went on in houses. Soon the sound of dogs and sirens were screaming for my blood. The forest was dark and with every step I took I fell over. I stumbled in the darkness following a light that would surely lead me out of the forest of junk booby traps. The sound of the dogs was getting closer.

I finally exited on the other side of the forest. I was entwined in all manner of obstacles. While I fought to free myself, lights flickered down the road. They drew closer. The sound of the dogs came from the same direction as the lights.

I turned around to run but found myself staring down the barrel of a gun.

"Move a muscle and I'll kill you, so help me God." The cop's voice was frightened. His hands shook; he was afraid. Blood poured from a wound on his head. It was the same cop that had ordered me to stop when I came out of the store.

The flashing lights at the end of the street drew closer and brightened the faces of angry white folks with dogs straining on leashes. The slime of vengeance dripped from the dogs' mouths as they barked and howled for some nigger meat.

"I'm taking him in," the cop declared.

"No, let's have him," a hefty white woman with a dog shouted.

"Lynch him. Make an example of him for any other niggers coming over here to rob," shouted a man. The lights shining on their faces made them look ten times meaner. The street was long and deserted. Police sirens in the distance were getting louder. The hornets' nest had been disturbed.

The cop fired his gun in the air which frightened and stunned the lynchers. The dogs barked even louder.

"He will be brought to justice," the cop warned.

"Our justice," a man hollered.

At that time I was praying for the cop to put me in his car. Approaching from the other side were more vigilantes. Many of those people had run away from black folks on the other side of the river. They weren't about to tolerate their bullshit on their island.

"Get in the car," the cop barked.

He didn't have to say it twice. Keeping my eyes on the angry faces I made my way to the car. The back door was already open. The cop slammed it as I slid inside.

The crowd circled the car and threatened to turn it over. Sledgehammers started beating on the car's bodywork.

The cop fired two more shots into the air. "You're all decent, law-abiding citizens. Don't get blood on your hands. The law will handle him."

"And let him go," shouted one.

"I give my word this one will pay," the cop shouted. He then referred to members of the group by their personal names, appealing for them to look at the situation rationally.

The crowd, after much persuasion, finally allowed the cop to take me in. As the car drove away and the lanterns faded in the dark the angry crowd became history, a nightmare that could only happen in a bad dream.

The car sped off down the lonely streets with a makeshift light on the top and sirens whining. The sirens attracted other police vehicles that joined the rush to jail.

More crowds had gathered outside Richmond police station. Some were dressed in their night clothes. It was as if they wanted to make sure that I was actually delivered to the station.

One million pigs surrounded me. They didn't book me in, my feet never touched the ground. I was whisked through the brightly lit station up a flight of stairs to a cage slightly bigger than a one-man shower unit. The cage was situated in the center of the room where the cops could observe me from all four sides.

The cop who arrested me was in a daze. He had been that way ever since he had been fired at. He stood at the front of the cage with blood pouring down his face onto his green army jacket. "Three of your friends are dead and one of my men is in the hospital on the critical list. If he dies then you can surely expect to get the chair."

"He's gonna get it anyway," said another of the many cops who stopped by the cage to intimidate me. "I heard the distress call from the other side of the bridge."

"What happened?" asked one cop.

"I responded to a store's SOS. Seems like this place has been held up quite a few times. When we arrived on the scene this man alighted from the store. I thought he was the only one inside. I ordered him to stop and fired two warning shots over his head. The next thing I knew bullets were raining down on me. I ducked behind a Cadillac and some son of a bitch tried to shoot me through the car."

Cops were arriving from all over the city. They were dragging in any black people they saw on the streets of the island.

They brought in one black man in his late teens. I had seen him standing at the bus stop when I entered the store.

"We arrested him in the area. He looks lost, could be the look-out man," one of the four cops manhandling the youth shouted.

They threw him in the same cage as me. He dropped on his knees, frightened out of his wits. "Please, brother, tell them I had nothing to do with this."

"What you talking about?" I answered.

The cops quickly disappeared, leaving us alone, hoping they would see something in the video camera trained on the cell and hear something through the bugging devices placed where we couldn't see them. All cops' stations were the same. I had been in enough of them to know their tricks.

Somehow I knew the cops were bluffing. The angry looks on their faces alone told me the other men had gotten away.

Two detectives walked up to the cell wearing long trench coats. "The officer you shot is now dead. Both of you men will be facing the electric chair."

The man in the cage with me pleaded: "I was waiting on a bus. I had nothing to do with what happened."

Cops continued to stream into the station, each one stopping to take a look at the cop-killers.

"Nigger, you gonna fry," said one pig.

"Rastafarian," said another.

"Just let me get my hands on him," said another.

This kind of activity continued until late into the night when a man with medium build and dark hair marched into the room. He was quiet and his eyes said it all. He just stood there digging me out with his cold eyes.

The cop who arrested me returned. "Give me someone I can contact for your friends in the morgue."

"Let the dead bury the dead," I answered.

The other man was released and I was taken into a room for the five-star treatment. The beating was severe, worse than I had witnessed at the hands of Batman and Robin. The beating lasted until the early hours of the morning when the cops decided that they weren't going to get any answers.

In the morning I was rushed to Richmond criminal court. The police had lied about my friends being shot. They all got away and I was left holding the bag. Mom and Destie were in court. Bail was set at $50,000. Mom only had fifteen hundred bucks.

That afternoon four other prisoners brought there earlier from Rikers Island and I were slung into a solid iron van known as a sardine can.

The driver was in a separate compartment. We were handcuffed in the back and given slight glimpses of the free world through a strip of glass in the side of the van.

The driver used the ferry over to Manhattan, then drove up to the Supreme Court where we were taken out and put into temporary holding cells.

I stood at the bars listening to men screaming for one reason or another. Through the screams someone shouted my name.

"Danny!"

"Yo, who's that?" I asked.

"You'll find out soon enough," the voice answered in a coarse Rastafarian dialect.

I knew this would be a prelude to some of the dangers that awaited me on Rikers Island.

"Where's your friend Bringle?" the voice inquired.

"What's that got to do with you?" I asked, remembering that Bringle had skipped the country shortly after Patrick's death.

"Bringle killed my friend and if I can't get him you're going to pay," the voice threatened.

A few prisoners friendly to my enemy shouted: "Hey, Rass, what's up? You got problems?" He was clearly popular among the Yankees and Puerto-Ricans.

"That new jack killed my Homeboy," he shouted.

"Hey, Chips, man, just chill. We rock his world when we get on the Island."

It was then I realized who my enemy was. It was one of

Jerome's soldiers known as Chippy, a short sunken-eyed man looking like he was undernourished.

Later in the night all the prisoners were shackled and taken in green buses to Rikers Island.

The city of my dreams faded out of sight. It was like a dream. The bodies that floated around in the cold night air were like intruders from outer space. They didn't belong outside and I didn't belong in that stuffy cigarette-choking van headed for a dank island.

Fortunately for me none of my enemies were in the van. The driver pulled up at a checkpoint before crossing the long bridge that connected Queens to the island.

The jail was in the distance. Bright bulbs lit up its different sections and also the cells where the prisoners had painted their bulbs blue and orange. It was like motel rooms at a lay-by station.

"We home," shouted one prisoner as the bus pulled up outside the jail.

Guards came out of the jail to meet the bus and escort the prisoners inside. Two at a time, the men were taken off the bus and led inside.

The distinctive smell of prison greeted my nose as I entered the building; the smell of captivity. The reception area was made up of three bull pens and some smaller cells for keeping the bug-outs and transvestites. The officers' desk was directly in front of the cells.

In one of the bug-out cells was a Rastaman in a straitjacket on the ground. It took some time for me to recognize him. It was Rano Dread. He was heavily drugged.

The new prisoners were thrown into one bull pen. The men who went from there to court in the morning were quickly processed and sent to their divisions.

The new jacks had to see a doctor and get processed before being allocated to divisions. Two at a time the men were taken from the bull pen, stripped, and given a robe to put on, then hurried in front of the doctor who took their blood and sent them back to the bull pen. Finally all the men were given a set of blue pants and shirt. Size didn't matter. Once dressed in the prison clothes we were marched into a hallway.

"Drop your pants and spread your cheeks," a black officer demanded.

"I ain't mooning for no one," one prisoner protested.

The CO walked over to him: "We ain't here to play games, sucker." He pounced on the man, aided by some more officers from the reception area. The man lay unconscious and bleeding on the ground when they had finished with him.

The COs walked down the line looking into every man's ass. Why was a mystery to me at the time. I later found out that men smuggled drugs up their butts.

After the shakedown we were led through a series of corridors to the Threes building. The new jacks were kept in Three Upper. Three Main was for the faggots and Three Lower was the segregation unit.

A CO buzzed the door and let us into the division. He was in a little control box surrounded by glass overlooking the cells. He gave each man a bag containing two sheets, toothbrush, toothpaste, a box of Bugle Boy tobacco, and cigarette papers.

The prisoners were at their doors catcalling and whistling as we made our way to the cells.

"You mine," shouted a husky voice of someone beating at the door.

"They got some fine bitches come in tonight," shouted another.

I was put in the same cell as a white youth who'd received the five-star treatment in the bull pens earlier. The cells were dirty and smelled terrible. I was on the side where I could see red lights from the landing strip on LaGuardia airport.

"Which bed you want?" the white youth asked nervously.

"The top one." I threw down my bedding.

"Looks like you're in bad shape."

"Don't look too good yourself."

He sighed. "I was beaten up in the bull pen." He offered me his hand. "My name is Bernie Pykett."

"Danny." I avoided his handshake and continued to spread the sheets over the bed.

That night I was overcome by hot and cold flashes. My body ached. I cowered under a horse blanket smelling of vomit and urine.

Late into the night I found sleep. Early in the morning I was woken by the sound of running water.

Bernie stood by the sink near the door. He was throwing water on his face and was dressed only in a pair of underpants.

The door knocked and a sour looking Puerto-Rican and a big black man stood looking through a strip of Perspex.

"Hey, superman, what's going down?" the Puerto-Rican asked.

Bernie quickly moved away from the sink and took his blues from the bed.

"Look at that girl wiggle. She mine." The Puerto-Rican was excited.

"I saw her first when she got in last night. Ain't that right, babes?" the black man said.

"Let's get the breakfast served. We can sort the girl out later," said another. The men ogled Bernie with intent before walking away.

Bernie was in his late teens with pimples on his face. He had shoulder-length hair and was quite tall. He gave a start as the door knocked and an ugly face smiled at him.

"Don't worry about those guys. They just having a laugh." The man had crooked teeth and was extremely black. His hair was short and rolled up like black pepper grains.

Bernie smiled nervously. Overcome by fever, I allowed myself to fall back in the bed.

"Would you like a cigarette?" the man asked in a friendly yet deceitful tone.

"Thanks." Bernie walked over to the door. He bent down and picked up a pack of cigarettes from under the bottom of the door.

"Keep it," the man said.

"Why, thanks," Bernie said delightedly. He'd made a friend, a thick, hefty one at that.

"Anything you want, just call me. My name is Face. I'm the number one on the house gang. Before I go, you want some cookies, soda pop, or candy bars?"

"Thanks, Face. I'll be fine." Bernie clenched his fist and smiled happily.

"Anyway, chill out, I got to rush. The breakfast is coming up." Face shuffled away from the door.

Bernie started whistling. He was confident, set on top of the world by the smooth-talking Face.

Twenty minutes later the doors opened for breakfast. I was in pain. The fever had taken charge of me during the night. Bed bugs and the unsanitary condition in the cell had also caused a rash to come up on my skin. Outside the cell men were screaming and chattering loudly.

Six prisoners dressed in white jackets stood over a hot plate near the control desk. The prisoners walked like zombies down the rows of cells. A queue had built up. I was about the eighteenth man in line. Bernie was before me.

Cold and shivering, I wrapped myself in the horse blanket from the bed. The line moved fast.

"Take care of my main man Bernie." Face smiled and emptied a ladle of grits into someone's tray.

"Any friend of yours is a friend of mine." The smiling Puerto-Rican gave Bernie two extra squares of butter.

Face stacked six slices of bread on Bernie's tray. "Don't worry. As long as I'm here you safe."

Bernie strolled off into the day room that was located beside the control box. He was smiling and bopping like a soul brother.

Face gave me a dirty look as I stood over the bread waiting for another slice. "Move on. One slice per man." He rocked his shoulders like a sumo wrestler.

I reached down and picked up three more slices.

"Hey, sucker, put that back." Face stepped around the counter.

"Let him be," said one of the house gang, a heavy-set good-looking man with a skifel haircut. "Man, you know those Rastas don't eat meat. Nothing wrong with letting the Dread have a little extra."

Face shook his head with an air of "I'll sort you out later."

The day room was slightly bigger than a double bedroom, with iron tables and benches secured to the floor. One side of the day room was a wall-length Perspex glass looking into the control room. There was a television on a stand and four high windows with bars.

There were only three white prisoners in the room. The others were either black or Puerto-Ricans. Instinctively the white prisoners sat on one table, each cowering in fright after having been solicited by the ass-hungry house gang.

The CO allowed us enough time to eat then ordered us back to the cells. He came out of the control box and shut each door, then turned on the radio that ran the length of the passageway outside the cells.

Bernie got on his bed with his shoes on. He crossed his legs and munched some chocolate-chip cookies while reading a paperback novel Face had given him earlier.

Feebly, I climbed up on the top bunk and looked out through the bars into a thicket where a red light flashed and the sound of airplane engines whirred in preparation for take off.

The sheet was just going over my head when Face started beating down the door. He'd turned into the exorcist. His ugly hippopotamus black face peered through the door. He was in a rage.

Bernie jumped from the bed and walked over to the door. He had a broad smile on his face, unable to comprehend what he'd done to upset Face.

"Yo, Homes, you got my cigarettes and cookies?" Face asked.

"I thought you said I could have them," Bernie said nervously.

"Have you gone crazy, motherfucker? Ain't nothing free in jail. Two for one or you got to bend over."

Bernie was confused. He stuttered: "I got some money coming in a few days. I can pay you back all I owe you."

Face was having none of that. His sodomite eyes sparkled. "Man, your ass is mine."

"Fuck that shit," Bernie protested, feeling secure behind the door.

Face was mad. "Hey, mighty whitey, you gonna pay for that." He looked down the passageway. "Yo, CO, crack number eleven cell."

There was a click and the door moved aside aided by Face's heavy hands. He moved around the cell like Muhammad Ali, boxing Bernie about the place. Four members of the house gang stormed in and helped him.

"Let's take him in the showers," shouted one.

"I'm first." Face had Bernie in a mugger's yoke.

"Rass, we know you brothers are religious so we ain't gonna disrespect you none or we'd fuck him right here," said the tall member of the gang with the skifel haircut. They dragged Bernie through the door, down the passageway, and into the shower opposite the day room.

I jumped off my bed and looked towards the control box. The CO had his head turned towards the next division on the south side.

Bernie's screams could be heard coming from in the shower. Ten minutes before they let us out for lunch they returned him to the cell. He walked over to the toilet and emptied his guts into the bowl.

The house gang came to the cell door and laughed as Bernie retched his guts out.

The CO came around at one stage, took a look at Bernie, and walked away.

Bernie sat on the floor staring into space. His world had been shattered. He didn't go out to eat at lunch time, he just sat on the floor rocking and staring into open space.

After lunch the doors were shut once more until three o'clock when we were let out for association in the day room.

Face came to the cell and ambushed Bernie as soon as the door opened. They disappeared into one of the empty cells at the bottom of the division.

The other two white guys in the day room were set upon by the house gang. One saw an opening and dashed out of the day room. He beat against the Perspex on the control-box window. "Get me out of here," he demanded.

The CO turned his head and peered at him through a pair of tinted sunglasses, his face impassive.

The house gang walked out of the day room as cool as a cucumber and bashed the youth in front of the CO, who again saw nothing. They dragged the screaming youth off to the showers and raped him repeatedly.

The abuse on Bernie lasted for four days. He finally ended his life in the middle of the night. The stench of blood awakened me in the morning. Bernie had cut his wrist and bled to death during the night. I started beating and kicking the door.

The night CO came around and took a look in the cell. He called for back-up before entering the cell. Blood washed the floor and soaked the sheets on the bed.

They put me in another cell and took away Bernie's body. The cell was locked up until an investigation was made.

The daily routine was always the same. Every night new men were brought in and some of the old ones got released on bail or moved on to other divisions.

I was alone in a cell near the control box. The rash on my skin had gotten worse. The flu had completely taken over my body with no signs of abating. Face allowed me a few extra squares of butter to put on my skin.

The days were long and cold. I waited for a letter from Destie. There was none. I was sick, appalled by the way men slept with each other in a way I never thought possible.

One week in the division and I was beginning to feel like I was alone in the world. I started to wonder if the cop had shot me that night and I had woken in hell. The sound of men screaming filled my brain. Outside was dark and only the red light from the airport's runway flashed. I wanted to escape. I prayed for one of the planes to crash on the building.

It was after nine one night when the CO slid my door open: "I've got one of your Rastafarian brothers to put in here."

A broad, smiling, coffee-colored man stepped into the cell. He had a limp and was quite tall. He chucked his pillowcase with his bedding on the bunk below.

"Have fun, Burke." The CO hurriedly shut the door and stood outside looking in through the Perspex.

Burke kicked the door. "Stinking piece of shit. While you're here fucking around looking into people's asses someone is fucking your wife."

"What's your problem?" the CO asked angrily.

"It hurts that I can't take a scum like you and push my gun under your chin and pull the trigger, feel your warm blood come running down."

The CO sniggered. "Being a Rastaman won't always save you from things that can happen to you inside here."

"Fuck you and your band of house gang budi-bandits. I've

got something for either man or beast, and don't give a fuck neither."

The CO smiled at him and strolled off, his footsteps making sticky sounds down the passageway. Burke looked up at me: "Brother, it seems like you were run over by a truck."

"Some cops beat me then I caught a cold here in the cell."

"Put down for sick in the morning and they'll give you some medication." He gritted his unusually large teeth as a pain seemed to surge through his body. He then put a foot on the toilet bowl and pulled up his strides around his ankle. His ankle was swollen and turned blue. "I was in a shoot-out with some cops on Fulton Street. The bullet is lodged in the bone. The doctor says I might have to cut off the leg. I would rather die." He shook off the pain and removed the horse blanket from his bed and threw it over me. "Here, take this. Sweat the cold out of you."

"Thanks." I moved about on the hard mattress. The light from outside in the passageway shone through the strip of Perspex in the door.

Burke rapped all through the night. He was quite humorous and managed to make me laugh. His case was in some way a comedy. He had gone down to Fulton Street to rob some Smallies who operated some gambling caravans along the street. The cops got involved when they saw the Smallies chasing him and his co-defendant down the block. Burke had fired several shots at the police, wounding one.

"They say I'm looking at a big sentence for my charge," I said.

"No way. Get a good lawyer and fight the case. Remember that little Dread who shot Batman and Robin? Well, they offered him seven years on a plea."

"I thought he died in Kings County Hospital."

"He's still alive," Burke said with much regret. "He's in the Bing with Natty Joe's younger brother, Jah No. Them motherfuckers make so much trouble that the warden has ordered them to stay down in the segregation unit permanent until they're sent upstate."

"Burke."

"Call me Bobby."

"How come the CO allow the house gang to rape the men every day?"

"He's afraid—as simple as that. He don't cause no ripples and he's safe. I was up here before and he had me put in the Bing on report. Now he's brought me back, hoping the house gang can finish me off." He got off the bed and handed me an ice pick that glowed silver in the dim light. "That's what they call a dang wang or jammer. It can go right through a man's body."

"Can you get me one?"

"It's yours. I always carry two. This is a dangerous prison. Most of the Fields posse are in here. They're on the kitchen gang and they get to walk around the jail as they like."

The following morning when the door cracked Burke limped ahead of me and joined the line of foul-smelling men who arrived through the night.

Face was ogling a new black guy with his hair cane rowed. His ugly face got hard as Burke picked up a whole loaf of bread. "Hey, motherfucker, what you doing?" He wanted to impress the young black man who cowered at the sound of his heavy bark.

Burke wasted no time. He dropped everything and pulled his dang wang. The prisoners quickly shuffled out of the way. He poked after Face with malicious intent.

Face started screaming: "Help! This motherfucker is crazy." He raised a hand to protect his eyes. The dang wang went straight through his hand.

Burke drew out the weapon and dried it on the arm of Face's white jacket.

The smooth-talking stick of dynamite on the house gang with the skifel cut raised his hands in innocence. "Rass, all that shit ain't necessary, brother. Chill out, Homes."

"Fuck you." Burke turned over the whole hot plate, scattering grits, bacon, milk, butter, and boiled eggs all over the place.

Face ran to the control box and beat against the window. "Call the riot squad! The motherfucker is going to bust up the place."

The six men on the house gang froze as I drew my weapon. The riot bell sounded like the world was coming to an end.

Burke snatched the weapon from me as twenty hefty men strolled in wielding night sticks and led by a black captain.

"Burke!" The captain was astonished. "I thought you'd settled down. You've just ruined my day because I was looking forward to coming up here and busting a few heads."

"Sorry to spoil your day, Captain, but he tried to touch my ass."

"He lying," shouted the big, soppy Face.

"Sodomy is a serious charge. But this is the first I ever heard of anyone trying it on with a Rastafarian. Burke, I'm afraid I have to put you back in the Bing. This time you might have to stay down there permanently." He reached out and calmly took the two jammers from Burke and led him off through the exit doors.

That same afternoon I was moved to Four Lower division on the other side of the building. The division was for those given the opportunity to go to school.

The CO was a hefty black man who spoke with a Southern drawl and ran an orderly division. He hand-picked his house gang who kept the place clean. Cells were scrubbed out when new men left. The clean bedding was neatly stacked up inside the control box. The shower rooms were scrubbed out each night and the day room was cleaned after each meal. Mail was handed out on time.

The inmate population in the division was 75 per cent blacks, 20 per cent Puerto-Ricans, and 5 per cent whites.

One of the house gang, a slant-eye Puerto-Rican known as China, took a genuine liking to me. His brother was also on the house gang. China was soft spoken with unusually pale skin for a Puerto-Rican. He was concerned about my health which was steadily getting worse every day. "I save some rice and green peas that was left over for you. Some butter is on the rice as well." He looked towards the control box and raised his hand. The door slid open and he stepped inside. "Don't worry, Dread, I will help you back on your feet. In here the Rastafarians and the Puerto-Ricans have to live good because the Yankees are our enemies so we have to stick together." He walked over to the radiator and put the food down.

The next day I was called for a visit in the afternoon. China rushed to my cell and gave me the good news. He was on the visit also. The other men were already standing by the control box waiting on me.

Two officers came down and escorted us up the stairs to the main floor where men were collected from other divisions. One of the other officers went up to Four Upper and another went into Four Main.

Further down the long stretch of hallway men were being collected from the other divisions and marched to the visiting room.

Three men from the kitchen pushed a trolley down the hallway. No COs were with them. Slowly the shape of my enemies came into focus. They were members of the Fields. They walked down the line of prisoners and looked into each man's face.

Chippy came to a stop in front of me. He was slightly taller than I, with shoulder-length dreadlocks. He was dressed in all white. He gave me a push that near dropped me on the floor. The other members of the Fields closed in with weapons drawn.

Chapter 28

Suddenly I was alone. Death had come to claim me in the dark and sullen chambers of Rikers Island. Glistening arrows of steel threatened to put me in that final tomb. The men's faces were bitter and rough, like the long and rugged road that had led me to this state of doom. I recalled the presages that spelled my destiny: there was the Dean who had predicted my days would be spent on Rikers Island, and Mom, who I had condemned to a barren desert to age in sorrow and drink her own brackish tears. Illuminated warnings embroidered with the blood and the tears of my struggle flashed through my mind. There was that milestone without a mark, a sign post with no direction: a merciless father who set me on my path of destiny on a lame mule and whipped us every step of the way.

China rushed from the front of the line and came to my rescue. His muscles bulged underneath a silk vest. "What's going on? Danny's sick." He spoke with his best Rastafarian accent that he'd adopted. A few of China's Puerto-Rican friends gathered around..

"He's a rat. He killed one of my friends." Chippy was awestruck. He didn't expect me to have any backing, especially some fierce-looking Puerto-Ricans.

"Chippy, man. Rastaman don't fight. Leave that to the Yankee boys," China said.

Chippy smiled on one side of his face. "What, you taking him under your wing?"

"He's sick. The beast boys beat him up when they arrested him."

"Hey, China, you know how we do things. All rats got to pay."

"Danny ain't no rat, Dread. I can give my life on that," China said.

The two visiting officers returned. The men quickly put away their weapons. They clearly didn't want to upset the Puerto-Ricans.

"We'll meet again." Chippy walked off pushing the trolley with the tea urns. His henchmen followed him down the hallway towards the notorious Six building.

The visit officers marched us down the hallway past the mess hall and dispensary. The men started screaming and going wild as the visiting officers stopped at the intersection to let a group of noisy transvestites pass. They were en route from the reception area and were heading for Three Main.

China stayed close beside me. "Here, take this. Chippy and his men practically run the jail. There are plenty of them and they have Puerto-Rican and Yankee backing." He handed me another dang wang. It was not as long as the one Burke had given me.

We were led through the labyrinthine hallway and into the visiting area. The visitors were separated by a glass partition. Every man was seated in little booths with a handset to talk through.

Destie was already sitting there when I walked down the line of men. She quickly picked up the phone. Her features were drawn. The whites of her eyes were swollen and crimson from crying.

The pressure of me being in jail had taken its toll on her. She'd given up the apartment and returned to her father's house. The members of my gang had all run away to Jamaica and there was no one out there to help her. The visit was short and I found myself looking back over my shoulder as the wardens led us away to the cells once more. Destie clung to the glass and waited until I was out of sight.

Within the next few days the fever left my body as mysteriously as it had entered. The house gang continued to look after me well. But the threat of danger still existed for me outside the division.

The smooth-flowing regime of the Four Lower division was interrupted when a young black man was transfered there. His name was Hi-God, a self-proclaimed Muslim Imam. Hi-God was a short, well-dressed man who carried his prayer cloth and Koran wherever he went. He had considerable influence on the blacks in the division. Many had turned righteous since coming to prison, the main reason for protection. Hi-God was aware of this and he wasn't about giving them an easy ride. He kept mass in the day room at nights and subjected those under his command to the study of the laws of Islam and also the laws of the Five percent Nation of Gods.

Hi-God's arrival in the division wasn't by chance. The Gods were a major force in the prison and they deployed their ministers all over the divisions.

Hostility soon built up between the pork-eating Puerto-Ricans and the Gods. The Rastafarians and the Gods were also at loggerheads.

Black prisoners entering the prison were given the option of joining the Gods or falling victim to the budi-bandits. The Gods weren't beyond raping a little ass and getting a blow job now and then. That was reserved for the likes of Hi-God and his enforcement officers.

The first Monday in January after the holidays I was taken to Richmond Court in Staten Island. Weatherman and Mom were there. He performed like the true champion that he was. His movements were somewhat restricted because Staten Island was out of his jurisdiction.

Mom seemed to have aged twenty years as she sat in the court while the charges were read out. "It was all lies," her eyes said in pleading mercy. The attempted murder on the cop was dropped and I was charged with armed robbery.

Bail wasn't met on that day and by the looks of things it wasn't going to be met. I had prepared myself for prison. How long was to be determined. Destie wasn't in court, which hurt me. Her letters had also slowed down.

I was returned to the Rocks. Two days later I was charged with another armed robbery in Brooklyn. The gold watch confiscated on my arrest was what gave me away. Weatherman, though convinced he could work out a deal with the DA, was pessimistic of my chances of keeping out of prison.

The DA in Staten Island was asking for a sentence of fifteen years if I took the case to trial. Weatherman advised me to cop a plea where he could get the robberies dropped to a D felony which carried the maximum of seven years.

Seven years without Destie seemed like a lifetime. "Both of those charges—I'm taking them to trial because I'm innocent."

"Danny," Weatherman said in a fatherly tone. "Think what you're doing and trust me. Here in Brooklyn is no problem but in Staten Island you won't stand much of a chance in front of a racist jury."

"More reason for me to prove my innocence."

"What if I can get the DA to have both cases run concurrent?"

"Trial."

Weatherman wasn't impressed by my performance. He had his own ideas as to my innocence. But he was getting paid to defend me so he had to comply with my wishes.

After court I was returned to the filthy bull pens. The tedious process of taking prisoners back to Rikers Island had started. The prison bus was a green version of the yellow ones that picked up schoolchildren.

I had a window seat. Night had fallen. The city rushed about outside. The bus trailed through the streets and crossed over the bridge.

On Rikers Island the men were taken off the bus in the usual manner. Officers, cold and rough, stood at the bottom of the stairs as I got off the bus. Directly behind them and chained to the gate leading into the jail was Lenny Chang. He was stark naked and his dreadlocks blew in the violent wind sweeping from the river. Shit ran down his legs and spattered all about him where he'd defecated and kicked it at the wardens.

I tugged at the new prisoner who was handcuffed to me and stepped towards Chang.

"Palmer!" bellowed a tall black CO.

"Tell him to suck his mother," Chang yelled. His skin was pale from the cold and his eyes were yellow like the moon.

"What's happening?" I asked.

"I shit in a bag and threw it on the scumbag captain, so he put me out here to suffer. They won't even let me inside to use the toilet."

I wanted to take off my jacket and give it to him but it wouldn't pass over the handcuffs.

The CO walked over and gave me a push.

Chang spat on him before I had a chance to respond.

The CO wiped away the slime from his face. "When I'm finished with you you'll wish you were never born."

"There's nothing you can do to me that hasn't already been done," Chang said.

The CO walked over to him and thumped him in the belly. The punch lifted Chang off the ground. The handcuffs had cut into his hands and the white of his bones was showing. He crumpled on the ground. Two officers also joined the assault and kicked him until he was unconscious.

More officers rushed from inside the jail and slung the prisoners inside like they were sacks of potatoes.

I was the last to be processed that night. Out of spite the officer sent me to Six building instead of Four.

The true anarchy of Rikers Island came to life in Six building. This side of the jail housed some of the most violent men on the island. They walked, talked, ate, lived, and looked bad.

I had one thing in my favor in that division. There were three Rastamen up there who were neutral in the war against the Fields. They treated me like a brother and gave me toiletries and the necessary things for hygiene.

The first full day on Six building was an experience in itself. Round about three o'clock five men dressed in silk shorts, vest, tube socks, and Pumas stepped out of the shower. They had baby powder spread lavishly under their armpits.

They walked into the day room like the black arms of death. Their wild eyes shifted around the room. There were no white prisoners. They'd all been abused and found refuge in protective custody.

"Budi-bandits." Junior slapped down a double six from his hand. He was a quiet Rastafarian from Queens. He was up on a murder charge.

The Puerto-Ricans looked at them suspiciously out of the corner of their eyes.

The budi-bandits had their eyes set on a black man sitting

alone with a pack of Bugle Boy tobacco and matches on the table. It was a crime in jail to be seen smoking the State free tobacco.

The black man backed up against the wall when he saw the bandits advancing towards him. His screams echoed around the day room as the budi-bandits laid hold of him and started beating him up.

"Take that turkey in the shower, get him scrubbed down," said one. They dragged the man through the day room and took him into the showers.

"It never fails. Three o'clock every day they want some ass. They just have to find someone to fuck." Junior chucked down four pieces of dominoes. "Key."

"What key?" protested Melaki, a quick-tempered Rastaman I knew from the streets but had never spoken to. He was slim built, quite tall, and had waist-length locks.

A Puerto-Rican shouted over in a jubilant mood: "Hey, Melaki, check all the pieces. Junior's a thief."

"Manny, you only sore because I gave you four love last night." Junior chucked a screwed-up piece of paper across the room where all the Puerto-Ricans were seated around the same table playing Spades.

The atmosphere between Rastamen and the Puerto-Ricans was magic. They shared one common enemy in jail and also both groups were handy with knives.

The budi-bandits returned the man after they had each sodomized him.

The Gods were the dominant force in the division. They were led by a slick brother known as Mustafa. He was muscular and revered for his street boxing skills. His coarse voice alone was enough to send fear through the new Gods who were forced to learn their lessons daily. Failure to do so could result in any number of punishments being handed out.

Mustafa would approach one of his followers at random and ask, "What's today's mathematics, God?" meaning which series of numbers taken from their supreme alphabet matched up with the day, year, time, and space. "Don't know" would bring a sparkle to Mustafa's eyes. "Brother, didn't I give you the lessons to study? Don't you know the black man is the original man?

The white man was grafted by Yacob and exiled to the European mountains. Brother, don't you know a God possess three hundred and sixty degrees of knowledge which is a circle which is the world, which is God and all things come from God, who is I."

This was the rap laid down by all the Gods throughout the prison system. They sent fear through the hearts of the young Yankee prisoners. The Rastas and the Puerto-Ricans weren't impressed.

Problems started brewing in the division when the main soul radio hosted the weekly one-hour reggae program. Speakers were screwed into the ceiling of the lobby outside the cells.

The cell doors started beating down and the Yankee cons yelled, "CO, turn off that jungle shit." The banging on the doors reached a deafening pitch. Eventually the CO was forced to change the station to WABC.

Grievances were ripe when the doors opened up for lunch. The Yankees seemed to be expecting trouble. The division was unusually quiet as the men ate that afternoon.

Manny walked over to our table. He had slick, black hair and was quite tall. "Motherfuckers disrespect us Dreads. They listen to the radio twenty-four hours a day every day and to allow you guys to have one hour is a problem. They some mean motherfuckers."

The following day, Sunday afternoon, the Puerto-Ricans requested the radio to be put on to the Salsa program that also lasted one hour. The doors started beating again. The CO changed the station after the noise continued for nearly fifteen minutes.

On lock-out the Yankees appeared to have scored a major victory. They got up to their usual daily antics. Some preached how they got to clean up the division and make it free of Gods.

The Puerto-Ricans and Rastas were armed. War loomed in the air of frustration.

On the Monday night the Puerto-Ricans took their shower and came into the day room dressed only in their shorts and vests. Each man had a toilet roll in their hand. They sat on one table and waited for the hour of eight o'clock. This, again, was their hour; they would watch the Irisis Chacon show on

Channel 35. The woman would parade on the stage half naked and sing seductive songs in Spanish. The Puerto-Ricans would take out their toilet paper and have a wank in front of everyone.

When the hour finally came around Manny walked over to the television and switched the dial.

Mustafa walked over big and bad. Manny was slightly dwarfed. "Man, we ain't watching this shit tonight. We got to eat in here and you guys are jerking off on the tables. That's nastiness." He turned the channel.

"Hey, what the fuck you doing?" Manny said indignantly. He turned the dial back on the Spanish station.

Mustafa changed the station once more. Manny did the same. Finally Manny chucked the television on the ground.

Mustafa danced back and jabbed Manny in the mouth and dropped him on the ground. "Chill out, sucker, or I beat your goddamn ass all around this room."

Manny picked himself from the ground and the other eight Puerto-Ricans jumped off the tables. One unwrapped a towel and produced eight dang wangs. The men were quickly armed and moved in for the kill.

The Gods outnumbered the Puerto-Ricans ten to one but still they cowered in fright. Mustafa looked about for some support but found none.

Junior picked up a chair and slung it across the room into the midst of the frightened Gods who allowed themselves to be held at bay by the handful of Puerto-Ricans.

Manny headed straight for Mustafa. The other Puerto-Ricans charged at the group of frightened Gods. Blood spilled on the floor and spattered against the walls.

Mustafa got stabbed. He fell on the floor and his body twitched as death beckoned him into its cold arms.

The frightened Gods made a rush for the door but it could only be opened from the control box. Finding no escape, they picked up chairs and started beating at the Perspex window. The Puerto-Ricans stabbed the Gods in their backs as they beat against the window that would allow them no escape. Cornered, they rushed to the walls hoping to melt into the solid concrete and have their lives spared.

The Rastafarians joined the Puerto-Ricans in what was later dubbed the Six Upper Massacre. Ambulances had to be called in from Queens to ferry the injured to hospital.

The riot squad arrived when it was all over. They made a blunder and went to the south side of the division. Realizing their mistake, they came over to the north side but it was all over.

All the Puerto-Ricans and Rastas were rounded up and taken to the Bing that very night.

Six Upper was heaven compared to the Bing. Some of the most notorious men in the city were housed there. They could not fit in with the regular flow of inmate population because of their uncontrollable resistance to law and order. In the Bing they were let out to roam as they willed. The warden had personally ordered those men to be placed in the Bing indefinitely and on no account were they to be allocated to any other division.

There was a knock on the door to my cell and a tall, light-skinned Rastaman stood outside. He resembled Natty Joe.

"Everything cool." He tossed back his heavy mane of locks that hung down in front of his face.

"I'm all right." I got up from the bed and walked over to the door.

"They call me Jah No," he said proudly. He knew without a doubt I had heard of him. The name of Jah No was on every prisoner's tongue. He ran Rikers Island and was a younger brother of the notorious Natty Joe. He had a Yankee posse on the streets who terrorized residents in the Buffalo and Sterling areas.

"Just come off the streets?" he asked.

"Yeah."

"Heard anything about my brother?" he asked offhandedly.

"He's in Sing-Sing on a few murders, the last I heard."

He nodded and a flicker of sentiment brightened his wild, gray eyes. "Don't worry about anything I run down here. They put some of the Gods on the north side. We got a treat for them when shower time come around." He stepped aside and made way for a hefty man with a bald head. The man was so tall he had to bend down to see through the glass.

"One of your Homeboys?" The man's voice was rough with a Harlem accent.

"He's one of us." Jah No didn't hesitate in making his decision.

"Just checking the hit list," he growled and walked off.

"That's Pontiac. He's from Harlem. Would fuck a man with the squint of an eye. He's on our side. Down here we stick together Yankee, Puerto-Ricans, Rastaman."

Chang made his way to the door. He was dwarfed by the much taller Jah No. "Those pussy holes are really gonna get it. I've been waiting for some of those Gods to come down here for a long time."

"Chill out, we rap later." Jah No put his hand on Chang's shoulder and marched off down the passageway.

That night the Gods were let out of their cells to take a shower. Jah No had arranged it with the CO because showers for the new men in confinement could only be given after being down there seven days.

While the men lathered themselves in shampoo and soap suds, the angels of death descended on them and plunged them with lethal arrows of steel. Their screams could be heard throughout the division.

The riot squad came down in full force. They took away those injured without asking any questions.

The following day I was in front of the captain to answer charges for rioting on Six Upper. I was found guilty and sentenced to one month's solitary confinement.

After a week Jah No had convinced the resident CO to let me out during the days to walk around. Every day he never failed to beat up someone or stab them up.

Chang was the baby in the group. He made endless trouble, knowing that Pontiac and Jah No would come to his aid.

One day a new officer replaced the resident CO. This officer couldn't understand why so many men were let out to roam freely. His first mistake was when he tried to put some men back in their cells. He was chased through the south side door by a Puerto-Rican with a knife.

The CO ran back into the control box and called the riot squad. In his haste he left the security door on the south side open. Pontiac, Jah No, and a few Puerto-Ricans were out at court that day.

The riot squad stormed into the day room shortly after getting the call. A short, stocky black captain led the charge. He walked over to Chang, who was sitting on the table sipping from a prison mug.

"Got a problem?" Chang looked sourly at the captain with his yellow, sick eyes. The Kings County Hospital had injected him with the hepatitis disease.

"Yes, I got a serious problem, you. I can still smell that shit you threw all over me." He twirled around a huge black key that was secured to his belt by a chain. Rumors were that he was transfered to the Island after killing a con with a similar key in the Brooklyn Tombs.

"Hey! Captain, let him be. How many times you gonna beat the brother," said a tall, bald-headed Yank. "You know Pontiac don't take too kindly to no one messing with his son."

"Neither Pontiac or any of you men run this prison, I do." The captain grabbed Chang by his shoulder and lifted him from the table. The riot squad closed in.

Chang screamed as the captain took a handful of his dreadlocks and dragged him through the day room door. The CO in the control room buzzed them through a set of doors on the north side of the division.

The door leading out of the division opened and an officer walked in with six men from court. The area between the two doors was about the size of a horse cart.

Jah No gave a start when he saw the captain manhandling Chang. Pontiac drew close beside him with equal astonishment. The officer that brought the men back from court quickly stepped into the control box.

"Step aside, Parker," the captain warned Jah No.

"Where you taking him?" barked Jah No.

"None of your business. Step aside or you might find yourself joining him."

"He's not going anywhere." Jah No's eyes narrowed. He looked beyond the little room where most of the squad were waiting eagerly to storm into the room and execute some agony.

With all the attention focused on the north side, a big, stocky white man from the south side took advantage of the door that had been left open when the CO was chased by the Puerto-Rican with the knife. He crept into the control box, yoked the frightened white officer around his neck, and put a knife at his temples. The officer was ordered to push the master button and let out all the prisoners from their cells. Men came out with pillowcases over their heads and armed with a variety of awesome weapons.

The riot squad looked about nervously as men resembling the Ku Klux Klan closed in on them.

Jah No wrenched Chang away from the captain. "If you don't want to see this place go up then lay your hands off him and fuck off back to the reception area."

The captain rested his hands on ample hips. "Parker, this jail ain't big enough for me and you. What do you really think you can achieve by this?"

"Most of us are in here for murder. One more won't make much difference to the sentences we're gonna get," Jah No said coolly.

"I will not submit to your threats." The captain was steaming.

Jah No stepped into the control box. "Release him," he ordered the man holding the white CO.

The officer shook like jelly when the man turned him loose. His face was pale and drained of color.

"What's the number for the Warden?" Jah No demanded.

The officer stuttered a few numbers. Jah No slapped him across the face and threw him back into the hands of the other prisoner. He picked up the phone and dialed. "Warden, get down here in the Bing fast before I execute some of your men. This is Leroy Parker, alias Jah No." He paused and leaned his ear to the receiver. "Enter from the south side. I give my word nothing will happen until you get up here, but make it fast."

Within minutes the Warden appeared with more of the riot squad, only these ones were in full riot gear with shields. He was a short man with sandy, receding hair.

"Warden, we're tired of Captain Willard coming down here and abusing Rastamen. Rano Dread was taken from down here a few weeks ago. Under Willard's instructions he was taken to the reception, tied up, and beaten. Chang is sick and dying and

Captain Willard once again took him from this division and chained him outside the building when it was ten degrees below zero. Now they want to take him again for doing nothing."

The Warden addressed Willard. "What seems to be the problem, Captain?"

"I'm responding to a distress signal from the riot alarm."

"And what was the actual purpose of that alarm?" the Warden asked suspiciously.

The captain looked confused—as though the answer was clear. "Men were causing a disturbance down here, sir."

"Men? More than one. Then why do you only have Lenny Chang? Did he play any special part in this disturbance?"

"No," the captain answered, stupefied.

"No!" the Warden exclaimed. "Then where were you taking him? These men were put down here for the safety of the prison and themselves. Under no circumstances should they have been taken out unless for obvious reasons." He turned to the CO manning the division. "I don't seem to recall seeing you before." He was puzzled.

"I have only been on the job one month," the officer answered, still shaken by the trauma.

"Preposterous. And you were left alone unsupervised to look over some of the most violent men in the prison system? Captain Willard, where is Officer Brooks?"

The captain stuttered: "Well, he had to take some time off, sir."

"And no one saw fit to inform me of these changes. Captain Willard, I suggest you report to my office. I go into retirement in two weeks. Nothing is going to spoil that. Am I making myself clear?"

The Warden resolved the situation. He left one of the riot squad officers to man the division. No one was charged.

Chapter 29

CO Myers requested my return to Four Lower two weeks after I had been sentenced to confinement in the Bing. News of the Six Upper Massacre and the Bing defeat of Captain Willard had spread throughout the prison.

Visits from Destie became less frequent. The letters had dropped from one a day to one a week maybe. She wasn't in court on my last few appearances.

Mom wasn't one for writing. She didn't visit either. Dad had forbidden her to come and see me. The long days without a visit or a letter started to affect me mentally. Slowly, I was being hardened and absorbing the prison that breathed through the four walls of captivity.

Rano Dread was transferred to the Four Lower division. He spent one day and was exiled to the Bing for turning over the hot plate. He was disgusted at the pork that was served every meal. The pork was only eaten by the bums and stragglers because the Muslims and Rastafarians in the kitchen had spat and discharged all over it before taking it to the divisions.

Chippy and his men stuck me up in the main mess hall one morning when I was going to court. They robbed me of my shoes and left me with one of their steel-capped boots. Four days later Chippy tried to rob me again. He was with one of Rano Dread's crimeys. They were pushing the trolley with the tea urns toward the Six building. They spotted me and left the trolley outside the Four building and slipped into the stairwell to ambush me. The CO was at the far end checking the other cons through.

As I entered the stairwell Chippy's hand went out to grab my cigarettes. I dropped everything on the ground and pulled the weapon. The cold edge of steel passed through his body without resistance. I poled him a few more times, not wanting to kill him, just damage him a little. His accomplice ran away when he saw him bleeding on the floor.

The Fields were after my head from that day on. The cat and mouse games in the hallways had started. The Fields, though popular, had made themselves some enemies among the other Rastafarians. One was Rano Dread, who they claimed was a madman. Any foe of the Fields was a friend of mine.

Jah No was at high tide with the rest of the Fields. He was intent on being the head man in the posse but came up against resistance from Chippy and another hard-core gangster from the Bronx named Lenky Roy. Jah No continued to carry out contracts for the Fields down in the Bing.

Both of my cases had been submitted to the Supreme Courts. I awaited trial.

Ingrid wrote me a letter and sadly informed me that Destie was having an affair with another man. I was bitter and for the first time in my life I had to face myself. There was a hurt inside that stayed with me and blocked my throat. I couldn't eat. I had restless nights, diarrhoea, headaches, nightmares, and all the other terrible symptoms that came along with losing someone you love. I lived only for eleven o'clock every day, when CO Myers delivered the letters. I stood by the door trying to make myself look busy so he wouldn't notice my distress. He would smile knowingly: "Nothing for you today, Palmer."

Finally a place was opened for me in the classes. The school counselor put me on a high school equivalency program. Going to classes during the days helped to take my mind off the approaching hour of eleven o'clock when the letters were passed out.

The Warden retired with his name intact and a new Warden, Mr Bishop, took his place. He was committed to following the ways of such men as Captain Willard and other unreasonable forces on the Island. Bishop was intent on cleaning up the jail and making a name for himself. He refused to believe that there were men that couldn't be controlled in the regular divisions and therefore allowed to roam in the Bing. His first move was to empty the Bing and house the men in divisions.

After one week Rikers Island erupted like a volcano. The riot bells rang nonstop. The riot squad found themselves running to two and three divisions at the same time. There was no end to the anarchy. Four officers had to man the control box. This further agitated the situation.

Finally, the old Warden had to be called back from out of retirement. It didn't take him long to sort out the problem. The men were quickly rounded up and returned to the segregation unit.

Jah No was shipped out of the jail in one of the weekly drafts to Elmira State Penitentiary.

Twenty-five members of the Renegade Posse were rounded up and put on the Island. The Fields were overjoyed their enemies had fallen into their hands.

The door to the cell opened one day and in walked a tall, red-skinned Rastaman with waist-length dreadlocks. His gray eyes wandered around the cell. He looked ruefully over his shoulder as Myers slid the door shut.

"Hey! I want the top bunk," he demanded.

I couldn't believe what I was hearing. I laid aside the magazine I was reading and stared into the wild eyes of the giant. He had a willowy frame, like most vegetarian Rastamen. "Take the bottom bunk and get used to it, because I ain't moving."

He looked at me puzzled, failing to understand why his towering stature failed to invoke any fear in my heart. "What's your game? Don't you know I could pull you off that bunk and take charge?"

I climbed down off the bed, slowly easing the dang wang from under the pillow. The giant pushed me against the wall near the toilet bowl. His eyes lit up when he saw the weapon. Slowly he backed up toward the cell door.

I lunged at him but the dang wang went through his shirt and pierced him in the side. The pain surged through his body and brought out the animal in him. His dreadlocks flew in the air in a mad frenzy and he threw himself at me.

We rolled on the floor. The weight of his body bore down on me heavily. The dang wang was in an awkward position and pointing at my heart.

The door to the cell clicked and Myers steamed inside. "What the fuck's going on? I thought you Rastamen didn't indulge in sodomy." He pulled the giant off of me.

I managed to slide the weapon down the front of my trousers as I rolled about on the floor.

"Get up, Palmer," Myers barked. He stood between me and the giant. His aftershave broke the prison stench. "Either you two cut the bullshit or I can arrange for both of you to be put in the Bing. What's it going to be?"

The house gang gathered around outside the door and looked in.

"Get away from here," Myers instructed.

"All right, Danny?" China wanted the new Rastaman to know I had backing.

"Cool." I waved him away.

"Well, what's it going to be?" Myers stood between us like a fight referee. "I deliberately put both of you together because I thought I was doing a good thing. There's a guy over there who shits and paints the walls with it and another one who says he sees little green men in his cell. I can put you both in any one of those cells."

The Dread looked at me as if saying "It's up to you."

"I hear so much crap about Rastamen don't fight each other and here you two is wanting to kill each other. Is it over?"

"Yes, sir," I answered.

The giant nodded.

"Guess you going to tell me you scraped your side on the bed," Myers said as the blood soaked through the giant's shirt.

"Something like that," the giant smiled.

Myers took the Dread out of the cell and had him taken to the dispensary to patch up his wound. Half an hour later the Dread was back in the cell. He smiled with much appreciation when he saw that I had moved my things from the top bunk and set up on the bottom.

"For a short man you're handy with a tool." He took the horse blanket from the bed and spread it on the floor as a mat.

"When you're short then you have to try that much harder so no one don't walk over you," I said.

He bent down and smiled. "The name is Big John."

"Danny Palmer."

That was the start of a brotherhood relationship between me and the giant.

Big John was one of the Renegades. He was picked up for being in possession of half a ton of Jamaican ganga. He was a learned man who spent hours on his back reading. Unlike me, he had several girlfriends who wrote to him regularly. One of his women I knew from outside. She was one of the new breed of Jamaican women who led their own posses and fired guns.

She wrote him some real sexy letters which he read to me.

I had given up all hope of hearing from Destie when one day I was called on a visit. Big John and four other men from the Renegade posse had visits also.

Five beautiful women from the dreaded posse turned out to meet the men. They wore African head wraps and long skirts.

Destie couldn't look me in the eye. She was guilty without a doubt. Her features registered no surprise when I confronted her about having another man. "It's a lie, Danny. I don't have anyone. You were the one to take my virginity. How could I ever sleep with anyone else?" she said in a voice almost too womanly for her age.

"Why haven't you been writing?"

"I lost my job and things were so hard." Tears rolled down her cheeks. Eventually she won my sympathy. The truth was I didn't want to believe that she was having an affair. I had always tried to convince myself that it was all a lie.

After the visit I was more confused than anything else. I went over everything she'd said, word for word, rewinding the conversation over in my mind. There were questions that I could have asked her that would have tripped her up but I didn't have the nerve.

Big John received a letter from his girl two days later. His boss Menzy was dead. He had died when he went to negotiate a drugs deal in Miami. The leadership of the Renegades was now in the hands of the young members, many of whom were not Rastafarians and hated Rastas.

Destie started visiting regularly once more. Each time she became friendlier with the Renegade girls. Eventually she started to dress like them and wore a beret to cover her long, shimmering hair.

I couldn't imagine in my wildest dreams that she had traded her beautiful hair for dreadlocks. She'd drummed up a relationship with Big John's woman, who recruited her into the posse. Her letters were facetious and she'd also started smoking. She was no longer my innocent little girl.

Big John was the one to give me the bad news. Destie was screwing with one of his soldiers, a man that once roamed with the Fields.

The true horror of prison revealed itself to me. Prison wasn't about being locked behind bars or sentenced to do time by a judge. It was about losing the ones you loved and not being able to do anything about it. This was the sentence that the judge couldn't pass. It was your loved ones who really turned the keys and locked you in mental slavery.

Though hurt, I pushed on. One day I would get even. Destie would pay like all my enemies. My visits had stopped. So, too, the letters.

The Fields started running battles in the hallways with the Renegades. They were desperately trying to get the Renegades into the Bing where men were ready to take them out in the showers.

Big John was wise not to fall into any of their traps. The other members of his gang had engaged in petty fights and ended up in the Bing.

Pontiac was forced to refuse a contract when Chippy wanted to pay him to fuck one of the Renegade dreadlocks men. Normally Pontiac would fuck a prisoner for free but he had genuine respect for the Rastafarians. He, like so many Yankees and Puerto-Ricans, couldn't understand why they were fighting.

Two members of the Renegade posse had to be taken to the outside hospital after Pontiac, Chang, and the other vultures in the Bing had turned on them.

Some of the problems eased when Chippy was sentenced to twenty-five to life for shooting a policeman. He was sent the following week to Elmira State Penitentiary in upstate New York.

Three weeks after Chippy was sent upstate I was sentenced to four years. A week later they woke me up early in the morning for the long journey upstate.

Big John stood at the door of the cell and chanted a psalm of guidance for me as I was led away that morning.

China stood by his cell door: "Take care, Danny." Tears were in his eyes.

By nine o'clock forty men were shackled and put on two Grayhound buses bound for upstate. Ten red-neck officers over six foot tall were sent to escort the prisoners.

Junior was on the bus and sat three seats behind me. The jury had returned a verdict of guilty and he was sentenced to twenty-five to life for murdering a gas attendant. He sat wide eyed as the bus wormed its way further and further away from the city.

We were on the road for nearly nine hours. Nine hours of watching skyscrapers and houses turn into mountains, forests, and farm land. The sun was disappearing beyond the brink of a white-tipped mountain when a sign read YOU'RE ENTERING THE TOWN OF ELMIRA. The bus drove along some country lanes and finally cruised through the quiet town of Elmira.

Summer evenings were long and the residents were out. The white folks watched the buses with a look of satisfaction on their faces. Many had never seen black people—only on television, and the weekly shipment of prisoners that passed through their town.

The prison was about twenty minutes into the town, set off by quiet tree-shaded avenues. ELMIRA STATE PENITENTIARY said a sign outside the front of the prison. Flowers and a recently cut lawn decorated the front of the prison. The building was structured out of red brick with towers. The sight was frightening.

The prisoners were led off the bus into a big room with benches against one side of the wall. On the other side was a long table where some hefty red-neck men sat with files in front of them. One by one the shackles were removed.

The officers wore different uniforms than those on Rikers Island. They called each man in turn and checked his mug against the ones they had on their files.

The captain, a hefty man wearing a white shirt with a gold pip on his shoulder, looked down at a file. "Newton Rose." He got up, walked around the desk and stepped over to Junior. With much distaste he reached out and took a handful of Junior's locks. "And what we got here," he said in a hillbilly accent.

Junior gave a toss to his locks and released it from the captain's grasp.

"Hey, boy, you got something about me touching your hair? Come morning you won't be seeing that no more." He took a few steps, then turned around and slapped Junior across the face.

Junior jumped up quickly and cleared the captain's feet from underneath him. He followed up with some punches to the face and head. Stunned, the other officers looked on before making their move. Riot bells went off instantly.

Giants came from out of the walls all over the place. The room was filled with some of the tallest men on earth. These men were bigger than any man I had ever seen in my life. Their necks were as wide as cows'. They pounced on Junior, pounding him with all the hate that upstate officers carried for black people.

"Take him to the strip cells and remove his clothes." The captain was on the floor still dazed. He wiped his mouth and looked at a trail of blood on the back of his hands.

The riot squad quickly bundled Junior away. The captain picked himself off the ground. "This here's not New York City or Rikers Island. Cons don't run this prison—we do, as you men will find out in the next few days. Give us any trouble and you'll just disappear—simple as that. Anyone who don't get visits or have any outside contact, I suggest you toe the line because no one will come snooping when you're gone. There's a wall that surrounds this prison. No question is asked if a man is shot trying to get over it. There's plenty of room in the consecrated cemetery."

The captain was bitter, having been humiliated in front of his men and the new cons. Every word that came out of his mouth spelled hatred. Speaking through swollen lips he informed the new cons that Elmira was an orientation center where the new prisoners would spend eleven weeks while being assessed as to which prison was best suited for them.

Cautiously, the captain walked around the room, keeping a safe distance from the new cons. "Tomorrow morning after breakfast each man will be given a haircut." His eyes caught my locks. "I hope you ain't going to give us any problems. I been hearing what you Rastamen got up to in the city, shooting police like they are targets. For your information, no more than three of you people is allowed in any one prison. Give the barbers any trouble in the morning and you'll find yourself joining Spence. He's been in solitary confinement for eighteen months for refusing to cut that shit from his head."

After the captain finished delivering his prologue the new men were stripped naked and taken into the shower. Three officers came around with canisters of bug spray. They turned the jets on us and sprayed our bodies from head to toe. After the spray had soaked into our bodies they allowed us a quick three-minute shower.

Each man was kitted out with prison clothes. This included four pants, shirts, underpants, vests, socks, and a thick coat for the violent upstate winters. We were no longer a name but a number that was stamped on each piece of clothing.

We were warned of the hot reception that awaited us on the division. "Men will be screaming and throwing down everything from shit to broken glass. You men will be locked on the ground floor. Remember your numbers and head straight for your cells. If you forget your cell number then get into any cell until the morning."

The men in the reception division roared with excitement. Fear gripped the hearts of every new man waiting to enter the jungle of discontent. Drums were beating and men shouting as we stood at the gate leading into the division.

The officer opened the gate and let us in like he was throwing food to hungry sharks. The new inmates clutched their clothing packages to their chests and scurried for their cells. Bedding and newspaper rained down from the tiers. The stench of urine and shit was unbearable.

I rushed for cell number sixteen, dodging missiles and concerned only about getting behind the gate. The men were screaming and shouting: "New jacks, new jacks."

Frightened, I stood behind the bars and looked up at the tiers. Men were pinned against their bars and screaming like wild animals. Fire burnt in the center of the division, directly outside my cell.

One hour later the men had thrown eveything from their cells and their voices had grown hoarse from continual screaming. The noise eventually quietened down and only the sound of men shouting across the tiers to each other, begging cigarettes or challenging each other with a showdown on lock out, persisted.

There was no sleep for me that night. I was afraid. Never in my life hàd I ever been given such a fright. I feared for the break of dawn. What could possess the men on the tiers to act in such a manner?

The following morning the prisoners were woken by a bell that rang throughout the prison. Trustees were let out to pass around hot water. To get this hot water you had to put your towel on the bars.

Twenty minutes was given for washing and making bed packs. The men were led from the sixth tier downstairs. They marched along the center of the first floor in single file. Officers stood on either side keeping the men in line while another led them through a set of iron gates at the far end of the division.

The men on the fifth tier followed in line. Men on the fourth tier were paraded outside their doors waiting their turn. As the men passed my cell I looked anxiously to see if there was anyone I knew. They all looked the same in the prison green uniform and bald heads.

Lagging behind the rest of the division on the third tier was Burke. His limp had gotten worse.

"Burke!" I shouted excitedly.

He looked around at the many cells on the first floor, then he saw me waving my white towel through the bars. "Danny!" he shouted. He still had that broad smile on his face.

"Burke!" shouted one of the officers keeping guard. "Keep quiet and get back in line."

"Go suck your mother." Burke stopped a little way from my cell. He couldn't say much because four officers came down on him with fire blaring out of their nostrils. He raised his hands and went peacefully into the mess-hall. The men on the second tier followed.

"Ones, fall out of your cells and stand by your doors," shouted the big voice of the area sergeant. He walked down the rows of men and inspected each man to make sure he was properly dressed. Satisfied, he gave the order for us to be marched into the mess-hall.

The leading officer led us around a series of corners. The lighting was dim and we could hear the eating utensils clattering and men chatting in the mess-hall.

Once again we were the center of attraction. Curious eyes looked up from their breakfast as we were marched into the huge mess-hall. There were rows and rows of tables. Men were seated opposite each other. Officers were in towers looking down over the men as they ate.

The kitchen was at the front of the dining area. Men in white served the food on trays that were neatly stacked at the front of the line. The food looked good and was well prepared. There was even fruit juice and plenty of fresh bread baked on the premises.

That was the best breakfast I'd had since being in prison. It was only a pity that I had to enjoy it in such a heavy air of tension. The atmosphere in the mess-hall was like a time bomb waiting to explode. Unlike Rikers Island, there were plenty of white prisoners, many from upstate. Gas bulbs were secured in the ceilings in case of a riot.

No sooner had the breakfast finished than the guards marched out the prisoners in the same order as they had been brought in.

I returned to the cell frightened by the thought of the gas in the ceiling. There was plenty of movement around on the tiers as the prisoners prepared for their daily programs. The new jacks were the only ones locked up.

The doors started opening one by one and each man was taken by two officers to the barber shop on the first floor.

There were three barbers, one white and the other two blacks. The shop was two cells converted for their convenience. There were three chairs and wall-length mirrors in front of each man. Two COs stood at the door to keep an eye on the proceedings.

I sat in one of the chairs knowing full well that to protest would be a waste of time.

One of the black barbers stood over me and looked at my locks with growing respect in his eyes. He took a handful of my hair and held a pair of scissors in the other hand. "I can't cut this brother's hair. It's his religion." He spoke with a deep New York accent.

"Cut it or get a ticket, plus lose your job," said one of the red-neck officers. He drew closer to enforce his command.

"I'll lose the job. Man, I see guys saying they this religion and that but only these here brothers got any respect for themselves. This is one order I got to refuse and I feel better for it too." He threw the scissors on the floor and took off his white jacket then walked back to the division.

"Hey, you, over here," the officer instructed the white barber. "I want all that shit cut from his head right now, hear me."

The white prisoner picked up the scissors and stood over me. He had warm blue eyes. "Sorry, Rass. That's the way they work their show." He spoke with a city accent.

One side of my head was shaved clean and my locks withered on the floor beside me. The officers in the shop gave a start when there was screaming and shouting coming from outside.

Some guards bundled a Rastaman and threw him on the ground. He was strapped in a straitjacket and his long dread-locks seemed to fall below his knees. The man slowly raised his battered head from the ground and looked at me.

"Here's Spence. He's just been returned from Matawan. The warden says he wants this shit taken from his head no later than today." The officer breathed heavily.

Tears welled up in my eyes when I saw the state of Jerome and how the prison system had mistreated him. I jumped out of the chair and got down on my knees beside him.

"Danny," he said in a drugged voice. "Don't bow, Danny. Eighteen months they've beaten me and put me in confinement but still they can't break me."

"Give it up, Jerome. Our locks can never wither. It's in our hearts."

He forced a smile and spat in my face. "Fucking traitor," he hissed venomously.

I got on my feet and wiped his slime from my face. Jerome would remain an enemy for the rest of my life. For no reason he'd waged a war against me and he was intent on seeing it through.

Chapter 30

The barber struggled with each individual lock until they withered in a heap beside me on the floor. I didn't even recognize myself in the mirror. Unlike Samson, I was strong and looked forward to returning to the world a strong man.

In the Elmira jungle every man looked the same until they opened their mouths.

Chippy was there along with some more of the Fields. At nights I could hear them shouting to each other across the tiers. They were on the sixth tier and had come to the end of their orientation period.

Burke passed by my cell one morning on his way to the mess-hall. He gave me a twelve-inch nail. I kept it with me at all times.

One week to the day after we arrived in the prison the new jacks were moved up to the second tier. It was our turn to initiate the new jacks coming in from the city. We aimed to make it as dreadful an experience as we had encountered if not worse.

Prisoners at the end of the tiers kept a look-out through the bars and informed the rest of the men what was going on.

"They bringing them up soon," shouted an excited voice.

Men were pinned to the bars straining their eyes, anxiously looking out for any signs of the new jacks. Some prisoners had broken pieces of glass on the end of toothbrushes so they could see for themselves what was going on.

"Here they come," the look-out man shouted. Each man knew the fear that was in the hearts of the new jacks. Silence ruled.

The CO opened the gate and let the new jacks into the division. The noise was greater than the night I first entered.

Fires were burning as the new jacks ran towards their cells clutching their parcels of bedding and clothes to their chest.

I threw down a bucket of piss that I'd been saving for one week. The smell was revolting. The men ran to their cells cowering in fright. I realized how foolish I must have looked on my first night.

In the morning one of the new black prisoners was found to have cut his wrist during the night.

The days had started to heat up and we were allowed out into the little exercise yard. The yard was slightly bigger than a tennis court. There were two basketball hoops on either end and four wooden picnic tables and benches near the north side of the cells. Each man was given a broom to sweep the yard before some basketballs were thrown out.

The New York Yanks, wanting to show off their dunk, hook, and dribbling tactics, rushed for the balls and displayed some Globetrotter-style ball play. The upstate Yanks, known as counry boys, just had to stand aside and watch.

I headed for a seat on the tables where some white prisoners were seated.

"Danny," shouted a familiar voice. The voice came from one of the cells on the ground floor where the new jacks were still caged in.

I walked over and bent down to look through the ground-level window. I recognized the straitjacket before I could make out Jerome. His eyes burnt with hatred. He resembled a young bird just hatching from an egg. His head was shaved clean.

He swore: "Keep on looking over your shoulder because one of these days I'm going to put a bullet in your brain."

"I would sooner charge for your murder than let you charge for mine."

"It's all right," he said with reservation. "I won't always be kept down like this. In fact, seeing you has just helped me to make up my mind to get out of here. As long as I'm in here scumbags like you will continue to talk shit."

"I got something for you." I bent down and hawked from the pit of my belly and spat in his face.

He jumped back but it was too late. "Guard!" he screamed and turned towards the front of the cell.

The tall black officer in his late forties came to the door and looked in cautiously. "What you want?" he barked.

"I'm ready to be orientated," Jerome said.

"Boy, what's that running down your face? Someone done slime all over your mug. Ain't no wonder you want to get out. You is one of the most vilest characters I ever did meet."

"Fuck you. The Warden said when I'm ready to go along with the regime of the prison I should send personally for him, not his shoe-shine boy."

"I'll personally recommend that the Warden send you so far into the sticks that your family will need to take an airplane if they want to see you."

Contented, I straightened up and strolled around the yard. Each time the white faces on the benches seemed to be talking about me and hatching some mischievous plan. In Elmira they outnumbered the blacks. Many were from upstate. The others were from the city and carrying heavy grievances from their torture on Rikers Island.

The third time round the yard one of the white prisoners put out a foot in an attempt to trip me up. I steadied myself and toyed with the nail that pierced my inner leg when I went off balance. My eyes made four with a blue-eyed white man who seemed to be the tallest man in the prison. He looked coarse. The name tag on his shirt labeled him as Frank Warner. His head was bald where his hair had naturally receded.

"Got a problem?" I asked.

"Sure, I got a problem. I don't like niggers." Four other white prisoners sitting on the table stared at me with malicious intent. This was a fight I knew I would never win. Warner drew closer. I stepped sideways towards one of the brooms resting on a metal railing. Before Warner could make another move I wrapped the broom around his head. It broke and left me holding only the handle.

Warner was unhurt. The white prisoners all jumped up from the table. The action on the basketball court stopped and some of the brothers gathered around. Warner rushed me but I side-stepped him and pulled the nail from my waist.

He growled like a big grizzly bear then spun around and kicked the nail from my hand. He had been trained in some form of martial arts. His heavy hands delivered a series of crippling blows to my body.

I dropped to my knees, overcome by pain. Warner gave me an upper cut and knocked me on my back. He jumped on me and wrapped his hands around my throat.

Things became blurry. I was slowly losing consciousness as he choked me. My tongue hung out of my head. The white prisoners urged him on. "Kill him, he's only a nigger. Nothing won't come out of it."

I had resigned myself to the land of the dead when one of the basketball players, a tall brown-skinned man, stepped forward and started slashing Warner about the head with a knife.

Warner quickly released me and screamed. His hands went to his face to stop the many cuts that targeted him with precision. The black prisoner moved about like a professional. He had a straight face and fine features. He turned around and faced the might of the white prisoners. The knife twirled around in his fingers like a cheerleader's baton.

The white prisoners were having no part of a crazy nigger with a knife. They stepped back and raised their hands in surrender. Warner was on his knees, blood pouring from his face.

I rolled over on the ground and picked up the nail. This man had to die. The nail went in and out of his body bringing out a chunk of meat from his neck at one instant. The sirens whined and I knew there would be very little time to kill him. Time was actually against me because the riot squad charged the yard with a force I had never seen before. The black prisoners quickly raised their hands and showed their neutrality before their heads got busted.

"It got nothing to do with us. Them the ones," shouted one brother.

My hand was caught in mid-air. The nail was set on course to go through Warner's skull. The guards quickly bundled me and the man who came to help me. The black officer who had recently spoken to Jerome had me around the neck in a yoke.

"Son of a bitch," he hissed in a nigger voice. "Blood is all over the place." The guards dragged us through the prison and around some corners to the security block known as the guard house.

The guard house was four single tiers overlooking a wall with barred windows. The guards stripped us down to our undergarments before throwing us into the smelly, roach-infested cells.

I stood by the bars and looked down the tier as the guards marched off. My partner in crime was thrown two cells down from me.

A white prisoner walked down the tier like he was parading his wares on Forty-Second Street. He had shoulder-length hair and a slim body. His voice was effeminate: "Anything you need just put your towel on the bars." He cocked out his ass and rested a hand on his hip.

I looked at him bitterly with all the hate that had built up inside me for faggots. He saw the dagger in my eyes and walked off down the tier.

"Hey, mighty whitey, what's taking you so long?" shouted a familiar voice from the cell to my left.

"Hang loose. The CO got his eye on me. Think he getting jealous." The pansy threw a kiss and moved on to continue his duties.

Before dinner the guards brought over a few articles from the reception area. I didn't have much—just a few bars of soap, toothpaste, and a Bible that I intended to read while sweating in the guard house.

The man involved in the incident in the yard with me identified himself as Gerald Addison. He moaned: "Man, I have been in an upstate jail in Rochester for one year and never got into trouble until I met up with another Jamaican." Though he was bitter his voice carried a hint of satisfaction.

The gut-wrenching smell of prison food crept up from downstairs on the bottom floor. Shortly after the faggot and the tier officer brought around white disposable trays with the food rations.

"I don't eat meat," I protested.

"Chuck it out if you don't want it," the faggot snapped.

"Give me a different tray, one that don't have no meat on it."

The CO, who appeared to have a soft eye for the pansy,

growled, "Take it or leave it. What'd you think this is—a catering service?"

I took the tray and threw it over the tier.

The CO removed a pen from his top pocket. "That just cost you a ticket."

"Fuck you."

"That's another one. Keep it up you'll never get out of this guard house."

"One cell is no different from the other!" I screamed.

"Yeah! I got a surprise for you." He smiled knowingly and walked off.

"Yo!" shouted the familiar voice from the next cell.

I drew up to the bars dressed only in prison undershorts and vest with the name tag above my heart.

"Yo," the voice growled once more.

"Yeah."

"Chill out, Homeboy. These cats don't fuck around. They got a strip cell at the end of the tier. They get you in there and you'll wish you were never born."

"I ain't bowing to none of these motherfuckers."

"Well," he said cautiously, "have it your way. But while you here let me have your meat instead of throwing it away."

"Take the whole tray."

"And what you going to eat? I'll see if I can get the trustee to steal some bread and butter for you. Might be able to get a little jam, too. What's your name anyway?"

"Danny."

"Don't seem to ring a bell. They call me Sugar Bear. I used to run with the Tomahawks gang."

"Bear."

"Yeah," he laughed.

"It was me and Dave Green who saved your cousin in the hospital when the gangs tried to shoot him."

"Well I'll be. Whatever happened to the footballer?"

"He's bad news. They bugged him out over there in Nam."

"Ain't that a bitch. He was one of the best ballers ever to come out of this city."

The faggot teaboy walked down the landing. He had a broad smile on his face. "You ain't ought to be running your mouth to those COs. They don't take no liking to city slickers." He walked off to Sugar Bear's cell.

"Homeboy. Ain't nothing going to happen to you," the Bear shouted.

"Are you ready now?" The faggot looked like he'd gone and put on some red lipstick.

"Man, chill out and move your nasty little ass. How could you want to suck my dick when I'm rapping to my Homeboy. Come back later or give my cigarettes back. And make sure they the same brand I gave you too."

"I'll come back later," the faggot said in a bitchy tone. He swaggered down the tier twitching his ass.

"Yeah, Homeboy. Chill out for a while. I'm gonna put my head down and have a siesta," the Bear said urgently.

"Before you go, what happened to Gold Tooth?"

"He in one of them State joints called Coxsackie. Me and him crimey's on a double murder." He cut the conversation quickly and slipped further into his cell.

I stood by the bars and looked up and down the tier. My partner in crime was silent. He was still chewed up about being in the guard house.

The faggot made a few rounds and returned to Sugar Bear's cell late in the afternoon just before the serving of the evening meal. Soon he was doing what he was paid for. I moved further into my cell, thoroughly disgusted that grown men could find pleasure from each other.

I timed the faggot and when he was passing my cell I spat in his face.

"Shouldn't ought to have done that." He wiped his face with the back of his hand and walked off in a huff.

Sugar Bear growled: "Hey, Rass, chill out. That there faggot got a lot of protection. They got guys in here would kill for the dude."

Gerald, my partner in crime, spoke: "Just can't keep out of trouble, can you?"

Someone with a mean voice shouted to the Bear from downstairs.

"Yeah," the Bear answered.

"Talk to your boy. He getting out of hand."

"Fuck you, I ain't afraid of no motherfucker!" I shouted.

"Hey, man." The voice was calm. "You just hitched a ride on the meat wagon."

"Now you really gone and done it," the Bear whispered.

"I ain't letting no one put the shits up me," I protested.

"Brother, you just a pint size. These dudes will chew you up."

While the Bear talked I hurried to my bed and ripped off the mattress.

"What the fuck you doing in there?" he asked.

I didn't answer. My fingers worked at the thin strip of metal that went around the frame of the bed. I needed a weapon.

"I hope you ain't hanging up in there," he said. "Man, you Rastas sure hot in the head. That brother Jah No is turning this prison upside-down."

There was a one-inch-wide strip of metal that went around the frame of the bed which held the springs in place. Five of the springs were now released, revealing a seven-inch strip of the metal. Keys jingled down the tier and I got up and rushed to the bars to check on the movement of the CO.

Sugar Bear was still on his bars with his mirror on the end of a toothbrush. "Hey, Danny, take it light. I don't want to see these guys do anything to you," he whispered as though afraid. "For now you safe. They give you a shower and association after seven days. That's when you got to start worrying."

Seven days. That should give me enough time to make a decent shank to defend myself. I didn't have no muscles but the one I had could only be pumped by blood. I had heart and that's what it was about on the street, so prison wasn't going to be any different.

The choking smell of the food caused me to rush back into the cell and put things back together. The CO and the faggot came around with the trays.

"I'm taking Danny's," the Bear said.

The faggot handed over the tray without checking with me first to see if it was all right.

That evening I drifted off into a troubled sleep and woke up with the end of a bad dream still in my head. Night had not yet fallen. Sugar Bear was on the bars negotiating some form of settlement on my behalf. He seemed to have gotten things under control.

The voice on the next tier down shouted: "I ain't looking to start no race riot but you know how it is in here."

"Like I said, the man is new. I'm gonna put him under the wing and set him straight."

"All right, Bear, I leave him up to you."

"Don't say nothing," the Bear whispered as he saw my shadow cast outside the cell. He went quiet for a while then handed me half a loaf of bread and some butter. "There's enough in there to last you a few days."

Night finally came. One day in the guard house was like ten in the regular population. Already I was missing the little things I had taken for granted. They didn't allow tape-players or radios in the guard house. There were three holes in the wall to plug in the cheap tin-can earphones that went with every cell. Two of the holes represented the local hillbilly stations. The other was for the prison's use.

Sugar Bear kept me awake with stories of his past. "The first person I ever killed was my brother. We were playing in front of our house when I found a gun in a hedge. My brother was only four and I was seven. We were getting ready to play cowboys and Indians and was glad to find the gun. I raised it and fired it at him and that was the end. The firestick was loaded. My parents shoved me into a home and there I stayed until I escaped and hit the streets."

Sugar Bear was yet another victim of the streets. He'd made it but fallen victim to the hard drugs. He'd lost his position as a feared gang leader and was now a slave to heroin.

The following day Gerald and I attended the adjustment committee. The court was a little office on the first floor. Two COs were there along with a lieutenant wearing a white shirt. The charges were read out.

The lieutenant spoke with a harsh voice: "You're lucky Warner isn't dead from all them stab wounds. This case will have to be recommended to the superintendent. Ninety days is the least you can expect for this plus another fourteen for misconduct on the tier. Take him out and bring in Addison."

I was escorted back upstairs where Sugar Bear anxiously awaited news of my fate.

"Superintendent proceedings," I said.

"Goddamn, you hit the big times."

Shortly, Gerald walked past my cell with a frown on his face. I didn't need to ask him what the lieutenant had recommended.

The days dragged. Each day I was driven further into myself. The writings on the wall told of the men who suffered mental torture there in that very cell. The tough fight against hard drugs and organized crime had netted some of the leading members of the underworld. Life sentences were introduced for the handling and distribution of the killer drugs. The law enforcement agencies, through their network of informers, had managed to pinpoint the Rastafarian Yard Men. They concentrated all their efforts in catching these young men and bringing them to justice, and the courts handed out brutal sentences to match the brutality of their captives.

On the seventh day we were let out with the other men to have association in a little room. I was expecting problems but Sugar Bear had bent over backward to set things straight.

I developed a fondness for the Bear. He had piled on a lot of weight since the last time I saw him. He kept me amused.

The superintendent proceedings was set for another two weeks. Day after day I paced the floor. Loneliness and thoughts of Destie were my worst enemies. There wasn't even a note from anyone outside to see if I was dead or alive.

I was into the fourteenth mind-bending, gut-twisting day. Early in the morning six guards came to the door and ordered me to pack.

"Where you taking me?"

"Just hurry and pack," one of the hefty officers growled. The six officers looked like a hit squad. I threw everything into a pillowcase and got dressed. I wanted to call Gerald but I wasn't given a chance.

Sugar Bear was awoken by the officers. He stood at his bars with sleepy eyes. "Hang cool, Homeboy. It seems like they taking you to another prison."

That was the last I was ever to see of the Bear or Gerald. I was put on a bus with some other men who were shackled to the floor. The bus traveled into deep countryside where only the pylons carrying electric voltage suggested any form of human life.

The bus drove for hours along country lanes. Evening had set over the countryside and the sun set low on the horizon, the sky a mass of purple through blue, orange to yellow. The bus entered into the town of Coxsackie. The prison was planted in the center of a vast area of farm land overlooking mountains as high as Mount Everest.

The outside of the prison resembled an old folks' convalescent home. Rows of pine trees on both sides of the asphalt drive led up to the prison gates.

We were ordered off the bus and led into the prison by some of the meanest-looking men I had ever seen. ALL GUNS TO BE LEFT AT THE GATE said a sign as we entered. Directly behind the sign was a display of weapons in a glass case that had been confiscated from prisoners.

The shackles were taken off and each man given their belongings that were taken off the bus by some trustee inmates. We were led through the prison to the reception area. The inside of the prison was like an old nuns' convent. The air was oppressive and dank. Darkness was present even though the lights were switched on.

The officers led us into a little reception room overlooking a small exercise yard. There were two iron doors at either end of the room. They led to the cells. Seven varnished wooden benches and matching tables were in the little room. The floor had red-brick tiles that shone with the sweat of some unfortunate prisoners.

There was hate in the air as well as an aura of medieval human condemnation. The COs were hillbillies and racist in their approach.

After a CO had delivered a brief speech on how the prison was run we were led to the cells to the right of the reception room. There were six cells opposite each other and the doors were solid with a little peep hatch. The cell was clean and had a toilet and wash basin. Still there was an air of doom that fell over the prison like thick fog.

Around nine o'clock the medication was handed to the men

who had medical problems. I was busy arranging the cell in some form of habitable state. The few bars of soap that I had taken from Elmira added fragrance to the room. They were laid out beside my Bible and pictures of Destie.

Outside my window bright floodlights blazed down on the exercise yard that was boxed in by four walls of the prison. There was a dead silence that ruled over the prison. I got down and did some push-ups. Thoughts of getting even with Destie gave me the drive to keep fit. She would realize one day that she had made a mistake.

There was a sixth sense warning me of danger. I stopped halfway down in the push-up and looked at the little box in the door. There staring at me were a pair of blue, hateful eyes. "On your bed," a big voice commanded. His face was that of death. He was tall and had blond hair.

"I ain't ready for bed," I protested.

"It's after twelve. Make sure you're on your bed by the next time I come around." He walked off, checking the hatch in the other cells before returning to a desk in the reception area.

I stood at the door and looked sideways into the reception area where I could just about see the CO at his desk.

The door leading out of the reception room suddenly flew open. In rushed an army of officers dragging a black prisoner. They threw him on the floor and beat him whilst shouting racial abuse.

Although I couldn't see fully inside the reception room I kicked my door in protest, hoping to wake the other prisoners and alert them as to what was going on.

Six officers rushed to my cell door, including the blond-haired blue-eyed devil who'd previously ordered me to get on the bed.

"On your bed before we put you down," growled the blond officer again.

"I ain't getting on no fucking bed. I can see what you doing to that man inside there."

The oldest of the officers, a shorter man with an aging tan, edged away the other officers from the door. "Lay on your bed, kid. It's not worth the bother." There was something in his voice that hinted of a far greater danger than just a beating.

With hateful eyes on my back I retreated into the cell. They turned off the light in the cell from outside and disappeared back to the reception area and slammed the door to keep down the noise.

The floodlights cast shadows of bars and barbed-wire fencing across the ceiling. I lay awake for some time until the dope they put into the food seeped into my system and commanded sleep. For the rest of the night I never even woke to take a piss.

Early in the morning I was woken by a kick on the door that snapped me out of a dream and stunned me with a sense of barbarianism.

A red-faced CO stood at the door. "Ten minutes to make your bed pack and prepare to go down to the mess-hall. Failure to do so will result in disciplinary action."

Ten minutes later the men fell out of their cells and stood by their doors. The CO marched us in single file, down the stairs and through the prison.

The mess-hall was big enough to feed a hundred men. There were rows of wooden tables and matching chairs. The foodline stretched from the front where the food was served back to the entrance where the officers stood guard.

The faces of the prisoners resembled men in a mental institution. They reflected the doom that shadowed the place.

While we ate the prison pansies were marched in. This made the men shout and whistle as the faggots paraded down the aisle for their food. They ranged in all sizes and colors. This was truly a nightmare. I wanted to blink my eyes and maybe it would be all over.

After the breakfast we were led back upstairs and put behind our doors. The exercise yard outside my window was now filled with the inmates who had had their breakfast.

I stood on my bed and looked down on the mass of bodies garbed in green uniforms. These were supposed to be some of the youngest men in the prison system but they looked old. They were unusually quiet and stood in their own ethnic groups. The blacks made up at least ninety per cent of the population.

The first person I recognized was Rano Dread as he emerged on the platform at the far end of the yard near the mess-hall. He walked straight down the center of the yard; the prisoners stepped aside to give way. Gone were his long dreadlocks. In their place were young, baby ones about half an inch long. He stopped under my window with a group of West Indians who'd remained quiet until he arrived.

I strained my eyes but couldn't see them. Something was clearly winding them up by the way they were cursing.

An army of guards stood on the platform at the end of the yard. "Shop parade. Fall out," the sergeant shouted through a loudspeaker.

There was no movement. The men remained still and turned towards the platform. Slowly, a tall black man stepped from amongst the black prisoners and walked towards the platform. He held a Koran in his hand and wore a Muslim prayer cap. He inclined his head and stopped in front of the platform. "We demand to know what happened to the brother that was taken to the reception area last night." The man was well spoken.

The sergeant with the loudspeaker spoke in an arrogant hillbilly tone. "He committed suicide," he said bluntly. "A note was found screwed up in his garbage pan where he clearly states that life was too hard and he took his life."

The black spokesman for the prisoners calmly said: "How could he have done so when his hands were handcuffed behind his back?"

"Obviously, he wasn't handcuffed," the officer said. There was a massive build-up of officers on the platform and leading into the prison.

"Since when is it a procedure to handcuff a dead man?" said the spokesman.

"Tell them, brother Akbar. Let them know they ain't getting away with no more of that shit," shouted one excited prisoner.

"Hold your head, brothers," Akbar said reasonably. He turned around and faced the sergeant once more.

"The Warden is on his way down here. All questions should be addressed to him. As to the handcuffs, I can assure you men that no force was used against that prisoner." He lowered the loudspeaker.

"On behalf of the inmate population and the Muslim brotherhood, we refuse to move from this yard until we have some answers and are satisfied as to what happened to that brother."

A heavy roar from the inmate population underlined Akbar's speech.

The loudspeaker sounded over the excited voices. "I will issue the order one more time. Fall out in shop formation."

The chanting grew more rebellious. I was caught up in the tension outside and nearly had a heart attack when one of the officers kicked the door.

"Get off the window and stay off. Failure to do so will result in a ticket." It was the same officer that had threatened me during the night.

I climbed from the bed and walked to the door. The musty smell of unwashed body lingered in the wake of his departure. The prisoners on the other side had their towels on the hatch. They were unaware of what was taking place in the yard.

While I sat on my bed Rano Dread's excited voice sounded through the window. He wanted more than just a peaceful demonstration. He wanted blood.

Chapter 31

Occasionally I defied the order of the CO and stole a glance outside. The prison chaplains were brought out to try and quell the disturbance. They too were a part of the system of hate. They came in the name of God but yet they stood beside the hungry, bloodthirsty officers who had claimed a man's life the night before.

The lunch hour came around. The cells were unlocked and the food passed around on disposable trays. My door slid open and the tall officer who was intent on causing me as much trouble as possible stood at the door. "What do you want? Bed service?"

"I don't eat meat."

"Who's asking you to eat it? Take the tray." He slung it down on the ground and stuck one foot through the door. "I don't like you, Palmer. Your kind don't last long. Slip up and you're mine." His eyes were like a raging fire out of control. He was in his late thirties and had a college boy haircut and a straight face that radiated evil. He removed his foot and slammed the door shut. As if that wasn't enough he stood outside and stared at me like he would like to kill me there and then.

The crackling of the loudspeaker summoned me to the window. The entire prison population was seated on the ground.

"This is the Warden speaking," declared a deep, authoritative voice. "I am asking you men to abandon this demonstration. I have it within my powers to call in the state troopers if this matter gets out of hand."

Standing beside the Warden was a tall, stocky black man

with a bushy beard. He was dressed in civilian clothes and held some papers in his hand.

The Warden's strong voice echoed through the prison. "Stanley Corbin committed suicide. The prison authority was in no way responsible for his death."

The highly disciplined stature of the Muslims' spokesman rose from the ground and strolled over to the platform. "Warden, we find it very hard to believe that Corbin took his own life. He was well known to many of us and had everything to live for. He was due for release next week."

The Warden arrogantly waved a few pieces of paper in the air. His hillbilly accent took charge of his professional speech. "According to this here letter he received from his mother only a few days ago, he was emotionally unstable, distressed."

Rano Dread's voice exploded: "A depressed man don't play soccer. He was all right when your captain led him from the main yard yesterday."

"That's right," shouted a few excited voices from around the yard. Akbar turned around, deafened by the uproar. He raised a hand. "Brothers, hold your heads. Don't be incited to do anything rash. Warden, we would like an independent outside inquiry into the brother's death. Also we would like the newspapers brought in." It was clear that his heart wasn't fully in what he was doing. He was a lip professor, like so many I had seen since being locked up.

The Warden frowned. "That just ain't on. I can't bring the newspapers in here on the account of you demanding to see them." He handed the loudspeaker to the black man beside him.

"Gentlemen." The voice was warm, sturdy, and comforting. "Being a counselor has in many ways brought me closer to many of you men. I would like to confirm what the Warden has said. Corbin was under a great degree of stress." It was as if he was reading a speech written by the Warden himself.

The men once again erupted in loud shouting of protest. The counselor raised his hands and brought them to order. "Brothers, don't do anything that might cause the Warden to bring in the men in orange suits. A reasonable settlement can be reached. Many of you know me as a man of my word. If there was any foul play as a result of brother Corbin's death then I personally would make sure that those responsible be brought to justice."

Akbar once again half-heartedly reaffirmed the need for the press to be brought in.

The counselor appealed to him personally. "Brother Akbar. The Warden has said what he thinks about the press being brought in. They can sometimes cause more problems than anything else."

"Counselor McCrossen. The men respect your word but we find it hard to take the word of a Warden who allows his officers to beat and torture inmates as they will. There has been complaints made about officers who come in during the nights drunk. These officers open cells at random and beat the inmates. There is a serious crisis in this prison. Brothers are being denied many basic rights. We ask only that the press be brought in to report on some of the atrocities taking place behind these walls. If we don't have access to the press then the Warden can call in the state troopers and they can shoot us down in cold blood like the inmates in the Attica riots. We are willing to die."

The Warden didn't seem bothered. He knew the leader was saber-rattling. He just stood there looking arrogant and unmoved just as he had when he was first called and informed about the disturbance.

Akbar had made a very impressive speech that was swallowed up by the men. They screamed and catcalled which seemed to swell Akbar's chest. Even from where I was standing there was something in Akbar's attitude that I didn't like.

The Warden and counselor disappeared into the building several times and returned to issue the same unedited speech of defiance. Each time the build-up of officers increased.

Six o'clock. A chill swept over from the Canadian border. The sun disappeared beyond the prison walls and the floodlights were turned on.

The Warden showed his head for the umpteenth time that day. His chilling voice declared: "This is the last chance for you men to come inside. Counselor McCrossen and I have given our word that a thorough investigation will be made. I know many of you men are hungry. The kitchen staff have prepared chicken and roast potatoes for those men wishing to come inside."

Akbar walked up to the platform once more. "Brothers!" His voice bore a strain of submission. "We're not cannibals. We don't seek blood for blood. What we seek is justice. Brothers, Mr McCrossen has given his word. In the past his word has always been his bond. He's been very helpful in securing many of our basic rights. The brothers who represent the Fruit of Islam along with myself have decided to allow the establishment time to investigate the matter before we take any further actions." There was an uproar of mixed feelings amongst the crowd.

Rano Dread and the men below the window protested wildly. They felt strongly that they had been sold out by Akbar and the Muslim brotherhood.

The men started rising to their feet and brushing dust from their prison greens. Swiftly they followed Akbar down the avenue of red-necks into the prison.

The blacks made up the majority of the prison population. With them gone the yard was bare except for an isolated group of whites numbering around fifty and twenty Puerto-Ricans. The West Indians below my window were still there.

The doors that emptied into the yard from the four corners of the prison opened. The guards stepped onto the platforms dressed in riot clothing.

A short Puerto-Rican wailed: "Man, we out here to risk our lives for the Morenos and they desert us for some chicken. I say we go inside. The next time those motherfuckers got a problem they stand alone."

The Puerto-Ricans took the same route into the prison like the blacks.

A tall, muscular white man in his early twenties with slick, black hair addressed his group who were standing in a corner at the far end of the yard near the platform.

The prison guards seemed quite content to let the remaining men in the yard be the recipients for their frustrations and pent-up anger through the day.

"The niggers and Spics have once again shown what they are

made of." He spoke in an angry Sylvester Stallone drawl. That voice was as distinct as Sugar Bear's. It was that of Dominico Vercotti from the Italian Destefano gang.

As the guards started to close in on the men the West Indians and the whites instinctively moved to the center of the yard instead of being pushed into the corner with their backs against the walls.

It was then that I saw Rano Dread and the other men who were under the window. Back to back the whites and the few Rastafarians with their weapons drawn prepared to face the might of the prison system.

Dominico yelled: "I might go down but I'm taking one of you pigs with me."

The guards marched in a tight formation. They were armed with night sticks and helmets. I feared for the safety of the men. They were outnumbered.

There was a sudden rush by the main gates near the platform. Counselor McCrossen rushed out onto the yard tearing his way through the guards in their slow march. "Hold it," he screamed. "If these men are willing to lay down their arms and come inside then they should be given the right to do so."

The men, defeated by the odds against them, threw down their weapons. Pieces of steel and daggers rattled on the asphalt. The counselor supervised the men safely back into the prison.

That day I had witnessed the failure of my own people to stand up for their rights. For a piece of chicken and some roast potatoes they had sold out the cause. As I lay awake that night filled with grief I was forced to think about the numerous black leaders that I had read about while I was on Rikers Island. Why were there no more Malcolm Xs, Garveys, Frederick Douglases?

The authorities didn't fear the black Americans. They knew how to control them. Later that night the remainder of the empty cells in the reception area were filled with men taken from the population area.

After one week I was allowed to join the population. I was put on C block. A red-faced hick known as Shannon ran the division. He was a heavy-set man with thinning hair in his late forties. Shannon thrived on discipline and ran a strict division.

He didn't tolerate noise and he did everything by the book, including the nightly showers.

The distance and time didn't cure my love for Destie. In fact, it only got worse as the days passed.

Mom kept in contact with tear-jerking letters and a few dollars to see me through. I had written Billy Weinstein but got no answer.

Thirty days after joining the population I met up with Rano Dread and three other Rastafarians. They'd been in solitary confinement since the day of the protest in the yard. There were a total of eight West Indians in the prison minus the one the guards had slaughtered.

Since the disturbance in the yard the West Indians were spread about the prison in separate divisions and often put in separate yards during the association periods.

Shorty Gold Tooth was there. He had put away his wayward lifestyle for one of righteousness. He was now a Five Percenter God known as Supreme Allah. The Five Percenters made up half of the black population. The Muslims made up the other half under the leadership of Akbar, a devout follower of Wallace D. Mohammed.

The two sides, though Islamic in faith, were like negative and positive. They shared only one view. Mohammed was the messenger of Allah.

After one year in the prison I had built up my own mental picture of the guards. I could predict the nights when they would roll on a division. It was one of those nights when they were out on the town drinking. I was awoken from a light sleep by the stench of alcohol on their breaths.

"Crack number fifteen cell," shouted a slurred hillbilly voice outside my door.

I jumped out of the bed and slid across the cell and stood to one side of the door. Slowly, the door cracked and there in front of me was the officer who had stalked me since the dawn of my arrival in the prison. He reeked of alcohol. No questions needed to be asked that night. I lunged at him and plucked out his right eye with my dang wang.

The guards were so far gone they must have thought they

were dreaming when they saw an eye on the floor. The officer screamed and cried out for mercy.

The whole division was woken up by the screams. They started beating on the doors. Normally they would have been too afraid to make a noise but that night they feared for my safety.

The guards dragged me up to the reception area where they had killed Corbin. They put me in the same dining room and beat me within an inch of my life. The doctor was near. They didn't want another death on their hands so quickly after Corbin's death.

The days in the guard-house were long. I was hungry and smelled like a water buffalo. To make things worse four of the faggots were locked opposite me and beside me. They'd assaulted a prisoner and bitten off his dick. They were always on their doors screaming at each other and sending semen in little packages to each other to eat.

McCrossen came around to see me a few times. He was working on my behalf. The officer who lost the eye wasn't supposed to be on duty that night. After the incdent he was rushed to an outside hospital where a high level of alcohol was found in his blood.

I had not seen McCrossen for three days and then John Bull shouted to me from outside in the exercise yard and told me he was dead. McCrossen had been found dead at his house. His head had been blown off by a 12-bore shotgun. The verdict on his death was the same as mine would be very soon.

The future of the prisoners in that little concentration camp was bleak. Day after day their screams and torture could be heard. I managed to throw a note to John Bull who smuggled it out the prison to my mother. The note told my mother that I was in danger and my life was being threatened.

Mom wasn't in the best of health but she got on a Grayhound bus and made her way to the prison. She went directly to Lieutenant Smithe, who was head of security, a racist and the main perpetrator of all acts of aggression against the inmate population. She told him if anything happened to me she was going to bring in the press because she knew everything that was going on in the prison.

I didn't see Mom because she spent the day trying to get through to see Smithe.

Smithe came to the door and informed me of my mother's visit. He was happy, having already hatched a plan to make me pay. His lean, red face peeped throuh the hatch. "Palmer, I'm putting you on protective custody."

"Bullshit," I protested. Protective custody was the dregs of any prison system. That's where they kept informers, child molesters, and cons who couldn't make it in the regular prison system. They were hated by the rest of the prisoners and were confined to their cells. Men in the kitchen pissed in their tea, put razor blades in the porridge, and abused their food. This Smithe was sentencing me to an indefinite period of confinement, a life of hell.

"This is for your own safety." He smirked and walked off.

"Hey! Come back," I yelled. Thirty days was the longest time I had ever spent in solitary confinement. It almost drove me mad. Now I was to be there indefinitely. One week of yelling produced no results. My skin scratched and my hair started falling out. Rashes appeared on my skin once more.

Finally I had to call the CO and rub a handful of shit into his face. This resulted in a beating but it got me to where I wanted to go, in front of the Warden.

The Warden flipped through pages of my past report. He shook his head in disgust. The teacher from the math class was beside him, plus two other civilians. The officer who had the shit thrown over him was also there.

"I see here," the Warden said in a rich, deep voice, "you seem to have gotten into more trouble since coming to prison than when you was a free man." He continued to leaf through pages of report, which was ali structured around stabbings and fightings. His eyes rested on the file that said confidential protective custody. "Protective custody!" he exclaimed. "The prison should be on protective custody from the likes of you. Who ever made this order?"

"Excuse me, sir, but may I have a word?"

"Speak," he said sharply.

I explained to the Warden everything that happened, starting with the arrival of my mother at the prison and her concern for my safety.

He picked up another file. "I see there is a deportation order on you after your release. You may not be aware but a hearing is scheduled for you in Attica State Prison in one month." He rubbed his chin and sat back in his chair with his fingers knotted in front of him. "Palmer, contrary to what you might hear, some of what is taking place in this prison is unknown to me. The prisoners have many grievances and they blame me. I can't be everywhere at once." He made a few notes on the files. "Time served."

The officer who had the shit rubbed into his face wasn't too happy when the Warden ordered me to be returned to the regular population and taken out of protective custody.

Two weeks after my release from solitary I was moved to Attica Prison along with four other West Indians. We spent three days on the wing where the Attica riots had started. Court was held on the fourth day in a stuffy room. An aging man in a tweed suit sat behind a wooden desk. His white shirt strained at the buttons and his enormous belly pushed in and out as he labored for breath. There was a little tape-recorder sitting on the desk in front of a woman in her early twenties who took notes. Beside me was the lawyer the state had appointed to me. He had a bushy ginger beard.

My mitigation fell on deaf ears. As a result the judge ordered my deportation on release from prison. He spoke with a slow, chilling voice of authority. "I am going to send you somewhere where these crimes of looting and shootings seem to be permissible. Such crimes will not be tolerated in the United States. I declare you an undesirable."

I was marched out of the court not fully realizing what had taken place. The judge had quoted offenses from section this and section that which all spelled that I was to be thrown out of the country. Exiled to Jamaica and the crowded tenements, poverty, and the heat of the sun.

The ruddy-faced lawyer was optimistic. He was allowed to talk to me briefly in the hallway while the guards stood at a distance keeping close watch. "This is not the end. I am going to lodge an appeal as of now. The deportation can't be executed once an appeal has been lodged."

Early the following morning four men with their dreams shattered were returned to Coxsackie prison.

Waiting for me was a letter from Destie. Tentatively I pulled out the pages. The smell of perfume reached my nose. I was afraid, as if the letter carried a sentence of death. Over and over I read the letter making sure each word was actually written by her hands. She cared for me and wanted me. I was the only man she ever loved. She could no longer resist the temptation of writing. Passion cocked my whole black being. I had completely forgiven her. Nothing mattered, I had what my heart really craved.

Destie visited that very Sunday. She arrived on one of the monthly buses that left from Grand Central Station and carried visitors to the many upstate prisons.

The visiting room was brightly lit, with round tables set out much like a huge dining room. A CO sat at the entrance and pointed out where the visits were located. The room was packed with excited children sitting on their father's laps and women stealing the precious moments to grope and kiss their menfolk.

Destie was there in the corner beside a picture window looking out on the sheds and picnic table in the yard. The prisoners were allowed out there on hot days to visit with their family. Passion carried me lightly across the room. My heart was beating fast.

Destie was like a stranger to me. We caressed and held each other close. Her little heart beat against my chest. She, too, was affected by the moment. Her long dreadlocks tickled my face. She'd turned into a Rastafarian queen and was dressed in the traditional African head wrap and a long skirt.

I was on a live wire with excitement. There was no time to talk about her having another man. I felt for what had been denied me so long. The smell of her sex, erotic and sweet, arose my passion.

That was the first of many visits that she was to make. She wrote many letters and sent plenty of private cash until my release nine months later. I had served a total of two and a half years.

Chapter 32

The Grayhound bus made its way from the prison gates on a crisp September morning. I was a free man. Slowly the tension that held me in mental bondage for two and a half years slackened its hold on my brain. The world outside looked a different place as the bus seemed to go back through time, rewinding, undoing the wrong that had been committed against me. I was about to get a free crack at the world once more. Smithe and the evil prison system were behind me, history.

The bus pulled up in front of Grand Central Station. Waves of bodies moved about in the afternoon rush. It took some time for me to come to terms with freedom. I expected to see an officer standing over me, shouting the next move. The black faces in the crowd all resembled someone I knew. Excited, I moved from each recognizable face to another only to realize I was wrong again.

I entered the subway station and took a train to Brooklyn. In my excitement I didn't realize the structure of the train was different from the rundown graffiti-stricken carriages that I used to jump on with my eyes closed.

Delighted, I got off the train when it reached Utica Avenue. This name I could never forget. I knew every inch of the Avenue. I shuffled up the stairs and into the evening light. The sun was high in the sky. People moved about in a rush. I was lost. At that time I began to wonder if I had gone mad. What had happened to Eastern Parkway and the area I once knew? Defeated, I wandered along the sidewalk until I saw Ingrid.

"Mister, is you mad?" The girl stared at me in wonder as I stood there holding a shoe box and dressed in a checkered jacket, gray polyester trousers, and black prison shoes.

While I walked around in a state of confusion someone

fingered the State check amounting to thirty-four dollars out of my pocket. All eyes seemed to be on me. For a moment I craved the security of confinement, if just for a short while, to get myself together. The prison system hadn't prepared me for return to the world. I was like a tamed bird set free into the wild.

Finally I asked the way to Eastern Parkway and Utica and got the right directions. The bus was crowded and I had to stand up and hold onto the metal support ring. I was unable to see outside clearly through the mass of bodies.

At the corner of St John's Place and Utica the bulk of the passengers got off the bus. The rundown tenements and the stench of poverty and dirty water in the sewers quickly brought me back to the land of the living. The area suddenly took shape in my brain. Only then did I sit down and relax.

I had gotten on the A train instead of the express or the number two train that stopped at Eastern Parkway and Utica. The area had completely changed. Black people had replaced the Jews. West Indian stores seemed to be everywhere. The Army and Navy store was still on the corner, so too the drug store.

As I walked the few blocks home I could see and smell the change. Garbage pans were piled high where the sanitation trucks hadn't been around. Fierce-looking men hung about on the corners. Gone were the quiet white folks that sat on deck chairs and talked softly to each other. The egg seller had gone. Anarchy ruled.

There was an army of young black kids on the block as I walked home. An old woman stood in Nathan's yard looking out and calling some young children. Her face was inflicted with many scars. It was Nadine. She was a total wreck.

Mom ran to meet me as I neared the house. She threw herself on me and wept. Some of the neighbors cried too. They tugged at my clothes and pushed in dollar bills to say welcome home. They saw in me the reflection of their own kids who'd gone astray and were either in prison or underground with bullet holes in their heads.

The house had been refurbished and looked a totally different place. There was a strange feeling burning deep inside me, something telling me I didn't belong in that house anymore. I took a bath and bathed away the prison stench.

There was something strange in Mom's attitude; she'd also changed. Her eyes were on me wherever I went in the apartment. She was short on words and avoided direct eye contact with me. It was as if I was a stranger.

I sat on the new settee watching a white 32-inch color television, afraid to move in case I soiled the settee or put any dirt on the lush red carpeting.

Mom stepped out of her bedroom. But before she could close the door I got a quick glimpse of Dad lying on the bed, his feet crossed and his hands tucked under his head. His eyes were fixed on the ceiling and all was tranquil with him but his thoughts. I could read his thoughts: "That damned boy has come back to wreck our lives, to shatter this calm and bring shame and disgrace on this house once more." I looked at Mom and could compose the continuation for myself: "To torment his mother who had gotten used to the fact that he was in prison and comparatively safe: safe at least from the horrors of the gun."

But I could also sense that deep down he respected me for surviving prison's horrors. He had often preached of prison whilst thrashing my hide, like his beatings were a blessing compared with the dreadful experiences that waited in the pen. Mom unfolded her fist. "Here's fifty dollars. Don't let Sonny see it," she whispered.

I took the money and chucked it on the floor. "After two and a half years in prison you give me that? What can fifty dollars buy?" The words stuck in my throat. It wasn't so much the amount of the money, as Mom's secretive attitude. I was being treated like a criminal just to receive a little help from my own family. It hurt. But I was no longer a child. They owed me nothing.

Mom's face hardened. "That's the best I can do. You drained all my money paying for the lawyer." She bent down and picked up the $50 bill.

Dressed in some old clothes that were still in the apartment from before I went to prison, I walked out of the apartment. The weight of the world was once again on my shoulders. I sat on the concrete steps outside the house feeling sorry for myself. There was no one to turn to for help.

Destie walked down the block shortly after the streetlights went out. She took me in her arms and patted my back. "Don't worry, Danny, I'll look after you. Next week I pick up my monthly pay of eight hundred dollars. It's all yours."

We went into the house and lay on my bed upstairs. Somehow the feeling of not being wanted dominated my senses. We took some bedding and went down into the basement. There was a mattress down there. Dad had started restructuring the place and all the junk was thrown into the only habitable room at the front. I laid out the mattress and Destie spread the sheets. Slowly she stripped, allowing me to feast on her beauty. The bright, unshaded bulb reflected on her body, a woman's body. She was no longer the little girl I once knew. I was hot for her.

We made love and it was a disaster. Her warm body and the smell of her sex excited me but I was unable to maintain an erection. I'd gone completely impotent. She was understanding, but for how long?

Later in the night when I knew Mom was asleep I slipped upstairs to get some food.

My father seemed to have timed my entry into the apartment. He stumbled into the kitchen and took a carton of milk out of the refrigerator. He took some time peeling back the flaps of the new container, whilst watching through the corner of his eyes. There was something uncharacteristic in his manner. His face was passive and warm; he was searching for some words that would not infringe on his emotions. Sensing I was about to leave he spoke, in a deep mellow voice.

"You could have been out here living good with your family but you chose to go and live amongst criminals and policemen." He wasn't being mean or offensive, that was his way of saying welcome home. Those were the most words he'd ever spoken to me without a belt in his hand. The years had taken the spur from his heels. He poured out a glass of milk and returned the carton to the fridge. Dad was a victim of many years working hard in the cold: it had made him a bitter man.

Something inside me wouldn't let go, wouldn't allow me to bridge the gap between us. Shakily he put a hand on my shoulder. "Here's four hundred dollars. Buy yourself some clothes."

"Thanks." I took the money, still refusing to look him in the face. No other words passed between us. He returned to his room having notched a place in my heart.

The following day Destie left for work early. I took the train down to Court Street to meet my parole officer.

He was a strict man in his late thirties and wore horn-rimmed glasses. He resembled Clark Kent in many respects. Entering the parole center was like being arrested all over again. There were bars on the windows and cops arresting parole violators.

Men and women just released from prison sat around waiting to be seen. Some looked down and out, worse than when they were behind bars. Slumped in a chair and sniveling was a man that resembled Akbar the Muslim leader. It was him, and he'd hit the scrag trail on his release. He was on the white horse that was riding him to hell.

I was to report to this parole office every Thursday and also to find a job. The warning was sufficient for me to realize what would befall me if these orders weren't carried out. Relieved, I left the office feeling worse than the first day I was released from prison.

The next day I took the train into the city and combed the employment agencies along Forty-Second Street. I spent seventy-five dollars paying the agencies to find me a job. They took the money and sent me to work in a seedy factory with non-English-speaking immigrants who slaved on production lines. The factory ran a scam with the employment agencies. For thirty-five bucks the agency would guarantee you a job. Once on the job the boss would give you the hardest work to do and force you to quit. In doing so you would lose your deposit and would have given the crafty boss a few hours of your labor. There was no rest for the wicked and poor. I had been suckered.

Frustrated, I took the express train home. The rush hour was on and people brushed shoulder to shoulder as the train raced through the underground tunnels smelling of burnt oil and corrosion. I rode past Utica Avenue and out to Saratoga Avenue.

Somehow I felt the answer to my problems lay in the ghetto.

My brain needed to be booted by the sickening stench of poverty and hungry black children searching in the gutters for food. It was like getting a look at doom before it struck you. A sneak preview.

Saratoga was just the same as I had known it, only there were no more gangs hanging out on the corners. The three hundred gangs that once ruled the city had dropped to only sixty-six. The winos, junkies, ass-peddlers, and petty hustlers were still there, wallowing in the bog of waste that swamped the streets.

I walked from Saratoga Avenue down to New Lots Avenue. There were no signs of the Rastamen that once hung out in the parks. Wars had driven them underground. Many had shed their dreadlocks and joined the many Jamaican posses that had sprung up as a result of the Rastafarian wars. The Yardies had moved into the sale of hard drugs and now controlled the streets.

My thoughts were far away when a little snot-nose girl about three years old stepped out of a rundown tenement.

"Mister, you got a dime?" She rubbed her eyes.

I dipped inside my jacket for my knife. Quickly I turned around and slashed violently at a man behind me. Eyes turned and stared as the man cried out for mercy.

He jumped back, pulled in his belly, and cocked out his ass as I slashed at his mid-section. He was a raggedy man with long nappy hair and he smelled like a bison. "Hey, mister, what's wrong? I was just going to collect my daughter." He looked angrily at the little girl. "How many times I tell you not to beg strangers, child."

There was no way I was going to be taken for a sucker twice in one day. Bouncing to the rhythm of the ghetto I strolled off down the block. Visions of the past when Rastamen used to ride on bicycles down those very same streets flooded my brain.

On the corner of Amboy Street I was quickly jerked from my stupor when a black chauffeur-driven limousine passed and splashed dirty water in my face. Inside the car were some dark-skinned Colombians with slick black hair and $2,000 suits. They'd taken over the ghettos. Many arrived from Colombia with their family, a suitcase of cocaine, no money in their pockets, and unable to speak English. They turned up in the ghettos and found the warring Yardies and their Rastafarian roots.

The Colombians, with the help of the Yardies and Smallies, were able to gain a foothold in the ghettos around the city. Soon they were millionaires and were able to match strength with the big cartels who ran Colombia and Dade County in Miami.

The Yardies had one aim in mind, and that was to get rich at any cost. Men like Chico Red and numerous other men from the past had taken a back seat and let the new men coming up from Jamaica handle the sale of hard drugs.

Brooklyn had changed. It was no longer a place for long-haired Rastamen. Las Vegas, Nevada, had come to the area with gambling houses, whorehouses, and go-go clubs that ran all night. There were also many dance halls where the Yardies hung out and paraded their wealth.

That night I stepped into one of the exotic clubs along Utica Avenue. The club was called the Salt and Pepper because the action inside was hot. Women danced naked on the bar in front of rapturous men with hundred-dollar bills waving in their hands. Reggae music was pumping like I've never heard it. That, too, had changed. The club was packed out with expensive-looking men and women who resembled walking jewelry stores.

There were many people who I knew in that club, including Rastamen who'd shed their locks and moved into the fast lane of hard drugs and organized crime. Several offers were made to me inside that club, men wanting me to join them as a hitman.

I was out of place in that club. Men who'd previously worked for me were offering me jobs to shine their shoes. I walked outside of the club and stood on the sidewalk. The club lights reflected shooting stars from the metallic surfaces of the foreign-made cars parked outside the club.

I must have looked like a reject from the Stone Age as I stood there under the night sky dressed like the Rastafarians of the early seventies.

Traffic sped up and down all six lanes on Utica Avenue. The

night was young. Once again I was in deep thought, unable to digest the full extent of the changes around me.

A Caddy Sevile pulled up outside the club and a handsome, straight-faced man peered out through an open window. I started to get nervous. I had no gun and I still had many enemies on the streets. The man looked me up and down with astonished eyes.

"Danny!" he shouted amiably. His pearly white teeth, studded with rubies, sparkled as I drew closer to the car. One hand rested on my pack as if I had a gun. "It's me, Nine Fingers." He no longer had his long dreadlocks and he was dressed in a white silk shirt with a few chains on his neck and a diamond-embedded Rolex that glittered from the many lights that danced around inside the car. He picked up his jacket resting on the seat beside him and invited me inside the car. There was a nine-millimeter resting on the seat when I got into the car. All manner of things passed through my brain, including being arrested for driving in a car with firearms.

"The Renegades," he declared, "they've killed most of my men but I'm not going down without a fight." He drove off towards the chain of street lights that led to King's Plaza. "The war is not like it used to be, Danny. People like Natty Joe and Chico Red is history."

Nine Fingers brought me up to date as to what was happening on the streets. Jerome was now leading his original gang made up of people from his area in Jamaica. They were known as the Ratchets. This was the trend the Yardies followed. Posses roamed the streets of Brooklyn like the days of the wild Wild West. They had names like Renkers, Shower, Samomacans, Disco Slime, Tel-A-Viv, Websters, Kirks, Rockfort, or Forties. These were just some of the leading names that ruled the streets of the city and were slowly branching out over the fifty states. They were answerable to no one.

Nine Fingers pulled up outside the Tilden Ballrooms. This was once an American blues club now turned into a reggae disco and owned by Jamaicans.

It took much persuasion for me to convince Fingers that I didn't want to go into the club. Eventually he looked at my rags and understood what I was talking about. Fingers knew what I was going through because he told me a story about Doc Holiday, who shot a man in the Salt and Pepper when he was released from prison. The man had offered to buy Doc Holiday a drink and Doc shot him because he said the man was taking advantage of the fact he had just been released from prison.

Fingers gave me five hundred dollars and asked me to come and see him the following day.

I departed his company with my mind already made up not to get involved in anyone's war.

I used two hundred dollars to buy a .45 automatic. I carried it everywhere, including to the probation office.

Destie followed me down to Delancey Street where the trading Jews had once closed their doors in the faces of black customers. Now they rushed to the doors and put on a reggae tape to thaw the cash in the pockets of their Jamaican customers. The Yardies had made their name down there by spending thousands of dollars on good clothes.

Four weeks out of prison I decided I needed a start in the fast and changing world. Petty armed robberies were no longer the in thing. I took a train out to Long Island in search of Billy Weinstein. His house was empty and a placard was poled into his garden. The house was up for sale. I wrote down the number on the placard and contacted the real-estate office handling the sale of the property. For a back-hander of two hundred dollars one of the workers gave me Billy's phone number in Mount Vernon. Destie went without pay that week so that I could have the money.

Henrietta answered the phone and insisted I went to their house right away. "Take a taxi. I will pay," she said excitedly.

The number two train took two hours to reach Mount Vernon. Billy was out and Henrietta entertained me until he got home.

Abraham had grown to a fine boy. "Are you my godfather?" he asked.

I picked him up and swung him around the spacious living room that appeared to be spun from gold. Henrietta had decorated the place herself.

Billy embraced me warmly when he got over the shock of

setting eyes on me once more. "No one would tell me what happened to you, not even Mom." He held me at arm's length and stared at me as though I would disappear. He'd added a few pounds and had a paunch that stood out in front of him. He'd also grown a designer beard.

Henrietta, sensing our need for privacy, slipped out of the room and went upstairs. Billy led me into a private study where he turned the key in the door and headed for an armchair behind a desk. He opened a drawer and took out a little brown package and threw the contents on a mirror on the desk. One nostril at a time, he drew the powder into his nose. "Pure sugar—there's nothing else like it." He shook off the stinging effect of the drug. "How could you be embarrassed to let me know you were in jail, for Christ's sake? Look where we're coming from."

"That's all history. I need help."

"Telling me! The world has left you behind, Danny. The days of selling marijuana is over. Cocaine is running this country. The Colombians went looking for business on the streets and you missed out."

"I'm ready to get involved. Cut me in on some of the action."

"Not so fast, Danny. Remember I'm a lawyer. First I got to arrange for you to work somewhere, get that probation off your back. One mistake in this game and you're fucked for life—and I mean life."

"How soon can you do something for me?"

"As soon as you're protected. Things are not the way they used to be. There are drugs wars waging all over the country. Everyone wants a piece of the cake. The war that is going to affect you the most is the one amongst your own people, the Yardies. They are hot cargo. Last month eight Colombians were gunned down when they went to deliver a consignment to members of the Ratchet Posse. That is only one incident. The Yardies replaced the gangs on the streets and they're making it difficult for any legitimate transactions to take place. They're shooting cops and anyone who gets in their way. At least with the Mafia if one family fucks around you know who to go and complain to. With the Yardies it's different. They are answerable to no one. To start you out in this business would be like giving you a gun to blow your own brains out. Get to know the streets again. Play fool and catch the wise. Get some good men behind you. If you need guns I will supply them. If necessary recruit men from Jamaica. I have a very good friend who works in the American embassy in Jamaica. He can arrange visas."

I left Billy's house with a .45 Ingram machine gun and $2,000 in my pocket. The following months I kept a low profile. Billy arranged for me to work as an assistant mechanic in a big Mafia-owned garage on Atlantic Avenue. Occasionally I went out to one of the many Jamaican clubs around the city. The posse members would often shoot up these functions.

August of that year carnival came to Brooklyn. Floats paraded along the length of Eastern Parkway. People were out in their thousands. Steel bands clanged away the rhythm of the West Indies. People were swigging alcohol, smoking grass, and dancing in the streets. The posses were out. They stood on the corners where they ruled their drug empires.

Many of the men who ran the posses were known to me from the old days when they wore dreadlocks and congregated in Screaming's basement. Some of the leading posses that I saw along the Parkway were the Rockfort Posse, Schenectady, Shower, Spanglers, Dunkirk, East 40s Renkers, Nineties, Super Studs, Waterhouse, Parasites.

Destie was by my side and we stopped on the corner of Franklin and Eastern Parkway where fifty members of the Renegades stood outside the old Cameo Theater. Music was blasting from Merritone disco, a Jamaican sound system. Giant speakers were out on the sidewalk in front of the Chinese restaurant. Backing the Parkway were rows of stone houses with steep steps leading from the sidewalk into the basements. Marijuana was strong in the air.

The Rockfort posse were standing on the walkway that divided the four lanes on either side of the Parkway. They stood where they could keep an eye on all the action around them.

I walked over to the Renegades where Lenny Skeng and Big John were standing. The last time I saw any of those men was on Rikers Island.

"Danny." Big John looked me up and down with a permanent screw on his face. "They finally let you out of prison."

"They couldn't keep me down." I suddenly felt vulnerable as members of the Renkers Posse looked over with intent. They were known for their brutality and drew their name from the stench of urine. Quickly I parted from the men's company and went back to join Destie.

She looked at me suspiciously because her former lover was standing beside Lenny Skeng. I didn't know at the time she was still having an affair with him.

Out of the forest of faces I caught sight of a fair-skinned girl who was slightly shorter than I. She smiled and did a slow, winding dance to the beat of the music. She was dressed in a tight bubblegum dress and had a short Afro and a sensual face.

Destie poked me in the side. "I see you looking at that girl." She was angry. She was a possessive woman. The incident was soon forgotten as we rubbed shoulder to shoulder with the merry crowd.

The otherwise happy occasion was marred by the tight faces of the bloodthirsty posse leaders who seemed to be there to settle grievances. Screaming had foreseen such dark and brutal days in store for the Jamaicans. The Fields were the first posse, followed by Natty Joe and his men, then the Renegades. To date there were four hundred posses, each armed and dangerous. The leaders of these posses were men I had grown with and smoked the pipe of peace with as brethren.

The girl in the bubblegum dress shook her hips to the sound of the music and side-shuffled over to where I was standing. She bumped me and handed me a piece of paper. As I read her name a light hand slapped me across the face. Destie's hand went up again, but this time I caught it and punched her squarely in the jaw. She fell down on the ground. The crowd scattered in anticipation of worse to come. I kicked her as she writhed on the pavement. Kicked her with all the venom that had stored up in me in those years of confinement.

Above the roar of the music gunshots rang out; one chipped the sidewalk on the ground beside my foot. Destie's lover had fired a shot after me through the heavy crowd. The needle scratched across the face of a record as people screamed and stampeded. The sound of gunfire seemed to erupt from every corner on the Parkway.

The pin had been pulled from the grenade. The posses turned their guns on the crowd. The crowd charged in all directions, knocking me from side to side. I pulled the Ingram from under my army coat and showered down bullets in the Renegades' corner. Fire spat from the muzzle of the gun like a firetorch. Men ran in all directions with their guns blazing.

There was no sign of Destie. People dived into the basements in an attempt to escape the shower of bullets that flew through the air like rain. The rest of the crowd stampeded like cattle on a range. The Parkway was on fire. Shots rang out like a chain reaction from one end of the Parkway to the other.

Cops ran around in the confusion, unable to pinpoint the area where shots were coming from. They, too, were under fire. The posses were intent on using the incident to mow down as many pigs as possible.

Guns blazed. Innocent civilians were forced to fire their legal guns to keep the stampeding crowd from trampling them. The crowd rushed about in a state of turmoil. The sound of gunfire shattered the air in a chorus of agonizing death.

People lay dead on the road and sidewalk. The tide of bodies carried me along. Eventually I was able to get off the Parkway.

A woman sprang from behind a car where she was hiding. She held onto my hand. "Help me, please," she wailed. Blood poured from many cuts on her body. Her clothes were torn and she stood with one of her shoes in her hand. She wouldn't let me go. "My six-year-old son, I can't find my car, friends." She was confused.

A crowd of people rushed down the road and knocked us aside, but still the woman held onto me for dear life. She was in her late twenties. Police cars screamed down the block. Had it not been for the frightened woman talking to me they would have stopped and carted me away.

I managed to calm the woman down and we went in search of her car. It was fifty yards down the block. She was in no shape to drive. I drove her to the 69th Precinct and left her there.

The carnival was described as a massacre. Word had gotten around about the way I handled the Ingram. Posse members showed me much respect as I moved amongst them in the coming days.

Chapter 33

Destie was no longer a part of my life. The wrong of a bad relationship had been set right. She was history along with all her dirty ways. I vowed never to let another woman have such a hold on me ever again.

The girl that gave me her particulars at the carnival turned out to be very discreet and conservative. Her name was Donna and she worked for Burger King in downtown Brooklyn. I was now having a steady relationship with Donna and she was seven months pregnant with my child.

The probation officer cut my visits to once a month. This was what Billy was waiting for. He gave me three kilos of 92 percent cocaine. The drugs were sold that very same day. He went on to test my distribution abilities by giving me fourteen kilos which were sold within a week.

I was invited to Billy's house one Friday night. There I was to get the shock of my life. Five Italians and three Colombians were sitting in his private study. One of the Italians was Dominico Vercotti. He embraced me warmly. Billy showed no surprise. He walked behind the bar and poured drinks for everyone.

"Toast." He raised his glass. "Gentlemen, my job is made easy. Mr Vercotti has personally vouched for my long-time friend Danny Palmer. I no longer have to put my head on the line to prove his loyalty."

The men smiled warmly but with reservation.

"Gentlemen, you asked for a man who knows the streets and has considerable influence with the posse leaders. I have found him." Billy rested his case and sat down.

Dominico stood up. "Danny, we can cut all the small talk. We're all here because there's a problem. We have the drugs and the Yardies have the streets. In order to get to them we need someone who can go amongst the different warring factors and offer them a deal."

"May I have a word," said a short, fat Colombian. He was in his mid-forties, pale skinned, suspicious eyes, and sandy colored hair. "Mr Palmer, we have tried doing business with the posses but they are sneaky and conniving. Over the past few months they have robbed and killed the Colombian distributors that offered them business. The Colombians are already involved in their own wars, much the same as the Jamaican war. To start another war with the posses would only add more fire to the fury."

I sat up in the armchair. "With all due respect, I will not betray my people if that is what you men suggest."

"No one is asking you to betray anyone," Billy said. "There are two main Colombian families operating here in the city. Mr Jaramillo over there"—he indicated the short, squat Colombian who had spoken earlier. "The other family is the Cifuentis, who, ironically, are working out of Jamaica. The island has been used as a shipping port for cocaine."

"If they are operating out of Jamaica I don't see how I can be of any help." The whole object of their plan started becoming clear in my mind although I was new to the game.

Dominico clinked his glass. "Let me be the one to shed some light on the proposition. Indirectly, the Cifuentis are supplying the posses with cocaine through their contacts in Jamaica. The DEA are hot on everything leaving the islands. We have the resources to move consignments of cocaine from Colombia without touching the Bahamas or West Indies. All we want you to do is talk to the heads of the posses. We'll make them an offer they can't refuse."

The proposition was plausible because there was no one out there on the streets that could go among the warring factors. They were all getting their consignments directly from Jamaica and were stubborn in their approach to change. The Colombians had learnt the hard way by trying to deal directly with them. They had even employed the services of Cubans as middle men, but the Cubans were no match for the Yardies.

"What about the Renegades? Their distribution of drugs will

dry up." I shifted around so I could look directly into the men's faces.

Jaramillo smiled, his plump face suffused with color. "Consider them history. From now on they will be tamed, because anyone will be able to touch them in a few days. As we speak posses loyal to us are on a mission of seek and destroy. That Labor Day shootout was no accident."

"What! You put the lives of innocent people at stake just to accomplish your aim? If you already have posses loyal to you then why do you need me?"

The men traded curious glances.

Dominico spoke. "It was not our wish that innocent people should get hurt. That was the only opportunity we had to get so many of them in one open space. It worked because they're on the run."

The meeting lasted for three hours in which time I accepted the proposition. I couldn't help feeling that I was being used for something far greater than cocaine distribution. Whatever the plan I intended to earn as much money as possible and get out of the racket.

That very same week I picked up twenty kilos on Knickerbocker Avenue. This area was controlled by the Italians known as the Zips. Men like Dominico Vercotti and the younger Italians arriving from Sicily had replaced the older heads of the Mob and were running the drugs racket. They were given the name Zips because of their fast tongues. Many of the men spoke very little English.

Getting rid of the twenty kilos was a matter of checking one of the main posses. Within a week I had sold a hundred kilos and had managed to secure eighteen posses who would take regular consignments.

The notoriety of the posses grew as they grew in wealth. There were now posses running that made the Renegades look like angels. Jerome headed the Ratchet gang. He refused to sit in the backseat and let the younger gangsters rule. He was active and had his own smuggling racket going on.

To boost their strength, posses recruited the fiercest and most merciless out of the Yankee population. Their war for turf and drugs was bloody.

Brooklyn, the city of churches, was now the new Vegas without the legal gambling houses. At nights the many lights of West Indian clubs lit up Utica, Church, and Flatbush Avenues.

The drug problem and the shootings brought the Feds closer to earth. Black officers from the FBI were trained to talk like Yardies and go amongst the warring posses. These undercover Feds found themselves caught up in the many shootouts that occurred at the reggae clubs and dance halls.

Jack Weinstein had earned himself the name "one-man army" for his fight against the mobsters and their desire to turn New York City into the number one drugs capital of the world. Jack set many traps for the rising posses—Italians, Colombians, and Cubans alike. He seemed to be succeeding in his war. He'd brought many posses to their knees and caused some of their leaders to take refuge in Jamaica. There the posse leader found no escape from the Jewish crusader. The Feds followed them to the island, often falsifying documents to secure extradition of the men and women they sought.

My first year being the drugs lord had turned me into a millionaire. I knew every inch of the city streets and I made use of that knowledge to expand my drugs distribution. My two and a half years in prison had opened many doors to me in the underworld.

I had eight distribution houses set up throughout the Nineties, New Lots, and Brownsville. Money fever eventually crept into me. It was a strange illness that shunted my thoughts down a green avenue and above my head a red cloud poured drops of blood down on me. I trusted no one, not even the money-counting machines that ran nonstop: every buck had to be accounted for. I became alienated and temperamental as a wave of paranoia swept in. My guns blazed nonstop like the burn-off stacks of oil refineries; I had to rival the Colombians, the Cubans, the Puerto-Ricans, and anyone else who might try to sink my empire. The Nineties, New Lots, and Brownsville had become resigned to my war of terror. Even the cops had to take caution when cruising past one of my drugs houses. Billy handled my finances and cleaned the money that was coming in like April showers.

January 1981 I married Donna. We had a son by the name of

Moses and we lived in my new $1.5 million house in Long Island. The grounds were secured by television cameras that relayed all activities to my private study where twelve television screens were stacked. I had an arsenal of some of the most sophisticated weapons in the country.

My gang was back in action with twenty more recruits. I hand-picked these men from the ghettos of Kingston, Jamaica. They were all Cuban-trained Brigadestas, experts in weaponry, men trained to kill. These men would not fire off one or two rounds and then run for cover, their power was firepower and they gloried in it. If they pulled a gun they really sprayed bullets: four hundred rounds or more. We had a motto: Fire one shot and a cop will arrest you, fire two and they will engage you in a shootout, but fire off hundreds of rounds and they'll keep well away.

Jaramillo called me one day when I was on the Expressway, en route to visit my parents who still lived in the same old house and refused to take any of my money.

"Sparrow C.," Jaramillo's crackling voice declared through the hands-free telephone system.

"Night Hawk."

"The roost at eight."

"Fine."

"How is the family?"

"Fine."

He rang off.

Dad was outside sweeping up the leaves on that September afternoon. He'd aged. His shoulders had stooped and he looked a mere shadow of his former awesome strength. I pulled up in a silver Mercedes Benz. Dad continued sweeping as if he didn't notice my presence. His eyes followed me as I left the car and made my way up the steps and into the house.

Mom hugged me as I entered the front door.

"What's this tears?" I cupped her chin in my hand.

She snuffed. "Oh, Danny, son." She held me at arm's length and stared awkwardly at my $3,000 suit. "I don't even recognize you anymore." She released me and strutted into the living room and slumped on the settee. With swollen eyes she looked into my face as I stood over her. "I had a dream. It's not the first time, but this time it's for real. I saw you drowning in a pool of blood. Shot down like a dog."

"I'm gonna live forever, Mom. Your son is on top of the world. Nothing can touch me."

"No man lives forever, Danny. I know you're a killer. I watch the documentaries on television about the Jamaican gangs. To think my own son's involved makes me sick. I can't even attend services, I'm afraid to leave the house. People look at me as though I've done them a personal wrong."

"I'm no murderer, Mom."

"You don't work, you live in a mansion and wear expensive clothes." She looked away. "You're not my Danny that I used to cuddle in my arms. You're a killing machine as cold as the instruments you use to carry out those heinous acts of violence." She stood up and pulled away my jacket where my gun was resting in a shoulder holster. She swelled up in anger, then turned and ran into her room and turned the key in the lock.

I knocked at the door with urgency.

"Go away, you're not my son. I can smell the blood on you as though I am part of your killing machine."

"Mom!" I yelled. I put my cheek on the door and whispered. "I need you, Mom." I pulled the gun and thought about blasting off the lock, but the sound of gunfire might give her a heart attack. Hurt and defeated I rushed out of the house. Dad stared at me as I got into the car and took out a small package of cocaine and drew up about five grams in my nostrils. The dust reached my brain fast. Nothing mattered at that moment.

Jaramillo and all the members of the syndicate were assembled in a seedy hotel room in Little Italy. I noticed something was wrong when Billy wasn't present. One thing I had learnt in dealing with these people was never to ask questions.

"The problem," Jaramillo said worriedly. He passed around the large table. "Jack Weinstein has been a long-standing problem for all of us present. He's not our everyday cop that can be bought. Several attempts have been made on his life starting with the Colombian cartels and a Cuban who rushed into a court room and opened fire on him. All has failed. Gentlemen, he's hunting for our heads."

The men in the room stared at me as though I held the key to the problem.

"This man has got to be eliminated, wiped out." Jaramillo dabbed his forehead with a handkerchief. "If he's not wiped out soon I don't see any of us in this room lasting another year. To make things worse, the scumbag knows all the tricks. He's a street man." He paused and his accusing eyes rested on me heavily. "Danny, I was told that your mother once worked for the Weinstein family."

"Leave my fucking mother out of this." I jumped up full of rage. Jaramillo took a few steps backwards. Dominico got up and held on to me. I had never really cared for Jaramillo. "What he's suggesting is that I be responsible for killing Weinstein. I don't want no part of it," I protested.

"I'm afraid you have no choice," Dominico said in a cold voice. His words weren't to be taken lightly. He turned me loose. "For Christ's sake, what are you? A cop lover? This motherfucker dies and the heat is taken right off our backs. The next man to take his place is someone we can talk to."

"The best hit-men in the city can't bump him off. Why are you so sure that I can execute such a mission?"

"The man is at your disposal. All you have to do is come up with a quiet location where it can be carried out. His death must be made to look like an accident," Dominico said.

This is what I had been groomed for all along. Billy had been used, now it was my turn. The stakes would be high if I didn't comply, I had learnt enough about these men to be actually frightened. They were strong and had a lot of backing around the city. There would be no escaping them. The carrot of those I loved dangled in front of my eyes. The looks on the men's faces in the room said it all. I would not get out of Little Italy alive if I didn't go along with their plan. The bullet could come from anywhere—maybe even a cop, a road sweeper, or a hot dog vendor.

"After I accomplish this task then I want out." I looked into all of their faces. As I stood there I made up my mind to make sure to kill Jaramillo as soon as Jack was disposed of. There was a saying mother used to quote: "A bird can't fly on one wing."

"What you request will be honored and quite handsomely too." There was a wry smile on Dominico's face. "That Jew son of a bitch will be sorry the day he was born."

Within a week I had devised an assassination plot for Jack Weinstein. During that week four members of the cartels in Colombia were extradited by members of Jack's men. A quantity of drugs was seized on Knickerbocker Avenue and some leading members of the Mob were in jail. Jack Weinstein had scored another major victory.

It was Abraham, Billy's son, who gave me the idea. He was excited one day and asked his mother if Uncle Jack would be coming to his birthday party. "He wouldn't miss it for the world," Henrietta had said. Jack was arriving on his Lear jet.

"A decompression bomb in the fuselage of the jet. Magnificent. Twenty minutes after the take-off then *boom*." Dominico's hands spread out like a mushroom. "Only you could come up with such a plan, Danny. I knew from the day you stabbed me in the Coxsackie yard that you were going places."

Jaramillo recruited a Cuban who serviced the planes out at LaGuardia airport. I personally gave the Cuban the bomb and sufficient instructions on how the job was to be done.

I was nervous for the next few days and drew close to a kilo of shit into my nose. The day finally arrived and the Cuban called to verify that the bomb was planted. I locked myself in the study of my house and paced the floor nervously. I felt like eyes were watching me. The cocaine was making me paranoid. To drown out the paranoia I snorted some more cocaine.

A red security light flashed and the cameras at the front of the house picked up Billy's sports car as it entered the driveway. He drove along the cobblestone pathway to the rear of the house. Ten minutes later he was in the study stretched out on a white leather settee. "Loneliness strangles the heart," he said wearily. "Henrietta and Abraham decided to fly down to Washington with Jack."

He'd just struck me with a sledgehammer. I froze. The brandy in my hand spewed out of my mouth and choked me.

"What's the matter? Looks like you've seen a ghost."

"It must be this cocaine."

"What, you snorting?" he asked excitedly.

"Yeah!" My eyes were locked in terror.

Billy shook his head and smiled as if saying "naughty." He took a sip of his drink. "Abraham is a fine boy," he said proudly. "He worships you, says you're the best uncle in the whole world, but he liked you better when you had your hair like Bob Marley. The kid is hooked on Bob Marley's music— he buys all his records."

I sat back in the chair, realizing that very soon Billy would be without a wife and the son he so loved. Jesus Christ!! If there was only something I could do. Cocaine was the only thing I could draw for at that time. I poured about four grams on the table, two for each nostril.

"Take it easy." Billy looked on with astonishment as the white dust disappeared from the table.

The time ticked away, each minute drawing closer to the destruction. Billy was content to just sit there and talk nonstop of his wife and son. My life was suspended on a live wire. The phone rang. I stared at it hoping the ringing would stop. The fourth ring and the phone seemed like it wanted to jump up and hit me in the face. My hands trembled.

"Hello."

"We got problems," said an agitated voice.

Sweat instantly washed my body. The phone went dead, leaving me gaping down the receiver.

There were a few moments of tense silence and the phone rang once more. This time I hurried and picked it up. It was an authoritative voice asking for Billy. He'd often transferred the calls from his mobile car phone to my house when visiting.

Billy took the phone. "My God," he screamed. His fingers went through his hair hysterically. The drink I was pouring spilled over.

Billy's breathing became irregular. He nodded solemnly into the receiver. In a state of shock he laid the receiver down, missing the target. "They're both dead." He looked off into oblivion with crazed eyes, then dropped to his knees and wept.

There in front of me was a man with the world on his shoulders. I bore the guilt. Suddenly nothing made sense any more. The wealth, the glamor, the big house, expensive cars. It was all blood money like my mother had said. I, Danny Palmer, had caused the death of two people who would never have lifted a finger against me.

Billy had always been weak. Henrietta and Abraham were his source of strength. They were gone. He folded into a ball on the ground and refused to move. I called a doctor friend who suggested he be taken to a hospital. Billy was in a state of severe shock.

Billy remained in a psychiatric ward for three months. During that time the cause of the plane crash was unearthed. Jack Weinstein, the pilot, and two members of his team had survived the crash. Parts of the bomb were uncovered.

Abraham's body was never found. Henrietta's body was unrecognizable. Billy pulled himself together for the funeral, which was attended by thousands of people, including law enforcement bodies and me.

Jack Weinstein concentrated all his efforts on crippling organized crime in New York City. The Mafia were brought to their knees in a series of seizures that stemmed the flow of hard drugs into the city.

The Yardies, ironically, were able to hold their heads up. The might of the Federal agencies had always been on them from the onset of their arrival in the States. They continued to party and have a good time. They were the wild cards in the lethal game of poker. No one understood them. Not even the young black Americans who now wanted to be Yardies.

Financially secure, I pulled away from the establishment and set up Danco shipping agency. Immediately I was involved in mass shipment of marijuana from Jamaica. Occasionally a Jamaican plane would be seized at Kennedy and the Jamaican government would have to pay a heavy fine to retrieve the vessel.

I ran into problems with Jerome who himself was a ganga entrepreneur. Jerome and members of his Ratchet gang ripped off two tons of marijuana destined for me on a trailer from Queens. They killed the driver and took the truck.

War once again loomed with my old rival. Working with the establishment had kept me out of his way, but my return to street-running of marijuana got me involved with him once more.

Two Saturday nights after the robbery I decided to pay Jerome a visit. A popular sound system known as Stereograph from Jamaica was scheduled to play at the Empire roller-skating rink. Dressed in green army fatigues I attended the dance with fifteen of my best men. Lights were flashing. DJs were rapping. Special requests were sent to this posse and that posse. Gunshots were firing in the air. Posses had turned out in their masses. Women danced in $1,000 dresses and gold chains. They were the gun carriers for the posses. Some of those women ran their own posses and fired their own guns. Law men were in the dance looking like civilians.

Jerome was there. He spotted me as I entered and turned an SMG on the crowd. People were screaming and hitting the floor. The Uzi in my hand blazed, clearing the way. Men and women were dropping like flies. The freebase pipe I had earlier was fueling a rage of murder inside me. Since the death of Billy's family my life had turned around. The shooting lasted for nearly twenty minutes. Jerome escaped.

I caught up with him inside the Salt and Pepper Club. Again shots were exchanged and there was a fierce gunfight out on the sidewalk. Two men who were with me died. We met up again at the Reggae Lounge where more shots were fired. The streets of Brooklyn had started to run red with blood because of the war between Jerome and me.

For the next two years Jerome's men and mine engaged in a bloody war. This included shoot-outs at discos, clubs, subway stations, and in crowded streets.

Django was eventually gunned down in the Empire roller-skating rink by Jerome. I flew down to Jamaica with sixteen members of my posse to give him a proper burial. The funeral was at the Dove Cot Cemetery in Spanish Town.

There was a big turn-out. The little church was packed. People had to gather outside. It seemed like the whole of Jamaica had turned out. This was due to the big wake that was kept in the Rema area and the thousands of dollars that had been spent in preparation for the funeral. I wanted him to go down into the grave in style. The procession was led from the church by the pastor and the pall bearers from Madden funeral home.

The pastor read Psalm 92 as the body was lowered into the grave. Women dried their weeping eyes. The Rema church choir were singing softly "Rock of Ages."

The sixteen members of my gang and I opened fire into the air with the rapid fire of gun salute. The sound of M16s, Uzis, and SMGs punctured holes in the balmy air. Thunder answered from above. Light rain drizzled as if the clouds were pierced by the gunfire.

The crowd suddenly started to hit the ground as if the bullets that came back down were loaded. Men crept up on the funeral procession and opened fire on them as they mourned. Blood spattered everywhere.

The pastor lay dead in my path as I jumped over his body. On the ground people were screaming and holding down little children. The bullets continued to rain on them.

Jerome had extended his war to not only Jamaica but to the funeral also. He sprayed mercilessly into the crowd with a sub-machine gun.

I wrenched away the AK-47 from one of my men who'd fallen beside me under a hail of bullets. Using the cover of cars and minibuses I went after Jerome.

Having made their mark, the men started to retreat to a fleet of cars parked in the middle of the red dirt-stained road that ran through the cemetery. They jumped over the dead and injured and knocked frightened women and children out of the way in the rush.

Jerome tried to escape me. Once more I was hot on his tracks. Police from the Denham Town police station near Rema had turned out at the funeral. They got involved in the gunfight, turning their guns on members of both posses.

Four cars now separated me and Jerome. Bullets were cutting through the air like miniature guillotines. Car windows were shattered and green leaves were shot from the trees.

One of my bullets hit Jerome in the leg as he turned on an M16 to clear his way to his car. The taste of victory was sweet in my mouth and the gun blazed as I rushed towards him to finish him off once and for all.

Suddenly there was an explosion from behind me. The weight of the world seemed to have fallen down on me. Darkness ruled.

I woke up two weeks later in hospital surrounded by members of the CIB. Things were still hazy.

The officer who shot me looked down at me in wonder. "You're lucky to be alive. I don't make a policy of wounding people." His voice was filled with hatred, so much so that I was forced to open my eyes fully. I had to make a mental note of the man who had shot me in the back and now stood over me proclaiming his expertise. I made up my mind there and then he would be the next on my list.

The full extent of what took place at the cemetery was read out to me by one of the detectives standing over me. Twelve people were killed and sixteen wounded. The dead included four of my men.

Donna flew down from the States with my three-year-old son, Moses. He wanted to climb into the bed with me.

Five months after being in hospital the police were paid off and I was on my way back to the States on Air Jamaica. On the plane I read a copy of the day's *New York Times*. Dominico Vercotti had been shot through the head at close range.

The FBI were there to meet me as I passed through immigration at Kennedy Airport. They hurried me through a side door to where their cars were parked. None of the four men who arrested me spoke a word. They took the Brooklyn–Queens expressway and headed for familiar ground. The car pulled up outside the 71st Precinct.

I had passed the stage of worrying. Whatever the problem my lawyer would get me out within the hour.

The men whisked me through the building, but instead of climbing the stairs they led me down into the basement. I was marched into a freshly painted room with fluorescent lighting. There were charts and maps of the city on the wall. Tables were set out in the room like a conference. Men in suits sat behind each desk. I was made to sit down; shortly afterward Jerome was brought in. He was limping where my bullet had shattered the bone in his leg. He was as surprised to see me as I was to see him.

A tall heavy-set officer got down to the details of why both of us had been brought there. The war between Jerome and me had claimed the lives of many innocent people. The Feds offered us a deal in a nutshell. Stop the war or face the consequences. The might of the United States government was about to fall on us with all its resources. They could have simply killed us both but that would only add fire to fury. The meeting lasted two hours. At the end Jerome and I shook hands. That was to be the end of a long-standing war.

As we left that meeting, each committed to our word, we knew something was wrong. This was another delay tactic by the State while they formulated a more devastating plan to rid the city of the Yardies. The future of Yard Men looked bleak.

One week after Dominico's death, Edgar Jaramillo lost his life, he too shot in the head at close range. Billy came to my house distressed and fearful for his life.

"Danny." His hands shook, the color drained from his face. "I'm afraid I'll be next. The other Colombian families are reaping vengeance for the trade we stole from them. The war hitting Dade County and the south coast has finally touched the city."

"Stay here with me. I'll get a few extra men down here if it will make you feel more secure."

"Thanks, Danny, you're a swell pal. I don't know what I would do without you. When Henrietta and Abraham died you were the only one I could turn to." Tears rolled down his face, his eyes stared vacant at the wall. "I can't stay here. I have a trial coming up next week."

"Take a few of my men to bodyguard you." For a moment I saw a look of resentment in his eyes. But it couldn't be. Billy didn't have an evil bone in him.

"Maybe I'm just being over-protective. How long can I continue to live under cover?" His face hardened, then was replaced by a fake smile as Moses ran into the room.

"Uncle Billy," he said excitedly, clutching his teddy bear to his chest. He rushed into Billy's somewhat reluctant arms. There was something strange in Billy's manner towards Moses, a cold and unfeelng air. I put it down to the stress that was barely allowing him to stay in the realm of sanity.

Three weeks later the killing amongst members of the establishment continued to mount. Each time Billy came round he was slowly deteriorating. He'd grown a beard and looked almost scruffy. I would sit and freebase with him for hours to relax him, take his mind off the killings.

Donna was quite fond of Billy but she started harboring resentment about the cold and uncaring way in which Billy acted towards Moses.

Billy came around to the house the second week into a hot summer when the city was basting in the heat. I had just picked up a consignment of marijuana from the airport and stashed it off in one of my warehouses in Queens. He was dressed in a long raincoat, his hair in tangles like when he was a hippie in high school. He reeked of alcohol.

Donna led him through the apartment to where I was sitting on the settee reading the papers about the latest happenings in the Yardie war.

Moses was at my feet playing with his train set and the air conditioner was humming. Moses rushed to Billy, much to my disapproval. Billy quickly jumped back and pulled a gun from under his coat. Moses didn't know any better. He loved his uncle and continued to rush towards him. In less time than it took to blink an eye Billy turned the gun on Moses and shot him in the head.

"Don't move, scumbag." He quickly turned around and pumped two bullets into Donna's head, ripping it completely from her body. Her headless corpse continued running and slumped beside the body of my son.

"I told you once, scumbag. This is a jungle. Not because the skyscrapers have replaced the trees." His voice was that of the Exorcist. "I loved you, you black son of a bitch, made you godfather to my son. My wife loved you. You even had the nerve to attend the funeral after you killed them in cold blood."

"I had nothing to do with their death." The sight of Moses lying on the floor tore my heart to pieces.

Billy threw a cassette on the floor. "Put it in and listen before you die."

He followed me to the study and stood a distance away while I put the cassette in the Hitachi stack system.

"Have a seat, scumbag."

I walked slowly behind my desk. The first voice on the tape was that of Jack Weinstein. He was about to interview Hernaldo Gomez, the Cuban who was hired to plant the bomb in the jet.

Hernaldo was picked up on a murder and drugs rap for which he was facing the electric chair in Kansas City. To save himself from frying he told the story of how he was propositioned by Jaramillo and me to plant the bomb in Jack Weinstein's jet.

Billy turned the gun on the speakers and blew them apart. "It took some convincing for Jack to agree to what I'd done, but like they say—blood is thicker than water. I killed all the rest, every fucking one. Didn't think I had it in me. Billy the softie, use him and abuse him."

Slowly I eased open the drawer where I kept a .45 automatic loaded with one bullet already in the chamber.

"Die, Danny. This is your last day on earth. Die." He raised the gun and fired. Two shots tore into my chest.

Through the darkness I managed to take the gun from the desk and fired repeatedly. Even in death my hand was steady. The gun in Billy's hand went limp and he staggered to the ground.

I got up unsteadily and emptied the magazine of the gun on the television monitors as they picked up the army of law men who'd besieged the premises. The house spun around my head, blood pumped from my chest. I was in pain, but not like any other pain. It was kind of sweet and somehow pleasant.

I staggered out of the house and flashes of light and explosion from the Federal guns broke the quietness of the suburban street. Visions materialized in my head. The area had turned into the Nevada strip. Neon lights were flashing. Donna and Moses were strolling merrily towards me. Mom was there, so too Jerome, Screaming, Patrick, Paul. Jesus Christ, it was one big happy family.

I fell in the middle of the street, breathing heavily. Blood poured from the corner of my mouth. The sirens hollered and screamed, whining in the nonstop cry of violence. Nathan was fiddling with the hydrant. I was young again on the block and infatuated by Nadine.